THE MAZE

THE MAZE

PANOS KARNEZIS

Jonathan Cape
London

Published by Jonathan Cape 2004

2 4 6 8 10 9 7 5 3 1

First published in Great Britain in 2004 by
Jonathan Cape
Random House, 20 Vauxhall Bridge Road, London SW1V 2SA

Random House Australia (Pty) Limited
20 Alfred Street, Milsons Point, Sydney,
New South Wales 2061, Australia

Random House New Zealand Limited
18 Poland Road, Glenfield,
Auckland 10, New Zealand

Random House South Africa (Pty) Limited
Endulini, 5A Jubilee Road, Parktown 2193, South Africa

The Random House Group Limited Reg. No. 954009
www.randomhouse.co.uk

A CIP catalogue record for this book is available
from the British Library

ISBN 0-224-06976-4

Papers used by Random House are natural,
recyclable products made from wood grown in sustainable forests;
the manufacturing processes conform to the environmental
regulations of the country of origin

Typeset by Palimpsest Book Production Ltd, Polmont, Stirlingshire
Printed and bound in Great Britain by
Mackays of Chatham PLC, Chatham, Kent

THE MAZE

In the shadow of a man who walks in the sun, there are more enigmas than in all religions, past, present and future.

Giorgio de Chirico

Historical Note

In 1919, in the aftermath of World War I, a Greek expeditionary force landed in Ottoman Asia Minor with the apparent intent of protecting the local Greek population from the hostility of the Turkish majority. The true aim of the expedition, however, was the permanent annexation to Greece of the Mediterranean Ottoman regions where a substantial Greek minority lived. The Greek occupation lasted until the summer of 1922 when the military tide turned in the Turks' favour. After a massive offensive that quickly turned into a rout, the Greek army was forced to retreat to the coast in disorder and evacuate Asia Minor.

PROLOGUE

In the peace of the dawn the tolling of the bells ought to have sounded all the more strange and out of place. Instead, the dull rhythmic knocks of their gigantic clappers – their ropes pulled by a feeble yet stubborn hand – accompanied the calmness of the morning like the beating of an elderly heart. The sound travelled over the tiled roofs and across the abandoned town, where dismembered artillery guns lay among iron bedsteads, oak tables and broken wardrobes.

A rush of wind sent a cloud of red dust towards a window where the shreds of its velvet curtains were flapping. The dust entered the vast salon, carrying with it sand from the desert, shrivelled rosebuds and brittle pieces of parched paper, all of which added to the unbelievable squalor of the once majestic room.

Of the aforementioned glory there still remained enough evidence: a gutted crimson sofa, the fringed corner of a torn carpet, a chessboard table whose mahogany top had been scraped spitefully by a knife. Against a wall was set a hacked-about armchair, its carved gold legs now nowhere to be seen. On the wooden parquet, next to a heap of compost and desiccated flowers, lay the skin of a snow leopard with no head, tail or paws. At the other end of the room, what seemed like the prow of a small boat was in fact the front of an enormous bathtub, in whose hull someone had expressed his absolute contempt by an irreverent act of defecation.

A sudden dash of miniature feet over the floorboards violated the silence: a rat navigated the delightful wasteland of the imperial room, stopping briefly to sniff the stale air. Across the blinding shafts of sunlight it went, then through a crack in the French window, until it came out to the veranda, where it was treated to a view of exceptional beauty – or ugliness if one were not a rat: the gardens that opened out before its eyes would have suffered less had they received a visitation of locusts. A meticulous stomping had crushed the beds of flowers and aromatic herbs without mercy, while a tall lilac bush had been stormed like a rampart. The trunk of a cherry tree had endured the attacks of an axe, only to die later of its wounds; with its leaves dried up and fallen off, it stood in the middle of the garden like a pleading hand. When the sun came out, a bevy of crows nesting on its branches took flight.

Propelled by the wind, uprooted amaranth shrubs tumbled down the dusty streets. Past an open conduit filled with dried excrement lay a maze of narrow alleyways – no one was to be found in those poorer houses either. In the square, the Town Hall had long since been set on fire and its roof had caved in. The crows flapped calmly towards the outskirts of the town. Some distance beyond the last houses, in the middle of the country road, lay the carcasses of dead water buffalo still yoked to wagons.

Old animals that had died of exhaustion, they were part of a caravan full of indiscriminate loot. In the back of the carriages, covered in sand, were pieces of furniture, a silent grandfather clock, a heavy Victrola. The crows ignored these; screeching, they landed instead on the dead animals whose flesh was in a stage of advanced putrefaction: the desperate exodus must have taken place several weeks earlier.

The sun climbed further and the wind passed through the wheels of the abandoned carriages. A pair of crows fought over a piece of rotten meat. The tolling of the church bells stopped. A beautiful spring day was beginning. Slowly, the desert erased a little more of the town from the eternal Anatolian landscape.

PART I

The Desert

CHAPTER I

Brigadier Nestor rubbed his eyes and sat up in his cot. His eyes were faint and colourless like paper watermarks, as if his eternal habit of rubbing them with the hard knuckles of his forefingers had slowly eroded their sheen. He yawned and unlocked the trunk with the keys that hung from his neck. The armoured trunk was packed with pressed and neatly folded clothes, some of which he had not yet worn on this tour of duty: a parade uniform with its medals and ribbons, a black one for evening functions with satin lapels and gold epaulets, a short riding tunic with coloured lanyards. He rummaged impatiently through the trunk; under his patent-leather boots with the silver spurs he found the bundle with everything his wife had sent him since the beginning of the war: Christmas and Easter cards, newspaper clippings, a postcard of a spa by the sea, a child's crayon drawing. He pulled off the rubber band that held the letters together and let them drop to the corrugated floor.

It was hot and dark in the back of the lorry. A thick canvas stretched over the roof and the sides, letting no light in or heat out. Brigadier Nestor felt nauseous and his throat was dry, but he craved neither a drink nor fresh air. He stood up and struggled to keep his balance while the moving lorry rocked from side to side. Stepping over his once precious correspondence, he leaned over the stove, lifted the lid of the steaming kettle with a pair of tongs, and removed the glass hypodermic syringe. He drew from a little vial, rolled up his sleeve, fastened the rubber band tight above his elbow, and finally injected the morphia.

The lorry continued its journey, moving in and out of the potholes in the dirt track; blasts of hot sand exploded on the tarpaulin like enemy potshots. The exhaust backfired and the smell of petrol entered Brigadier Nestor's nostrils, causing an unwelcome awakening of his senses. The sun cast the shadow of the vehicle on the saltpetre; it resembled a crawling scarab. There were dunes of soft, gold sand all round, and on the side of the track were the bleached bones of birds and camels. Feeling the morphia in his blood, the brigadier rolled his eyes and smiled like a child. Soon the drug had erased both his tiredness and his thirst. The suspension creaked and a tin cup rolled across the floor. The wind carried over the padre's voice.

'. . . *When the poor and the needy seek water and there is none, and their tongue faileth for thirst, I the Lord will hear them, I the God of Israel will not forsake them.*'

For a moment the brigadier forgot the horror and felt as if adrift in a tranquil sea, the sea that was their destination – albeit not the ultimate one; that was the motherland. But if they reached the coast – anywhere along the coast – they would have a good chance of salvation. His eyes watered from the petrol fumes. Only now did he register the explosions of the battered exhaust and his intoxicated reason misinterpreted them. Were they being fired at? he wondered, but with little alarm, as if an ambush were not a threat but a mere inconvenience. While the lorry was driving round a bend on the road, a little light came through the crack of the hatch and the dust in the carriage sparkled. Outside, the vultures circled the walking soldiers and croaked impatiently.

'I will open rivers in high places, and fountains in the midst of the valleys. I will make the wilderness a pool of water, and the dry land springs of water.'

The brigade had been on the move since dawn. What time was it? Brigadier Nestor only knew it was daytime, it was hot and they were still in the desert. How long ago had they entered this maze? Had he been sober he could have answered, but his memory had now been swallowed by the quicksand of the morphia. On the horizon whirlwinds of dust shot upwards. The old officer coughed; his eyes grew heavy and he dropped back on his cot.

'I will plant in the wilderness the cedar, the shittah tree, and the myrtle, and the oil tree; I will set in the desert the fir tree, and the pine, and the box tree together.'

The reciting voice became distant and the brigadier sank slowly into a dreamless sleep.

In August the waiting had been over. That morning the sun had risen red and ominous to inaugurate the fateful day. Under the sun the line of the horizon had appeared gradually, like a line made of sympathetic ink, and soon the rest of the Anatolian steppe was revealed, an endless plateau interrupted by a few hills, shrubs of myrtle and ancient ruins. Then it began. The artillery barrage, thundering like an untimely storm, had signalled the beginning of the enemy offensive. The guns had pounded the trenches long enough for the soldiers to think that the gunners were set on levelling the hills and opening new gorges and caves in the prehistoric landscape. The batteries had ceased fire and shortly, from the pall of smoke, the infantry had emerged. There were ten divisions at the front and the soldiers came in waves behind their bayonets, panting. They ran across the barren plain, up the fortified hills, and neither the barbed wire nor the machine guns could stop them. The dead piled up in the gullies that ran down the hills, but more men came until one after another every stronghold was overwhelmed.

Brigadier Nestor had been in bed when the offensive had begun. The evening before he had attended a dance at a nearby town that had continued well into the night. It had been a pleasant soirée. He had welcomed the invitation, presented to him by the president of the local social club, for the long uneventfulness on the front had also caused a stalemate in his disposition. For sure, he had strong views about the situation and had made these known to his superiors: namely, that the present inactivity was not prolonging peace but increasing the likelihood of a great disaster. But for some time his frustration, like that of many other officers and soldiers, had given way to a fatalistic apathy. Accordingly, at the dance, when ambushed by a cheerful group of educated ladies and prosperous merchants, he had refused to discuss the status quo, saying only that in his opinion the front line was the sharp edge of a knife stuck into the enemy's side, and those who believed that there could be peace without it being carefully removed were

14

deluding themselves. That evening he had devoted most of his energies to the plundering of the inexhaustible buffet, and only after midnight, when the brass band had played *Rosen aus dem Süden*, had he allowed himself to yield to the pleas of a luminous young beauty and had made the brave, for a man of his age, decision to dance in the rapid Viennese style. That waltz was still ringing in his ears when the enemy bombardment began at dawn.

It was all over in two days. On the barren landscape now lay decomposing bodies, abandoned garrisons and telegraph poles with cut wires. What remained of the army split into lawless units that ignored their leaders' orders and fled for their lives. The war in Asia Minor had been lost. In the whirlpool of the defeat Brigadier Nestor's decimated unit, less than a thousand men, had preserved its discipline and was trying to find a way out of the maze and to reach the sea. They had to avoid contact with the enemy; they had been travelling for days, changing direction every time they suspected an ambush ahead, but there had been no sight of the coast as yet. Furthermore, communication with General Headquarters had been lost, and many suspected that the rest of the Expeditionary Corps had by now evacuated the peninsula.

In any case, Brigadier Nestor refused to raise the white flag.

The first thing the brigadier did when he awoke was to hide the syringe under his cot. It was late afternoon and the column had halted. There was the snorting of horses outside and the occasional clop of a shod hoof on stone. Brigadier Nestor sat back and crossed his hands over his belly. He felt contented, even though he knew well that his emotions were only due to the generosity of the morphia – he had grown to accept its effect without shame. After a while he sat up and with a bayonet attempted to open a sealed cigar box. He was still struggling when a younger officer climbed into the lorry and gave a casual salute. His uniform was caked with dust, his kepi was missing its cockade and a towel was tucked into its back to cover the nape of his neck. Brigadier Nestor looked fleetingly at his subordinate – it was enough for his eyes to register their disapproval of the man's beard.

'It's you, Porfirio – I mistook you for Don Quixote.'

His Chief of Staff wiped his face on his cuff. Through the open hatch the sand of the desert blew in, settling on the blankets, the maps, the smoking coffee pot on the stove. With his face clean the major looked much younger.

'Is it time?' the brigadier asked.

The radio-telegraph was in a corner, next to the old bicycle that drove its magneto. Without replying, Major Porfirio sat on the seat and began to pedal with a burdensome sense of duty. He looked like someone arriving for a long but uncomplicated shift – a night porter or a watchman. The rear wheel, kept an inch above the floor, was set in motion with a hissing sound. There was a certain desperation in the task, which was supplemented perfectly by the assortment of dusty utensils, the small stove, the table with the yellowed maps.

For the next hour Brigadier Nestor sent messages

and waited for a reply, but the only thing he heard in the headphones was electromagnetic noise. He gave up with a shrug of his shoulders; his Chief of Staff wiped his forehead and stopped pedalling. They had failed again. For the past week they had been trying to contact General Headquarters, but the only replies they received were a message from the enemy calling on them to surrender or face total annihilation and a prayer to St Varvara keyed by the operator of the wireless on board a Greek cargo ship nearing Suez. The brigadier sighed and poured two coffees. As soon as he took a sip he grimaced.

'Unsweetened coffee could have been the punishment of Sisyphus,' he said. [*]

He had awakened that morning to discover that the tin with the sugar had disappeared. At first he had suspected his orderly, but according to several witnesses the boy had spent the night in the infirmary, recovering from a snakebite. Brigadier Nestor threw his hands in the air: Major Porfirio raised his eyebrows. The mystery had caused the old man a disproportionate glumness – one might have thought the fate of the sugar concerned him more than that of the brigade itself.

'A breakdown of discipline. If only I knew who had stolen it.'

He set his cup on the floor and took the cigar box

---

[*]In Greek mythology, Sisyphus was a king who enraged Zeus. The latter condemned him to the lowest region of the underworld, where he was forced for eternity to push to the top of a hill a stone that always rolled down again.

in his hands again. On its lid was the picture of an African wearing a fez, with smoke coming out of his ears. The brigadier tried to break the seal again with the bayonet. It slipped and cut his finger, the box hit the metal floor with a dull sound and the old officer set to sucking his finger. At his feet the caricature of the African stared at him. Brigadier Nestor felt his disposition balance on a tightrope. The major lifted up the box, took a switchblade from his pocket and worked its tip into the groove of the seal. When at last he heard the metal break, the brigadier let out a sigh of relief and welcomed the scent of tobacco. For a while the two men smoked.

'I miss reading the papers,' said the brigadier.

'There would be nothing to read. When the situation took a turn for the worse, they started printing the old stories with the names and dates changed.'

Brigadier Nestor agreed that the heavy censorship had affected the quality of the news. But any newspaper would still be better than none at all. He shoved his hand under his cot and revealed a large leather tome. The spine read *Lexicon of Greek and Roman Myths* in fading letters. In its thick creased pages several lines had been underlined by a passionate hand. He closed the book and tapped the burgundy cover with his finger.

'A most pleasurable read. The padre is incensed that I know more of this by heart than the Bible.'

The major glanced at the heavy book. Behind the desk the rusty bicycle stood like a relic of old, carefree times. At that moment the experience of pleasure felt to the officer like a very distant memory. He put out his cigar, hid it in his pocket and spread a map over his knees. He ran his hand across the gridlines, then stopped and rubbed the nape of his neck.

'Well,' he announced. 'We're lost.'

His commanding officer received the news without surprise.

'There is always the possibility of divine intervention.'

A bird's cry came from afar, sounding like a curse. Feeling queasy from the heat, Major Porfirio put down his cup.

'I didn't like this campaign from the start,' he said.

The brigadier closed his eyes.

'Discipline is needed now more than ever, major.'

The major let his eyes wander from the kettle on the stove to the envelopes strewn across the floor, to the leather belt with the holstered revolver that hung from a crossbar of the roof of the lorry. Brigadier Nestor sneezed.

'The dust is giving me an allergy . . . Naturally, I understand your disappointment – under the circumstances.' He took a deep breath and summoned the last reserves of his optimism. 'But rest assured this story is not over. Now we are down – but.'

The major went back to studying the map.

'Not to mention our Christian brothers here in Anatolia,' continued his superior. 'They shall need our help again.'

The brigadier tapped his boot on the floor. The morphia had unearthed a rare eloquence in him – he felt as if he were not sitting on his cot but standing on a marble plinth. He looked a few inches above the major's head, to the past.

'Once there was an empire, major.'

The younger officer arched his eyebrows. 'An empire?'

'The Byzantine Empire.'

'A long time ago, brigadier.'

Brigadier Nestor raised his forefinger.

'History is what happens over centuries – not yesterday.'

He gulped his coffee. The sun was setting and he asked for his greatcoat. Through the open hatch he watched a scudding cloud with a castaway's expression. He took the cigar out of his pocket, lit it and savoured the mentholated smoke.

'This cigar is not bad. But the coffee tastes like my mother-in-law.'

He handed over his cup and cracked the joints of his fingers. The drug had afforded him its brief windfall and was now receding – if only he could maintain that feeling a little longer . . . Brigadier Nestor tried to recall the time he had no need of the services of chemistry, but it was like trying to remember how it had once felt being a boy. His subordinate poured the remains of both cups back in the pot. 'Any orders?' he asked.

The miracle of the morphia was evaporating. Brigadier Nestor wrapped himself in his coat and waved the major away. 'No. Dismiss.' When Major Porfirio turned to leave the old man spoke again. 'One moment.' He gave his subordinate a tender look – there was a hint of honest concern in what he said next.

'Don't forget, Porfirio. In the aftermath of defeat the firing squad works overtime.'

The old officer waited until the footsteps had faded away, then buttoned up the flaps of the tarpaulin and found the syringe he had hidden under his cot. A whistle blew outside, and the order to start again travelled down the column. For a quiet moment Brigadier Nestor held the syringe to the light and smiled at it with disaffection.

'A little more,' requested Father Simeon shyly, holding his mess tin with both hands. His left eye looked straight at the cook, while the other was trained somewhere to the right and above the man's head.

That eye was made of glass – Father Simeon had lost the one given to him by God during a barrage of artillery fire in the first year of the expedition when, despite the repeated warnings of the soldiers, he had rushed to administer the last rites to a cavalryman lying in the field. A piece of shrapnel had hit the ground near them, penetrated the belly of the man's dead horse and caught the padre in the face. For several days Father Simeon had worn an eyepatch with some embarrassment, until the brigade had liberated the next town. There the padre had promptly bought one of the eyes of a stuffed jackal from a local taxidermist.

Father Simeon held out the tin.

'The day of saints Michael and Gabriel is coming up, friend.'

The cook looked at him.

'The patron saints of soldiers,' the padre explained. 'I'll put in a good word for you.'

He was in his fifties, but his skin was resisting the attacks of age with success. Despite the eye wound and the clerical beard, his face was still handsome and lively. For many years he had been the pastor of a small congregation in a village that offered few opportunities for sin. Indeed, boredom was one reason he had volunteered for the campaign despite his age — the other was his sense of not having fulfilled the requirements of his vocation. As a young priest he had toyed with the idea of joining the Orthodox Mission in Africa, but then he had chanced across an illustrated novel which showed an explorer in a boiling cauldron and natives dancing all round him. All at once his ear had turned deaf to his divine calling, a decision that had left him with an eternal sense of guilt.

The cook puffed with impatience. 'Not a drop, Father,' he said and shooed away the flies with his ladle. 'The mechanic needs it for the lorries.'

The padre raised his eye to the sky.

'Lord, forgive him. He is betraying the souls of his comrades for some pistons.'

He refused to go away. A buzzard landed at the nearby rubbish heap and began to walk towards the rotting matter cautiously, keeping an eye on the man with the ladle. Other birds big and small plunged from the sky into the remnants of the afternoon mess, hesitantly at first, more bravely after a while. Father Simeon counted the months that had passed since it had rained: under his feet the sand felt hard and dry. Suddenly he tried to imagine the life of the old Christian hermits, and the old sense of worthlessness came over him. While he struggled with it, the cook picked up a wire brush and started cleaning the stove. Father Simeon rocked on his feet from side to side.

'How about that oil, friend?' he asked again.

The cook continued his work.

'Against orders.'

'When we get home I will personally ask the bishop to reward you for your piety.'

The cook opened the oven door and put his head inside.

'Not even your patron saints know whether we'll make it.'

Father Simeon did not contradict him. Instead, his eye fell on the cook's back and he frowned: the man's trousers were ripped at the seam. The padre murmured his displeasure.

'What now, Father?' the cook asked.

'Wider than the Straits of the Dardanelles.'

Without removing his head from the oven, the cook felt the seat of his trousers, grunted indifferently and resumed his work. Father Simeon walked round to the other side of the stove in order to avoid the spectacle.

'Five,' he finally murmured.

The cook took his head out of the oven and grinned.

'Ten.'

'Seven, sinner.'

The cook agreed. He wiped his hands on his apron, picked up the burned pan and filled the padre's tin to the brim. Father Simeon looked searchingly around: on the rubbish heap the scavengers buried their beaks in the trash and flapped their wings – there were no soldiers in sight. He unbuttoned his tunic, took out a manila package and handed it to the cook. The latter passed it under his nose and smelled it with eyes closed.

'Sweet as communion wine.'

The padre blushed and contemplated the packet with sadness.

'I may burn in Hell on their account – but life is a matter of priorities.'

The transaction finished, he took hold of the mess tin with both hands and walked away. The air was cool, yet the sand was still hot. On the other side of the camp was a shabby tent, patched up with old uniforms and tablecloths. Above its entrance was a tin inscription that read, HOLY ORTHODOX CHURCH OF THE CAPPADOCIAN FATHERS. Once inside the padre poured the contents of his mess tin through a tea strainer, funnelled the clean oil into an earthen pot and topped up the lamp that hung in front of the altarpiece. Then he sat on the floor with a sigh and poured himself a cup of jasmine tea. He thought: imagine; having to bargain for oil for the lamp. He drank slowly, nodding his head to register his disappointment in human nature.

The penury of the makeshift temple somehow added to the holiness of the place. Almost everything had been fabricated by the padre's inventive hand: the broken lectern that was fixed on a machine-gun tripod, the cases of artillery shells now filled with sand and used in place of candelabra, the four doors hinged together to make an altarpiece. He sipped his tea and studied his work with pride. Breaking his rest, he searched for something to do, and in a minute he set about sweeping the floor. When he had finished it was almost time for vespers. In the middle of the tent was a large brazier filled with charcoal; he kindled it with a bundle of handbills daubed with methylated spirit. While waiting for the fire to build, he glanced at the little pieces of paper he had found that morning pinned on the entrance to his tent. They were handbills advocating insurgency. Similar pieces of paper had been appearing throughout the campaign under trunks, knapsacks and saddles.

The first had been distributed the very day of the landing. No sooner had the troopship with the first detachment of the brigade dropped anchor in Anatolian waters, than its decks were swarming with those little paper squares the soldiers would soon grow familiar with. Blown by the wind, they had reached the promenade of Smyrna like a cloud of butterflies, where thousands of Christians had assembled to welcome the liberators. It had been an embarrassing incident that had almost cost Brigadier Nestor his command. Since then a number of inquiries had been undertaken, but none had revealed the culprit. Father Simeon had fulminated against the treasonous handbills from the pulpit on several occasions, but they continued to appear.

It was time. The padre took his tunic from the hanger and brushed it inside and out. He removed his liturgical cross from his breast pocket and wore it over his uniform, then put his stole about his shoulders. He dressed with slow movements, whistling and taking his time to pluck the loose threads of his old stole. Having lived alone all his life, he had invested his domestic and religious chores with a transcendental quality. Daily tasks had the ability to take his mind off his loneliness – they were the buoy that kept him on the surface of life, whose darkness terrified him. That was the reason why, when he had joined the expedition, he had promised himself that he would carry on as if he still lived in his village.

When he was ready he stepped out of the tent and shook his handbell. No one came. He knitted his brows and rang the bell louder, but as soon as he stopped silence returned to the camp. He tried a third time. A dog squirmed out from underneath a lorry and came towards him, its ribcage swinging to and fro.

'What's the matter, Caleb?' the padre asked.

Breathing thirstily, the dog raised its head and looked at Father Simeon with dull eyes. The padre rubbed his beard – in truth he was not surprised at what was happening. Once he was convinced that no one was coming to mass, he removed and folded his stole, dropped his cross in his pocket and put on his skullcap – his gaiety had evaporated and he was now upset.

'It's useless, Caleb. They have offered themselves to the devil.'

He had been looking forward to vespers. A month ago more than forty soldiers would come to the evening service, but by last week that number had dropped to ten. The evening before he had said mass to a congregation of one deaf bombardier. Father Simeon snapped his fingers and the dog sprang to its feet. Together they walked across the camp. There was a forest of stacked rifles, rows of tents and several fires where coffee pots simmered: the soldiers were resting after another day of continuous marching. The hobbled dromedaries and mules in the corral watched the man and the dog without emotion. The padre wiped his forehead with the back of his hand.

'A great misfortune, Caleb.'

He puffed, and looked deep into the dog's eyes for some sign of sympathy.

Major Porfirio unfolded the chair outside his tent and searched his pockets for the half-smoked cigar. He struck his lighter and lit it, then crossed his legs and exhaled the smoke. The day was burning out – over the hills an enormous red sun was setting. The officer observed it without thinking, until a voice brought him back from ecstasy. It was his orderly; he was dressed in a pair of oversize breeches and a shirt whose buttoned-up collar almost choked him. A towel hung down from his forearm – he had somewhere seen a waiter once carry one that way. It was not only because of his age, or the bad fit of his clean uniform, but also because of his tormenting clumsiness that he always reminded the major of a play-acting boy. Speaking with discretion, the orderly informed his superior that his meal was ready. Major Porfirio looked at him almost with affection before asking for a glass of wine.

'I'm afraid there isn't any, my major.'

The major frowned. He could remember perfectly well that the last time he checked there were still several bottles left.

'That's true. But they have gone missing.'

The boy was a distant relative of his. When he was conscripted his family had implored the major to keep him out of harm's way; Major Porfirio had interceded with the brigadier and the boy was assigned to be the two officers' joint aide.

'I kept the bottles under my cot,' the orderly said. 'It

must have happened the night I was in the infirmary.'

'The brigadier will be very troubled by this news,' Major Porfirio said.

He finished his cigar and received the tray with his meal. He lifted the tin covers and inspected every plate: two slices of cornbread, a boiled corn cob and a cup of thick soup whose main ingredient was corn kernels. Major Porfirio's face assumed a gloomy expression.

'The cook is even less imaginative than our strategists,' he murmured, before wiping his knife against his sleeve and doing the same with the fork.

Having eaten everything on both plates he skimmed off the crust of dirt in his cup and drank the lukewarm soup slowly, helping down each sip with a piece of hard tack – it was the fifth day in a row they had had corn. Interrupting his meal to swat the flies, he thought about the thefts of the wine and the sugar. He was intrigued that in the midst of this direst situation the men would concern themselves with profiteering. 'When the boat is sinking,' he said by way of an explanation, 'the rats come up on deck.' He drank the last of his soup and put down the empty cup with a sigh of relief.

He caught sight of Father Simeon walking across the camp in the company of his dog, and raised his hand in a greeting. Immediately the distant pair of silhouettes changed course and came towards him. Waiting for them, the major felt the loneliness of the corn in his stomach.

'Lost, Father?'

The padre nodded. 'In the labyrinth of sins. I run a church that has no congregation.'

Major Porfirio pushed a stone with the side of his boot and offered a smile.

'Don't blame them. They don't know whether they'll be alive tomorrow.'

'Even more reason. The Lord can take away the fear.'

The major called to his orderly to bring the padre a chair. Father Simeon accepted it with thanks. As soon as he sat down the dog crawled under it, and he gave the animal a fatherly glance.

'If dogs could talk,' he said, 'they would teach the world humility.'

The dog beat the dust with its tail a few times. Major Porfirio turned his head and looked at the animal with an expression of disbelief. He could not think of it as a creature in possession of moral supe-riority, but he did appreciate its instinct to treat evil merely as a natural occurrence – like something that could not be prevented but which one could still run away from. A dog is like a happy madman, he thought. He pushed back his cap and prepared to watch the sunset as if it were a theatrical performance. The air was warm and silent, with a velvet texture. Next to the spectacle of his defeated troops the beauty of the landscape seemed as inhuman as it was absolute. He contemplated with melancholy the sun burying itself in the sand.

'The fact of the matter is, Father, that this world would still be the same whether you and I were above ground or six feet under.' Night was coming and above their heads the birds hurried away. 'I would offer you a glass of my wine, if only I knew who had the bottle.'

'Oh.' The padre twisted a strand of his beard. 'Stolen?'

Major Porfirio rubbed his eyes.

'If the brigadier catches the thief he will set him at twelve paces.'

The padre looked away. 'We ought not let our personal grudges get in the way of our mercy. After all, what are a few bottles of wine . . .'

'You don't understand the rules of the army, Father.'

The padre made a face.

'The army would be run better by the Ecumenical Patriarch.'

Above their heads flies always circled, almost invisible in the dusk. The major clapped his hands and inspected his palms with triumph: a small red smear was on his fingers.

'If you hear anything at confession,' he said, brushing his hands on his trousers, 'you will of course let the brigadier know.'

Father Simeon shook his head in refusal.

'The contents of a confession are not to be disclosed. But I promise to try and dissuade the sinner with all my pastoral powers.'

The dog whined. Father Simeon stretched his arm and stroked it. Across the camp the fires burned and the mules nickered in the corral. Beyond the hills the moon was rising; it was not long before the bugle would be sounding lights out.

CHAPTER 2

The brigadier knelt down with a sigh and looked at his correspondence scattered across the floor of the lorry. The sight of letters and postcards lying in the dirt caused a sadness in him, as if he were looking at a flock of dead doves. He sat on his cot and began to smooth everything piece by piece, with patience, brushing off the dust with his palm. When he finished he raised his eyes and looked out: the landscape was a vast wasteland, littered with ditched lorries and decommissioned artillery guns. Soldiers and animals walked about in silence, seemingly without a purpose, as if still dazed by the overwhelming defeat. But suddenly, in the dusk, small fires began to appear one after another across the camp. A little hope stirred in Brigadier Nestor's heart – perhaps they stood a chance after all, he thought. He opened a random envelope from the bundle on his lap, read a few of the hand-written words he almost remembered by heart, and at once evoked the memory of his wife.

They had first met at a Christmas ball thirty-four years earlier, in one of the most fashionable hotels of the capital, when First Lieutenant Nestor had trodden on the lace train of her dress. When his sincerest apolo-gies had been met with her benevolent smile, he immediately knew he had chosen well. Because, in fact, their encounter had been the product of a Byzantine conspiracy perpetrated by a professional matchmaker. Unbeknown to her, the young officer had already noticed the fair maiden months earlier. His enquiries had revealed that although she was indeed available, she was the beneficiary of a European education – a benefit to a man, but to a woman of a marrying age an unmediated anathema. Why, she even condemned the feudal practice of arranged marriage! First Lieutenant Nestor had been all the more fascinated. In his attempts to woo her he applied the principles of modern warfare he had studied at the Academy; finally, his decisiveness and imagination had paid off.

It had been a marriage of peaceful routines. There had been the occasional liaison, of course. Thinking about these, Brigadier Nestor now shrugged his shoulders self-righteously: it was impossible for a soldier away from home for such long periods not to succumb. But nothing of substance ever. He would have told her about them if she had been capable of comprehending – but it was different for women, he understood. He had long since absolved himself. He licked his thumb and, as he turned the page, a photograph fell out: a child dressed in a sailor suit, riding a tricycle: Brigadier Nestor's grandson. The old officer held it at arm's length for some time, squinting and smiling with pride, before he returned it into the envelope.

Finally, he found the letter from his daughter, which announced the terrible news, and confirmed the date of his wife's death from pneumonia: a year ago tomorrow – he had to arrange the memorial service. 'Orderly!' he shouted in the direction of the hatch, and when the boy appeared: 'Ask the padre to come and see me.'

He blew his nose in his handkerchief and then, as soon as he placed it in his pocket again, he detected the smell of putrefaction. He traced it to under his cot, where he saw a dead snake. Kneeling down, Brigadier Nestor observed his discovery thoughtfully, as if trying to interpret an omen. The snake lay in the dust in an unnatural position, twisted in the shape of the numeral eight. Someone had hurled it there, the brigadier thought, stroking his chin. He opened his trunk and used his ceremonial sword to retrieve the reptile. He noticed that its head was crushed. Holding up the snake, skewered from the tail, he studied next the patterns of its skin.

'It is wrong to kill a creature with a skin more intriguing than Euclidean geometry,' he said. 'Orderly!'

The hatch to the driver's cabin opened. When the soldier saw the snake, his eyes opened wide too.

His commanding officer asked, 'Who did this?'

The young man shrugged, while his big brown eyes remained fixed on the dust-covered carrion. Through the hatch Brigadier Nestor saw the evening desert framed by the dirty windscreen, vague and all of a single dark colour: a few broad strokes on a canvas left otherwise unfinished. He looked back again, made an expression that indicated he did not believe his aide and passed him the snake.

'I do not care what the Bible says. You are not to kill another serpent.'

As soon as the hatch closed, he cleaned his sword and put it back in the trunk, under a stack of starched and ironed shirts which had lost their freshness a long time ago. He locked both the enormous padlocks and sat at his desk. Buried under his maps were the pair of compasses, the ruler and a pencil as small as a cigarette end. In his breast pocket were his spectacles. 'Now,' he puffed, and fixed the wires of his glasses behind his ears, 'let's find out where the hell we are.' He licked the blunt tip of his pencil with gusto and started.

For some time he was absorbed in the geodetic calculations he did on the margin of the maps. He only had a break in order to fill his cup with coffee and search for the protractor. He sipped the bitter coffee with a sentimental craving for sugar. More than an hour later he put down his infinitesimal pencil and read out the depressing news.

'Three hundred and twenty-two yards west of our last position. Plus or minus eleven.'

He removed his spectacles, fixed his eyes on the leather holster hanging over his head and at once recalled the legend of Damocles' sword[*] – he had read about it recently in his book of mythology.

'And we are headed away from the coast,' he added.

A gentle voice from outside brought him back from his grim reflections.

'I could come back later,' the padre said softly.

---

[*]Damocles was a courtier of the tyrant of Syracuse. When the tyrant heard Damocles commenting on the grandeur and happiness of rulers, he invited him to a luxurious banquet. As soon as the meal ended, Damocles noticed a sword hanging above him by a single horsehair. Placed there by the tyrant, it made Damocles realise that insecurity might threaten those who appear to be the most fortunate.

Brigadier Nestor waved him in.

'Come in, Father. My job won't be any easier in an hour.'

The padre climbed into the back of the lorry, smiling. He found a stool, sat down, undid the button that held the stiff collar of his tunic and exhaled. Then he started talking in a pleasant manner. He apologised for being late – it was because that afternoon he had caught a soldier eating corned beef. Brigadier Nestor looked at the padre with weary eyes.

'Is that an offence now?'

'Eating meat on Wednesday,' the padre explained.

The brigadier nodded. There was a sweat stain on the map where his palm had lain: like the territory they had annexed during the three-year expedition, it soon began to evanesce. Brigadier Nestor contemplated the old map – he would have called the whole venture a waste of time if it were not for the dead, the dispossessed, the refugees. No: it had been an outright catastrophe. Father Simeon was still talking.

'What is the point of fasting if not for acquiring discipline, I told him. I had to produce the tin during confession to stop him denying it, my brigadier – took me more than an hour to absolve him.'

Brigadier Nestor left his desk and lay on his cot. After a while he suspected that Father Simeon must have asked something because he had suddenly turned silent.

'Excuse me, Father, I didn't hear you. I was thinking about my funeral.'

The padre raised his eyebrows and repeated the question.

'You wanted to see me, brigadier?'

The officer remembered.

'Oh, yes. I need your services, Father.'

'A . . . confession?'

The padre sat on the chair and leaned forward: he was like a thirsty man bending down to drink from a tap. But it was dry. Brigadier Nestor scratched the crown of his head with bemusement.

'My confession now would taste like raw meat. Still too much blood in it, you see.'

Father Simeon assumed an expression of gloom with as much speed and accuracy as if he had rehearsed it countless times. But he was not pretending; since the collapse of the front he often thought of himself as a heavy sack of ballast in a rapidly descending balloon. The brigadier reminded the padre that it was a year since Mrs Nestor's death. In yet another automatic reaction the padre offered his condolences.

The officer asked, 'A memorial service perhaps?'

'By all means, my brigadier.'

Brigadier Nestor thanked him and added, 'I should have been by her side . . .'

'How could you have, my brigadier?'

Brigadier Nestor rubbed the furrows of his neck.

'This war . . .'

'Everyone has a cross to bear,' said the padre in his usual way.

'A cross,' Brigadier Nestor echoed, and gathered as much humour as was there in his heart. 'At my age I shouldn't be bearing weights, Father.'

'It's a steep ascent to Calvary.'

The brigadier chuckled bitterly.

'It's not the ascent I mind, Father, but the cruci-fixion afterwards.'

The man of God could offer little more than a smile.

'It's natural to be afraid. But salvation could be round the corner.'

'There are no corners in this Field of Blood.'

Father Simeon took out his Bible and riffled through it.

'*Touching the Almighty, we cannot find him out,*' he read out. '*He is excellent in power, and in judgement, and in plenty of justice.*'

The brigadier puffed with exasperation. A draught had found the lamp on his desk with the maps and toyed with it – the flame flickered but did not go out. Held down by the lamp, the old maps crackled and fluttered like birds beating their wings against the wire of their cage. Brigadier Nestor said, 'One of these days, Father, you have to explain to me that whole lily business.'

Father Simeon frowned.

'The lily?'

'The lily of the Annunciation. Just how on earth –'

'A miracle, my brigadier. It was a miracle.'

The officer nodded.

'A miracle. I see – exactly what we need now. Could you arrange one for us?'

Father Simeon did not reply – he knew better than to stoke the coals of discontent with too many moral pronouncements. Like a stone thrown in a lake, the ripples of the irreverent comment travelled across the silence and slowly faded away. Feeling he was no longer welcome, the padre stood up and turned to leave, but the brigadier suddenly spoke up.

'Is it a sin to kill a snake, Father?'

'If it were going to harm you I should think not. Isn't it . . . the same in battle?'

They shook hands and soon the padre was walking across the camp. His shoulders sloped under his great-coat and the cross on his chest swung from side to side. Lying at the entrance to his tent was the dog, waiting for him. Father Simeon did not let it in. He pulled down the flap and went and sat on the edge of his cot. If only people trusted in God, he thought. Maybe that was the reason they had lost the war: the enemy had a blind faith in Allah and was not afraid of death. The enemy truly believed in Paradise – his own paradise, a barbaric notion, of course. He wondered: how many of his fellow Christian soldiers believed in salvation? He looked at a coil of rope on the floor and for a moment remembered the conversation about the snake.

'God save us from the serpent,' he murmured with apocalyptic fear.

From underneath the cot he produced a candle and pushed it into a bucket filled with sand. He lit it and slowly a foul smell filled the air: ever since the paraffin had run out he had made candles from cattle fat. A scorpion crept in from under the tarpaulin and raised its tail. Father Simeon gave it an indifferent glance and wrapped himself in his blanket. His eye wandered across the wooden altarpiece. On it was a John the Baptist, a St George on horseback and an Entry into Jerusalem where Jesus' donkey had the padre's face. It had been meant as an innocent jest – perhaps even as an exercise in humility, but the humorous painting now appeared as a sanctimonious, blasphemous and conceited act. Father Simeon thought again about his religious failings, and those of his congregation.

'Science,' he said unexpectedly.

His face reddened and he stood up. In situations like this, when the weight of self-recrimination became too heavy to bear, he would attack his favourite hates. With his hands made into tight fists he began to pace his tent, head bent, mumbling. Science was the new religion in the Western world, he thought. The vainglory of professors, the grandiosity of lecture theatres, the doctrinal language of scientific treatises . . . How did those people dare challenge faith? He had seen photographs of laboratories and it had struck him how much they resembled medieval torture chambers. The preposterousness of it all! Take for example the ridiculous theories of that German Zionist physicist. He scratched his head, trying to remember the name in the newspaper not long ago.

'*Enistan,*' he said like a profanity. Yes – that man was becoming more popular than that other enemy of Orthodoxy, the Catholic scoundrel, the Pope. Father Simeon clasped his hands behind his back and maintained his planetary orbit round the sombre religious furnishings. 'It only goes to prove that science is the fifth column of the Jews,' he grumbled.

He was feeling out of his depth. The frustration of not knowing exactly what he was talking about only fuelled his vexation. 'The Enlightenment,' he pondered scornfully, twisting the tip of his beard. 'The scourge of Logic!' The fortunate Ottomans had missed all that. And now . . . Father Simeon stopped his incensed walk and curled his lip. '*Blessed are the poor in spirit*,' he said, panting. '*For theirs is the kingdom of heaven*.' He bowed his head and added with despair, 'As for us, we'll simply burn in Hell.'

The forest of stacked rifles gleamed in the twilight and in the glow of the fires burning under the coffee pots. Somewhere a flint was struck to light a cigarette or a pipe. Sitting cross-legged on a Muslim prayer rug, the corporal studied the chessboard, rubbing the stubble on his chin, making brief sounds with his nose: he was thinking. The cold of the desert night had begun to overwhelm the camp; it would soon be impossible to stay outside. The corporal puffed, stood to wrap himself tighter in his military coat and sat again on the rug. It was a small square rug with tassels at both ends, a beautiful tendril design all round it and an inscription in Arabic in the middle. The corporal never let it out of his sight. That night, for example, he sat on it not because the ground was too hard or cold – after all, he was a cavalryman and his lower body was used to the daily obstinacy of the saddle – but because he wanted to make sure that no one would steal this precious memento from him. In violation of the forgotten orders that strictly forbade looting, he had taken it from a house in an abandoned village the brigade had come to during its final advance into the Anatolian heartland, almost a year earlier. He would not tell anyone, but the rug was intended as a present for a special person back home.

On the other side of the chessboard the medic sighed, adjusted his Red Cross armband and gave him an impatient look.

'Let me remind you that we are still playing chess, corporal. If I didn't know you were Christian, I would have assumed you had forgotten our game and were praying to Allah.'

The corporal did not raise his head, but took his hands out of his pockets and cracked his fingers in a gesture of great resolve. But as he was about to touch his rook he noticed something in the arrangement of the pieces on the board and his hands retreated hastily into the deep pockets of his greatcoat once again. The wind blew the smoke from the coffee pots in their direction − a smoke without aroma: the coffee had been cut with chicory.

'Your bishops have been acting like a band of brigands,' the corporal said. 'Against every rule of war.'

The medic abandoned the game in order to urinate. His opponent rested his chin on his fists, filled his chest with air and studied the chessboard. When the medic returned he was already putting the pieces away.

'Let's play draughts − a democratic game where all the pieces start as equals.'

The medic made a gesture of indifference, sat on the ground and crossed his legs. His puttees were soiled and shredded, his tunic was missing its buttons and the stitching of his sleeve was coming apart at the shoulder. But his temperament did not accord with the condition of his uniform − none of the horror and disenchantment of the war seemed to have contaminated his clear eyes: in the midst of the grief and fear of the camp he reminded one of a wise, impartial judge presiding over the trial of a horrific crime.

He was a university student of medicine who had suspended his studies in order to join the army. He was no political animal – indeed, he would have been indifferent to the Cause if he knew what it was. His aim from the start was to gain experience in shoe-string surgery, which he planned to practise after the war in a remote part of the homeland. Medicine was his religion and politics, and he wished to attend to it like a hermit. The day they were about to sail to Asia Minor he had declared to the chief medical officer that he would be following the trail of blood, and he meant it. He treated friends and foes the same, in defiance of the rule that priority should be given to one's own casualties. His attitude had earned him the public disapproval of his comrades, but, at the same time, their secret admiration too.

The medic pushed a draughtsman; in the next move it was going to be crowned. The corporal acknowledged the inevitable development with a bite on his moustache. He sat back, lit his pipe slowly and filled his cheeks with smoke.

'With luck like yours,' he said, puffing smoke moodily, 'you ought to try the lottery.'

After a moment he leaned forward again and studied the board under the fog of tobacco.

'I meant to ask you, medic. Last spring, why did you order the military police to cordon off that brothel?'

The tobacco smoke still hovered an inch above the chessboard, just like stratus clouds over a flat piece of land. Through the soft rolls of smoke the medic observed the black wooden draughtsmen scattered on the board and thought about the town with the brothel. The event that had taken place there had required the full austerity of his character. Such had been the seriousness of the situation that he had had to threaten the crowd of soldiers with a loaded pistol to stop them from entering the house of pleasure.

The medic frowned – sometimes he felt as if he were not a doctor but a herdsman of wild cattle. He raised his hand and pushed the smoke away from the chessboard.

'That place was a conservatory of every disease suffered by man below the waist.'

The corporal raised his head.

'Would you have fired that gun?'

His opponent met his eyes and spoke with a calmness that left no doubt.

'I would kill in order to save life.'

The corporal shuddered – the cold had begun to pierce the thick woollen coat and it hurt like needles. The call of the bugle offered him a way out of his imminent defeat. 'Lights out,' he declared and jumped to his feet. He rolled up the prayer rug and tucked it under his arm. 'This game is officially a draw.'

The medic collected the draughtsmen and, with the board under his arm, headed for the infirmary. It was a large round tent pitched in the middle of the camp, with red crosses painted on its tapering roof and its sides covered with crude paintings of wild animals, laughing clowns and acrobats in mid-air. The medic pursed his lips. They were lucky to have it. The tent had belonged to a roving Armenian circus, which the enemy had bombed from the air by mistake. When the brigade had stumbled across it, the soldiers had been confronted by the heart-rending spectacle not of dead men and women – *they* had managed to escape – but of their slaughtered wild beasts. A disembowelled elephant lay on its side like a beached shipwreck, several monkeys were bleeding to death while still chained together, a male lion with a singed mane and broken hind legs was crawling towards the burning carcass of his mate, growling. It had been a horrific sight. They had buried them all, and had demanded that Father Simeon say mass. It was peculiar how the suffering of animals always aroused more sympathy among the troops than the death of human beings, the medic reflected. He heard whining behind him: it was the padre's dog. He bent down and gave its receding coat an examining look. '*Alopecia areata*,' he diagnosed after a moment and patted the animal on the head. Caleb wagged his tail and sat down to scratch his flea bites, and the medic went to make his rounds.

Immediately he entered the enormous round tent he was greeted by the smell of antiseptic. Wounded soldiers lay in the cots, which were arranged in a circle round the edge of the tent and in straight rows in the middle. The medic walked among the beds. One soldier had a bandaged head, another had his leg in a plaster cast, a third had his face buried under layers of compresses. The medic stopped briefly now and then to examine a patient. He pressed his palm on someone's forehead and nodded with satisfaction. When he held up another's wrist and felt his pulse, he screwed up his face, lifted a gauze dressing soaked in pus and studied the wound until the nurse came up to him.

'Gangrene,' the medic said. 'Amputation first thing in the morning – before we start marching.'

The nurse nodded. He was a big man with a child's smile and arms as thick and rippled as the branches of a centenarian oak – he would have seemed more at home in a fairy tale than the field infirmary. Before the war he had been a sponge fisher and had suffered the bends countless times, but had survived thanks to a stubborn constitution. He had hoped to enlist in the navy but had not been given the choice – the infantry had a greater need for men. He often dreamed of the Aegean island he came from, and whether he would ever see it again. His love of his home was equalled by the great respect he had for his superior. He had served under his command from the start of the campaign. The medic had not only taught him the principles of nursing and surgery, but had also unearthed from his nurse's gigantic calloused fingers a miniaturist's preciseness the latter had not known he possessed.

He had used a simple method. At first, the embroidery exercises had seemed ridiculous to the nurse and so embarrassing that he would take the pharmaceutical gauze, the needles and the cotton thread and go and hide in his tent, cursing his superior for the demeaning tasks he was being given. But the medic knew what he was doing. Somewhere under the frustration at the botched designs, the pricked fingers from learning the chain stitch, the blanket stitch and the feather stitch, the sore eyes from mastering the French

45

knot, the satin cross, the cross stitch and, even, petit point, the nurse had turned into an invaluable surgical assistant.

The mosquitoes fell like bullets against the oil lamps that hung from the beams of the roof. On the earthen floor a small traffic of mice had already started, which no one paid any attention to. A few hours had been enough for the desert rodents to discover the temporary encampment. But instead of being sinister the mice had a bizarre, contrary effect. They reminded the men of their homes – the nibbled cheese in the larder, the torn sheets in the linen closet, the hole in the corner of the kitchen wall: the war had invested an otherwise mundane and foul presence with an almost moving notion of domesticity.

The medic continued his rounds, giving more orders in a discreet whisper. He indicated which casts could be removed, pointed out the dirty bandages which had not yet been changed, reminded the nurse to place an order with the carpenter for more splints. The nurse followed close behind with his hands in the pockets of his apron and his sleeves rolled up, revealing an uninspiring anchor tattoo on his forearm.

'Some cases are terminal, doctor. Perhaps we could save drugs . . .'

The medic pursed his lips.

'I'm not in charge of the firing squad.'

He immediately regretted having reproved his assistant. He turned round, patted him on the shoulder and tried to smile.

'I'll set up the laboratory,' he said.

The announcement made the nurse happy.

'We need sedatives, chloroform and aspirin, doctor.'

His superior shrugged his rickety shoulders.

'And the philosopher's stone – I promise to do my best.'

His quarters were in the next tent. They were furnished with scientific frugality – a black-lacquered desk and chair, and a cot covered with a rough wool blanket. On the desk were an earthenware set of wash-bowl and pitcher, a small mirror, a bar of soap, a shaving brush and a vial of pure spirit, everything arranged like surgical instruments. A wooden cabinet with labelled drawers was the medical archive, while the rest of the space was occupied by crates marked with the emblem of the International Red Cross. The medic put the chessboard on top of the filing cabinet, sat on the chair and no sooner closed his eyes than he was ambushed by sleep.

And then he dreamed. He was in a vast laboratory, a room with high ceilings and many rows of wooden tables, on which were laid beakers of every size, glass tubes, precision scales and sterilised instruments. He was dressed in a lab coat and he was looking through a microscope. He was alone for a long while and then the door at the far end of the room opened and an old man in a dark suit, starched collar and black bow tie walked towards him. He knew that face – not just the clothes, but also the white beard, the large fore-head, the trimmed grey hair. The man looked exactly like the photograph in the academic textbook, the medic thought in his dream: it was Louis Pasteur. The old man approached and leaned over the bench.

'Well?'

The medic raised his hands in the air and sighed.

'It is impossible, doctor.'

'The germs, my son.' Doctor Pasteur patted him on the shoulder. 'Think of the glass of milk. The process of fermentation. Disease develops in a similar way.'

The medic looked through the microscope again.

'Such a small organism and yet . . .'

The wise scientist nodded.

'Quite. It could bring down a vastly larger one.'

'How can we beat it?'

'Inoculation. It worked with septicaemia, cholera, diphtheria, tuberculosis, smallpox, hydrophobia . . . And we are only at the start. There are so many other diseases.'

'But what about the war, doctor?'

'The war? *You* have to discover the vaccine for that.'

The medic chuckled bitterly.

'There is no vaccine against foolishness, doctor.'

The old man shrugged and reminded the young man of one of his most notable successes.

'Oh, yes. That was what they said about rabies too.'

The medic woke up as suddenly as he had fallen asleep. He checked his watch: only a few minutes had passed. For a moment he fixed his eyes on the illusion of his dream, and only after it had totally disappeared did he begin to open the crates. In them was the equipment of a rudimentary laboratory, a benefaction paid for by wealthy expatriates. He unpacked the tubes filled with chemicals and read the label on each before placing it on the desk. He was more careful with the heavy Carl Zeiss microscope. At the bottom of the crate was a wall chart of the periodic table. He spread it over his desk, turned up the lamp and sat down to study it.

A voice behind him said, 'The bugle called lights out an hour ago. You are in breach of the regulations.'

He turned round. In the middle of the tent, with his thumbs hooked in his belt, stood Major Porfirio.

'You are fortunate I'm not the enemy. You could have had your throat slit.'

The medic gave him a weary glance.

'I can't remember the last time I set eyes on the enemy. By now I suspect we are a fairy tale to scare their children with.'

'The war is not quite over yet.'

The medic returned to studying the periodic table.

'They call it the theatre of war,' he murmured, 'but I think it rather resembles a circus.'

Major Porfirio remembered the reason for his visit.

'I need to borrow your razor. I seem to have misplaced mine.'

'Are you losing your beard?'

'The old man disapproves of it.'

'We have one foot in the grave and all he thinks of is personal grooming.'

The medic leaned over his desk and rolled up the periodic table. But no matter how much he looked for his straight razor he could not find it anywhere. He was perplexed.

'But it was there.' He pointed his finger. 'Right there. I always keep it between the shaving brush and the surgical spirit.'

Major Porfirio leaned over the desk and immediately recalled the recent thefts of the sugar and the wine. Surprise but also anger turned his face crimson: the brigadier was like a drowning man crying for help, and all someone did was put stones in his pockets. The medic gave the major a puzzled look.

'Stolen,' Major Porfirio explained, still looking at the empty spot on the desk where the medic's razor should have lain. 'Just when we thought that things could not get any worse we have a thieving spree to stop.'

As the moon emerged from the ruffled sand and rose above the desert, the wind quietened and the birds went to perch on the barren hills. Caleb walked across the camp at a lazy pace. The air stood like sheets of glass. His breath puffed up from his snout and his sad eyes moved from side to side with instinctive vigilance. Occasionally, one of his pointed ears turned in the direction of some noise and he immediately lifted his muzzle and sniffed the air. His tail had lost its hair and it now seemed as if he was dragging behind him a piece of torn rope.

His disease was not the only instance of bad luck in his life. The day he was born under a minaret in Istanbul a refuse lorry had run over his mother. He had suckled another dog and grown to be a fierce hunter of rats and cats, until a warden from the Board of Hygiene had caught him in his net. He was thrown in a cargo ship with other strays and carried across the Sea of Marmara to a small island off the Anatolian coast, where he was let loose to die of thirst and starvation. But no sooner had the funnel of the tramp steamer disappeared over the horizon than Caleb had entered the water. The Asian coastline loomed several miles ahead – he did not mind. Behind him the other dogs howled with fear and desperation – he paid no attention. Many days later he entered the town of Bursa all but dead from exhaustion. It was there that Father Simeon had come across him in the first year of the war.

Caleb stopped and scratched himself for a long time. When he had finished he had added another bald patch to his coat. Someone whistled and the dog walked up to him and let him stroke him. But when the man shook a bone with some meat on it Caleb walked away – he trusted only Father Simeon's hand to feed him. The stars had come out and he raised his head. He was bored. He whined. If only he had a companion . . . He yawned and let his tongue catch the moisture in the air. One of his incisors had rotted and fallen out. Outside the church he sat down and rested his muzzle on the sand. Under the moonlight a squad of soldiers was heading for sentry duty.

The night passed slowly in the camp and over the hills. Some time later Caleb heard footsteps and saw a man approach. Immediately, he stood up and began to snarl with a sense of duty, but when the man came closer he recognised his master. He tried to follow him into the tent but the padre forbade it. For a while an incomprehensible murmur came from inside while the shadow of Father Simeon wrapped in a blanket moved about. The candle went out and only the glow of the smouldering brazier remained. A little while later a stormy snoring began inside the tent.

Chapter 3

Brigadier Nestor emerged from the makeshift church with his mood unchanged. Neither the consolations of the mass commemorating his wife, nor the early-morning shot of morphia had helped him. He put on his cap and shook hands with Father Simeon, thanking him for his services. The sun had not yet appeared, but a line of blue light slowly grew across the horizon, as if the purple sky rose like a heavy curtain. The vultures had not arrived either, the wind had quietened, the earth was still cool – a brief moment of peace administered daily like medication. But it was a medicine that was only intended to soothe rather than cure: the army remained lost. The brigadier stood for a moment and contemplated the horizon with his hands in his pockets, while around him the preparations for the departure of the brigade continued. In any direction he turned, he saw no sign to suggest a way out of the labyrinth. Since Anatolia was east of the Aegean they could go west, of course, and eventually reach the coast. But a journey across land was not a simple problem of plane geometry. What was the condition of the terrain ahead? Perhaps the sea was closer if they travelled south or south-west. Above all: where was the enemy at that moment? One thing was certain: they should not head east.

Eastwards: not too long ago that had been the direction of their advance. For more than two years the towns of the Asia Minor heartland had surrendered to the Expeditionary Corps one after another . . . Enough of such thoughts, Brigadier Nestor suddenly reprimanded himself. He put his hand in his breast pocket to retrieve his compass, instructed his orderly which direction to follow (one of the latter's duties was also to drive the brigadier's lorry) and at last gave the signal to march.

Slowly the column started: another day of blindfolded marching was beginning. Brigadier Nestor's lorry led the way, followed by the vehicles carrying the wounded, others with ammunition and food and those loaded with water. Behind the motorcade the soldiers walked in silence, at a funerary pace that had also something of the unsteadiness of a drunk returning home. From the entire brigade at the beginning of the enemy offensive, there remained only two incomplete infantry battalions, a company of *evzones*[*] dressed in filthy skirts and boots with torn pompons, a squadron of horsemen and an artillery battery. Behind the troops came a long train of mules and dromedaries, laden with more provisions.

Sitting on the edge of his cot the brigadier rubbed his face with both hands. He had slept little the previous night. Following the conversation with the priest, he had taken to bed and spent the night adrift in a sea of abandon. At one time he had seen his wife's

---

[*]Soldiers of an elite Greek infantry unit used as assault troops.

ghost, suspended an inch from the floor, and later, after she was gone, the snake with the crushed head appeared crawling up the chimney of the stove. Worse was to come. A little before dawn he had been enveloped in a phantasmagoria of more dead coming alive: the ashen faces of friends who had passed on long ago, fellow officers in torn uniforms and with rotting skin who had been killed in action, his own soldiers and those of the enemy with blood oozing from their fatal wounds, headless cavalry horses, drowned sailors from sunken battleships . . . As if that were not enough, a constant and chilling clamour of incomprehensible whispers had accompanied the macabre carnival. When Brigadier Nestor had finally returned to the world of the living his body ached as if it were bruised all over.

During a brief rest to repair a flat tyre, Major Porfirio came to see him. They were in the middle of discussing their route when the brigadier noticed that his subordinate had only clipped his beard; he frowned.

'I thought I made it clear a beard does not befit an army officer. If you are so fond of it you should have joined the navy or the clergy.'

Before explaining the reason for not having shaved, Major Porfirio reported the disappearance of the wine bottles. Then the theft of the razor from the medic's quarters made a more dramatic impact. Brigadier Nestor scratched his cheek and pouted – unlike his subordinate's, his face was closely shaven and rewarded with perfumed lotion. He connected the thefts of the sugar, the wine and the razor in his mind as if joining the dots of a puzzle. The result pointed towards the obvious conclusion. His Chief of Staff articulated it.

'I feel it was taken by the same person who stole your sugar and my wine, brigadier.'

The brigadier nodded in agreement.

'A repeat offender.'

He took his handkerchief from his pocket, and while wiping his forehead remembered his discovery under his cot.

'Someone who doesn't like snakes.' He stared at his handkerchief. 'This is turning into a cheap detective novel, major. We have to put a stop to it.'

Outside, the troops marched past and the day grew hotter. The orderly lifted the wheel of the lorry off the ground with a jack. A long gash ran along the side of the tyre, wide enough to show the deflated inner tube that had to be repaired. There were other cuts on the same tyre, from older accidents, that had been sewn together with leather thread. While the orderly worked, the long column of soldiers continued to pass by, but they neither paid any attention to the lorry nor to the man squatting next to its front wheel. As the lorry began to tilt to one side, the two officers inside held on to the steel bars of the roof. The table and the heavy stove started to slide downwards, while the mechanical jack continued to creak. Brigadier Nestor felt seasick – a bitter substance from his stomach rose to his mouth, and he had to swallow several times and keep his lips tight to stop himself from vomiting. At last the jack stopped. With relief, the brigadier heard his orderly undo the wheel nuts. Slowly, his nausea faded and his mind returned to the matter of the thefts.

'I remember a case in the first company under my

command,' he said while the colour was returning to his face. 'When I caught the thief I had his arm amputated at the elbow. He was grateful I didn't have him shot.'

The smell of dung reached their noses. From the back of the lorry the brigadier watched the mules walk by, delving their heads into their nosebags as they went. With the halters round their necks they gave him the impression of a line of innocents on the gallows wearing hoods and nooses. Life, it seemed, was an enormous privilege once bestowed by a ruler, who sought to revoke it as soon as he realised the extravagance of his offer.

'There's a time and place for everything,' the brigadier said. 'And thieving is a peacetime pursuit.'

His subordinate agreed with a nod.

'We have to keep our wits about us,' the brigadier went on. 'If these thefts continue, morale will deteriorate even further. There is always the business of the handbills.'

Only two days earlier the agitator had struck again, after a brief truce which must have had to do with the disarray that had followed the collapse of the front. This time the handbills had been even more poisonous and incendiary than before. Brigadier Nestor had walked across the camp shouting at his men not to touch them while he frantically collected the handbills with a pair of tweezers. It had been more than a symbolic gesture. In his panic that morning, having read the articulate thesis which accused the military and political leaders of being responsible for the disaster, the brigadier had quickly come up with an ingenious story in order to stop his troops from reading them: the agitator was an enemy spy who had daubed the paper with arsenic to inflict casualties. It had not worked. By that afternoon the word had gone round that they, the soldiers, had been the victims of the politicians' eternal struggle for power, as well as of the incompetence and apathy of their generals in the field. Brigadier Nestor had despaired.

He now said, 'The only way to stop them from discussing what was written in those handbills would be to cut off their tongues.'

'I could reopen the handbill inquiry,' Major Porfirio offered.

'From now on I will conduct all inquiries person-ally. It's the only way to stop the heat from stewing my brain.' The lorry was still tilted. Brigadier Nestor looked out. 'That boy. He only had to change the tyre, not overhaul the damn engine.'

He ordered his Chief of Staff to see to it. When he was alone again he took to his cot, in a futile attempt to rest. Not only was the heat suffocating him but also, because of the tilt, he kept rolling off his cot. He decided to leave the lorry and walk instead. He climbed down at the moment the cavalry squadron was passing by and despite the slow pace of the horses he was at once overwhelmed by the clamour of the hooves, the stirrups and the sabres hanging from the side of the saddles. Such was his confusion that for a while he stood like a pedestrian frozen with fear in the middle of a busy street, while every kind of automobile, horse carriage and streetcar rushed past him, raising clouds of dust, sounding their horns and cursing him. It was the corporal who brought him back from his stupor.

'Be careful, my brigadier. My horse has a grudge against the army.'

He was riding a chestnut gelding with white shins and a cropped mane. Brigadier Nestor raised his head and gave the animal an inquisitive look: the intent gaze of its eyes, the tight mouth, the raised neck, gave him the feeling of being received in audience by an emperor. A proud animal, he thought. No – pride was a human trait; a horse had no sense of dignity or value. In the same way, it felt neither arrogance nor conceit. And what satisfaction could an ungulate take in achievement or possession? Brigadier Nestor regarded with contempt the fairy tales about sentient, talking and reasoning animals, but at the same time failed to recognise the anthropomorphism of the gods in his beloved myths.

'He will never forgive me for depriving him of his virility,' the corporal said.

The horse snorted and shook its head from side to side. The brigadier caressed its forelock.

'Sometimes I, too, feel like a eunuch, friend. At my age, even mandrake does not work.'

The corporal squeezed the reins, held on to the pommel and pressed his boots in the stirrups against the gelding's belly. He told his commanding officer that many a time in the heat of battle the horse had unexpectedly dug its hooves into the ground and sent him headlong into the enemy trenches. Nervous on account of its rider's posture, the gelding neighed. 'One of these days it's going to snap my neck,' the corporal said. 'But it is still better than going on foot in this heat.'

He saluted respectfully and rejoined his comrades. Some had an arm in a sling, their head or chest wrapped in bandages caked with blood, others were missing an entire limb. Watching them, Brigadier Nestor felt again the weight of his responsibility for keeping them alive. He removed his kepi and wiped his forehead with the back of his hand. It was nearly midday and the heat hung in the air like drapery. On the few trees the cicadas emitted a drone like a desperate, recurrent radio-telegraphic message. The old man shielded his eyes with his hand and surveyed the uneventful landscape. Beyond the humpbacks of a range of hills he detected some ruins – an ancient temple? It was quite possible; the Anatolian land was littered with them. They were the scattered pages of a book no one wished to read.

He could not then but recall that time when the army had been ordered to build fortifications in order to defend some town from the attacks of the Muslim brigands. Not far away, on the site of the other, the ancient city, there had been an Alexandrian citadel, whose walls still held out against the weight of time, the vortices of earthquakes and the fanaticism of winds. The arrival of Brigadier Nestor's retinue at the ruins had been greeted by two monumental marble lions, one male, the other female, lying on their sides in the undergrowth like a pair of predators after a successful hunt. When the officers had come closer they had not failed to notice – despite the thick lichen – the intricate detail of the chiselwork and the faded paint (the scarlet of the tongues, a little yellow on the broken tails) that gave those statues an all the more lifelike appearance. They were not therefore much surprised to discover in the shadow of one of the lions' bellies a litter of orphan wolf pups trying to suckle its stone teats.

The conquerors had entered the citadel through a secret aperture in its wall, whereupon, once their noses had accustomed themselves to the torpid breath of hibernating time and their eyes to the sepulchral darkness, they had been further amazed by the remarkable columns, friezes and mouldings that still decorated the defunct city, as well as by a self-sown copse of fig trees that had unexpectedly grown in the cracks of the floor tiles and now bore enormous aromatic fruit. Brigadier Nestor had ordered the army cartographer to sketch everything for the benefit of future historians and archaeologists, before giving, with a pain in his heart, the order to dynamite the whole place, so that they could use the stones to build the required fortifications round the modern town.

His orderly finished changing the tyre and began to lower the jack. They had to hurry – up ahead, like a vessel adrift, the brigade had moved on, roaming blindly across the endless maze of sand and dust. Brigadier Nestor sighed and headed for his lorry.

'What a torment,' he said. 'Being the captain of the Ship of Fools.'

Not long after, the column stopped again at a well – a low wall of uncut stones placed on top of each other without mortar, a rusty pulley on the end of a wooden pole and a frayed rope hooked on to a goatskin. The brigadier leaned over the hole and could not resist shouting through his cupped hands: 'King

Midas has ass's ears!'[*] A fading echo repeated his words down the dry shaft. Resting against the well he then contemplated the desert with watery eyes. At that moment Father Simeon walked past, holding in his hand the tin megaphone he used for his sermons. His beard was coated with dust and his boots had started to disintegrate.

'You spend too much time in the sun, Father. Even a Bedouin would get sunstroke on a day like this. You are crazy.'

The padre gave him a conceited smile.

'That's what they used to tell St John the Baptist.'

His piety did not impress the brigadier. He pressed his temple with his hand, then touched his brow before rubbing the bridge of his nose. The two men stood under the sun like numbers in an equation that has no solution. It was a stroke of genius to found a religion on the embrace of earthly suffering: no promise needed to be fulfilled in this life. Brigadier Nestor tried to think of faiths that actually exhorted the immediate gratification of carnal desire – hedonism, in other words. If they ever existed, had they survived – or would they – as long as Judaism, Christianity or Islam? He could not answer his question – he knew next to

---

[*]Midas was king of Phrygia in Asia Minor. When, as one of the judges in a musical contest between the gods Apollo and Pan, he favoured Pan, Apollo changed his ears to those of an ass. Midas managed to conceal them from all but his barber, who, not being able to keep the secret, whispered it into a hole in the ground. Every time the wind blew, the reeds growing over the hole repeated the story.

nothing about the religions of the East and was equally unsure where his ancient gods stood on the matter.

'Do me a favour, Father. Get in the shade. You can have your head served on a platter when I am not in command.'

'Life these days gives a priest few chances to prove his faith. I have to fulfil the demands of my vocation.'

'The way you carry on, Father, the only thing you will end up filling is a coffin.'

Reluctantly, Father Simeon went away. Brigadier Nestor screwed up his eyes and watched the man of God until he climbed into the back of one of the lorries. The brigadier shook his head. 'What an army. They are either thieves, traitors or martyrs.' Suddenly a sensation as discomforting as indigestion took root in his belly. Soon it felt as if a snake had made its way inside him and was now squirming slowly. Then the symptoms became akin to the snake nibbling his innards. He knew what all that meant: he was having a premonition. He immediately forgot about gods and religions. Now, *there* was something he believed in profoundly. He looked round him with apprehension but the only thing he saw, propped up against a tree, was the old postman's motorcycle his Chief of Staff had requisitioned after the death of his horse. On the small island of shade under the tree Major Porfirio had stopped to shave. For some time Brigadier Nestor searched with his gaze for a sign that something was wrong, but the landscape offered him nothing out of the ordinary. Yet he remained convinced of the imminence of some unusual event; he only questioned whether, whenever it happened, it would prove to be good or evil.

But he had little time to ponder – he remembered he was supposed to be having a word with the medic. At once he went to see him. He found him having his meal alone in the driver's seat of his Red Cross lorry. When he saw his commanding officer, the medic put his mess tin on the dashboard and wiped his lips on his sleeve.

'I hope I have arrived in surgery hours,' the brigadier said.

The medic smiled.

'There will come a time when people will get sick only when us doctors tell them to. Until then, we stay open all day.'

The brigadier removed his cap and climbed into the cabin of the lorry.

'Please, finish your meal, doctor. I can wait.'

He turned the rear-view mirror towards him, wiped off the dust and looked at the reflection of the crown of his head.

'And one day, you doctors will be able to raise the dead too,' he said, running his fingers through the thin strands of his hair. 'But you still won't have found a cure for baldness.'

'The matter will be settled by the process of natural selection,' the medic remarked. He broke a piece of hard tack, dipped it in his bean soup and chewed it slowly. Everything in the way he ate indicated that he was a man at ease with his conscience. He was not a pharisee – he knew exactly the limitations of his character and of his abilities. But he also knew he was doing his best under the circumstances. He was that rare species of man who is not responsible for the

ugliness of the world and who can thus sleep peace-
fully even inside the hottest cauldron in Hell – not
that he would ever end up there. Only perhaps that
his godlike heart, as clear and perfect at first sight as
Bohemian glass, could also hide the flaw of cruelty
that is sometimes associated with perfection, Brigadier
Nestor thought. But who could say that the old man
did not at that moment simply envy his subordinate
for his own failings? The brigadier unbuttoned his
tunic and breathed out with relief. That morning, in
an attempt to lift his spirits, his orderly had brushed
his uniform, sewn back the shoulder straps which
were about to fall off, darned the holes in the pockets
and polished his boots with petroleum jelly. The boy
had spent more than an hour on his undertaking, but
to no avail: the brigadier had not noticed. While
waiting for the medic to finish his meal, Brigadier
Nestor finally did see that his clothes were in perfect
order.

'Well,' he exclaimed. 'For a moment I thought I was
wearing someone else's uniform.'

The medic looked up from his mess tin.

'It could have been worse. You could have thought
you were someone else wearing your uniform.'

This was his opportunity to talk to his superior
about the matter that greatly worried him: malnutri-
tion. He explained that an ever-increasing number of
men were exhibiting its undeniable symptoms. The
fact was that the perpetual diet of corn was giving
rise to pellagra. Its first symptoms were fatigue, lethargy,
insomnia and weight loss; after exposure to the sun
the skin roughened, reddened and became scaly;

painful mouth lesions also developed; then came loss of appetite, caustic indigestion and unannounced diarrhoea. And it could go on to affect the nervous system too; later symptoms included headache, vertigo, muscular tremors, even dementia. Shaking his head, Brigadier Nestor listened to this list of horrors with diminishing attention.

'Dementia,' he echoed. 'As if there weren't enough madmen in this army already.'

He considered the medic to be his friend, ever since that day in the first year of the expedition when he had summoned him to his quarters. He had already heard good things about the young man: he was fulfilling his duties with enthusiasm and remarkable skill; he was treating bullet and shrapnel wounds, sewing up bayonet stabs, carrying out amputations; none of his patients ever developed septicaemia. That day the brigadier had needed his services too. 'I have developed a certain . . . ulcer,' he had said. The medic had asked where the lesion was. After a moment's silence, Brigadier Nestor had locked the door, pulled the curtains and unbuckled his belt. He had then dropped his breeches.

'The plague of artists and poets,' the medic had diagnosed as soon as he had seen the chancre. 'Syphilis.'

Brigadier Nestor's face had maintained its serious expression.

'Impossible. I'm a happily married man.'

The medic had been quick to catch the drift of the argument; he had had another peek.

'Perhaps they are infected bedbug bites, after all.'

Only then had the brigadier smiled.

'That would be my guess too.'

The medic had nevertheless prescribed a course of Salvarsan. Sitting next to him Brigadier Nestor now remembered the incident with gratitude.

'You were the only person I could turn to. I would rather have died than visited the chief medical officer. Our wives play pinochle together.'

The medic shrugged off the little favour he had done some time ago, and observed his commanding officer with curiosity – he had the impression he was circling round the true reason for his visit without taking a peck at it.

'Do you want your blood pressure taken?'

'Thank you. But my heart can withstand the pressures of a train boiler.'

Brigadier Nestor rapped his fingers on the steering wheel. The sun moved a little and the cabin was flooded with light. Soon he could hold back no more.

'I need morphia,' he said.

The medic was not surprised at the request: almost everyone had heard the rumour that their commanding officer was addicted to the potent anaesthetic. When the medic had first heard it himself he had refused to believe it – besides, he alone had a key to the drug dispensary, and the inventory showed no morphia unaccounted for. But his experience of army life had taught him that the more preposterous a story was, the more likely it was to be true. How had the rumour started? he wondered. He traced in his mind the line of clandestine information that began with his nurse and disappeared in the darkness of the lower ranks, like a railway line leading into a tunnel. Suddenly he remembered: the handbills. Of course: they were the source of every rumour, or – as almost everyone believed by now – the truth. He nodded.

'How much, brigadier?'

His superior requested an enormous amount that made the medic's eyes open wide.

'That could put a pachyderm to sleep.'

But Brigadier Nestor was not embarrassed by the rising demands of his condition.

'Believe me, my friend. My troubles weigh more than an African elephant.'

He had to admit to the doctor, with a penitent's voice, that he was a regular user of the narcotic, but denied that he was an addict. He said that in the past he had obtained his medicine from civilian pharmacists, but the brigade had not been near a town for over a week. He explained that morphia was his lifebuoy in the stormy seas of the current situation, and promised the medic that as soon as things improved he would give it up. He justified his need by saying, 'Camomile infusions don't stop me from wanting to blow out my brains.' The medic listened to the argument with medical composure. Finally he accepted it, not because he agreed with it, but rather because he instinctively believed that man and his environment were separated only by a thin, permeable membrane, through which evil moved in one direction or the other. How could one retain one's own sanity when everything was falling apart? It was the principle of osmosis. He jumped out of the lorry and a moment later returned with a large bottle. Holding it in his hands like a newborn baby, the brigadier remembered the other reason for his visit.

'I understand you have been the victim of a recent theft.'

'It was not of any value. And I know how to shave with a scalpel.'

The brigadier hitched up the bottle under his arm and opened the door of the lorry.

'Nevertheless,' he said, jumping out, 'it's another link in a chain of worrying incidents.'

The heat was propelling him towards the shelter of his own lorry when he had that premonition again. He looked behind his back but still nothing seemed strange: he saw only lorries, horses, dromedaries and artillery guns. Dazed by the sun his soldiers marched on. He squeezed the morphia bottle under his arm and took a deep breath. With his eyes he searched for his orderly and saw to his dismay that his lorry had resumed its place at the head of the column, way ahead. Without warning his knees started to give up their support and his ears became blocked – he heard a distant sound that could be his heart or his breath. He recognised the symptoms of sunstroke. But what about that premonition? His eyes stung and every-thing appeared as if he were looking from behind a yellow screen. He tried to breathe but his chest deflated like a balloon. He felt so tired. If he could reach his lorry . . . It was the desperate wish of a cast-away. He had to have his shot soon, he thought. The morphia bottle slipped from under his arm. Blinded by the heat he bent down to search for it on the sand. This heat . . . His carotids throbbed like frightened snakes held by the neck. He was going to faint. The last thing he remembered before losing consciousness was someone seizing him by the armpits and lifting him up from the burning sand.

Major Porfirio wiped the blade on his shirtsleeve and folded the borrowed razor. For a brief moment he looked at his reflection in the mirror with something resembling surprise, then he brushed and put on his tunic. He sat on his motorcycle and began to pedal. Soon he was puffing, but the motor still gave no sign of coming to life.

'If all postmen ride a piece of junk like this,' he said, 'it would explain why the mail is always late.'

He carried on pedalling but without success. Some time later he was interrupted by the arrival of the corporal on horseback, who came to inform him of the brigadier's collapse.

'When I found him he was lying face down in the sand. Thanks to me he's still alive. I deserve a decoration.'

Major Porfirio received the news calmly. Without quitting his attempts to start his motorcycle, he nodded.

'You might have been doing him a favour if you had left him there. Better than the stupor of the drug.'

The corporal dismounted.

'I wonder where he gets it from.'

'There is no shortage of offers when one wishes to die. It is one's will to go on living that puts the world to inconvenience.'

Major Porfirio stopped pedalling and caught his breath for a moment under the shadow of the tree.

On the branches the cicadas suddenly stopped, without a reason. The officer could hear his heart beat fast from the physical effort. He thought of what he had just said. Life was like a stone on one's shoulders as one attempts to swim across a rapid — what if one simply surrendered oneself to the currents? He looked at the horizon: there was nothing there. Oblivion — it was, he had to admit, a terrifying thought. The horse stretched its neck to chew some leaves but the corporal, in a spiteful reaction, gave its reins a yank. The major frowned.

'Don't do that. Horses are a decent species. Alas, whoever invented the motorcycle gave it the head of a mule.'

A carbine was slung across the corporal's chest, a sabre hung from his belt and his riding boots were peppered with dust. The horse pushed a hoof in the sand and continued to eat from the tree. The cicadas started again and brought the major back from his musing. He took hold of the handlebars, opened the throttle and at last managed to start the motorcycle. For some time he revved the engine lest it stalled, and then put on his goggles and set off, leaving the corporal behind.

The lunar landscape extended as far as his eyes could see. When he caught up with the column he heard the padre in the back of a lorry speaking through the tin megaphone — that day he was reading from Deuteronomy.

'. . . *The Lord your God which goeth before you, He shall fight for you, according to all that He did for you in Egypt before your eyes. And in the wilderness, where thou hast seen how that the Lord my God bare thee, as a man doth bear his son, in all the way that ye went, until ye came into this place . . .'*

The troops marched silently in the sun, paying no attention to the sermon. Major Porfirio raised his eyes to the sky and contemplated a swarm of migrating cormorants almost with jealousy.

Inside his lorry Brigadier Nestor was recovering from sunstroke. He lifted the lid of the kettle and watched the glass syringe sink slowly into the bubbling water. He covered the kettle again and, rubbing his hands together, sat down at his desk with a superhuman effort. In front of him were the maps. He propped his head against his arm and gave them a brief, impatient look. They were covered with a multitude of lines drawn in pencil, each a little further inland from the Aegean coast like beach marks left by the tide: they showed the front at different stages of the expedition. Where was he the day his wife had passed on? He was unable to remember. He turned one of the maps round and on the back he drew two columns with his pencil. One he labelled *Name of suspect* and the other *Piece of evidence*, then he started filling them in. He had not worked for long when he felt his throat dry. He stopped, poured himself a glass of water and gulped it, but it was warm and gave him little release from his thirst – he would give anything now for a block of ice. He did not have another glass but instead reached for the kettle. No sooner had he rolled up his sleeve than he heard shouting coming from outside. With the syringe in his hand he moved the flap of the tarpaulin aside, and when his eyes adjusted to the glare of the afternoon sun he saw at last the reason for his premonition.

CHAPTER 4

Air Lieutenant Kimon rested his elbows on the edge of the cockpit and surveyed the ground with his binoculars. He was always happy when he was flying; the air at that altitude was cool and clear. More importantly, he did not have to look at his squadron leader's handlebar moustache, which he displayed in the officers' mess as if it were the stuffed head of a big-game kill. The shadow of his biplane rippled over the perpetual saltpetre hills like an enormous ray. Flying seemed to Air Lieutenant Kimon not dissimilar to swimming underwater: the only sound one could hear in the aquatic silence was one's own breathing – in the air it was the noise of the engine; and then there was the boundlessness of both media, the welcoming aloneness one felt, the sensual experience of being wholly immersed in fluid . . . Had he been afraid of heights, Air Lieutenant Kimon would have become a deep-sea diver.

For a while he searched the terrain, and then, on an impulse, put away his binoculars and removed his leather helmet; the wind blasted his forehead and hair. Keeping his eyes shut, he experienced a brief moment of exuberance, as if he were not on a military mission but an aerobatics display. How he wished he could take part in an air show – after the war, as a matter of fact, he intended to buy his own aeroplane and travel across Europe performing death-defying stunts for astonished audiences. With a youthful contempt he laughed heartily at the prospect of death, then covered his head again and turned up the throttle; the exhaust pipe backfired and petrol sprayed his face. Ahead of him an eagle, frightened by the noise of the engine, rose towards the sun. The airman observed it from behind his goggles, squinting and grinning. Rocking from side to side, the biplane raced ahead.

He had taken off that morning from his base on an island in the Aegean, on his daily reconnaissance mission to look for survivors of the catastrophic defeat. He had been searching for several hours but so far had discovered nothing. One month on since the collapse of the front, he believed that if there were any troops alive they would by now have been captured by the enemy. His mission was a waste of time and fuel – he had told his squadron leader so earlier that week.

'You send me to look for skeletons.'

His superior had twisted his moustache.

'Don't underestimate the eternal survival instinct of our race, lieutenant. Dismissed.'

'Quite. The missing-in-action are now discussing the eternal nature of their survival instinct with the soldiers of Alexander the Great.'

In any case, he preferred these missions to his creaking rocking chair on the veranda at the airfield. When he could see the eagle no more he turned and realised he was headed for a stratus cloud. He pushed the control column and the biplane began to descend; the air became warmer and immediately he thought that he was probably flying too low. No sooner had he cleared the cloud than he was caught in a violent sandstorm. He only had time to cover his mouth and nose with his scarf, before the biplane plunged into the soaring sand. He grabbed the steering column with both hands and pulled it back with all his strength. Buried in the storm he could see nothing, but felt the wind one moment pulling the plane down, then pushing it sideways, then letting it climb higher. The airman recalled the liquid simile again: it was exactly like being in a small boat hit by the waves of a hurricane.

It lasted only a minute, and then the biplane emerged from the darkness. Air Lieutenant Kimon cleared his goggles and inspected the damage: the sand inside the cockpit was up to his knees and the fabric of the wings had holes in it, but all the struts and wires appeared intact. He looked over his shoulder: the rudder was slightly bent but still operational. Only moments earlier he was thinking of death with disdain, but now his bravado had abandoned him and he crossed himself. He was still thanking God for His benevolence when the engine started knocking, and at once Air Lieutenant Kimon knew that the sand had choked the carburettor. A moment later the engine stalled altogether, and the biplane began to lose altitude.

Father Simeon screwed up his only real eye; something had caught the dog's attention and it was running towards it. While he followed the animal to the top of a hill, a prickling sensation grew on the nape of his neck. Was it something good or evil he was about to discover? He tried not to think about it, the way someone crossing an old suspension bridge would rather not assess the strength of the frayed rope. When he reached the ridge of the hill he stopped to catch his breath, and he saw it. He shielded his eyes and checked his panting.

'Hosanna!' he cried. 'It's ours!'

It was a yellow biplane with a blue-and-white cross painted on its tailplane. A moment later it passed overhead, and Father Simeon's only eye made out its silver nose, the struts of its wings, the silent exhaust pipe. He frowned: it *was* silent. He had once been invited to an airfield to bless the squadron and sprinkle the aeroplanes with holy water for good luck, and afterwards he and the other guests had been treated to a display of take-offs, landings and aerial manoeuvres. What had overwhelmed him that day more than the antics of the daredevil pilots had been the infernal noise. This aeroplane above his head was as quiet as a leaf in the wind. In the sky the yellow biplane continued its silent flight. It was circling the camp, the pilot looking for level ground on which to land.

Soon everyone in the bivouac had noticed. The soldiers dropped their mess tins, left behind their boots and ran barefoot on the hard saltpetre towards the descending speck, shouting and waving their arms with joy. They made it to the flat piece of land that the pilot had chosen as his landing strip the moment the biplane touched down. But with its engine cut, it had been descending too fast; its wheels sank in the sand and, executing a somersault, it finally came to rest upside down. There was instant silence – the aeroplane, the soldiers, Father Simeon, the dog, were all quiet – but that lasted only a moment, because then there was a large explosion and the biplane went up in flames.

The tragic spectacle was too much even for the pious priest to bear. It was one of very rare occasions of his life so far when his grip on his religious convictions was loosened. 'Have You no mercy, Lord?' he murmured, averting his eyes from the disaster. 'Why do You give the thirsty an empty flask?' The failure of his faith lasted only an instant. With a sense of shame he recovered his composure and looked round him: thankfully no one had heard him.

The soldiers rushed to the burning wreck. They pulled out the airman, carried him to safety, removed his goggles, his helmet and the buckskin jacket that was singed by the flames, and then waited for the medic to arrive. He came with his first-aid box, which contained nothing more than a bottle of ether and one of pure alcohol, a wad of dirty cotton and some old stained bandages that had been washed several times over. The box was like a priest's portable altarpiece: its contents had more of a symbolic than a remedial value. It was not only faith in religion but in science too, the medic had discovered during his long apprenticeship on the front line, that could heal. He held the ether under the pilot's nostrils and it was not long before the airman opened his eyes and took a deep breath. Still feeling the heat in his shirt and trousers, he looked round him with pale, confused eyes. Not far away his biplane burned with a bright red fire and a dense billow of smoke that stretched out into the desert sky. He sat looking at the path of soot like a traveller at the end of a long journey contemplating the road he has arrived from, while the medic felt his body for wounds and fractures. The doctor was surprised to discover that his patient was apparently unhurt.

'Not a scratch. You are as lucky as a rabbit's foot, lieutenant.'

His words brought the airman back from his morbid contemplation.

'It's the eternal survival instinct of our race,' he said cryptically.

Despite the medic's attempts to dissuade him, asking him to wait for the stretcher in case he had suffered a concussion, the airman insisted on being helped to his feet. When he stood up he asked for a drink, and they handed him a water bottle; he brought it to his lips with shaking hands. The water trickled down his gullet, blistered by the fumes he had swallowed during the accident, and caused more pain than relief. The soot in his mouth was washed down, and a moment later an acrid tang rose from his stomach; everyone standing near him had to pinch their noses – he, on the other hand, winced but did not stop. While he drank, Brigadier Nestor's voice was heard in the crowd. 'Out of my way!' The soldiers moved aside to let him through, and soon the old man appeared, panting, dressed only in his vest and breeches. As soon as he was confronted with the burning wreck, he pushed back his cap and watched it for a long while in silence with the sentimental eyes of one attending a funeral pyre. Then he turned to the airman and gave him a scornful look – his condition did not concern him the least.

'What news of our withdrawal, lieutenant?'

The airman gulped until the water had extinguished

the fire in his stomach, and only then did he take the bottle from his lips.

'It's over, sir,' he replied, coughing. 'They are discussing the terms of the armistice now. This was meant to be my last mission to locate survivors.'

The brigadier turned and looked at the fire again.

'And you succeeded splendidly in that.'

The smoke rose thick and black in the air, attracting the attention of the vultures. They flew in circles around it, intrigued by the chips of wood and shreds of fabric carried away by the wind: it was not food. Shrieking with frustration, they soon headed back to the camp. The smoke passed in front of the afternoon sun and Brigadier Nestor's disappointment eclipsed his anger.

'I could hear them singing our dirges,' he said. 'It is finished.'

The fact that the country would from that day on consider them perished made everyone feel the way a dead man does on awaking to the predicament of life as a ghost. Father Simeon did not need his confessor's intuition to read the crowd's mind. He put on his cross and opened his Bible; its spine was broken, the cover was torn and all of Genesis and half of Exodus were missing. Done some months earlier, the damage had not only been a heinous sin, but also a cause for personal disappointment to Father Simeon: its perpetrator had been no other than a playful Caleb seeking at the time to entertain his glum master with an overdramatic display of his hunting skills. After seven days of sulking, the padre had forgiven him.

Caps were removed and heads bowed. Slowly the flames died down, and of the biplane all that remained was its charred frame. Father Simeon leafed through the Bible, took a deep breath and started. While he read a rain of ash began to fall quietly over the camp and settled on the kepis of the men, their shoulders, the open Bible and Father Simeon's beard. It fell throughout the recitation of the Gospel and was still coming down when, some time later, while the congregation was singing a psalm, the airman touched his forehead, went pale, and collapsed with a thud on to the dust that was peppered with ash.

The medic passed the time of the brief afternoon halt for rest and repairs in the Red Cross lorry with a stack of old medical journals. He read lying on the floor, occasionally turning back a few yellow pages to verify the data in a chart while picking his nose; there was a deep cut in his cheek from the scalpel he had used to shave. The lorry had no windows – its interior was lit by the glow of the sun through the canvas. He heard the flap being raised but did not take his eyes from the article.

'Anything interesting?' the padre asked.

The medic turned the page and reattached his finger to his nostril.

'Hardly. These journals date from the time of Hippocrates.'

Father Simeon sat on a stool and removed his sidecap. Outside, hot gusts of air pushed against the taut fabric of the lorry like angry hands – it seemed as if the wind, too, was desperately seeking shelter from the heat. The padre folded his cap in two and mopped the sweat overflowing the deep furrows in his forehead.

'In olden times medicine and religion were inseparable,' he said.

Lying on his back, the medic dropped the journal to the floor and lifted another from the pile.

'The average life span at that time was one half of today's,' he said.

As soon as he held up the journal and bent back the cover, a cloud of fine dust fell off and sprinkled his face. He coughed without surprise and brushed the pulverised paper off him.

'Ever since the censorship officer let loose those monsters, they have been feasting on my medical archive.'

Father Simeon shrugged his shoulders.

'Introducing bookworms to curb the dissemination of clandestine literature seemed a good idea at the time.'

It had been another of Brigadier Nestor's absurd decisions, made when his rage had defeated his reason. After a year of having failed to find the source of the handbills he had taken delivery, from God knows where, of a bucketful of beetles, which he released in the barracks with the insane hope that their larvae would seek and destroy the hidden reserve of paper used to print the seditious mottoes. But the coleopteran solution had soon backfired: the bookworms had nibbled through maps, telegrams and starched collars, while the flood of handbills had continued unabated.

The medic scooped up the confetti of crisp yellowed paper.

'This was a case study of acute appendicitis.'

'One of these days they will catch the traitor who circulates them,' Father Simeon said.

The medic blew the paper out of his cupped palm and watched it settle on the metal floor.

'Ever since the thefts began, the brigadier has forgotten all about the handbills.'

All the while, the padre had not ceased suffering from the heat; he felt as uncomfortable as if he were sitting in a dentist's waiting room. His gaze moved round the interior of the lorry in a random orbit, but nothing caught his attention.

He asked, 'How is the man who fell from the skies?'

'He will have a bad headache when he wakes up and might suffer from amnesia.'

'Amnesia,' repeated the padre.

The remark and the infernal heat opened a door inside his brain, one he had kept locked for a long time. Something distorted his face then, his lips started to move and a moment later out came the words.

'There are certain things I wish I had forgotten myself.'

The medic knew he was referring to the massacre.

'Whether you remember them or not, Father, those things did happen.'

Father Simeon rubbed the nape of his neck.

'A sin not confessed is a yoke across the shoulders.'

'We are swimming in a sea of sins and you are worried it might rain.'

'Every evening I wait in church for someone to come to confession . . .'

'Have you at least absolved yourself?'

Father Simeon wove his fingers together into a tangle. He heard the dog bark in the infernal afternoon – probably at a vulture. The stench of his sweat and the smell of disinfectant on the medic's clothes added to the conspiracy of the afternoon. While the padre thought of Hell, the fleeting shapes of soldiers appeared on the translucent canvas of the lorry, like cardboard puppets in a sinister shadow play. An unresolved feeling simmered in his stomach. The medic lowered the journal and observed him with his medical eyes.

'Funeral rites wouldn't have done them any good,' the padre murmured as if talking to himself. 'They were not Christians.'

The medic pitied him.

'Better forget it. Even you cannot raise the dead, Father.'

Father Simeon stood up to leave. Before climbing down from the lorry he stopped and looked down.

'Maybe this present misfortune has something to do with divine justice.'

The crumpled shoulder straps of his uniform were braided with the emblem of his eternal faith, the Christian cross. There was a hint of pleading in what he had just said – he longed for someone to agree with him. The man on the floor gave him a look and denied him that grain of consolation.

'Or with a broken compass,' he replied and returned to his journal.

After leaving the medic's lorry the padre wandered along the column. The intense brilliance of the sand made him feel dazed. He walked like a man the morning after an overnight binge: unsteady, oblivious, headachy – and a little regretful. He shielded his eyes with his hand and surveyed the landscape. Some ragged tents were pitched in neat rows on the level ground, lorries were parked in straight lines, smoke was rising from the stack of the field kitchen – a town existing in a precarious transience. He resumed his walk. Anywhere else such silence would be unnatural for such a large gathering – it was the curfew of the heat. Father Simeon surprised a vulture wandering about with a limp.

He remembered with longing his house in a small village lost in the mountains. A single-storey house made of stone, it had a tiled roof and a small veranda, and had been built by his father on the land brought to him by his bride. Father Simeon had not married himself. It was neither a coincidence nor out of self-reliance that he had not done so: after cancelling his plans of becoming a missionary, he had nurtured the ambition of training for the office of bishop instead, and to achieve that he had to preserve his celibacy. How haughty his old aspiration now appeared to him! When at last he had relinquished that dream too, he had felt he was both too old and too cowardly to embark on the deadly adventure of courting.

After his death the house would pass to his sister. He was pleased there was someone to survive him, but could not help but wonder: did his sister consider him dead already? A sense of nausea seized him at the thought of being erased from a loved one's memory – to purge it, he considered the vanity of thinking of oneself as a critical gear in a colossal and intricate machine that would cease to work if it were removed.

He thought more of home. He compared the permanence of his old church to the flimsiness of his makeshift chapel here in Anatolia, and for the first time since the landing he understood the impossibility of the task bestowed upon the Expeditionary Corps: they were invaders. Even he knew that one after another the empires dissipated, slowly but inexorably: the Dutch, the Hapsburgs, the Ottomans . . . The motherland had gone to war, looking back with desire to her own long gone but not forgotten imperial past.

He came across Brigadier Nestor's orderly who was filling a radiator from a steel can. The young man turned and looked at him quizzically. Deep in his thoughts, the padre made the sign of the cross in his direction and carried on.

The sight of his tent intensified his glum feelings – he had given orders to set it up in case anyone wanted to pray. The wind had loosened its ropes and the heavy tarpaulin was slack and covered in dirt, like the skin of the septuagenarian Indian elephant with the sawed-off tusks he had seen once on a trip to the provincial capital. The wooden cross on the roof was tilted to one side. An even more unpleasant surprise awaited him inside: the draught through the rips in the seams had toppled the altarpiece and buried it under a thick layer of sand. For a while Father Simeon surrendered himself to the spectacle of destruction, and then he started tidying up submissively. He fetched a spade and carried out the sand, removed the sheet from his cot and cleaned it with the carpet beater, then raised the fallen altarpiece and wiped it patiently with one of his shirts. Last, he swept the rugs. Once everything was in order again, he undressed and lay down on his cot with a sigh.

At least it was cool inside his tent – the wooden

altarpiece cut down some of the glare of the sun through the canvas. A cloud of flies circled noisily over Father Simeon's head. He listened to the sound of his breath – he breathed forcibly and quickly, in little puffs, as if trying to fill a balloon. He was tired; he had tidied his quarters with an energy his heart normally would not have allowed. He closed his eyes but the dust in the air was making him sneeze. Soon he abandoned his efforts to sleep and lay with his hands folded under his head, observing the flight of the insects above him. It was the perfect opportunity for his conscience, which had lain in ambush all day, to make its attack – Father Simeon could no longer avoid thinking about the massacre.

It had happened more than two years earlier. The padre recalled the entry of the brigade, fresh from a bloody but ultimately victorious battle, into the small town. A long time had passed, but the place now appeared in his memory like a coloured postcard: the wooden mannequin in the tailor's window, the striped pole outside the barber's shop, the yellow signboard of the haberdashery. The week before, in a battle that had taken place not far from the town, the enemy bombs had hit the artillery batteries of the brigade with unusual accuracy. Several times Brigadier Nestor had ordered them moved, but they could still not escape the deadly shelling – someone had been divulging the position of the guns. In the small town the padre had watched nervously while the soldiers searched every house. It was not long before they discovered the telephone, and they assumed it was what must have been used to inform the enemy.

There were tamarisks round the square where they had herded the people and a dry fountain in the middle. No one had admitted treason during the inquiry. The shooting had lasted a long time – the square was too small to line up more than fifteen at once. It had been a horrible sight, yet Father Simeon had watched without emotion – the ordeal of the battle had hardened his heart too. How could he have done nothing to prevent the murder? he asked himself now with shame. For a long time after the event he used to think of his conduct that day as more a failure of some vague professional obligation rather than the complete bankruptcy of his compassion. Lying on his cot, he felt his only real eye water and covered it with his forearm. Only recently he had truly begun to question his integrity, and it was exhausting his soul. He felt the tingling of a fly on his wrist. Somewhere someone was trying to start an engine. He was sailing too close to the wind of self-loathing when a torpid sleep at last rescued him.

Standing a few yards away, a vulture flapped its wings a couple of times and watched the young orderly with curiosity. After several attempts, the man let go of the crank and wiped his forehead.

'The padre ought to write a prayer for the starting of internal-combustion engines,' he said.

He lifted the bonnet wearily and unscrewed the spark plugs, cleaned each one carefully with a steel brush and bent their electrodes closer, then placed them back. He went to the front and grabbed the crank again.

'In the name of the Father, and of the Son and of the Holy Ghost!'

He gave the handle a good yank and this time the engine sprang to life. Frightened by the noise, the vulture took flight and began to circle the camp. Turning its naked head from side to side, weighed down by its enormous hooked bill, it inspected the humans and the draught animals with frustrated appetite. It was evening – another day had passed in which the bird had to placate its hunger at the rubbish heap; it wondered whether following the troops had been the right decision. The long shadow of the flag-pole in the middle of the camp traversed a row of tents and faded over the sand eastwards. Other birds joined the vulture and croaked a greeting. The vulture did not reply; it was eyeing a large round tent with red crosses on the canvas from where a delicious smell was rising. It had almost forgotten the smell of fresh blood – now that the war was over, they would begin to bury the dead again. The vulture did not under-stand war; all it knew was that after three good years it was once more hard to find carrion. It croaked back at the other birds, but it was something more like a curse than a greeting.

The orderly raised his eyes to the sky and gave the birds a brief look. Hovering with their wings spread out against the colourless sky, they reminded him of marks inscribed on paper to represent the signatures of the illiterate. He prided himself on being able to sign his name – it was the frontier of his rural educa-tion. He opened the door of the lorry and threw the crank on the seat; from his breast pocket he took out a stethoscope and auscultated the engine. Happy with the health of the valves, he lowered the bonnet, turned off the engine and cleaned his fingers on his trousers. Presently, the nurse walked by and stopped to share a cigarette.

'We chop more meat in the infirmary than in an abattoir,' he announced. He took a puff and passed the cigarette. 'An amputation every other day. On average.'

The thought of severed limbs set a whirlpool in motion inside the orderly's stomach. It felt like water in a sink when the plug is pulled – he was going to vomit. The nurse gave him a sidelong glance and immediately noticed his discomfort.

'In fact, today we did an operation so urgent, we sawed off a patient's arm before he had time to sign his will.'

'Awful.'

The orderly refused the cigarette and patted his chest to stop the rising vomit.

The operation had created a legal conundrum, according to the nurse. The advanced gangrene had killed the unfortunate soldier soon after the completion of the emergency procedure, and his will had been left unsigned.

'I had to pick up the arm and sign the will with it myself. His hand still held the pen – the will was, after all, signed by the testator's hand.'

He took pity on the young man and silenced his mouth with another puff at his cigarette. Gradually, the orderly began to recover from his nausea and changed the subject.

'Have you heard about the thefts?' he asked.

The nurse replied that he had – but there was nothing interesting about them. In any case, he did not own anything worth stealing – it was the officers who should be worried.

'Besides, this weather is just too hot for solving mysteries.'

But the young orderly insisted. He wanted to know what the other soldier thought about the matter.

'It could be anyone,' the nurse said. He paused and looked at the orderly through narrowed eyes. 'You, for example – you're the one closest to the brigadier.'

'I am the brigadier's most trusted man. I have vowed to serve him.'

'The infirmary is full of soldiers who had vowed never to abandon their position, and each has a bullet in his arse.'

The young man blushed.

'Is a contract signed by a hand not attached to a body valid?'

The nurse rubbed his chin. His education was hardly better than his comrade's, but his voice had an authoritative pitch.

'It is. When three witnesses are present – according to the Roman Law.'

When the cigarette was so small that he could smoke it no more he dropped it, stepped on it out of habit and left. The orderly had to go too – soon the brigadier would rise from his afternoon nap and he had to have his coffee ready.

He climbed on to the back of the lorry, where he took the lid off the tin and saw that the coffee was running out. He poured in some chicory and shook the tin well. Then he stirred two spoonfuls of the mix in the water and lit the fire under the pot. He always followed his routine so blindly that he even opened the trunk to take out the sugar before he remembered it had been stolen. A sense of gloom came over him at that moment, as if he had been responsible for his superior's life losing its only specks of sweetness. His dedication to his duties resembled religious vows: he abode by them unquestioningly.

Lifting the pot and putting it down again he let the coffee boil three times before taking it off the fire. Whistling, he poured the coffee into an enamelled cup, placed the cup on a saucer, filled a glass with fresh water and put everything on a tray. Brigadier Nestor's pocket watch was on the desk with the maps. The orderly picked it up by the chain and read it: it was time. The completion of his task gave him a sense of great achievement. There was only one more thing he always served his commanding officer along with his coffee, and he stretched his arm under the bed. Casual at first, his expression soon changed to one of concern, and then to a panic that dilated his pupils; hastily, he dropped to his knees and had a furious search.

Some time later he was entering his commanding officer's tent with a slight tremble and a solid lump lodged in his throat – somehow he had to break the news to him that the box of his precious cigars had also disappeared.

CHAPTER 5

The old circus tent glowed in the sun and the temperature inside rose steadily. After travelling in circles for two days, the brigade had halted and scouts had been sent out. They were gone for a day already – enough time to pitch the infirmary tent and look after the wounded. A mechanical fan with enormous blades, like an impossible flying machine, hung from the truss that supported the canvas. No one operated its handle. The sun cast the shadows of the red crosses and animals painted on the canvas over the earthen floor and the cots: the dark silhouette of a prancing tiger with sabre claws, an elephant with a raised trunk that rather resembled a teapot, a cobra with flared hood that danced to a charmer's flute, a kangaroo wearing boxing gloves . . . They were like the projections of a children's carousel lamp. Hitched to the foot of every cot was a progress chart that showed a flat curve. The cots were covered with coarse flaxen sheets stained with sweat; they had not been washed for weeks. Under the sheets, dressed only in their underwear, the wounded lay with the patience of those sentenced to life in prison with little chance of a pardon – the perpetrators of some terrible crime for which there could be no forgiveness. A mere glance at the human debris was enough to affirm that a crime had indeed been committed – but was that of these men's own making? Next to each patient, hanging from a metal stand, was a drip. It should have represented hope, the possibility of recovery; instead, each stood like a rudimentary cross above a shallow grave. In one of the beds a soldier with his head wrapped in bandages was trying to understand his progress chart. After a while he held it up. 'Can anyone explain this to me?'

In the cot opposite, a man with his leg in a cast kept high in a sling sat up with difficulty. He put on his glasses and squinted at the chart across the aisle. Encrusted with tartar and full of decay, his teeth resembled a miniature piano keyboard. 'If that monitored a stock price,' he replied, 'I would advise you to sell right away.'

A few cots away the airman slept quietly with a water pouch on his head. Resting on the sunken pillow, his face bore the signs of mixed lineage: light brown skin, blond hair and – if his lids were not shut at that moment one would have seen it – blue eyes. While his exact ancestry would be anyone's guess, one thing was perfectly obvious to everyone that lay in the squalor of the infirmary: he was definitely an aristocrat.

He was the sole heir to a fortune that was large enough to bribe fate several times over. His father, an Alexandrian widower of a Germanic belle, had never remarried but had devoted his life to the unsentimental trade of premium cotton, with offices in Piraeus, Marseilles and Manchester. The boy had a lonely child-hood of starched sailor suits and garden mazes, endless seasons of boarding-school incarceration and loveless hours spent on decreed pastimes: piano lessons, fencing, equitation, European languages. It was not until he started taking flying lessons that he escaped the gravitational field of paternal discipline.

He was a student of classics in Vienna when, during a long walk in the Prater (where he went whenever he felt the ethereal need to memorise some verses of Catullus), he had chanced upon the landing of a brightly coloured triplane on a level meadow with daisies. The noise of the engine and the thick soot of its exhaust had immediately won him over from Latin lyric poetry. Some time later the Anatolian expedition had been announced and he had returned home at once to volunteer for the Air Corps. It was a decision taken more out of his love of flying than out of patriotic fervour. All his father's connections could achieve then was for the air lieutenant to be posted to a reconnaissance unit rather than a raid squadron.

At that moment, however, the young aristocrat could remember none of this because of his concussion. Suddenly he opened his eyes. Standing next to a stretcher on wheels, a monumental man in a white apron looked down at him. The nurse held up a trephine and began to demonstrate its use with a grin.

'This will take away the bad dreams, lieutenant,' he said.

Air Lieutenant Kimon stared at it in horror but was unable to speak. He could hardly part his lips – they felt as if they were sewn together. His condition had caused his brain to lose control of his muscles. Where was he? He heard the snoring of the other patients and the noise of a spade digging far away. He thought of a grave and a body thrown in it, without a coffin, without even a shroud – his mother's marble mausoleum did not seem at that moment such an ugly denouement. Cramming his skull like cotton stuffed into a ball, his dizziness allowed for a while only morbid thoughts to filter through. Then he remembered being caught in a sandstorm – but when had that happened? The nurse patted him on the shoulder and prepared for the operation. Whistling, he whetted a razor on a leather belt. When he had finished he daubed some gauze in chloroform.

'Anaesthesia,' he explained. 'Without it your head would hurt as if you had sat through one of the padre's sermons.'

The airman looked at him with the helplessness and panic of one buried alive. From the far reaches of his memory came the echo of an engine – was he travelling on an aeroplane when the accident happened? It took him several seconds to give himself a positive answer, but it was impossible to recall what that aeroplane looked like, or whether he had been a passenger or its pilot. He was still trying to make sense of his predicament when the nurse pressed the gauze with the chloroform on his aristocratic face. A saccharine taste burned the airman's throat and numbing vapours blocked his nostrils. He began to faint.

The nurse hummed and lathered his patient's head before taking the sharpened razor. After he had shaved a patch of his hair he lifted him from the cot and put him on the stretcher. He was ready to leave for the operating room when the medic walked in, dressed in surgical attire.

'Are we ready yet?'

When his nurse nodded, the doctor leaned over the stretcher.

'We have to relieve intracerebral pressure, lieutenant,' he said. 'Or your head will burst like a balloon.'

Holding up his hand to his patient's face, he squeezed the thumb and forefinger together to indicate a minute amount of a substance.

'A little bleeding between your encephalon and your cranium – nothing to worry about.'

The last thing Air Lieutenant Kimon saw before his eyes shut completely was the medic beckoning his subordinate.

'Bring him in,' he heard him say. 'While he is still alive.'

The moon rose silently. Inside his tent Major Porfirio yawned, moved the torn flap aside and observed the camp from end to end, turning his head slowly, as if it were the beam of a lighthouse. Lit by the moon, spread out against the black backdrop of the desert sky, the camp seemed no more real than the two-dimensional props on a theatrical stage. Major Porfirio thought this an appropriate simile: he was an actor in a production that had foundered despite his brave performance. And this uniform . . . He put his hands in his pockets – he loved the army, but the expedition had left him feeling that he was dressed in a cheap costume. A cloud appeared over the hills and moments later a wind started that made the camp resound with a circus of noises: unlatched lorry doors banged against their frames, tarpaulins flapped on their poles and the

Christian cross on the end of the flagpole spun like a weathercock. Major Porfirio pulled his head inside, sat at his desk and poured himself a glass of cordial – it was the only drink left, apart from warm water and weak coffee. While he drank, one of Brigadier Nestor's favourite aphorisms came to his mind: *Only waxen wings will take us out of this hell.*[*]

He was young for a major and even more so for Chief of Staff, but the bayonet slash he had received across his face early in the campaign gave him an austere mien. There was a deeper cut hidden inside his heart: he had always thought this war purposeless. But he was a soldier and had complied – not unlike a child ordered by a stern father to empty his plate. He finished his glass and immediately filled it again. The yellow dust that covered him from head to toe made him seem like a sepia figure out of an old photograph. He felt tired. He drank the liqueur and had another look outside: three tattered flags hung from the mast in the middle of the camp. Two were the flags of the infantry regiments and were embroidered with the Virgin and the names of the victorious battles of the Balkan Wars – a mission he had also taken part in and one he had every reason

---

[*]Daedalus was an architect who designed the labyrinth for Minos, the king of Crete. The labyrinth was a prison for the Minotaur, a man-eating monster that was half-man and half-bull. When Daedalus helped the hero Theseus to slay the monster, the king imprisoned Daedalus and his son Icarus in the labyrinth. Daedalus made waxen wings and they both escaped, but Icarus flew too near the sun. His wings melted and he fell into the sea.

to be proud of. The third and smallest flag, with St George slaying the dragon, belonged to the cavalry regiment. When the wind changed speed and direction the flags turned too, with a lashing sound. Satisfied no one was near, Major Porfirio returned to his desk and took the cover off his typewriter.

He had only managed a sentence when the sound of footsteps interrupted him. He removed the paper from the cylinder, hid it under his tunic and only then did he give permission to enter. The corporal walked in and saluted.

'All quiet.'

Major Porfirio relaxed.

'Up at this hour?'

The corporal removed his cap and used it to brush the dust off his clothes. His shirt was missing some buttons and a half-empty cartridge belt crossed his chest. In his arms he cradled his carbine and his pockets sagged with bullets. There was an intensity about him, as if the wind had set his limbs in motion.

'I'm on patrol.'

'Good. Then we'll do it tonight.'

The corporal sat down. He kept his eyes fixed on the entrance and listened to the wind. He started tapping his foot on the floor like a traveller waiting for a much-delayed train. There was so little one could do in a railway station, he pondered. One could only wait. There ought to be rides and acrobats and other amusements to shake off the boredom of the platform – a Ferris wheel perhaps? Now, there was an idea. Inane thoughts, the corporal had discovered, kept his mind from ruminating on the fear he felt before every secret mission.

After a while he said, 'If this weather continues, there will be no dust left in this desert by dawn.'

His commanding officer rocked back and forth in his chair, listening calmly to the wind as it buried the lorries and tents under the dust. He was thinking about his men with fondness. Lying in their cots, wrapped in their greatcoats, they could do nothing but wait, like during a barrage of artillery fire. His first and utmost responsibility was towards them. All his secret efforts, aimed at enlightening them and inspiring them to assume their responsibility towards society, arose from his layman's humanism. Alas, the corporal had been his only convert. He shook his head dispiritedly.

'One fellow traveller out of a thousand men. Some achievement.'

The corporal shrugged.

'You tried your best, comrade.'

'What a waste of time. Our handbills are fodder for the mules.'

The major snorted with annoyance and stared at his typewriter. His disappointment was justified – the only person the handbills seemed to affect deeply had been the brigadier. Working on the wording of one of his circulars, Major Porfirio could not help but feel he was personally addressing his superior. After all, Brigadier Nestor was the most avid reader of his incendiary declarations. If only the rank and file were half as interested . . . He used to think that the worst that could happen would be for the soldiers to ignore his exhortations, but the recent thefts had delivered his clandestine undertaking a death blow.

'Now the men think the petty thief and the writer

of the handbills are one and the same person,' he said. 'If only I knew who had sullied our cause.'

A storm lamp on the desk gave the two gaunt faces an amber tint. A few mosquitoes had discovered the source of light and were circling it like planets orbiting an enormous sun. It was a fundamental law of existence that life operated by a hierarchy of size, quantity or overall strength − the insect, the lizard, the beast, the man: the latter ruled on earth now, Major Porfirio thought, but in the scale of the universe he was still of infinitesimal importance. It was the natural order in people he denounced − the one according to wealth.

The corporal searched his pockets and found the medal he had received in the first year of the war for supreme courage. For a while he fiddled with it and then held it up to the light.

'So, I have to give this back.'

The major nodded.

'All decorations should be returned as a protest against the imperialist policies that led to this war.'

He remembered one of his comrade's recent enquiries and produced a pamphlet from under his tunic.

'Before I forget. This will answer your questions regarding the concept of surplus value.'

The corporal put the pamphlet and the medal in his pocket and blew out his cheeks. The storm had no intention of waning soon. Sand crept in the tent from underneath the tarpaulin, and a passing sense of menace came over the cavalryman, as if the storm were a wily beast trying to break into his shelter. He soon realised that far from being his enemy the weather was his ally: no one would be out that night.

'We should have gone when we had the chance, major. Our comrades at the railway would have helped us.'

'You could have, corporal. I don't agree with the Party on this one. As long as the brigade exists I cannot abandon it.'

It was getting cold in the tent. The corporal hugged himself and glanced round with boredom. He saw the major gazing at the storm lantern, and it suddenly crossed his mind how different the two of them were for fellow conspirators – and not simply because the other was an officer. He was right. There was an essential simplicity in the corporal's manner. If his attitude were made of solid matter it would float on water – like pumice. The major, on the other hand, was a slab of granite. It was intriguing how that tormented but talented man could share the same beliefs with a simpleton like himself; the young cavalryman began to feel flattered that he was on that good man's side. He spoke up.

'I have to continue my rounds.'

'Put some stones in your pockets. Or the wind might blow you away.'

Their embrace was both affectionate and ceremonial.

'Come back in an hour,' Major Porfirio said. 'I should have everything ready.'

Only when he was alone did the major notice that the constant glow of the lantern had branded his eyes. It took him a long time to rub off the persistent illusion of the flame with his hands. His quarters became a darker place then, and he even sat with his back to the light, trying to penetrate the darkness with his smarting eyes. His coat dangling from a pole seemed for the first time like a reminder of the fate that awaited him if he slipped off the tightrope of his mission – a cowardly thought, he scolded himself. He had to print the handbills. He took out the sheet he had hidden under his tunic and fed it into his typewriter again. A mimeograph was in a crate and when he finished typing he put the machine on his desk. Yawning from sleeplessness, he mounted the typed sheet on the cylinder and fed paper squares through it. He worked with the habitude of a professional printer – yet there was something defeated in the way he turned the handle, at the same time humming the hymn of the Third International.

Air Lieutenant Kimon awoke from his surgical sleep in the dark, with the taste of chloroform in his mouth. He spat several times on the floor to be rid of the chemical, and then sat up in his cot and studied his surroundings. A few oil lamps across the tent threw their light on what he thought were arms tied in splints, legs in plaster, necks kept straight by wooden collars. He could not see clearly: the concussion was almost gone, but the anaesthetic had left a mist over his eyes that was slow to dissolve and gave his surroundings a haunted quality – as eerie as an early-morning walk across a dilapidated cemetery with mossy crosses and urns and statues. This was the airman's first encounter with the misery of war. Throughout the campaign he was always based more than a hundred miles behind the front line, in the complacent comfort of temporary airfields set up on requisitioned farms and country estates. He had witnessed several battles, but all of them from the air, from where the bloodiest charge would seem little more than the opening of a game of chess. Such was his ignorance that when the mist in his eyes finally went he nodded calmly at the spectacle of Hell and refused to believe it was real. Accordingly, he felt not pity for the human suffering around him but a sense of puzzlement about how it resembled a certain Dutch painting he knew – only it was much worse.

'Hieronymus Bosch was a foolish optimist,' he declared.

It took him a while to realise that he was not in Hell but in the infirmary. He raised his hand to his head and felt the square patch of shaved hair, and in the middle of it discovered the metal disc that plugged the perforation of the trephine. He shivered: his head had been marked as if it were a piece of pottery or some pewter cup. Air Lieutenant Kimon felt like someone returning home to find the place ransacked. Disregarding the fact that the operation had probably saved his life, he thought of it as a violation of the sanctuary that was his body. He was young enough never to have had a serious health problem before; until this moment, the helplessness of disease had not entered the calculations of his life.

Around him the other patients continued their snoring discourse. If the suffering did not touch him, it was the proximity of human beings that made him uncomfortable: the gurgling noise of obstructed windpipes, the stench of sweat, the sudden discharges of disagreeable flatus. The imposed intimacy of shared accommodation always repulsed him. Being an only child and having been sheltered from the world in the formative years of his juvenility by private tuition, he was furnished with a certain fastidiousness that had persisted throughout his later years at the Swiss boarding school and the Austrian university where his verbal powers of persuasion – and those of his paternal purse – had always secured him individual accommodation. Furthermore, he suffered from paruresis. In the airfield barracks, in fact, he had been given permission to build an anechoic toilet, a windowless cabin coated with thick layers of cork and felt, where he could defecate and urinate in complete and blissful secrecy. It was therefore not surprising that he now felt an overwhelming urge to escape this twilit dungeon that smelled of antiseptic. The wind had already begun to circle the thin oilcloth walls of the infirmary when he climbed down out of his bed.

He found his clothes – the singed trousers, the scarf, the goggles, the leather flying helmet and jacket – and dressed quietly. When he slipped out everyone was still asleep. Immediately, he experienced a sublime sense of liberation that was not dissimilar to flying his biplane. He was pleased to feel the blustering wind against his face, but not over the patch of tender skin on his head; he quickly put on his leather helmet and fastened the chinstrap. Caught in the whirlwind, he tasted the saltpetre on his lips before wrapping his woollen scarf round his mouth. The mounting storm swept across the camp like a herd of frightened animals, carrying away torn pieces of tarpaulin, empty cups and pots, the cold ashes of the campfires. The most marvellous incident happened when the wind snatched some officers' tunics that had been washed earlier that day and had been left forgotten on the line, and they flew away in a cloud of dust, sleeves flapping and pockets bulging with sand. (In fact, some days later the uniforms would be seen crossing the sky at low altitude above a coastal town. When the townspeople recognised the colours they would instantly be divided into two groups: the Christians would bid the souls of the dead soldiers farewell on their long journey towards heaven, while the Muslims would throw stones at them and wish that the ghosts would roam the Earth for ever as a punishment for the evils they had committed.)

No such thought entered the airman's mind as he watched the tunics disappear in the whirlwind. Instead, he simply pitied the orderlies who would, without fail, be in trouble for having neglected their duties. He would not be surprised if they were locked up – a grotesque reasoning often operated in times of extreme seriousness. When bravery, religious faith and patriotism failed it was discipline that offered some consolation: the proof that there was still order in the world. And this could be achieved at such a small cost: polish a pair of muddied boots, replace some missing buttons, sew back a torn epaulette.

He had experienced the insanity himself too. Not long ago his squadron leader had reprimanded him for not having shaved one morning, while, on another occasion, when he was ordered to scramble at dawn, he had been caught as he was about to climb into his biplane wearing his silk pyjamas instead of his military suit underneath his leather coveralls. He had almost been cashiered. Air Lieutenant Kimon wondered what such tragicomic incidents must have taken place on board the *Titanic*.

He had the idea of sharing a cigarette with the sentries. He expected there would be guards at the corral, but when he came to it he saw there was none – they had probably taken shelter, waiting for the weather to clear. Behind the fence the dromedaries sat quietly on the sand, ruminating, oblivious to the explosions of wind around them. It was different for the other animals. Not accustomed to the habits of the desert, the mules and horses brayed and neighed, choked on the sand and tried to free their legs from the hobbles. In their blindfolds they seemed to the airman like a row of the condemned awaiting the discharge of the firing squad. He felt for the horses; he had ridden horses before he had even sat on a tricycle, and had grown up if not to love them – he scratched his head: he had not agreed with himself upon a satisfactory definition of that word as yet – at least to respect them. He always maintained that horses had no place on the battlefield and was privately pleased that the new discipline of automotive engineering would sooner or later emancipate his favourite quadruped (he did not, however, extend his benevolence to the mule or the donkey).

As soon as he took out his cigarette case the wind snatched it from his hands. He went down on his knees and felt about in the dark. He was still searching for the platinum repoussé box when he saw, among the legs of the horses, those of a man. Air Lieutenant Kimon did not stand up; he continued observing the pair of legs moving about as if searching for something. Finally they stopped. In the moonlight Air Lieutenant Kimon saw the man remove the blindfold from a horse with a cropped mane, and then the hobbles from its white-shinned legs. The man had only a moment to pat the horse before the animal realised it was free, whereupon it cleared the fence with an easy jump and, galloping at a breathless pace, raced towards the top of the dunes and disappeared into the desert night. Having watched the animal's flight, the man left the corral quietly.

Only then did Air Lieutenant Kimon stand up again. He had made no effort to stop the other man. From the first moment he saw his face in the moonlight he had recognised him, but was so intrigued he decided not to raise the alarm. He found his platinum case and lit a cigarette, shoved his hands in the pockets of his flying jacket and set off again on his walk, thinking of what he had witnessed. The storm offered a truce and the sand began to settle on the bonnets of the lorries, the roofs of the tents, the artillery guns. The regimental flags still hung from the mast in the middle of the camp, but the mast, battered by the winds, now leaned on one side. One by one the soldiers emerged from the tents and examined the sky with mistrust. An order was shouted out, and they set about digging out the lorries buried in the sand. But it was a purposeless activity – soon the storm was heard approaching again. They hastily secured everything they could, tied the lorry doors and tarpaulins with rope, covered the gun muzzles, took down the glorious flags, and then the wind arrived.

But this time something unexpected happened. The whirlwind did not just bring sand to the camp, but what seemed at first to be – on account of its white appearance – a flock of seagulls. Such was the power of the illusion that the more excitable of the men began to shout that the sea must thus be near, only to fall silent a moment later when they were inundated with a sea of the familiar handbills, each one justifying carefully and with ample exclamation marks why the war was an imperialist undertaking and why the government was entirely responsible for the mess the brigade was now in. But apart from the familiar proclamations, the handbills this time also included a fierce denunciation of the recent thefts, calling them the act of a ruthless and counter-revolutionary traitor.

CHAPTER 6

It was the first night in many weeks that Brigadier Nestor, succumbing to an unbearable homesickness, did not sleep in his uniform. On nights like these he had the habit of unearthing the civilian nightshirt, a loose white garment with flared sleeves and wooden buttons down the front, that his wife had packed in his trunk in order to remind him of their matrimonial four-poster. He had laughed at her suggestion then, but three years had passed since he had left home and the garment never failed to work its magic on him.

His wife had taken the secret of its alchemical powers to her grave. She had boiled the fabric in an enigmatic stew of dried sage, thyme and mint leaves, cinnamon and cassia bark, cedar and sandalwood, rose and violet petals, anise and caraway seeds, orris root, orange peel, camphor and myrrh, before turning the heat down and adding several pellets of precious ambergris, the secretion of a spermaceti whale caught in the Tropics. It was this last ingredient that made the brigadier feel a little like the terrified prophet Jonah whenever he dressed himself in the magic nightshirt, before the unique perfume sent him to sleep and released the sentimental memories from the confines of his senile forgetfulness.

Wearing the nightshirt was, therefore, a custom that profited his soul. But on cold nights like this it little helped his rheumatism, and Brigadier Nestor was feeling uncomfortable. He stood up with a sigh and, rubbing his hands, went to his trunk where he searched for his woollen nightcap. Despite wearing his dusty greatcoat over his nightshirt, the cold still gripped his chest like a vice. 'Poor Bonaparte,' he reflected, shivering. 'You stood no chance in Russia.' With the cap pulled down over his forehead and ears, he returned to his cot, blew out the oil lamp and buried himself under an avalanche of blankets. The wind continued to perforate the defenceless tent – an old tarpaulin stretched over a simple framework made of two poles and a few lengths of rope. Brigadier Nestor tried to shelter from the cold with the desperation of a soldier caught in crossfire. It was during an unexpected interlude of calm, when the storm slowed down, that he managed to fall asleep and, sure enough, he was soon dreaming.

At first he dreamed he was back home and the war was over. He had been demobilised with the rank of lieutenant general and lived quietly in the capital on a handsome pension. For a while the brigadier enjoyed the serenity he could not afford while awake. But it disappeared abruptly and he found himself in that town again: he was dreaming about the massacre.

It was a town of single-storey houses round a small square. It was raining and the whitewashed houses seemed as if they were sinking into the mud. There was a ring of soldiers in the earthen square, while in the middle, herded together like livestock, were the villagers. The soldiers wore their coats and helmets, but the people stood knee-deep in the mud, half naked, drenched and silent. Brigadier Nestor twitched in his cot and his breathing became heavier; in his dream the soldiers fitted the bayonets on their rifles and the rain gathered strength. The brigadier knew what would happen next: an order was going to be given. Sweat collected on his forehead, and he shuddered from fear as he struggled to prevent in his nightmare something that in reality had already happened . . . His recurrent dream took its usual course.

Some time later – he did not know how long – he awoke with his face in a puddle of sweat. Immediately, his eyes opened wide in terror: his demons had escaped his nightmare and stood in the flesh now, at the foot of his cot. He pulled the covers up to his nose and let out a plaintive, high-pitched sound – but it was another of the cruel games of his dream: he was, in fact, still deeply asleep. When he truly woke up, he searched the tent with his eyes suspiciously: he was alone, thank God. Since the collapse of the front he had seen countless ditches overflowing with bodies, but they were mostly military casualties. For these dead from either side he felt nothing any more – apart perhaps from a certain curiosity regarding the manner of their death: they appeared no more human to him than the mummies in an archaeological museum. On the other hand, the memory of the town of his shame was different: those had been civilians and it was he who had ordered their execution. He buried his face in his blemished palms. His guilt was a beast that needed to be fed so as not to turn against its master.

He had searched long and hard before he had at last discovered his only source of solace. He sat up in his cot and massaged his eyes: it was time for his morphia shot.

The dawn found him at his desk, shaven and dressed in his breeches, vest and boots. With the pair of compasses, ruler and pencil in hand he was leaning over the maps. He worked with a frenetic energy, evaluating the scouts' reports – his night torment had left its dark circles round his eyes, but the morphia had conjured up its miracle. Not only had it inflated his disposition, it had also given wings to his inspiration. But the problem he was attempting to solve required more than good will and stimulation; like an inexperienced explorer his enthusiasm only led him ever deeper into the jungle of his algebraic calculations. Still, he refused to turn back; he went on scribbling, his chances of finding the egress in the countless equations in front of him diminishing with every jot.

He was still fighting against all mathematical odds when someone asked permission to enter his tent.

'Come.'

Major Porfirio walked in and saluted. His hollow cheeks were at last shaven, but for a well-trimmed moustache that turned upwards at the sharp tips. The brigadier could not but notice the groomed moustache, the skin that was tanned by the desert sun, the dark eyes – it could well be the face of the enemy. The idea suddenly struck him that it was quite remarkable what a difference a uniform made. Without the unlike colours it would be almost impossible to tell the two armies apart. At least in the animal kingdom

. . . But he knew that the notion was false as soon as he thought of it: cocks peck each other, rams butt heads, a dog would bite another. Brigadier Nestor nodded at his Chief of Staff approvingly, but was feeling uneasy.

'Good, Porfirio. That beard was too thick – I could hardly hear what you were saying.'

The major shook his head – a gesture more of obedience than accord. Brigadier Nestor was quick to notice. He lowered his eyes in slight embarrassment. Where his breeches ended, a pair of scrawny legs protruded downwards and disappeared into his unlaced boots. Without socks or leather leggings his feet seemed ridiculously small – Brigadier Nestor felt he was some grotesque character in a fairy tale for children.

'In any case,' he added, 'I thank you for indulging the fancies of an old goblin.'

But Major Porfirio did not indulge his superior's modesty. He merely shrugged his shoulders and removed his solar topi. The previous night he had ventured briefly out of his tent to give the corporal the handbills, and the wind had snatched the kepi from his head – no doubt it had met the same fate as the officers' uniforms hanging on the line. He sat on the edge of the brigadier's cot and immediately noticed the signs of a tormented sleep: the blankets were in a jumble, there were sweat marks on the pillow, his nightcap was on the floor. While he examined the evidence with as much discretion as curiosity, the brigadier began to change into a clean uniform.

'What month is it?' the old man asked.

'September.'

'Of course. Pestle and mortar to my bones.'

Brigadier Nestor had suffered from rheumatism for years, but the privations of the long march had caused his condition to deteriorate further. He folded his nightshirt and placed it neatly in the trunk with a silent promise to never wear it again unless he was lying in his bed at home. He slung the braces of his breeches over his shoulders, sat in his chair and started rubbing his knees; then he bent down to tie his laces. His undertaking was as sentimental as an act of penance.

'I am turning into a fossil,' he joked.

At last the major granted him a glance of sympathy. He was surprised by what he saw then. The brigadier had certainly aged much during the campaign. Major Porfirio felt like someone seeing a loved one after a long time. Ageing was not a stairway but a landslide – a period of corporeal stability followed by a sudden subsidence: the appearance of wrinkles, the greying of the hair, presbyopia, breathlessness. All that could have happened to his commanding officer during the previous night. Was it his obsession with the recent thefts that tormented him? The major opened his mouth to say something but his superior started first, as if he had read his mind.

'It is a direct challenge to my authority – everyone knows how much I like cigars.'

'A horse also went missing during the storm,' the major said.

But his commanding officer paid no attention. He had already forgotten his geodesic calculations and was now mulling over the loss of his personal effects – like a child at play, his mind cast aside a favourite toy for a new one. He twisted the tip of his moustache.

'I have compiled a list of suspects. At present, it is longer than the catalogue of the library of Alexandria, but I will pare it down. The only things aplenty in this desert are dust and time.'

A mild rage inside him pressed against his chest, like a caged animal that knew it had no chance of escaping. A pleasant wind, the last remnant of the previous night's violence, shook the canvas of the tent and slowly brought the old man back to reality.

'Oh yes, the storm. I understand it caused problems, major.'

His Chief of Staff had already compiled a list of the damage to the materiel — a long table on a scroll of paper, where neat rows and straight columns had been filled in by a miniaturist's hand. The brigadier gave it a look full of boredom and did not let his subordinate read it to him; he bowed his head and started to rap his fingers on his desk without speaking. At that moment of silence an uneven reaction took place in the two men, sitting so close to each other in the confines of the tent: one, the brigadier, was beginning to relax, the other to suffocate. Ever since his recruitment to the Cause a certain radius had been established around the major, which defined how close he could sit to someone without making himself nervous: he was uneasy lest he be found out. The brigadier, on the other hand, welcomed company. For many years he had shared his living space and his needs with a wife, a daughter and a maid — it was good when someone could take off his shoulders some of the burden of life. And, besides, he had no reason to hide – everyone of course knew *his* own secret, the massacre. After a while he stood up.

'Someone once told me,' he began, 'that on some island or other a seasonal wind exists that can drive you insane. When it blows everyone takes to their houses at once. The instant madness of those caught in the open causes them to hang themselves, throw themselves off a cliff or drown themselves in the well.'

He clasped his hands behind his back and began to walk round his desk with a serious expression on his face.

'That is what he said. Of course, it could all just be a myth concocted by the islanders to cover up the punishment of molesters, adulterers and sheep stealers.'

He took a deep breath.

'But no matter how evil that wind is, no one has ever reported it carrying away a grown horse – or, even worse, putting Bolshevik ideas into people's heads.'

It was the child again, discarding its second toy for yet a third one: his mind picked up the conspiracy to consider now, but his body was not up to the task. He felt his strength drain away quickly, and he sat back in his chair, already suffering the beginnings of a bad headache. Flies flew in through the entrance of the tent. The wind had stopped and the heat grew. Brigadier Nestor felt as if a corkscrew were being driven into his temple. He mopped the sweat from his forehead with his cuff.

'Dissemination of anti-national literature in wartime is high treason, and therefore punishable by death.'

He took a handbill from his pocket and looked at it with obvious disgust, but also the apprehension of handling perhaps an unexploded grenade.

'The Red Scourge. So, it thrives on the desert climate, too. I thought the bloodbath of our retreat would have satisfied the traitor, but the hatred of whoever writes these is unquenchable.'

He crumpled up the piece of paper into a ball and tossed it away defiantly; the paper grenade did not explode – it rolled under his cot and went out of sight. Brigadier Nestor sat back and crossed his hands over his belly.

'More and more this adventure reminds me of *The Odyssey*.'

Outside a soldier slung his rifle over his shoulder and began to pace up and down in an attempt to rid his legs of their numbness. Walking back and forth at regular intervals, he was like the statue in a bell tower set in motion by its clock. It was an image of peace – the delicate chiming of the bells in a town square somewhere in Switzerland or the Netherlands, places the devastation of war would perhaps never reach. So much absorbed was Brigadier Nestor in this fancy that he failed to notice the soldier who entered the tent.

'This is the man whose horse has disappeared,' Major Porfirio informed him after a moment of awkwardness.

Deep in the narrative of his imagination, it took the brigadier some time to hear his Chief of Staff.

'What horse?'

In front of him the corporal stood to attention and saluted. His uniform hung on the wiry frame of his bones like clothes on a scarecrow. He lowered his hand and waited, rigid, the smell of onion coming from his mouth. He wore his long cavalry boots, which were really not made for walking – but now that his horse was gone, that was what he would have to do until they reached the sea. Brigadier Nestor waved the corporal at ease.

'Have any witnesses come forward?' he asked.

The major replied that there had been none. Brigadier Nestor could still not forget the Bolshevik conspiracy.

'Do you know anything about the other incident last night – the handbills?' he asked the corporal.

The non-commissioned officer gave a negative answer. Brigadier Nestor pursed his lips.

'It was a bad storm, my brigadier,' apologised the corporal. 'We had to take shelter.'

'A storm?' Brigadier Nestor tried to concentrate. 'The storm. Of course – you took shelter.'

His craving for morphia was lessening his ability to think properly. He tried to pull himself together. In that morning's roll-call, which he had ordered across the whole brigade, it had been established that only the dead were missing – whoever set the horse loose had stayed behind.

'There's only one explanation,' he said. 'An act of sabotage by the Bolsheviks.'

But the storm had not finished with the brigade. The morning calm was only a brief truce, like the return of a terrible disease soon after a long and painful treatment. Indeed, the wind began again, without a display of its strength yet, but nevertheless threatening.

Brigadier Nestor felt it in the barometer of his joints. He rubbed his knees and coughed nervously. The elements he could not harness – at least, if the enemy were close, the weather would be as cruel to him as it was to the brigade. Thinking about the storm reminded him of the lost cavalry horse; he rubbed his chin.

'The release of that particular animal may well be of some significance.'

The corporal shrugged and tried to think of something useful to contribute to the investigation.

'It did yearn for its testicles.'

Brigadier Nestor looked at him earnestly. Was there any connection between the animal's ability to procreate and its escape? His intuition was telling him to pursue that line of enquiry further. But all this would have to wait. As if the rheumatic pain were not enough, his head, too, had all but mutinied against his reason in anticipation of the syringe.

'Thank you, corporal – you too, major. Both dismissed.'

After leaving the brigadier's quarters the corporal wandered about the camp, not knowing where to go until he saw the corral. He came to the fence and leaned against the wire with a sigh. His mood was made even worse by a fruitless search through his pockets for a cigarette. The disappearance of the gelding had had a profound effect on him. It was not merely the fact that he was on foot now. The actual fact was that he felt lonely; only now did he understand that the animal offered him an invaluable, under the circumstances, sense of companionship – one could impart to it some of the affection denied by the protocol of masculinity. Even the padre had a dog, the corporal thought, and what about the cook who scattered the leftovers after mess and sat to watch the rats come and eat for hours? He felt a sense of shame at having treated his horse with contempt and cruelty – that animal had been a present taken back from an ungrateful child.

Solitude was his Achilles' heel. As a matter of fact, it was his loneliness that had led him into the arms of the Party. Having been conscripted early in the second year of the expedition, he had become desperate for company within a few weeks. His reaction was to place an advertisement in the personal column of a national newspaper back home, asking to correspond with young women. He had written: *Decorated hero* . . . even though at that time he had only seen the front line through his binoculars – with his abilities it was surely a matter of time before receiving his first medal. He had; and was also promoted to the rank of corporal, before his only reply arrived from a woman in Salonika.

They wrote to each other fervently and frequently, but no matter how many times he asked her she never sent him her picture. He, on the other hand, had soon enclosed a beautiful photograph coloured by hand and mounted on black cardboard. It showed him in parade uniform in front of an oriental landscape, cap under his arm and elbow on a gypsum pillar. After a few letters she had mentioned the political situation, a topic the corporal had found uninteresting at first. But as his affection for his correspondent grew, he started not only to agree with her but also to add to her radical views in order to please her. Then, in her ninth letter, she had revealed Major Porfirio's name – he was the commissar secretly in charge of indoctrinating the brigade.

Standing at the fence of the corral, the corporal observed a soldier going from horse to horse to brush them, denying the mules and donkeys his affections. With his newly found compassion towards animals, the corporal was struck by the groom's unfairness. The lowly beasts loitered about, eating a few briers, staring at passing soldiers, shooing the flies with their tails. The breeze wafted the reek of their skin to the corporal. There was something of the homeland about it. Suddenly a thought crossed his mind: he must go to Salonika and find his correspondent – she loved him, he convinced himself, she would not deny him. But would he make it out of this maze alive? It was the flight of his gelding that gave him the bold idea. It would be difficult to find his way out of the desert alone, he admitted, but one man could travel faster than a whole brigade, what with its heavy guns and the wounded and the lorries breaking down every few hours; one man could slip easily through enemy lines – the brigade would have to engage in a situation like that, and many would die, of course.

The corporal felt euphoric. He had to plot this well, he told himself. It was desertion: if caught he could expect the firing squad – but nothing could wipe the confident smile off his face. When he walked away from the corral he had already begun to plan his escape.

The storm seemed to have set the sky in a perpetual rotary motion. All day, drawn into the centre of the immense whirlpool, clouds had slowly gathered, and by late afternoon they had filled the sky, arranged in concentric circles. Behind the leaden, low-hovering clouds the sun was merely a glimmer, like a distant lighthouse. The air was humid. In the evening the first drops fell and soon the rain grew into a tropical storm that melted the dry earth. For several hours the soldiers struggled to save lorries and artillery guns, before the mud engulfed them entirely. Only when the equipment stood again on firm ground were the troops allowed to rest under the incessant rain. Autumn had arrived: travelling would be more difficult now.

Standing in front of the stove the cook was crying. With tears in his eyes he looked above his head where the canvas canopy had begun to sag from the weight of the rain. The ropes stretched and the poles creaked, like the rigging and masts of a sailing boat. Wondering how long it would be before something snapped, he continued peeling the onion with a sharpened bayonet. Thick, grazed and with their tips burned by his long apprenticeship to the stove, his fingers seemed like half-smoked cigars – yet their injuries had impaired none of their dexterity. After chopping the onion the cook threw it into the frying pan, wiped his tears on the corner of his apron and started to hum. While the onion sautéed, he removed the fuzzy layer of mould from an open corned beef tin and added its contents to the pan.

The smell of fat and onion was making his mouth water. He felt happy; a man of simple tastes, he was in the fortunate position of being able to satisfy them even here in the wasteland. He was of the sensible opinion that those who insisted on skimming off the fat and the scum from life would inevitably go hungry – he, on the other hand, took everything it had to offer with gratitude.

The rain poured from the edges of the canopy in long streams that gleamed in the lightning like quicksilver, and thunder cracked not far away. Stirring the meat with a wooden dipper, the cook remembered life before his conscription. He used to work in the kitchen of an old steamship that twice a week did the round trip from Piraeus to the islands – a life that was so simple it could almost be wise, if it were not for the cook's eternal endeavour to tame his appetite. That was why at that moment he recalled neither the blue-eyed mermaid who had surfaced once briefly on the starboard bow, nor the night when the tail of Halley's Comet had brushed against the Earth, nor even any of the divine sunsets that had burned a hole in his comrades' hearts like a magnifying glass. Instead, he remembered fondly the time he had cast a line through the porthole and caught an enormous, and later proven succulent, swordfish – he could almost taste it now.

A breathing noise interrupted his reminiscing. Caleb had arrived, followed by the padre. Father Simeon caught sight of the sagging canvas roof.

'What do you intend to do about this?'

The cook assessed the growing problem above his head.

'As soon as I've had my meal.'

Caleb sat upon his hind legs and fixed his eyes on the cook. It was a trick he had learned from his master: Father Simeon had the ability to shrink his body several inches in height and width, as if by dislocating his joints under his uniform and twisting his limbs in the manner of the most talented contortionists; having assumed this stance he would direct an intense look of supplication towards the cook, with enough emotion in his only eye to make up for the glass emptiness of the other one. Only then would he ask for a drop of oil for the lamp, or a dollop of fat to make his candles. In contrast, all Caleb could do was wag his tail.

'Maybe something for the dog?' asked the padre.

Without taking his eyes from the cast-iron pan the cook made an irksome face and gave the padre the rusty corned beef tin. He then wrapped a towel round the handle of the pan and tossed the food a few times. An oblique burst of rain landed on the stove and its sizzling startled the dog. There was still a little meat left in the tin.

'There are maggots in this,' said Father Simeon.

The cook put down the pan and threw the towel over his shoulder.

'Then you have to give it back. The medic pays a dozen cigarettes per can of worms.'

'The medic?'

'They eat the germs in the wounds – he economises on carbolic.'

Father Simeon looked at the writhing maggots with fascination. They were only the larvae of blowflies which had laid their eggs in the decaying meat of the open tin, but to him they represented a miracle. He thought: behold the Lord's infinite wisdom – the visitation of worms could quite possibly be God's gift, now that the medicines had run out.

'The spontaneous birth of worms in rotting matter is a phenomenon godless Darwin never managed to explain,' the padre said.

The cook took the tin from his hands and put it in a safe place. He removed the pan from the fire, served himself half the fried beef and ate standing up. Next to him Father Simeon could not stop thinking about the maggots. The rain soon put out the fire in the stove. The stream down the edges of the canopy was beginning to resemble a glass-bead curtain. The two men and the animal squeezed round the stove that was already cooling down. Holding the mess tin at his chin, the cook ate with his fingers.

'Provisions are running out, Father. Soon you will have to show me how Christ fed the five thousand with seven loaves.'

'Miracles only happen in exceptional circumstances.'

'I consider my death to be an exceptional event too.'

'Let me suggest that you take the Holy Sacrament and pray — and not just for your own good but for the salvation of the whole brigade too. Such a big task I cannot manage alone.'

The rain came down heavily, hitting the flooded roof like lead shot. The hungry dog curled up at Father Simeon's feet. The padre continued.

'Speaking of miracles, once it rained fish in a neighbouring parish. If I hadn't seen it with my own eyes I wouldn't have believed it.'

'Fish?'

'Whitebait — the human mind cannot begin to comprehend God's ways.'

The cook nodded and continued to eat.

'Once, Father, I caught a swordfish the size of a rowing boat – it tasted good too.'

He served himself the rest of the food and smacked his lips. Father Simeon studied the enthusiasm with which his comrade masticated, and could not help himself from feeling he was the leader of a congregation of sheep. How appropriate it had been to represent Him as the Good Shepherd, he thought.

'Do you ever wake up at night, cook?'

A dark shadow passed over the other man's face – he knew very well the padre was referring to the massacre. The truth was that the ghosts of the dead had also been appearing to him – but he, instead, preferred to attribute their presence to the slices of toast he fried in lard before turning in for the night.

'I generally sleep well.'

'And the memory of the events which –?'

'I'm here to cook, padre,' the big man interrupted him. The only authority I am invested with is what to serve tomorrow.'

He spat out a piece of bone he found in his food and added with irritation, 'All other decisions I leave to my superiors.'

Father Simeon raised his eyes with the intention of contemplating the night sky, but all he saw was the tarpaulin two inches above his head, laden with rainwater and sagging dangerously.

'How I envy you, friend. *My* superior lets me make all the decisions myself.'

'I see,' the cook said with his mouth full. 'The bishop?'

'No. Our Creator.'

The cook nodded with indifference. He stretched his neck out of the canopy and drank from the pouring rain while the water struck his face like a whip. The wind travelled between the camp and the hills, bringing back more sand, dust and gravel, to mix up with the rain. Under the canvas roof the two men could only wait. A moment later the padre unbuttoned his pocket and took out a bundle of folded paper: the Genesis and Exodus pages Caleb had torn from his Bible. Father Simeon had tried to glue them back with starch but it had not worked and he had since kept them close to his heart. Rubbing his eyes he searched through the loose pages and cleared his throat.

'And God said unto Noah, the end of all flesh is come before me. For the earth is filled with violence through them. And, behold, I will destroy them with the earth.'

He had no time to read more – a loud crack like thunder interrupted him. He had only just turned his head and noticed the snapping pole, when the canvas canopy slowly began to rip from its edge. Then it burst open like the belly of a gutted animal and let loose a momentous torrent, which fell over the two men and the small dog, throwing all three instantly face down into the mud.

CHAPTER 7

When will this torment end? Major Porfirio asked his reflection in the mirror – a sharp wedge of glass whose silver backing was flaking off. It was an expression of uncompromising displeasure he was looking at: the narrowed eyebrows, the small furrow in the bridge of the nose, the curled, stubborn lip. Like most men of authority he had sculpted that face all by himself, patiently and meticulously, during the early years of his commission. But he did not like this now sour expression, and he began to rub his face with his callused hands, the way one tries to erase a sketch that has turned out wrong. Having only succeeded in making a smudge of it, he abandoned his efforts and pulled the leather braces off his shoulders; his trousers immediately dropped to his ankles, heavy and limp like a large bird shot dead while flying, and raised a cloud of dust. He felt not only tired but also disheartened – he had to admit that the propaganda operation he had carried out all this time had failed. There was not much point in continuing with it – he only risked being caught. The sound of rain against the tarpaulin generated some sort of comfort in him – as long as my tent does not flood tonight, he thought. He raised the wick in the oil lamp a little and, looking closer in the mirror, inspected the shadows of his

cheekbones, the stubble on his chin, his long moustache with curiosity: it was the portrait of a beaten
man.

His underwear consisted of a tattered undershirt and
a pair of soiled long johns. He removed his undershirt. The sun had baked his face and neck, but the
rest of his skin was soft and white, save for some patches
of hard-crusted dirt. It was more a peasant's body than
a warrior's, he thought not without contempt. Indeed:
the brigade were a thousand labourers who ploughed
the desert with the wheels of lorries and artillery guns,
with the hooves of pack animals, with their boots.
They had not fired a shot in weeks; just marched in
circles. Throughout the war the major had maintained
his ideological opposition to the campaign without
once doubting his convictions, yet in battle he would
throw himself at the enemy with the enthusiasm of a
young officer: fighting was his vocation. He found a
stiff brush. From the pole of his tent hung a cavalry
tunic with a stand-up collar, a sword with threadbare
tassels and a rimmed helmet dented by shrapnel. His
riding uniform reminded him of his horse, the brown
Turk with the white star on her forehead. She had
bled to death in the first week of the withdrawal from
a bullet she had taken in the neck intended for her
rider. Major Porfirio's face darkened: if only he had
had time to save her or, at least, deliver her from her
pain – but the enemy had been coming like breakers
on to a shore. Rubbing his back with the brush, he
thought of the gentle animal with fondness; now he
was riding a postman's motorcycle . . .

Suddenly, from not far away, came the noise of

ripping canvas and snapping wood – probably a roof, collapsing from the weight of the rain. He thought he heard the padre's voice followed by a sudden cry from his dog, but his mood had tied such a heavy millstone round his neck that he paid no more attention to it: he had his own misfortunes to care for. Under his desk were his riding boots and next to them a crate containing a library of second-hand books. The lettering on their spines read, *Socialism: Utopian and Scientific . . . Critique of Political Economy . . . Imperialism: the Highest Stage of Capitalism . . .* There were several others. Major Porfirio picked one up and thumbed the pages slowly. He had trouble understanding the full argument of these books, but still knew in his heart of hearts that they upheld a momentous and valid thesis – he would have to be deaf and blind not to notice the unfairness of modern society; his reaction to injustice was an instinct. He put the book back and chose another; he had to search through two more before discovering the leather pouch. Major Porfirio took it out and spread it open on his desk.

It contained his medals from the Balkan Wars. He had been a second lieutenant fresh from the Academy when he had been sent to Macedonia. During that time not only had he been promoted to captain, but also his badly drawn portrait had decorated the walls of coffee shops in the villages liberated by the company under his command. It had been the labour of love of a journeyman painter, after the army had found him hanging upside down from a mammoth oak, with his hands tied behind his back, his dried hog-hair brushes stuck in his orifices and a placard round his neck that read, *This is the generous payment I have received in return for painting our great Sultan in the likeness of a cow.* Captain Porfirio had ordered his soldiers to take him down, untie him and remove the brushes. When the blood had flowed back to his appendages the self-taught artist had placed his precious tools in a fodder bag and kissed his saviour's hand.

'Hail, Alexander the Great,' he had said.

'And you must be Leonardo da Vinci,' the officer had replied drily.

For the rest of the war the painter had followed Captain Porfirio and his troops across Macedonia, expressing his gratitude through his fanciful art. Perhaps his wall paintings of a man in an ancient helmet and body armour, shield and javelin, with a pistol hanging from the belt round his waist, could still be seen in some of those places, Major Porfirio thought with embarrassment.

He arranged the medals on the velvet lining like pieces of jewellery, starting with his favourites: a splendid silver cross on a ribbon with light blue and white stripes, and a bronze cross with crossed swords on the end of a red and deep blue ribbon. The former had been awarded to him when the War Minister had heard of the young officer at the front who had thrown himself on top of a live grenade that had rolled in the pit where he and several of his men had taken cover. The grenade had turned out to be a terrified tortoise blown into the pit by the nearby explosion of an artillery shell, but that did not stop the minister from pinning some days later the Silver Medal for Valour on the brave officer's chest. The other decoration, the

War Cross Third Class, he had received after capturing a submerged Ottoman general who was hiding in a flooded marsh with a reed in his mouth.

Recollecting these and other adventures, while still rubbing his back with the hard brush, Major Porfirio could suppress neither his pride nor his sadness — he had to return all his medals when the expedition was over and resign from the army for the sake of politics. It had been a difficult decision but these were exciting times Europe was living through, he told himself — what with the founding of the soviets . . . When will I see home again? he suddenly wondered. He had done his duty, even though he disagreed with the campaign — it was his responsibility towards his men that made him remain at his post. Yet now the war had been lost, and, while the generals were back home, he was still in that inhospitable land. It was a fate he did not deserve. Major Porfirio felt like one who has come early to the depot but still missed his train.

He thought about the only soldier he had managed to convert to communism and chuckled bitterly — the corporal had been seduced into joining the Party by a woman. The idea that the Party should reply to soldiers' advertisements in the personal columns of the national press had been the major's. How would the corporal react, he considered now, if he knew that his correspondent was not the young woman of his dreams but an overweight and amply bearded commissar in Salonika?

Major Porfirio had been scratching his back for some time, absent-mindedly, when he checked the hard brush and saw it was soaked in his blood. He hid it away and put on his greatcoat; then he took down his helmet, removed the glass cover from the storm lantern and held the helmet over the flame. When it was so hot he could hold it no more he put it under the blanket. Waiting for his cot to warm up, he sat at his desk and took from the crate a book titled *Origin of the Family, Private Property and the State*. Pencil in hand, it was not long before his head slowly came to rest on the well-thumbed pages, and he began to snore with a whistling noise.

Moments after the canopy had caved in, a squad of drenched *evzones* wearing short tunics and ammunition belts across the chest passed near the field kitchen. Unaware of the disaster, they would have carried on had they not heard the yapping of the dog. When they realised what had happened, they stacked their rifles and rushed to save the men.

First they unearthed the cook and sat him on the ground. He had to take many deep breaths and spit out a bucketful of mud before he could speak.

'The padre – save him! If you can find it in your hearts to forgive the boredom of his sermons.'

Caleb was already digging into the mud with a fiery energy. The weight of the flooded canopy had toppled the stove and the dog's master lay under it. Finally, the soldiers managed to lift the cast-iron monster and pull out the padre.

'Father? Are you alive?'

He was shaken. Little by little he recovered, and the first thing he did was to feel his pockets.

'My Bible – find my Bible, sinners!'

Covered in mud, his face seemed like a clay mask. Behind it his left eye moved from side to side in panic. Father Simeon shook off his helpers and began to move in circles, uttering loud and indecipherable croaks. It was a terrifying sight. The soldiers stepped back and watched him in awe, thinking that the rain must have entered his skull, perhaps through his ears, and flooded the poor man's brain. He was like an entranced dancer at the height of some pagan ritual. Was he enacting an etching from some illustrated novel of his youth about cannibals – the one that had dissuaded him from his dream of becoming a missionary? The padre continued to move in circles with his head bent, and then suddenly he fell to his knees and turned silent – his bizarre choreography was, after all, an erratic search for his Bible. At his feet was a small heap of pulp. As soon as Father Simeon took it in his hands it broke to pieces.

'Ruined . . .' he mumbled. 'Now we are *truly* lost.'

He meant what he said with all his heart – he always considered the Book to be one's only map in the journey towards salvation. He looked at its remains with utter despair. He would have been less devastated had the brigadier's Geological Survey maps met a similar fate. He stood up, but the asphyxiation he had almost suffered in the mud had left him with vertigo. He wavered, and the soldiers had to support him again lest he collapse in the mud.

'The Lord,' he stammered, 'shall never allow unrepentant souls out of Hell.'

His words fell upon the men with the gravity of

prophecy. They raised their heads and contemplated the silver strings of the autumnal deluge like explorers searching for the source of a mysterious river – but they could not go beyond the barrier of the clouds: they were as dark and heavy as the smoke from the chimney of a factory. The padre observed the wet faces round him carefully, with an eye that was as haunting as it was full of pity.

'Mother of God! I am surrounded by dead men.' He trembled with fear. 'Am I dead, too?'

The cook cupped his hand. When it had filled with rainwater he washed the mud from the padre's face. This he repeated several times, with increasing affection, until the clerical beard, the ploughed forehead and the cracked lips had recovered some of their energy.

'Take him to the infirmary. The nurse might have a shot that cures madness.'

'Leave me alone!' the padre hissed. 'I have to go to church. I need to pray for your worthless souls.'

The *evzones* took a step back – there was still some authority left in Father Simeon's old priest's voice. Then he picked up his cap slowly, wrung the water out and followed his legs in the direction of his tent, like a somnambulist. The dog went with him, close behind.

'Leave him,' the cook said. 'He will be fine in the morning – unless he blows his brains out during the night.'

The padre did not appear at the next roll-call, nor was he seen anywhere in the camp all day. Only those who happened to walk past his church of the

Cappadocian Fathers heard his voice: a weak and suppliant whimper that was a far cry from the usual vociferations of his sermons.

News of the accident and the effect it had on the padre spread fast, and after evening mess the major was asked to report to brigade command. Brigadier Nestor was sitting at his desk when his Chief of Staff entered. He was making cigars from a bundle of tobacco leaves. Immersed in his task he did not notice his subordinate until some time later, when he raised his head and saw the slender silhouette on the fringe of the radiance of the lamp. Major Porfirio promptly stood to attention; the old officer did not return his salute.

'Come closer, major. This toothless dog cannot bite.'

There was a crude cigar press on his desk, made out of a screw clamp and the two halves of a split pistol barrel for a mould. It was like a miniature torture implement, Major Porfirio thought; a finger would fit in it perfectly. Brigadier Nestor wrapped several leaves together and attempted to roll them, but they were too dry and they cracked in his fingers. He bit his lip and started again, with the petty stubbornness of a child; every time he had to use his hands to perform some delicate job, his rheumatism made it feel as if he were wearing gloves. It took him several failed attempts before he finally surrendered.

'Useless,' he puffed, and examined his hands with exasperation. 'A crab would do a better job with its pincers.'

He produced a pipe from his breast pocket and filled it with the tobacco confetti scattered on his desk. He sat back in his chair and smoked, relighting his pipe at regular intervals and drawing at it with all the strength of his lungs. He seemed to have forgotten the major; his eyes wandered around the interior of his tent. His maps were on the floor under the table, where they had fallen when he had cleared his desk to make room for his cigar press. On his cot his private letters were mixed up with his twisted blankets. A small woodpile – broken branches, a bunch of fodder, some dried asphodel roots – had collapsed when the old officer had stumbled upon it the night before, at the height of his intoxicated phantasmagoria. It all helped to give the place some sort of domesticity: thanks to an innate untidiness, the brigadier could turn his fleeting quarters – his tent was put up every evening when the order was given to camp and taken down the following morning before marching again – into an almost cosy abode. Major Porfirio glanced at the mess – it was like the finds of an archaeological excavation. He thought: if the sandstorm had buried the brigade alive last night and an archaeologist came across it centuries later, he would be able to guess the magnitude of our defeat just by the squalor of our personal belongings. Brigadier Nestor's voice interrupted his thoughts.

'I don't see much future in cigarettes. They are nothing but paper and hay – and a pinch of the cheapest tobacco in the middle.' He puffed out a cloud of smoke. '*I* would put my money into the pipe-making business.'

The cured leaves emanated a delicious smell that made it impossible for the major to return to his macabre dream. It was the incidental pleasures that made living bearable – they were the rare stones that turned the string of life into a precious necklace: music, food, a beautiful landscape, dance . . . It did not cross the major's mind to include love in his list, too.

'So,' Brigadier Nestor said. 'The padre went insane. An interesting development.' He began to chuckle but it quickly turned into a cough. 'He brainwashed himself by reading the Bible night and day.'

'His Bible was all but ruined by the rain,' Major Porfirio informed him.

Brigadier Nestor welcomed the news with a mirthful slap on his thigh.

'Peace and quiet at last. His megaphone was worse than the Furies.'*

His pipe went out and the brigadier lifted the glass cover of the lamp and lit it again.

'I always thought his attitude was detrimental to troop morale,' he added.

The fragrance of the tobacco was making Major Porfirio's mouth water – the cigarettes he himself had been smoking were of such bad quality they almost scraped his lungs.

He had always been critical of the extravagances of wealth. Before the war he had been stationed in the capital, where he led a spartan life, even though his salary could afford him many of the metropolitan

---

*Three avenging deities who lived in the underworld, from which they ascended to earth to pursue the wicked. Just but merciless, they had no regard for mitigating circumstances, punishing all offences against human society.

indulgences that were on offer. Now, standing in front of the brigadier, enveloped in the cruel smoke, he at last started to yearn for the daily pleasures of peacetime: the coffee and newspaper at the street café, the afternoon stroll in the Royal Gardens, the evenings by the fireplace in the Officers' Club.

Brigadier Nestor picked up a map from the floor and tore off a large piece in which he wrapped the tobacco leaves.

'I shall carry this tobacco with me at all times. It is the only way of making sure that no one steals this too.'

The major looked at the torn map with a frown. His commanding officer waved his hand in a sign of nonchalance.

'Don't worry about these, Porfirio. They are worse than Columbus's maps.'

The major asked permission to leave; feeling his way through the thick tobacco fog he found the exit.

It was a night of clear skies speckled with dim stars. Two days earlier it had been a bright, full moon, but the crescent now was sallow, ugly and grim, as if it were a gash in a fine piece of black fabric. Major Porfirio felt suffocated. Not only had his mission of enlightenment kept him busy during the long days of the retreat, but it had also helped him preserve his sanity. Now that this task had failed, he wished he were home as much as his men did. He raised his eyes to the sky. If only they could follow the stars to the coast, he thought. But it was impossible: the terrain forbade travelling in a straight line, and they had to make countless detours. He made out the constellation of Scorpius and traced his finger north-east to discover Lyra. Vega, its brightest star, seemed that night no more brilliant than an ordinary firefly. It was as if a paper screen stood between heaven and earth – or a thin burial shroud. When he lowered his head he was surprised to see the soldiers still sitting round the campfires, talking. He lit a match, checked his watch and pursed his lips: the bugler should have called lights out a half-hour ago. After a brief search he found him sitting under the flag post, talking to the airman. Immediately he saw his superior, the bugler sprang to his feet, put the bugle under his arm and saluted.

'My major – I was about to commence.'

Major Porfirio looked at the bugle. There were patches where its brass coating had rubbed off and its gold-threaded cord had lost its tassel. In its bell was the dent from the night the bugler had brought down his instrument on the head of a brigand, intending to murder him. Major Porfirio waved him at ease.

'We were discussing my demobilisation, my major,' the bugler said. 'The lieutenant is kind enough to promise to help me find a job in a cabaret when all this is over.'

'I am sure such a placement would be extremely useful. You are likely to make the acquaintance there of some of our most eminent citizens.'

The soldier raised the bugle. He was so nervous that he blew off-key.

'Lights out, if you please, bugler,' the major reproved him without anger. 'Not a spirited foxtrot.'

Before the call had ended the fires were already disappearing and the camp slowly erased itself from the saltpetre plain. It was after the bugler had retired that the incident took place, which some time later would have such grave consequences.

It is often the case that ominous events are wrapped within a soft shell of innocence: the eating of the forbidden fruit, the dipping of the baby Achilles into the River Styx, which made his body forever invulnerable but for the heel by which his mother held him (and which was the exact spot where he was ultimately wounded by a fatal arrow), or, less fabulously, a child at fascinated play with a box of matches. In this instance, it was Air Lieutenant Kimon taking out his case and offering the major a cigarette. The latter observed it in silence before his lips began to contort in an expression of disgust. The scant moonlight was reflecting upon his face like an interrogator's lamp from the platinum case; he was unable to hide his indignation and soon the airman noticed it – but guessed the wrong reason for it.

'No, these are not rationed,' he said genially. 'They are the best Turkish. Go ahead, major.'

But in actual fact it was the expensive case Major Porfirio's eyes were observing with such contempt.

'I've seen whole families killed for less,' he said.

The young lieutenant knitted his eyebrows and nodded sympathetically.

'Yes, we heard the stories at the squadron.'

The major looked at the night sky with bitterness: he did not see constellations up there now; he saw oak-panelled boxes above the enormous stage that was the desert.

'War must be a lesser affair from up there,' he said.

'Lesser?'

'One does not witness the horror.'

'I almost died trying to find you, major.'

'A blind man would have done a better job.' Major Porfirio lowered his eyes to the cigarette case. 'Don't wave this around, lieutenant. There has been a series of thefts.'

The airman smiled.

'Couldn't I at least trust an officer?'

The major felt he could not be more different from the aristocrat – and not just because of his beliefs; his own dark eyes, black hair and olive skin were the opposite of the younger airman's Teutonic beauty. He watched himself, minute and distorted, in the mirror of his opponent's eyes.

'Even officers are sometimes human, lieutenant.'

But the airman's armour was impenetrable to the wooden arrows of such sarcasm.

'My experience shows otherwise,' he replied.

His impertinence served only to enhance Major Porfirio's anger. Until that moment his contempt for the aristocracy had been little more than a theoretical abstraction: the bourgeoisie, the government, the foreign imperialist powers. But now it had found a face. Here at last was a man on whom the major could vent his resentment. The great revolutionary leaders had for some time been the object of his affections – but a doctrine needs both its gods and its demons. It was very dark now across the camp. The constellations were a few bright specks in the irises of the two men: not enough to reveal the emotions behind their eyes, but sufficient to present each of them with a conspicuous target for his shooting practice. Major Porfirio fired another insult.

'War!' he sighed. 'A hunting expedition for the ruling classes!'

He was treading on the edge of the precipice; his revolutionary vernacular could easily betray his clandestine mission. Biting his lip right now offered him plenty of a painful sensation but little help in covering his tracks. The airman did not notice. He scratched his head under his leather helmet.

'Report to the medical officer in the morning and volunteer your services,' the major ordered. 'Let's hope you are better at emptying bedpans than flying a plane.'

Not even his inborn aristocratic nonchalance could hide the fact that at that moment Air Lieutenant Kimon reached the furthermost reaches of his patience. Insults he did not mind, but he would hold his palm an inch above a lit brazier rather than follow orders.

He suffered from an incurable aversion to authority. It originated in the sins of a supreme autocrat of a father, who treated his only son the way he dealt with his clerks – namely, as if they were not in his pay but, rather, a gang of thieves who every month stole their salary from the safe in his office. Decisions at home, the airman remembered, were announced like imperial decrees arriving from a faraway seat of power: suddenly, with little justification and without the sugar coating of the paternal reassurance that 'Father knows best'.

Among other practices, his father had enforced bathing in icy cold water – because he had found that it was eminently beneficial to a man's constitution; he had banned the reading of modern poetry because it incubated the grave danger of melancholy; and as for the solitary sin of onanism – which the vigilant patriarch had once caught his offspring committing in the coach house while at the same time goggling at the darkness between a mare's buttocks – he had shipped all the way from England a patented contraption that restrained its unwilling user, so that he would not turn overnight into a blind and degraded idiot.

Air Lieutenant Kimon pouted. Then he stood to attention sharply and saluted his superior.

'As you wish, major.'

When a little later the two officers walked away in opposite directions, each had made an implacable foe.

Suddenly the lamp flickered and the shadows that had been projected on to the canvas of the tent started to dance like cinematographic images. Father Simeon unscrewed the bottom of the lamp and added a few drops of oil. Lines of string above his head ran from one end of his tent to the other; held with clothespins, the damp yellowed pages of his Bible hung down like perching bats. The padre put on his glasses and examined several of the pages closely, grinning with a near demented satisfaction; under the ink blotches most of the text was fortunately discernible. He pulled down a few pages and hung the oil lamp round his neck. As soon as he found his megaphone among the jumble of his kit he made the sign of the cross and left the tent.

Not far away, covered up to his eyebrows with the blanket, the brigadier was dreaming he was on board a luxurious train travelling across a vast expanse of olive groves on a cloudless day. Sitting alone in a private compartment of plump leather seats he was smoking an enormous cigar. With his thick tome in hand he was lost in the labyrinth of Greek and Roman myths, while on the polished table in front of him a crystal goblet half filled with absinthe chimed to the hypnotic vibrations of the car. As his mouth chugged like the speeding locomotive of his dream, Brigadier Nestor felt a rare pleasure akin to watching a fine operetta for the first time. But in a moment a distant voice intruded upon his happy journey like a conductor's announcement.

'Yet thou shalt be brought down to hell, to the sides of the pit. They that see thee shall narrowly look upon thee, and consider thee, saying, Is this the man that made the earth to tremble, that did shake kingdoms; that made the world as a wilderness, and destroyed the cities thereof; that opened not the house of his prisoners?'

The brigadier raised his head from his pillow and rubbed his eyes – it took him some time to persuade his senses that he was, in fact, awake. Holding his breath he listened.

'But thou art cast out of thy grave like an abominable branch, and as the raiment of those that are slain, thrust through with a sword, that go down to the stones of the pit; as a carcass trodden under feet.'

'In the name of mercy,' the brigadier said, half asleep, when he realised who the voice belonged to. The invisible narrator continued gravely and monotonously as before.

'Thou shalt not be joined with them in burial, because

thou hast destroyed thy land, and slain thy people . . .'

When the padre moved on and there was silence again, Brigadier Nestor was left shivering. His feet jutted out from his campaign cot, and he immediately imagined himself strapped on to Procrustes' bed.[*] It was too much for him. Losing control of his reason, he started to bestow the most elaborate profanities on the military cleric. Only after he had exhausted his vocabulary of vulgarity did he shut his eyes again. He had not yet fallen asleep when somewhere across the camp another headache was already being conjured for him: also lying on his back, with his hands folded under his head and his eyes open, the corporal was calmly planning his escape for the night of the next new moon.

---

[*]Procrustes was a highwayman on the road to Athens, who tortured his victims by cutting them down to fit his bed if they were too tall, or hammering and stretching them if they were too short. He was eventually killed by Theseus in the same way the robber had been torturing his victims.

PART 2

The Town

CHAPTER 1

The *hamam* was located in a quiet street behind the market. It was an ochre building with a dome of peeling plaster and the modest façade of a country chapel. Immediately past its entrance was a square court with cubicles round a stone fountain, each with a bench and a row of shelves. The baths themselves were a large steamy chamber whose floor was decorated with geometric mosaics. An archway of pencil-thin columns ran round the room, where the coal furnaces used for heating were. In the middle of the chamber, lit by shafts of daylight through the bottle-glass windows of the dome, was a marble platform. On it at that moment, enveloped in dense clouds of steam, prone and naked, lay the schoolmaster.

He turned around, dipped the wooden ladle in the pail and sprinkled the coals with slow, stupefied movements. Hot vapours and the smell of essential oils rose from the grate and covered his body. He closed his eyes and folded his hands over his belly. Motionless and prostrate under layers of steam, he gave the appearance of a corpse wrapped in a shroud. After a brief moment of inertia he sat up and began to feel the signs of maturity on his body. There were certain things that age had given him in abundance: nasal hair, flaccid skin under each arm, an enormous concertina in return for his once flat belly.

'The only thing life is not tight-fisted with,' he reflected, 'is flab.'

He collapsed back on to the marble and his skin stretched over the flat surface like dough worked with a rolling pin. In his young days he had taken up traditional wrestling after seeing a match between two giant Turks smeared with olive oil at the annual fair. The schoolmaster remembered how, when the physical education teacher had found out, he had reprimanded him: he ought to be practising the sports that fostered the classical ideals, he had said, not taking part in what was nothing more than a street brawl . . . The boy had thus been forced to adopt the Graeco-Roman style.

It was during an athletics tournament in Smyrna in his penultimate year at school that he had met the love of his life. She was already a graduate of the Central School for Girls, and one of the young women holding the silver trays with the laurels and scrolls at the medal ceremony. The moment he climbed the highest step of the podium and their eyes met he blushed as if his leotard were too small for him.

Together they had experienced the brief fantasies of their adolescent imagination – that is, talking of marriage and comparing notes as regards its consummation. She was the first to awake from their mutual delusion: before the tournament had ended she had run away with his physical education teacher.

An acid gas rose from his stomach, lifting the memory of that morning's coffee and boiled eggs to his mouth, and the schoolmaster belched heartily. The bitch, he thought; not only had he never married, but also he had done not a minute's exercise since, therefore being reduced to the pitiful state he was now in. He wiped the sweat on the bald patch on his head with a sponge and surrendered once again to the soporific steam of the baths. Some time later the creak of the door awakened him. The schoolmaster squinted at the moving shadow behind the thick steam.

'Is that you, Yusuf?'

'At your service,' replied a cheerful voice.

The young attendant approached the platform with an effort that was not compatible with his age: deformed by a teenage attack of tuberculosis, his back had a large hump. On his dark Arab face his eyes shone with a combination of brightness and humility. He put down his wooden pail and smiled. Even though they knew each other well, only now did the schoolmaster see with surprise that the enamel of the Arab's teeth was as bright as the whites of his eyes. He felt like one who raises his head to notice for the first time the high façades in a street he has been walking down for years. The pail contained a large towel, a copper bowl with a handle, a bar of soap and a brush.

'Isn't Mr Othon asleep?'

The schoolmaster closed his eyes and waved to him to proceed. The attendant rolled up his sleeves, filled the pail with hot water and started rubbing the other's back. He was like a baker, kneading with his bare hands, occasionally sprinkling the dough with water, working his way through the soft mix in a systematic fashion, while his eyes travelled along the painted frieze that ran above the columns and across all four walls. At first sight it had appeared to depict an elaborate

floral scene of acanthus leaves and branches of pome-
granates, but after several hours of absent-minded
observation the paintings had yielded their secret to
Yusuf: between the discreet decorative pattern lay
hidden images of ecstatic and multiple lovemaking.
The young Arab smirked; he took profound pleasure
in being the sole possessor of such scandalous knowledge. After washing out the suds with tepid water, he
massaged the skin for a long time before, finally, filling
the pail with cold water and splashing it over his
customer. Instantly, the schoolmaster jumped off the
platform and began to rub his buttocks.

'Brother!' he exclaimed. 'Did you bring that water
all the way from Antarctica?'

He wrapped himself in the checked towel and when
his teeth had ceased chattering asked for his clothes.
The attendant shuffled his slippers towards the door,
carrying the pail in his hand.

'Yusuf,' the schoolmaster called after him. 'In my
cubicle you will also find my bag. Bring it to the
garden, please.'

The attendant nodded.

'Does Mr Othon want his *narghile?*'

The schoolmaster smacked his lips.

'An excellent idea, Yusuf.'

He made his way to the garden, whistling. As soon
as he stepped into the courtyard he found that the
weather approved of his euphoria. It was a sunny afternoon with a light as mellow and golden as honey:
autumn had finally arrived. The garden was surrounded
on all four sides with plastered walls the colour of
peach, on which illicit ivies had cast anchor over the

years, while in the honeycomb holes at the top of the walls pigeons had made their nests. The garden itself was planted with hibiscus shrubs, above which rose a narrow juniper heavy with berries. At that time of the afternoon its shadow fell over the oval pond teeming with algae and enormous goldfish. In the green water the fish swam lazily, never touching each other. The schoolmaster carried a chair to the shadow of the wall.

In a moment Yusuf came with his clothes, the wreckage of a leather satchel and the *narghile*. Mr Othon's suit betrayed his marital status – a series of repairs done to it over the years had clearly not been vetted by a spouse's eye: the worn collar of his white shirt had been replaced by a beige one, the stripes on the extra piece of fabric sewn on the seat of his trousers ran at right angles to the rest, and on his jacket a bent paperclip stood in for a missing button. Humming, the bachelor dressed with the help of the Arab.

'They don't make suits like this any more, Yusuf,' he said. 'I had it sewn when I was promoted to school-master.'

His finger searched for the collar button but it, too, had fallen victim to the anarchy that ruled his domestic life. He thought it must have fallen off earlier when he undressed carelessly in the *camekan* before entering the steamy baths in all his naked glory. He pouted in an expression of acquiescence, tightened his necktie over his loose collar and asked for his jacket. Yusuf held it up for him.

'This fabric is as exquisite,' Mr Othon said and pushed his arms into the sleeves, 'as it is impenetrable. It has survived fourteen years of daily student bombardment.'

He felt indeed like a medieval knight helped into his armour by his devoted squire. He put on his white felt hat all by himself and checked the time on the stone sundial that stood among the hibiscus, before sitting down in the shade and opening his satchel. Tied with an elastic band, the thick paper bundle contained the answer sheets to the problems he had set the previous day on the laws of gravity. He put on his glasses and had only had a quick look through the papers before knitting his brows and making reproving sounds with his tongue – his expectations had been confirmed. 'Those cretins,' he said, referring to his students, 'made a preserve out of Isaac Newton's apples.' He sucked the tube of the *narghile* and addressed the attendant of the baths.

'Look at this, my friend – and they claim to be direct descendants of Heraclitus!'

Yusuf acknowledged his comment with a grunt. Unlike his customer he himself was dressed with less consequence but more prudence for such a warm afternoon: a simple shirt without a collar, a pair of slack linen trousers and his old slippers with the rope soles. Standing on the edge of the pond with his hands on his hips, he observed the water in such silence that the schoolmaster assumed he was praying. After a while the Arab went back inside and returned with a bucket and a long stick with a net on the end.

'The fish have grown very big,' he announced.

As soon as he sank the net in the water the fish rushed to hide under the lilies.

'Do they taste any good, Yusuf?' the schoolmaster asked absent-mindedly from where he sat.

The attendant shook his head from side to side, while ploughing the water with his net.

'No good – many bones. They're only good for the mayor's cat.'

The schoolmaster continued marking the exam papers.

'I don't see why you look after that useless feline. She can't even catch a lame rat.'

Yusuf replied with a perfunctory nod. Catching a goldfish in such murky waters was quite a challenge, especially with this bad back of his. He narrowed his eyes and steered the net smoothly towards an orange silhouette under the surface. He stopped humming, held his breath and struck in a flash. A pigeon sitting on the garden wall took flight with a few irritated beats of its wings. Yusuf raised his net slowly: a large quivering goldfish was caught in it. He looked closely at its sparkling scales and gave a triumphant smile that exposed his marvellous teeth.

'You're too fat to pass through the gates of Paradise,' he said, and shook his head with disapproval.

'But not too fat for the cat's mouth,' the school-master said from his seat.

Yusuf transferred the fish into the bucket and lowered the net into the pond again. He asked casually, 'Is it true the mayor is going to marry Madame?'

On the margin of an answer sheet the schoolmaster wrote in crimson-ink letters: *If the distance between the two bodies increases then their force of attraction should decrease as the square of that distance!* Then he capped his fountain pen, removed his glasses and rubbed his eyes.

'It would be inappropriate for a man of such a high office,' he answered with a sneer, 'to associate himself with a fallen woman.'

The Arab accepted the schoolmaster's argument, but that did not mean he had ceased to hold the prostitute in high regard.

'She's a fallen angel,' he said, 'but the mayor has the face of a donkey.'

The schoolmaster stroked his chin.

'Under her auspices he will run a formidable election campaign,' he said bitterly.

Ever since the schoolmaster had heard the rumours about the wedding he had begun to wake up during the night – oh how he wished now that his students were playing a prank on him with the alarm clock! They had violated the sanctuary of his bedroom on more than one occasion before. One time the little wretches had nailed his blanket to the bedstead, and in the morning he had waited for more than an hour before a neighbour had heard his cries for help and rushed to the house to release him. Another time he had awakened to see wooden boards an inch above his nose and had assumed the heartless devils had buried him alive, but thankfully they had only moved him underneath his bed while he slept.

But the reason for his current insomnia was more grievous. The truth of the matter was that he worried he would lose Violetta for ever. As the schoolmaster raised the tube of the *narghile* to his lips and nibbled at its tip a butterfly entered the garden. His eyes followed its meandering among the hibiscus shrubs with a clandestine sentimentality. Soon the attendant of the baths suspended his attempts to capture another goldfish and leaned on the rod of his net.

'I remember the day she arrived,' he pondered. 'I thought she was the queen of Sheba.'

The woman had come to the town eleven years earlier in the sacred hours of the afternoon rest, in a landau pulled by two lazy water buffalo. Dressed only in his trousers and a sleeveless undershirt, the schoolmaster had come to his balcony in time to witness a head covered by a hat trimmed with flowers emerge from the window of the carriage. Violetta had stretched her long neck adorned with a number of diamond chokers and sniffed the air; immediately she had grimaced in disappointment.

'*Ah non,*' she had sighed in the silence of the afternoon. '*Une autre ville qui sent la merde.*'

She had instructed the driver to dismantle the pyramid of her buckskin luggage with the utmost care. On his balcony that overlooked the town square the schoolmaster had stopped breathing and had watched . . . To this day he still remembered her embroidered bolero sewn with pearls, her small purse and chatelaine draped around her waist, and – when she lifted her skirt for her foot to find the step – the horrific inch of three pleated petticoats she wore underneath. As soon as she was standing on firm ground she had pulled out a lace handkerchief from her cuff and sprinkled it with cologne. Having purified her pale cheeks from the miseries of the journey, she had then addressed her maid.

'*Annina, ma petite, on est arrivé chez nous.*'

In the shade of the oriental garden Mr Othon

fingered the ivory mouthpiece of the *narghile*. The attendant had invoked memories that poured oil on the flames of his heart; the schoolmaster deservedly made him now the butt of his irritation.

'The Queen of Sheba indeed,' he scorned. 'The problem with you Turks is that you are excessively sentimental.'

Yusuf was not offended – he was privy to the tormented affection the schoolmaster felt towards the Frenchwoman. He shook his head and steered his submerged net towards another lazy goldfish.

'I am not Turk, Mr Othon,' he grinned. 'I'm Arab.'

The grocer sat on the bench in the shade across the street from the baths and stroked his grey goatee – he had decided to take a digestive walk after lunch because the barley and yoghurt were giving him trouble again. Rubbing his belly, grieving over his alimentary misfortune and blaming his wife, he had found himself in the streets behind the market. He was still fending off the detonations of his bowels when he caught sight of the schoolmaster coming out of the *hamam*.

'According to my wife, teacher,' he called at him from across the street, 'that establishment represents pure Ottoman decadence.'

The schoolmaster crossed the earthen street and joined the grocer on the bench.

'Women are suspicious of anything that puts a smile on a man's face,' he said. 'Even laughing gas.'

The grocer rubbed his aching belly with tenderness and told the schoolmaster that of his wife's sins the barley-and-yoghurt soup was the most unredeemable

– others were the quails she insisted in roasting in a pool of olive oil and melted butter, and the *pilaf* with cracked wheat she overcooked by seven whole minutes. Mr Othon nodded sympathetically but hardly a word made it as far as the labyrinth of his ear. This skill of listening without hearing had taken him years to perfect – it was invaluable in the classroom. He patted his friend on the shoulder.

'The Bible tells it wrong, teacher,' the grocer continued, and slackened his belt with an expression of agony. 'The serpent did not give Eve an apple – it taught her to cook.'

'I never understood why you married,' the schoolmaster said agreeably.

The grocer made a gesture of helplessness.

'The evil woman tricked me with her *baklava*.'

It could not have been further from the truth. Everyone knew that he had fallen prey to love at first sight. He was a silversmith's apprentice in a small Armenian town when his future wife had walked into the shop and asked him to repair her late grandmother's ring so that it could fit her. He had obliged and done the job for free, but in a moment of inspiration he had also decided to engrave his name on the inside. Some days later her mother had discovered the unauthorised work and he had promptly been dismissed.

It was the eve of the century. Soon their town was to be inundated by the tidal wave of massacres that drowned Armenia in blood – as it turned out, the couple's elopement not only saved their love but also their lives. No sooner had they arrived in their new home than they married; the keepsake had become the bride's wedding ring.

The grocer took out his watch: it was time to open the shop. The two men walked towards the town square through a maze of alleyways that was the Muslim Quarter. From the open balcony doors came the peaceful noise of snoring. Somewhere a treadle was started and a sewing machine rattled in the afternoon silence like a distant train. Lizards criss-crossed the two men's path and climbed the whitewashed walls, while a bead curtain in front of an open door was blown about by the wind like lifeless tentacles. On either side of another door pots of geranium stood guard. The alleyways were not wide enough for both men to walk side by side, so the grocer walked ahead. Behind him the schoolmaster paused to switch his satchel to his other shoulder. The walls carried his panting away – only a moment later he heard it somewhere behind him. He found his handkerchief and mopped his brow, admitting to himself the burden of wearing a suit all year round – but he did not question his habit; a schoolmaster ought always to appear respectable.

'If this is the quickest route,' he asked, 'how come one needs a ball of thread to find one's way out?'[*]

---

[*]When the Greek hero Theseus came to Crete as one of the victims that the Athenians were annually required to offer to the Minotaur, Ariadne, the daughter of Minos, fell in love with him. She gave him then a ball of thread, which he fastened to the entrance of the labyrinth and unwound it as he went along, until he found and killed the Minotaur. He escaped from the maze by rewinding the thread.

'A straight line is not always the shortest distance,' replied the grocer without stopping or turning round.

'Pythagoras would disagree, of course,' said Mr Othon, breathing heavily.

A whiff of cooked food was sieved through the mosquito screen nailed on some kitchen window. The schoolmaster shoved his handkerchief back in his breast pocket and hastened to catch up with the grocer.

The shop stood in a corner of the square opposite the Town Hall. It had a conspicuous signboard that boasted from afar THE CORNUCOPIA GROCERY, above a wood-sculpted horn of plenty. The grocer unlocked the patched-up door and walked in. 'Watch your step, teacher,' he said. The schoolmaster froze at once, resting himself on one leg while the other remained hovering over the threshold, as if he were attempting a silly imitation of a stork. Only when the Armenian had lit the lamp did the schoolmaster see the reason for the warning: scattered across the sawdust on the floor were mousetraps baited with cheese. The grocer took down his white coat from a nail on the wall and in its place he hung the heavy key. A cloud of flies circled the oil lamp that hung from the ceiling. The schoolmaster put down his satchel and rubbed his back. His eyes followed the orbiting insects as he would have observed a merry-go-round.

'Lord have mercy on me,' he sighed. 'I'm teaching centripetal force next week.'

The shop was well stocked and its merchandise neatly displayed. On the shelf behind the counter the bread loaves were arranged in size, and on the table next to them stood the coffee grinder. Underneath were tin boxes with rubber seals for the coffee beans, and on the counter two scales with their weights. Despite the delicacies on display all round, one smell dominated the shop and it was coming from the barrel of salted cod. Standing behind the counter the Armenian felt like a captain on the bridge of his ship. But his stomach had yet to recover; he dissolved a spoon of baking soda in a glass of water and gulped it down. Only then did he offer the schoolmaster a seat.

'I hear the mayor is getting married,' he said, uncorking a brandy bottle.

Immediately, the schoolmaster adopted a surly expression.

'One cannot marry without an Orthodox priest.'

From the window of the grocery they could both see the azure dome of St Gregorius Theologus and its belfry, rising above the ceramic roofs of the town. Once the church had a devout priest, two psalmists, a sexton and a pious congregation. On the feast day of its patron saint it held a week-long fair with food, music and strongmen from distant Asian lands. Then the priest had fallen ill and when he had recovered he had immediately announced his retirement. Sensing the sand in his hourglass running out, he had decided to visit the Church of the Holy Sepulchre in Jerusalem. (He had not lived to complete his long pilgrimage; he had expired on seeing the biblical walls of Jericho.) The answer to the town's request for a new priest had come in a letter written in the hand of the Ottoman governor. He was a moderate man who maintained many a fond memory of the town fair he attended every year and had developed a deep affection for his infidel but hospitable subjects. In his letter he explained how the political situation in the Balkans was developing. He predicted a flood of Muslim refugees into Asia Minor following the end of the Great War and the ultimate defeat of the Empire, and the violence that this would spark between them and the local Christians. He admitted that it would be impossible for him to prevent it – but there was one solution: the town could distance itself from its religion. *Therefore, my dear friends*, he had concluded his sincere letter, *do ask yourselves: does the salvation of the soul take precedence over the preservation of the flesh?* His calligraphic question mark had coiled itself round the townspeople's necks and squeezed them for days. Finally, they had taken a unanimous decision not to insist on their request for a priest.

Years had now passed since the church doors had been locked for ever and its Byzantine windows boarded up. Not long after it was abandoned, a legion of rats made it its home. Having eaten everything inside – from the candles left in the candelabra to the drapery of the altar and the carpets on the floor – they had begun piratical raids against the grocery and had become the Armenian's biggest headache. His repeated protests had resulted in the mayor buying a cat, but she preferred to perch on the windowsills of the Town Hall rather than satisfy her predatory instincts.

The grocer poured two brandies and gave the schoolmaster a sidelong glance.

'A priest is the least of the mayor's worries. The

next town is only three hours away, and there's an Orthodox church there.'

The schoolmaster grabbed his drink without thanks and downed it.

'If there's a priest inside it, he'll probably be swinging from the chandelier.'

He punctuated his sentence with a thud of his empty glass on the counter; the Armenian duly refilled it.

'Anyhow,' the grocer said, 'the mayor is determined to get married. Whether by a priest or by an *imam*.'

The schoolmaster raised a forefinger loaded with malice. No sooner had he opened his mouth than the sound of hooves on the cobblestones cut through the silence of the afternoon and stopped him short with its urgency.

The lobby of the Town Hall was a vast room laid with chequered tiles, from which a double flight of sweeping steps led up to a gallery of offices. Time had stripped off most of the lacquer from the drawbridge-like doors, and the bare cedar-of-Lebanon planks exuded the last drops of their ancient fragrance. On one such door a handwritten sign was pinned that read, *I am not in*, but a thundering snoring coming from the other side undermined the veracity of the declaration.

Sitting at his desk with a large pillow behind his head and his hands clasped over his belly, the mayor paused to gulp in his sleep and then resumed his snoring. On the dirty windowsill, under the pane that vibrated to the gurgling noise of his gullet, his cat also slept, lying on her side. Presently, the mayor opened his eyes and rolled his head in the direction of the window. A row of blossom-covered tamarisks stood in the courtyard round a marble bust. All night the wind had shaken the trees and now the square was a sea of pink flowers; two men were crossing the square, knee-deep in the blossoms. The mayor recognised the Armenian and the schoolmaster: they were probably on their way to open the grocery for the evening.

The air in the office was hot. Still dazed with his slumber, the mayor looked around him. The flaking paint, the chipped pilasters and crazed tiles caused him a fleeting melancholy. The small town had managed to escape the prow of the war but had been caught in its backwash. Since the landing of the Expeditionary Corps state funding had been suspended, and for the last two years the treasury had remained empty. The mayor puffed and rubbed his rosy nape that was stiff from his nap. Why did living have to be so difficult? his mind protested to no one in particular. As soon as he recovered his faculties, he stood up and went to the other end of his office where two easy chairs were arranged on either side of a mahogany Victrola. A stack of dusty phonograph records was on the floor and he riffled through it. He put one on, turned the crank and waited for the music to start before he returned, humming, to his desk. On the windowsill the cat yawned, stretched her legs and promptly began to miaow. The mayor gave her a brief glance of adoration and opened a drawer. There were the cast-iron punch, his black satin oversleeves and an alabaster inkwell in the shape of a swan. He remembered when he had received it several years earlier, a present from the Ottoman governor in recognition of his administrative services – he had collected more tax on behalf of the central government than any other local head across the province. A cursory search under a pile of official letters revealed a smoked herring wrapped in the arts pages of a Levantine newspaper. He sliced off the head and tail with a paperknife and gave them to the cat. She accepted them with a regal manner, without thanks, as if the mayor were somehow indebted to her. He did not mind: his was an unconditional love. He wiped the paperknife on his trousers, licked his fingers and wrapped the rest of the fish back in the news-paper.

'A meal fit for a queen, my little bureaucrat,' he said stroking the cat.

She was a beautiful Abyssinian with a ruddy coat and a white chin. The mayor had bought her via mail order, after having made his decision with the help of an illustrated book of cats in the town library. While she ate he talked to her with affection; she, in turn, ignored him. In a moment the door opened and a man entered with a pencil stuck behind his ear. It was his secretary; with eyes that had long since exhausted their tolerance he observed the familiar spectacle of his boss stroking the creature.

'That animal has domesticated its owner,' he sighed.

No sooner had he said it than he sneezed loudly and started sniffing. While he was wiping his nose with his handkerchief his eyes began to fill with tears.

'Cats are the proof that the Devil exists,' he said and went and opened the glass door to the balcony. The fresh air slowly ameliorated his allergic reaction. 'We spent the last few coins in the town's treasury on that beast,' he snapped, 'while I haven't been paid for over a year.'

The head of the town did not take his eyes from his pet.

'Her ancestry goes back to the time of the Pharaohs. You, Procopio, don't even know whether your father was the butcher or the barber.'

His secretary shrugged his shoulders – his patrilineal origin was indeed a mathematical problem he had not as yet solved.

'Everyone says that I have the cleft chin of one and the pointed nose of the other.'

In the square the wind shook the tamarisks, ruffled the sea of flowers on the ground and carried some petals through the open balcony door into the office, together with their vague fragrance. The mayor thought about the state funerals he had attended over the years, where the same rose petals were used time after time to pave the way for the hearse with its eminent corpse. After a few ceremonies the petals would become shrivelled, colourless and fetid like pieces of paper in a wastebasket. He thought: *sic transit gloria mundi* . . . When his mind landed again in reality, he noticed that the music had come to an end and the needle of the Victrola was scratching the inside of the revolving record.

'Now that the war is over,' he said and went over to switch off the motor, 'things will soon go back to normal.'

His amanuensis unleashed a protracted guffaw.

'Only a man who has slept continuously for the last three years could have come up with such a statement.'

His boss replied with a patrician silence. When the

cat finished her food and miaowed again he opened another drawer, took out a bottle of milk and filled her tray. The cat was no more grateful this time than before.

'Feed it as much as you like,' the secretary said, 'it will still sleep in the *hamam* at night. The Mameluke is its true master.'

The mayor frowned and pointed his finger in the direction of the baths.

'It has nothing to do with him. She goes there because the steam preserves the elasticity of her bones.'

The cat slurped her milk. When she had finished this too it was time for her afternoon cleaning routine. The mayor gave her a smile and lay back in his chair. Tapping his fingers on the carved arms he remembered the damage done by the recent storm.

'Oh yes,' he said. 'Tell me what has been done about the roof.'

'I have the report right here.'

His secretary put his hand in the back pocket of his trousers and took out a folded piece of paper. While he was unfolding it the mayor observed him: the pencil stuck behind his ear reminded him of the Armenian. The mayor's face gradually twisted to a pout.

'After eleven years on the job, you ought to stop behaving like a grocer and start acting like a civil servant.'

A few days earlier the arrival of autumn had been announced by a sudden and violent overnight storm in which the town had been caught like a ship sailing in the open sea. The rain had flooded the streets, the balconies and many of the shops, and then the torrent had found its way into the abandoned church. Not long afterwards, from every cleft in the wall and every hole in the boards, thousands of rats poured out in an endless flow, making their way to higher ground. They climbed above the carved spandrels of the church doors, past the parapets of ceramic tiles, and in their panic they did not stop when they reached the safety of the roofs of the apses, or the shelter of the enormous dome, but continued, squeaking and clawing, towards the weathered belfry.

Draped in rodents, the church had turned into an ugly and ominous spectacle, but the real damage would happen some time later when the wind set upon the warehouse of the Co-operative Association. After an hour of futile resistance its masonry beams had snapped with a nightmarish noise and the roof had begun to rise above the building it had covered for over half a century. For a moment it had floated in the air, until the wind admitted it was impossible to carry it away and let it drop to the ground. No sooner had the roof turned into a pile of broken tiles and wood, than a rotating column of air had found the bales of dry tobacco leaves and blown them out of the warehouse, in the direction of the desert.

The secretary studied his crumpled piece of paper while chewing the end of his pencil.

'According to my calculations,' he announced, 'we lost one-third of the crop.'

'One-third,' the mayor contemplated with relief. 'If the storm had lasted a little longer we would all have to go down to the coast and beg for handouts.'

During the war the town had lived in peace and

relative affluence; even the secretary who remained unpaid for sixteen months lived well from the produce of his garden and his chickens. The thought of poverty was enough to rob him of most of his inexhaustible sarcasm.

'From what I hear, that would have been purposeless, mayor. Following the end of the war, those hands that aren't cut off are busy scraping the bottom of the barrel.'

He cast his gaze in the direction of the open balcony door with an idle intention, but an unusual sight immediately caught his attention: a chestnut horse with a cropped mane was trotting round the square, cutting furrows in the tamarisk flowers with its white shins. From outside the grocery the schoolmaster and the Armenian watched it with their hands on their hips. In a moment a window opened somewhere, then a door some place else, then another, and men and women in nightdresses and undershirts stood and observed the horse in astonished silence. It had no tack on, and when it passed under the balcony of the Town Hall the secretary noticed to his puzzlement and horror that its croup was branded with the emblem of the Expeditionary Corps.

CHAPTER 2

He uncorked the bottle, poured himself a measure as generous as the size of his glass allowed and raised the drink, careful not to spill any – but his hand betrayed him. The moment his lips were about to touch the brim his fingers began to tremble as if they had suddenly decided they were handling not a chipped tumbler but a heavy salt shaker, and his drink spilled on the table. He waited for the shakes to subside with the patience of one caught in an earthquake. When they did, he licked his fingers that were wet with alcohol, wiped his lips with the back of his hand, filled his glass again but with less exaggeration this time and sipped his *raki* quietly, while observing the street from behind the closed window.

The furnishings of his room had been chosen according to the necessity of their function. There was a chair on either side of a table, an unmade bed with a spring mattress, a chipped washbasin, a chest of drawers and on the wall a mirror under a dusty crucifix. A shared lavatory was at the end of the corridor outside, but for those nocturnal impulses of the bladder a chamber pot also sat underneath his bed like a guard dog. Forever shut, the windows preserved the humidity of that afternoon's sleep together with the previous night's, and many more sleeps before them. Outside the wind blew briefly.

Dangling from the balcony railings of the façade facing the street, each tied with a piece of rusted wire, a row of blue tin letters tinkled and proclaimed HOTEL SPLENDIDE in vain – the grandeur of the sign was not enough to disguise the advanced dilapidation of the small hotel. The war correspondent let out a sigh of misery.

He was unshaven, with a spiny stubble that was about to turn into a beard. His hair was tended with no more care either; without any combing cream its parting was quickly becoming a thing of the past. He ran his fingers through his hair and emptied his glass hastily – the next drink was awaiting its turn. His unbuttoned shirt was soiled with sweat and the aftermath of one of his drunken sprees. The war correspondent refilled his glass.

The end of the war was the worst thing that could have happened to him. A few weeks earlier he was on his way to the front, riding on the back of a slow-moving cart drawn by a pair of buffalo, when the devastating news of the collapse had met him at this very town. It was the moment to admit the imprudence of spending a whole week in Smyrna playing roulette in a clandestine casino. Not only had he parted with a substantial part of his life's savings, but he had also lost the opportunity he had bet his whole career on: to witness the battle that would tilt the scales of the war. Under the circumstances there was only one sensible option left to him: to lodge at the local hotel and take to the bottle.

Once, he had been a cultural correspondent for a popular national periodical. A decade into the profession his career had yet to move forward – its highpoint remained the weekly dispatches from the national tour of a septuagenarian toothless elephant. During the war he had watched with envy his colleagues leave for Asia Minor, and later read their articles that related the early victories of the Expeditionary Corps. Soon every one of these men had become famous, and it had made him think. The idea that was born then in his mind had taken a long time to grow wings and even longer to learn to fly. But eventually he had resigned, withdrawn all his savings from the bank – they were supposed to last him until he would start selling his articles – and booked his passage to Smyrna.

The journalist sipped his *raki* and his eyes wandered about the simple room. The truth was that he had nothing to go back to. On top of the wardrobe a spider was slowly wrapping its web round his typewriter. On a ledge on the wall his Autographic Kodak lay open, its bellows and lens gathering dust. He finished his drink, hitched up his braces and searched for his shoes. They were under his bed where he had kicked them the previous night, together with a dusty heap of unsorted socks and a cardboard suitcase tied with a piece of rope he had not undone since his arrival in town. No sooner had he solved the riddle of his socks and picked a green pair, than he regretted his bachelor's negligence. He should have kept them in a drawer: subjected to the repeated visitations of the rats, his socks had been reduced to an assortment of colourful shreds. The war correspondent looked at them for a brief moment, in silence, before putting his shoes on his naked feet and leaving the room.

In the lobby he encountered the hotelier entering the hotel with a folded umbrella under his arm. In the

shopping net dangling from his hand the journalist iden-
tified with misery the perennial ingredients of his hotel
dinners: cabbage, sweet potatoes and pigs' trotters. The
hotelier stopped on the threshold and greeted his
customer with a brief smile before cleaning his shoes
on the foot scraper.

'Flowers!' he said with exasperation. 'The autumn is
drowning us in rotten flowers!'

The war correspondent did not understand – he
observed with a momentary bafflement the man trying
to remove the petals stuck under his soles. The thought
of boiled cabbage and pickled trotters again that evening
defeated the ragged remnants of his optimism.

'Better than the mud,' the journalist said. Fat dripped
off the dirty claws of the pigs' feet in the net. 'When
the rains start I suspect this place will turn into a pigsty.'

The hotelier inspected the soles of his shoes. Satisfied
they were clean, he entered his establishment. He put
the shopping net behind the reception desk and hung
his dry umbrella on a bronze hook shaped like a horse's
head on the wall.

'Not this town,' he replied without a trace of affront
in his voice. 'The soil is eternally blessed from the time
the very St Gregorius travelling on foot happened to
lose his way and pass through these parts.'

He removed his jacket and hung it from the hook
too. He wore a shirt underneath buttoned up to its
frayed collar, a pair of women's garters over his arms to
keep his sleeves from sagging, and on his trousers a
leather belt where over the years he had punched several
extra holes. The war correspondent felt the need for
another drink.

174

He said, 'I have yet to be in a village where a miracle hasn't happened at one time or another.'

The hotelier unbuttoned his cuffs and rolled up his sleeves.

'In our case there is undisputed proof. The print of the saint's sandals can still be seen on a rock on the side of the road – it is something you ought to write about.'

The war correspondent put his hands in his pockets. The dream of becoming a celebrated journalist had finally given way to the familiar nightmare of staying for ever a hack.

'I wonder how on earth, despite a miracle being reported every other day, the nation heads from one hell to another,' he said.

'God is testing us because He loves us exceptionally.'

Suddenly the hotelier noticed that his customer wore no socks, and wondered whether he would ever be paid for his services – but he was a polite person.

'Dinner is served at eight,' he announced cheerfully. 'On the menu tonight fresh cabbage soup, seasoned pork and sweet potatoes for dessert.'

When the journalist stepped out of the hotel the distant hills had already begun to hide the sun. It was a calm, warm evening. The town was built on the edge of the desert, where the sand petered out to a land blessed with fertile mineral salts. Scattered across the crescent of the lunar hills the houses resembled from the distance boats moored at a tranquil anchorage. The war correspondent walked down the street towards the centre of town. As soon as the square came into view he thought he had slept that afternoon through an excessive carnival: a thick carpet of flowers extended from the Town Hall to the shops opposite, while under-neath the naked tamarisks a large crowd of excited townspeople was gathered. A professional feeling of curiosity stirred in him and he quickened his step. He opened his way through the crowd, pushing the chil-dren aside with his foot, tapping the adults on their shoulders with authority, until he came face to face with a silent horse. A man was bending down behind its croup – by the blue charm against the evil eye on the lapel of his waistcoat and the gold watch chain the journalist guessed who he was.

'Well,' the mayor said and stood straight again with much effort. He struck his hands together to clean them. 'I can confirm that this horse is the property of the Expeditionary Corps. I can also tell you that it has no testicles.'

The crowd began a loud murmur. It had been a while since the armistice had been signed and both sides' prisoners had returned home – what was the horse doing here? they asked each other, and their surprise was transformed into a chorus of unsubstantiated opin-ions. Some suggested it had simply survived the collapse of the front and wandered the desert for weeks. That would have been impossible: not only was there little food or water in the desert – and the animal appeared reasonably well fed – but also no jackal would have declined such a succulent meal for so long. It was more reasonable therefore to assume that the horse carried the invisible ghost of a cavalryman killed with a treach-erous shot in the back who now, understandably, was searching for his murderer. This thought made everyone cringe, but not as much as the proposition that it was a marble statue from the ruins of some ancient temple that had come to life during the tragic collapse of the front. The deliberations continued with the gelding watching with expressionless eyes while slowly shaking its tail.

'Enough,' said the mayor at last. 'You're louder than our annual bazaar. Furthermore, you're scaring the little ones.'

Only then did the men and women notice with shame the sobs of their children who had been listening to the macabre stories. The only person immune to them was the war correspondent; before long he detached himself from the excited townspeople and took a seat at one of the iron tables of the *lokanta*. The waiter, lost in the crowd, was nowhere to be seen and the journalist had to fetch the bottle himself. He had just started his evening routine – which hours later would culminate in his attaining a state of intoxicated oblivion – when the mayor joined him.

'I understand you have a photographic apparatus,' he said.

The war correspondent shut his eyes and sipped the first drink of the evening. The alcohol almost made him happy again – it was the only magic he believed in. He let out a sigh of intense glumness.

'It is true,' he replied.

'Then you ought to take our picture with the horse.'

The journalist had used his camera to photograph the landmarks of Smyrna – the Olympia Theatre on the promenade, St Anthony's Catholic Hospital, the English Commercial School, the Armenian and Greek cathedrals – and then had aimed its lens at the camels and buffalo he had chanced upon in the exotic landscapes of the Anatolian coast. But most of his expensive and hard-to-procure film he had spent on the unusual poses struck by the female employees of the cheap hotels near the docks – these printed plates remained hidden in his suitcase under his bed. He shook his head in response to the mayor's request.

'It's out of the question. I cannot waste my last cartridges on ridiculous mementoes.'

The mayor curled his lip.

'I have to warn you that I am vested with rights of impoundment.'

It was a brief but convincing argument. Not long afterwards the mayor, surrounded by his fellow citizens, flattened his hair with his hands, folded his arms and stared at the lens with a seriousness not unlike that of the bust in the courtyard of the Town Hall. Someone brought a rope, tied it round the horse's neck and gave it to the mayor. He pulled the rope firmly and ordered the photographer to release the shutter: many years later, when everyone present in the square that day had long since been transformed into a heap of dust, visitors to the War Museum in the motherland would stop briefly in front of a faded black-and-white photographic plate of a small crowd posing awkwardly on either side of a big horse, whose reins were held by a little man in a white shirt and a black waistcoat.

No sooner had the photograph been taken than a young woman left the square in a hurry – it was Annina, Madame Violetta's maid. Late in preparing her mistress's dinner, she cut across the labyrinth of the Muslim Quarter. She navigated the alleys with confidence, often

178

scraping through a tight cleft between the adobe walls, undaunted by the shadows of the last daylight that obscured her path. She paused only once, and very briefly, to find a pin in her pocket and fix a loose strand of her hair. She appeared to be a woman who dismissed her own beauty: there were more pins in her hair than spines on a hedgehog, she wore no jewellery, she used no cosmetics save for olive oil soap and her bosom was trapped under a corset like a heraldic breastplate.

Her appearance complied with her mistress's orders. When Madame had said that she liked her, Annina had attempted to kiss her hand with sincere gratitude but Violetta had withdrawn it; there was one condition of employment.

'There cannot live two beautiful women under my roof.'

The poor girl had not understood.

'It's not vanity, my dear,' had said Madame, 'but simple commercial sense.'

She went on to explain that in her line of work competition was fierce and she had no intention of inviting it in her own *boudoir*. The young woman had blushed.

'I'd rather die than —' she had protested. But immediately she foresaw herself drowning in the sea of her poverty and had thrown herself a lifebuoy: 'How could I? I have none of Madame's charm and elegance.'

She was offered the job on the condition that she dressed like a nun. In fact, it mattered little to someone whose life had so far been a novel worthy of Victor Hugo's pen. She had been born in the hold of a barge moored in a muddy estuary twenty-three years earlier, and suffered from sudden attacks of vertigo which she would attribute to the rocking of its keel on the day of her birth. The truth was more prosaic: minutes after she was born her father, who during the delivery had been puffing at his pipe while pacing the deck, was summoned below to wash her. In a momentary lapse of concentration, he had removed the pipe from his mouth to place it in his pocket when the baby slipped from his big hand – callused and scarred by the chores of his job – and landed headlong on the wooden floor thus permanently damaging her cerebellum.

It was the first of countless visits which misery would pay the girl during her early life. Then, when she was fourteen, a sudden storm had detached the iron weathervane from the spire of the cathedral the moment her widowed mother was entering its gothic porch (she had come to pray to St Vincent de Paul for the saint to break the vicious cycle of their poverty). The sharp arrow of the heavy weathervane had pierced the poor woman's heart: she had died instantly, leaving her daughter alone in the world.

So, no; humble clothes were not a problem. Neither was changing her name, at the request of her mistress, to Annina, after a character from the latter's favourite opera (she later discovered that Violetta was also the name of the protagonist of *La Traviata* and assumed her employer did not go by her real name either). Walking down the narrow alleyways of the Muslim Quarter the maid considered once again the unfairness of life.

But the fact was that Madame had saved her. When she had knocked at her door Annina had been living on the fruit she gathered from the gutter after the closing of the street market. Several months would pass without a hot meal – and even that would always be a bowl of vegetable soup without the vegetables. Annina considered with amazement how she had succeeded in surviving the years of ordeal when, as during a fast observed with rigid devotion, she had transcended reality and had existed in a permanent state of haziness. In those days, she recalled, she was not part of the world; she had become an outsider looking in from behind the screen of her destitution. Yet her suffering had not appeased God or cleansed her soul – quite the opposite, in fact: it had poisoned her innards. The dome of the obsolete church towered above the flat roofs of the Muslim Quarter. In a reprieve from her bitter thoughts Annina turned and gave it a quick glance, with the uneasy feeling of one who senses she is being observed. Before carrying on, she spat on the ground – a visceral response to the smell of excrement that blew in her direction at that moment, or a demonstration of her contempt for the Divine? (The former: she still believed in God – only now she thought of Him as either a cruel or an incompetent alchemist.)

Oh yes, she was grateful to her mistress. At the same time, in no way did she approve – or even condone – Madame's occupation. Even on the treadmill of her fate, she herself had not once forsaken her virtue. And there had been opportunities to do so when she lived in the streets and even more afterwards while working for Madame Violetta in Paris – despite the spinster's dress, the shapeless shoes, the tamed hair: the overweight physician, for example, who used to treat her mistress, or the retired general with the caster fixed to his wooden leg (a hero of the Battle of Verdun, but only thanks to a shell that had gone astray), and what about that vermin of an ambassador whose country, as Annina understood it, had ceased to exist after the Great War? What buffoons they had all been – the maid could not suppress a brief sensation of maidenly pride that for a moment cancelled her very virtue.

At last she came out of the maze of alleyways. Pinching her nose, she stepped over the open sewer that encircled the Muslim Quarter like a moat. Madame's house could be seen ahead, beyond the shops on both sides of the street. A recent storm had carried away several terracotta tiles from its pitched roof and exposed the rafters – Annina should not forget to ask Yusuf to replace them.

The white stucco house had two floors of tall glass doors and windows designed to provoke curiosity. At the same time, two lines of defence protected its interior against the sun and the intrusive eyes of the townspeople: when the wooden shutters were open to air a room, a heavy purple curtain was drawn across its window. Complemented by grand balconies of white balusters and scroll-shaped brackets, the villa would not have looked out of place on the Riviera. It had a brief but interesting history. Built by a contractor who had made a fortune from the construction of the railway, it had passed to the Ottoman governor of the province even before the paint on its walls had dried – everyone rightly surmised it was *baksheesh*. For years the governor would come and stay for the duration of the January fair, but no sooner had Violetta arrived in town than she moved in. The governor never came back – the townspeople had made assumptions on that occasion too, which were confirmed when the foreign woman began to visit the seat of government at regular intervals.

The house stood in the middle of a beautiful garden. Orange trees blossomed on either side of its iron gate and more behind the building where ornamental annuals and perennials gave their place to a multitude of herbs arranged with the exactness of a military encampment. The maid closed the gate and, after a brief stop to smell the roses, walked round the back. She normally entered the house through the kitchen door – sharing the main entrance with her mistress's clients caused her an uncomfortable sensation. In the vegetable garden a man was weeding quietly; the moment she saw him, Annina forgot the urgency of her domestic obligations.

She said, 'I didn't see you in the square.'

The Arab started. But when he turned his head his surprise was transformed into happiness – nevertheless, he pouted.

'The mayor sent me home.' He dug his hoe in the soil. 'Even the eunuch horse was in the picture – but poor Yusuf no.'

The woman wrinkled her forehead in an expression of compassion – it often occurred to her that the world was a clock in which people like her and Yusuf were just the cogs behind its dial. She pointed in the direction of the front garden.

'The roses smell wonderful now. You can raise the dead, Yusuf.'

The gardener shrugged.

'The secret is buffalo dung – more shit, more fragrance.'

Annina smiled affectionately.

'You could build the Hanging Gardens of Babylon, my dear Yusuf.'

'Maybe,' the gardener said, and his chest now inflated with a little pride. 'If only I was given a little more money.'

'When Madame marries, you'll be able to buy all the plants you want.'

Yusuf shook his head in doubt.

'The mayor's fist is as tight as a cork in a bottle.'

'Don't worry. It's not his money he'll be spending but the town's.'

The Arab beamed at the thought and showed his perfect teeth.

'Then I'll dig a pond and plant water lotus – to remind me of home and the great River Nile.'

The woman looked round her: there was no one. She reached out and touched the gardener's humped back.

'Sweet Yusuf,' she whispered. 'What will happen to us?'

'*Allahu akbar*,' the Arab replied and squeezed her hand. He tapped his fist on his chest. 'And if not, then I'll find a solution.'

He continued to weed with his hoe and she watched him, neither of them saying a word. After a while the Arab looked away and spoke up.

'Coming tonight?'

Only then did the young woman remember she had to cook for her mistress. She nodded in agreement, with as much shyness as the question had been asked, and walked away in a hurry. As soon as she crossed the threshold of her kitchen she heard her mistress's voice coming from upstairs.

'. . . *Peut-être d'un injuste effroi ma tendresse est alarmée / Écoute, amour, et dis-moi, si je suis encore aimée.*'

The aria, weighed down with redundant sorrow, seemed to expire after each line only to pull through at the last moment. When the kitchen door was shut the song was allowed to rest briefly.

'Annina?'

The maid bit her lip – more than the preparation of the dinner she was concerned about her mistress discovering her affair with Yusuf. She need not have worried; Violetta had indeed observed the clandestine couple from the window of her bathroom, and not for the first time, but she was a more tolerant and compassionate person than she would ever let others know. While Annina examined her clothes and hair in front of the vestibule mirror, the song upstairs resumed its martyrdom in the hands of the merciless voice.

'. . . *Un seul object avait rempli mon âme je ne voyais / Que lui dans ce vaste univers.*'

There was a light knock on the door and the maid entered. The room was dominated by a cast-iron bathtub the size of a rowing boat. Coated with a thick layer of vitrified white enamel, it sat on four lion paws that pushed the wooden floorboards to the limit of their strength. On its side was stamped the manufacturer's logo: *L. Wolff & Co., Chicago.* The tub was so big that after the movers had carried it upstairs they had had to knock down the wall to get it into the bathroom.

Madame stretched her neck and for a moment looked at her employee like an ostrich, before disappearing again under the rim of her bathtub.

'*Grâce à Dieu*,' she said. 'You are back. When my dear husband went for a walk seventeen years ago he forgot to return.'

That bathtub had travelled further than the Wandering Jew. Its first journey had been by train from its manufacturer to Mexico City, where it was installed in one of the numerous bathrooms of the National Palace, only months before the Constitutional Army would occupy the building. A year later it had somehow found its way to the warden's house in the infamous penal colony on the *Île du Diable*, off the coast of French Guiana. For a long time the mentholated vapours of the majestic vessel were the only consolation in the life of the solitary bureaucrat who, in addition to being tormented by chronic dysentery, had also contracted the virus of humanity. His superiors were therefore very suspicious when, six months after a political prisoner had escaped, the said bathtub was found washed ashore at a Panamanian fishing village: the desperate convict had managed to sail the bathtub along the entire northern coast of South America. It was such an impressive feat that the warden had been duly dismissed.

When the mayor had discovered it behind a heavy curtain of cobweb at the back of a second-hand shop in Smyrna, he had been told other stories too. Some he believed credulously but others were too macabre for him to accept – like, for example, the one about the wealthy Portuguese owner of a vast cotton plantation high up the Zambezi who had drowned his wife with his own hands in that very bathtub, after having caught her civilising an ignorant savage repeatedly in the nuptial bed. The mayor had pouted.

'And how was all this knowledge divulged to you?'

The merchant had nodded: he had anticipated the query. As it happened, he had met the dying murderer during one of his regular trips to the Dark Continent, where he went to plunder the bazaars of cheap trinkets he later sold at twentyfold prices back in the Levant. Tormented by remorse, the Portuguese had sold his estate and spent his fortune and the rest of his life making amends to God for his crime. He travelled the wilderness barefoot, yoked to the indomitable bathtub, which he set in the middle of every village he happened across and filled with holy water from the steel cans he also dragged behind him. Then he would lure the puzzled locals with pieces of mirror, strings of glass beads and oddments of colourful fabrics, and baptise in his lavish font as many idolaters as he could fit in at a time. It had been a severe and sincere act of repentance but it had not worked, because it never crossed the sinner's mind also to beg forgiveness for his other crime: feeding his spouse's African paramour to the crocodiles.

In any case: the haunted bathtub, further decorated with silver Greek key patterns and gold-leaf rosettes by order of the mayor, adequately represented his exultation at the moment his perpetual wedding proposals had at last received an affirmative answer – Troy itself had fallen after a shorter siege. Besides, his lavish engagement present had cost him only a brief letter with which he had informed the Ministry that the large sum received before the war for the construction of a covered conduit for the sewage in the Muslim Quarter had been diverted to fund an alternative sanitary project. He had not mentioned that this project was a new bathtub that did not leak for his bride-to-be.

Annina sat on a stool opposite Madame and rested her interlaced fingers on her lap.

'I was detained in the square, Madame. A –'

'Fetch my brush, please.'

The maid took the brush with the wooden handle from the wall and handed it to her mistress. Then she took a deep breath and launched into an animated speech regarding the sudden appearance of the army horse. Scratching her back with the brush, Violetta showed little interest.

'The mayor was there too,' Annina said.

Her employer paused to dip the brush in the water and absent-mindedly continued her cleansing routine.

'I'm not surprised,' she said. 'That man has put his face in more pictures than Our Lord Jesus Christ.'

Annina blushed.

'You shouldn't talk that way about your future husband,' she ventured.

Her mistress turned her head and looked out of the window. In the garden the Arab was pruning the trees with a pair of rusty shears on the end of a long pole which he operated with a string. Madame shuddered, suddenly being reminded of the *guillotine*. When she recovered her humour she remembered they had been talking about the mayor.

'For an enamelled bathtub I would even marry our hunchback.'

Annina felt as if a snake had bitten her.

'Monsieur Yusuf is a fine gentleman.'

Madame dropped the brush and picked up the sponge that floated on the soapsuds. She squeezed it over her back and felt the soap trickling down her perfect shoulders before she shrugged them innocently.

'*D'accord*. A gentleman – but with the back of a camel nevertheless.'

Blood rose to her maid's cheeks again, but she said nothing.

'What do you call a camel with one hump?' her mistress asked. She stretched out her arm for the tin pitcher placed next to the tub. Her maid did not help her.

'A dromedary, Madame.'

'*Un dromadaire*. But of course.'

Violetta filled the pitcher from the bathtub. Pouring the water over her shoulders she began to sing again.

'. . . *Mais je sens qu'elle approche et va finir mes peines / Le poison des douleurs a coulé dans mes veines.*'

She stood up in the tub and washed off the lather from the rest of her voluptuous body. When she had finished, her maid was still staring out the window; she snapped her fingers to summon her attention.

'*Allons, ma petite* – my robe!'

The command erased Yusuf from the maid's eyes but not from her mind. The moment she took the cotton bathrobe that smelled of lavender from the stand in the corner of the room, the doorbell began to ring. Madame checked the time on the clock on the wall.

'*Putain!*' she sighed. 'I can't stand these rustics. Soon they'll be calling on us at breakfast.'

Annina placed the stool next to the tub so that her

mistress could disembark. Once she had helped her put on her bathrobe the maid made a move to answer the door – but Madame stopped her.

'Leave it. Whoever it is, he will go away.'

He did not. Violetta dried herself in her bathrobe, changed into a silk kimono with a cherry-blossom pattern, pulled out the hairpins that held her hair in a neat cone and sat at her vanity to perform her toilet. All the while the bell did not stop ringing.

'See who it is,' she said eventually, in a serene tone which suggested that by then she knew the answer. Indeed, moments later, when Mr Othon was standing at the bathroom door, panting from having climbed the stairs in a hurry, she did not even turn to look at him. Instead, she finished combing her hair, picked up the powder puff and dismissed her maid. The schoolmaster watched her with a deep frown of disapproval.

'See if dinner is ready, *jolie*,' said Violetta as her maid was closing the door.

The moment they were alone the schoolmaster came forward to embrace her, but no matter how many times he tried it proved impossible – Violetta fended off his attempts like an animal tamer. Conceding defeat, he ran his fingers along the enam-elled lip of the bathtub.

'Your thirty pieces of silver,' he said with contempt.

The woman opened her blusher set. Religious metaphors normally tired her, but this time she did summon Mary Magdalene to help her retort.

'If you wanted your feet anointed you came to the wrong place, *mon ami*.'

Mr Othon rubbed his chin and decided that sulking

had been the wrong strategy. Presently, he manoeuvred his forces to accomplish a lesser objective.

'There's no reason why we shouldn't preserve our' – he coughed – 'discreet association, under the changing circumstances. To our mutual benefit, of course.'

It was another tactical error; at once, Violetta swirled round on her stool and hit him across the face with the blusher brush.

'*Ce n'est pas une façon de s'adresser à l'épouse d'un représentant de l'état, Monsieur!*'

The brush left some blusher on Mr Othon's cheek. Quickly, the rest of his face turned crimson too – under his skin his blood was simmering. The fact that he had no French and had understood not a word of his former lover's detonation only added to his fury. He lifted his hand in the air reluctantly, the way an army would raise a white flag.

'So be it,' he said. 'The forces of evil have won. I wish you both a harmonious matrimony.' But he could not surrender without a parting shot. 'Only remember this, my sweet. When –'

He did not have a chance to complete his oracle. At that moment they both heard the sound of a distant drum; for the second time that evening Violetta imagined the *guillotine*.

'*Merde*,' she murmured and tried to suppress a morbid sensation. 'What fool said the Devil plays the violin? His favourite instrument has to be the executioner's drum.'

The former lovers remained silent and motionless, listening to the drum. It beat rhythmically, a slow tempo suitable for a military march as well as a funeral. They could not tell where it was coming from − the square, the Muslim neighbourhood? For a moment the school-master had the impression the sound was blowing over from the direction of the desert. He quickly dismissed the idea − that would have been impossible, there was no one out that way. Ever since the harmony teacher had left to invest his savings in a plantation in the Belgian Congo, Mr Othon had also taught music at the school, and out of habit he tried now to determine the metre of the march. The playing was erratic, almost childish: it was the way an untrained pair of hands would play − or an exhausted one. He noticed that the sound was coming closer. Suddenly the maid called from the other side of the door: '*Madame! Madame!*'

Her voice brought both back from their trance. Tying the string of her kimono, Violetta opened the door. Annina waved to her to come to the window across the landing that faced the front of the house; Mr Othon followed nervously.

'What is it, *ma petite*?' Violetta asked.

Her maid had only to pull the heavy drapery aside for her mistress to receive her answer. As soon as her eyes adapted to the twilight she saw them: an endless file of soldiers on foot and some on horseback, stretching back to the distant sand dunes, was entering the town. Their uniforms, boots and faces were covered with so much dust that for an instant Madame could not suppress the haunting belief that they were men made out of clay.

Chapter 3

The sun penetrated the square panes at an angle, casting skewed shadows on the floor that were like a riddle of crosses or some sort of a religious mosaic. Round the room the furniture – chairs, cabinets, a marble conference table – stood anyhow, covered with dust sheets, reminding one of the ridiculous ghosts seen in cheap theatrical productions. Beyond the shut midday windows the world was warm and silent. Soldiers strolled across the town square, rifles slung over their shoulders. If they happened across an officer they looked down. It was a display neither of insubordination nor of contempt, but of embarrassment that had loomed large ever since the disaster had begun. The officer would do the same and hasten away; in his quarters he would lie on his cot, away from the eyes of his men and the glare of the sun pouring in through the windows, and perhaps write another letter home it was impossible to post.

Brigadier Nestor paced round the marble table. He was alone in the room – he and the ghosts in dust sheets. He had every reason to feel content; lost in the desert for weeks, the brigade had eluded the scythe of death on numerous occasions: the heat, the thirst, the enemy. And suddenly, salvation – almost. The army had occupied the small town the way a crew of shipwrecked mariners might cling to a raft. There was food and fresh water here, and the sea – at last they knew for certain – was not far. If only their luck would last a little longer. But the discovery of the town was not only the gift of luck; it was also an achievement that was in large part his, and Brigadier Nestor was entitled to feel proud. Instead, he felt something akin to despair.

The paws of the enormous table crept out from underneath the filthy dust sheet. Outside a cart rolled by, tearing up the afternoon silence like paper. Brigadier Nestor noticed a smell of oleander emanating from the distant corners of the vast conference room. He thought: someone has recently sprinkled it with rat poison. The dried ink stains on the floor attested to the fact that the fading but still majestic surroundings were once a thriving habitat of clerks and councillors; now they were but the silent and shady interior of a forgotten mausoleum. The prospect of his own body being entombed for eternity made the old man shiver.

His campaign cot was set among the commanding furniture together with his desk, his folding chair and the maps. Next to them lay his trunk with its impenetrable lid open – his shirts and trousers were scattered across the floor or hung down from its iron rim. Brigadier Nestor looked at his trunk as he would have observed the gutted carcass of a large animal. Suddenly he remembered; he found his parade boots and poked his hand inside – there it was: from his left boot he retrieved a small bottle.

'Hiding like a rat,' he said.

He found the box he kept the syringe in and lit a

match, held the flame briefly under the needle as a rudimentary means of sterilisation, filled the syringe and, at last, emptied it in his vein. Not waiting for the drug to take effect, he gave himself another shot in the other arm. Now he could rest.

He had taken up his residence in the Town Hall when the brigade arrived in the town three days earlier. Standing on the steps to the entrance, the mayor had welcomed the brigadier with a sentimental address that had not quite disguised his deep suspicion. Together they had walked inside where the mayor had insisted on giving him a tour of the building. The blindfolded journey through the desert had ransacked the brigadier's resolution and he had not enough strength to decline. On the ground floor he was shown into the room that housed the modest municipal library. It had been a pleasant surprise; on the feeble stacks, behind the dusty webs of an empire of spiders, arranged in alphabetical order, was a forgotten treasure. There were first editions of the classics, several volumes by the Alexandrian poets, a Ptolemaic Septuagint and parchments with maps that showed the Titan Atlas bearing the earth on his back in great detail. The brigadier had forgotten his exhaustion and studied them with fascination. On the counter the lending register had lain open; his host had blown off the dust and run his finger down the ancient list of entries.

'The last person to borrow a book here was Moses,' he had said. '*The Commandments*. According to this he never returned it.'

The tour had been resumed. In another room Brigadier Nestor was prompted to appreciate the artistry of the invaluable Byzantine icons brought to the Town Hall only days before a neighbouring monastery was destroyed by arsonists. Then upstairs his eyes had fallen on a top hat of black silk kept inside a glass cabinet; he had enquired about it.

'We bought that from a conjuror at the annual fair,' the mayor had explained morosely, 'with the intention of starting a rabbit colony. But we haven't as yet managed to pull out a single animal.'

He had quickly guided the officer in front of a wall of framed honorary diplomas, the awards from various international trade fairs to the Co-operative Association for its excellent tobacco. The mayor had unclasped his hands and tapped his fingers on his sternum.

'It has been demonstrated beyond doubt, my brigadier, that our tobacco not only delights the senses but also soothes chest pain. Let me show you –'

For a while the old man had been nodding impatiently.

'Enough, my dear mayor. Is there anywhere in this Pharaonic tomb I could set my cot?'

Naturally – if only the brigadier would follow his host down the corridor. When they had reached the door of the conference room the mayor had tried to open it, but it had been locked.

'Procopio!' he had called over the railing.

His secretary had climbed the stairs lazily.

'Bring me the key to this door.'

But the extensive search had failed to locate the missing key and in the end they had to break the lock. A stagnant pool of air that had lost its flavour had

awaited them inside. They had lit candles to avoid trip-
ping over the forgotten furniture, which had been
covered when the war had begun and the governor,
declaring a state of emergency, had dissolved the
council. The mayor had instructed his secretary to
prepare the brigadier's quarters.

'And listen,' he had whispered to him. 'Don't spare
the rat poison. It would be very unfortunate if they
stripped the brigadier's flesh to the bone while he
slept.'

The morphia propelled Brigadier Nestor towards a
chair; as soon as he landed on its protective covering
he was enveloped in a cloud of dust. Between coughs
and sniffs he contemplated his naked arms, scarred by
the perforations of the needle. He shut his eyes to
avoid the spectacle of his tragedy and recalled again
the village massacre as clearly as the day he had ordered
it. His conscience assured him that he would carry the
crime on his back like a tortoise its shell, and for
the first time since it had happened he considered the
likelihood of his shame outliving him. The thought
pierced his ribs and reached his heart – it was not
vanity: hopes of a glorious reputation after death had
not been in his daydreams since the stalemate that
had followed the initial advance of the Expeditionary
Corps during the first year of the war; it was his legacy
to his grandson he worried about. The boy would
grow up to suffer the consequences of shame: the butt
of schoolyard jokes, the refusals to furnish him with
references, the unavailability of scholarships – in short,
it would be a pariah's existence.

He thought: the enemy of course knows what has

happened, but our academicians could easily dismiss that as propaganda. The real problem was his own troops. Sooner or later there was bound to be some soldier who would talk to his family, a friend, a stranger in the coffee shop. Then it would be only a matter of time before the press . . . But what if the brigade never reached the sea? The thought entered his mind like an amorous fantasy. He mulled it over: he himself had little to lose — how many more years were left in his hourglass? Two, three — five perhaps? A blink of the eye at his age. Besides, he would not make a tame pensioner: a lonely, savage existence (oh, how he missed his wife now) and a burden to one's progeny. Suddenly the possibility of encountering the enemy lost some of its dread.

The creak of the door startled him and Brigadier Nestor reached for his pistol — despite the large dose of morphia, his survival instinct had not completely abandoned him.

It was only his orderly.

'A civilian insists on seeing you, my brigadier.'

Brigadier Nestor relaxed his grip on the wooden handle of the revolver.

'When they demobilise you,' he said, 'you should get a job in the House of Horrors.'

A pair of fragile eyes looked back at him with the obedience of a domesticated animal; they reminded the old officer of his grandson again.

'One of these days you will scare me to death, orderly — if you are lucky, that is. Because I might shoot you by mistake.'

The room draped the two men in its gloomy light.

One was young, tall and lean, well groomed and smooth-skinned with a permanent expression of excitement and the trepidation of an athlete at the starting line. The other was old, short, ample and weary, dressed in a khaki tunic whose untidiness would not be forgiven were it not for the unquestionable authority of his insignia.

'Anyway,' Brigadier Nestor sighed, 'who is it? That blabbermouth of a mayor again?'

It was not he; his orderly handed him a creased and soiled calling card. Brigadier Nestor took out his glasses to study the baroque coat of arms printed on it: a shield with an open scroll underneath that declared, *Lux in Tenebris*. He pursed his lips.

'Light in darkness,' he translated. 'Just the thing we need in this room.' He removed his glasses and twisted the tips of his moustache. 'Very well. Show him in.'

The journalist entered the conference room with such aplomb that the brigadier expected him to be accompanied by a large retinue. When he realised he had come alone, Brigadier Nestor waved his orderly away and sized up his visitor with suspicion. The war correspondent introduced himself.

'The fourth estate,' Brigadier Nestor said. 'Even in the pits of Hell there is bound to be one of you reporting back.'

The journalist had just enough experience to anticipate the customary resentment towards his profession.

'But of course, my brigadier. His name was Dante Alighieri.'

His appearance that afternoon bore no resemblance to the man run aground by alcohol only a few days earlier. His cheeks had the smoothness of a prolonged hot-towel treatment, his hair had been moulded with copious amounts of perfumed ointment and his finger-nails were manicured with a silversmith's riffler borrowed from the Armenian grocer – this resurrection at the hands of the local barber could only have been achieved on generous credit.

Brigadier Nestor gave him a brief look. He had little respect for history but his admiration of fable knew no bounds. Easing his contempt, he clasped his hands behind his back and walked up to a window.

'A genius of allegory,' he said while looking out. 'Not many of our people are familiar with the Italian poet.'

The journalist sensed he had detected his opponent's Achilles' heel and could not refrain from giving himself his warmest mental congratulations.

'Our family name is included in the Register of Nobility of the Venetian Republic,' he said.

Brigadier Nestor's forehead wrinkled as he placed the accent: the journalist was a native of the Ionian Islands.

While the rest of the country had been conquered by the Ottomans, the western archipelago had had the relative good fortune of passing into the possession of the Venetians. The near-benevolent occupation that had lasted almost four hundred years had forever infected the locals with a fervent passion for culture as well as a streak of loftiness. The brigadier did not let the opportunity to score off his visitor pass him by.

'Oh yes – the Register of Nobility, of course. Alas, people today pay more attention to the cash register.'

The journalist granted the brigadier the satisfaction of the last word – after all, it was the bitter truth. But he had come for a reason; he said he had heard about the adventure of the brigade – which he declared 'an unbelievable feat of military ingenuity' – and asked with sincere interest how the brigadier had led his broken army through the devious routes of the desert.

'Pegasus,'* the brigadier replied immediately. 'I trust you are familiar with his story?'

The journalist said that he was, and listened as the brigadier narrated the caprices of fate that had led to the army's salvation. About the gelding that loathed the army, which someone had let loose on a night of biblical storms, and how that horse – and therefore the detail sent to bring it back – had chanced upon the town that had proved the exit from the labyrinth. Brigadier Nestor paced round the room and the bare walls echoed back the sound of his boots on the parquet.

'If I catch the man who released the horse I won't know whether to shoot him or decorate him,' he concluded.

The war correspondent rubbed his chin.

_____

*A winged horse, son of Poseidon and Medusa. All longed in vain to catch and tame him, until the hero Bellerophon succeeded with the help of the goddess Athena. Pegasus proved to be of great help to the hero in his adventures, but then Bellerophon, overcome by pride, attempted to fly to the top of Mount Olympus and join the gods. The horse threw him and left him wandering about, hated by the gods. Zeus then entrusted Pegasus with carrying his lightning and thunderbolts.

'I see . . . Your soldiers followed the tracks of his hooves.'

He was wrong – often it was impossible to pick up the horse's tracks because a treacherous wind would sweep them away.

'In fact, they followed the trail of shit,' Brigadier Nestor admitted with modesty, and explained how the horse had helped them unintentionally by dropping dung at regular intervals.

'Thank God it didn't suffer from constipation,' he added, raising his arms in the air. 'Then we'd all certainly have ended up as food for the vultures.'

For the next hour Brigadier Nestor recounted the other events of their impossible journey, not refraining from mentioning the incidences of theft that had plagued his unit during their withdrawal. Suddenly he was talking with the relief of a sinner who had met a sympathetic confessor. He dropped his voice to a whisper.

'I believe the thief and the emancipator of horses are one and the same person. Soon we will know. I'm tightening my grip.'

The journalist licked his lips; the amazing story was whetting his professional appetite. Only three days ago he was down on his luck, anaesthetising himself with cheap alcohol in provincial squalor – hell, he would even have had to borrow money if he had decided to commit suicide. But all that stood now firmly in the past; he was already thinking of newspaper articles. What if he called the whole series *Diary of the Maze*? In creative silence he considered other titles too. And he would naturally need several photographs to accompany his dramatic account – how glad he was that he had had the prudence to save some film. Following the embarrassment of the disaster in Asia Minor, the return home of that lost army would be an event of immense proportions: an opportunity for the nation to feel proud again. And *he* would be there as the brigade's official and only chronicler. He felt like a prospector finding the first nugget in his pan after years of searching.

'My brigadier!' he uttered, unable to curb his enthusiasm. 'With your cooperation I promise to make you more famous than Odysseus of Ithaca.'

The officer shook the offered hand with reluctance – a pact with the Devil, he thought. But the more he considered it the more he liked the idea. If the brigade were to be depicted as a heroic army – and it undoubtedly was, except for that unfortunate episode of the massacre – then it would be in this journalist's interest, and the government's, to suppress any uncorroborated stories regarding a ridiculous crime. In addition, he himself would be venerated – what better legacy for one's family? The proposition had begun to improve his mood, as well as adding leaven to the dough of his vainglory.

Despite its size, the church of St Gregorius Theologus was a melancholy sight. With its mute belfry, its mossy steps and fossilised doors, the enormous church was akin to a felled colossus: a monument whose vastness time had spared, while robbing it of its significance.

Not according to Father Simeon – the view of the church from the window of his room offered him precious solace. He was billeted with the Armenian grocer and his wife, in a house conquered by wistful trinkets. He had failed to persuade his hosts to allow Caleb in too. In the end, he had negotiated a place for the dog in the abandoned chicken coop in the backyard, but Caleb lay there whining and sulking until Father Simeon agreed to let him out in the streets – but not before he had extracted from the animal the promise to return to the coop every evening.

Father Simeon looked round his room and scratched his head. Hanging in prominence was a portrait of the wife's grandmother in a heavy gilded frame. It was a fitting tribute – her death, after all, had sparked the sequence of events that led to the two young people meeting. Scattered around the room were traditional musical instruments (a Turkish crescent, a zither, a *surna*), scratched gramophone records, brass thimbles, dull knives, threadbare carpets, framed goat heads . . . The unbelievable clutter exhausted the padre's eyes. He attempted to decipher the purpose of a contraption underneath a round table with a crystal ball on top, a device consisting of cranks and pedals which when set in motion lifted the table silently in the air. He remembered that his hostess had a reputation as a necromancer and surmised that what he was looking at was a cunning levitation apparatus. On another shelf was a dusty concertina with a smiling turbaned face painted on its folded bellows. When the instrument was expanded the image transformed into a chopped head dripping blood over the words FREE ARMENIA. Father Simeon carefully returned it to its place. On the table stood his heavy altar cross, a small censer, his folded stole, and a stack of ruffled pages hooked on a piece of wire: the remnants of his copy of the Scriptures.

'What a tragic accident,' he murmured, recalling the incident that had led to the demise of his Bible.

A stuffed eagle on the wall, frozen in mid-flight, eyed him through its yellow glass-bead eyes – once again the padre thought about fallen empires and felt he was suffocating. He left his room and, with the melancholy of the fusty objects over his shoulder, went downstairs to where the Armenian woman was preparing dinner. The small kitchen had not escaped the couple's mania either. It was evident that none of the wooden and brass mortars on top of the cupboards had ever fulfilled its vocation, and neither had the beautifully carved ladles on the walls. The woman's true tools were kept without fanfare or appreciation inside the warped drawers.

'Ah,' the padre uttered, smelling the air with admiration. 'The alchemy of flavours!'

The woman emerged from the pall of steam wiping her hands on her apron. She offered him a seat.

'Men throw away fortunes in search of depraved delights,' she said in the melody of her unshakeable accent. 'What they don't know is that pleasure can be found even in the heart of an artichoke.'

Father Simeon was uncertain how to respond. He agreed that carnality was the quickest route to damnation but, on the other hand, the woman's thesis seemed to promote the deadly sin of gluttony.

'The iniquities of the flesh,' he ventured, 'include those of the stomach.'

The woman shrugged her shoulders and returned to her artichokes. They were as big as newborn babies, the padre commented admiringly, and asked her where she had bought them from. She replied they came from her garden and – cutting short the priest's compliment – explained that the earth was blessed by St Gregorius' feet. Father Simeon immediately knew he had found a sympathetic listener.

'Before arriving in Anatolia I undertook a substantial study of the ancestral descent of our mortal enemy,' he began. 'My investigation revealed several facts worthy of dissemination. Maybe you would be interested to hear about it?'

The woman left the stove and sat on a narrow wooden chair. It was another of the pair's sentimental acquisitions; its peremptory geometry made her seem as if fitted with orthopaedic splints.

'Tell me, Father.'

And so Father Simeon began his learned discourse. He explained that the race of their enemy was a diabolical amalgamation of the Mongols with other anthropomorphic subspecies that used to live in the mountains of northern China, creatures renowned for their brutality and bestial instincts. For generations they walked the Earth dressed in hides or more often naked, eating roots and nuts, rodents and other beasts they killed with bludgeons or even their bare hands. One day a civilised man taught them the arts of war and thus, thanks to their innate savagery, managed to create a formidable army which soon conquered Asia, Byzantium and a part of central Europe too.

'Have you heard about the Huns?'

'The Huns,' mumbled the woman, transfixed by the dramatic narrative.

Father Simeon's reason might have abandoned him, but oratory was his ever-faithful praetorian.

'The first thing they did when killing an enemy,' he explained, supplementing his yarn with copious gesticulations, 'would be to slash his throat and drink his warm blood.' Having run his finger across his neck to indicate the motion of the blade, he proceeded to beat his breast with his fist. 'Then they would rip open his chest and devour his heart with delight.'

'Cannibals,' grunted the woman.

The padre rewarded her with a paternal smile.

'Our present enemy is the descendant of those undisciplined, bloodthirsty and merciless hordes once led by King Attila.'

'The Scourge of God.'

Father Simeon confirmed the fact serenely.

'Indeed. According to contemporary historians he was a short and ugly man with a flat face, a head without a neck and a pair of the cruellest eyes. What a contrast to our heroic and' – he paused to turn over the pages of the thesaurus of rhetoric in his mind – 'pulchritudinous general, Alexander the Great. Wouldn't you agree?'

The woman did so with a quick succession of nods.

'I have accrued these facts from undisputed historical sources,' said the padre. 'During the campaign I endeavoured to educate our troops through my daily sermons. Alas, only a few would listen. But I didn't give up in the desolation of the desert and shan't do it in this oasis of Christianity either. I'm convinced it's the Almighty's true and wholehearted wish.'

'Amen,' said the woman.

Father Simeon consulted the pendulum wall clock with Mount Ararat painted on its dial. He admired the hand of the traditional artist but not his knowledge of history: stranded on the snow-covered peak was a ship with smoking funnels.

'But where is your husband?' he enquired casually.

The woman sighed and returned to the sink to nurse her vegetables.

'The depraved delights, Father.'

The padre had just registered the woman's reply when the door opened and the grocer walked in, whistling and playing with a string of beads. He was dressed in a pressed dark suit, smelled of a woman's perfume and had his tradesman's coat under his arm.

'Good evening, Fa –'

As soon as he saw the artichokes his heart sank.

'How many times do I have to say it?' he addressed his wife. 'Madame Violetta has the greatest respect for you.'

His wife began to place the artichokes in the boiling pot with defiance.

'Don't mention that name in this house.'

'I visit her only for the therapeutic effects of her services.'

'And so are these,' the woman said indicating the artichokes. 'Therapeutic.'

On hearing the couple's argument, the padre bit his lip and sprang to his feet.

'I thank you for your hospitality. Now, if you'll excuse me.'

He felt he could not stay in the house for another minute. Upstairs, he placed his liturgical equipment in his army backpack and left the house. The street received him with suspicion. Tamarisks lined the sides but the colour of their flowers was lost in the dusk. The signs above the shop doors were also illegible in the dark. During the day lavish merchandise gushed from those doors and the swarms of musical birds in the trees hawked it to Father Simeon's delight. But in the evening the streets seemed to him more endless than the corridors of a barbaric prison.

He approached a house with white stucco walls that was surrounded by a wondrous garden. The growing darkness failed to subdue this beauty – quite the opposite, in fact. The illicit odours of jasmine and lilac offered the padre some consolation. But when he saw the line of soldiers his gloom returned promptly. Leaning against the wall, smoking and talking calmly, they awaited their turn with civil patience; some greeted him.

'You should all be attending evening mass,' Father Simeon said. 'Even the deepest darkness cannot conceal a sin – the Lord is watching.'

A succession of checked laughs saw him off from the vicinity of the brothel. The dusk and his frustration made the padre lose his direction. Not long afterwards, while groping his way in the dark, the ground under his feet appeared to give way and he splashed into a ditch. The nauseous smell he had been paying no attention to until now convinced him he was standing in a sewer. He looked down and tutted with sadness. The moon shone in the slow current of the conduit.

'O God of infinite justice. Why did You cast Your humble servant in the filth?'

It was with both feet in the excrement that he experienced his personal revelation. The first shadow appeared on a crumbling wall not far from where he stood, and it began to move furtively from one house to the next, pausing for a moment at each door. Soon it was joined by another and then another, until there were more shadows on the whitewashed walls than windows, and the alleyways of the Muslim Quarter echoed with intermittent whispering. Father Simeon shuddered and held his breath. When they at last came nearer, he discovered they were people dressed in tattered and patched-up clothes and barefoot.

They failed to see him. Father Simeon's supernatural fear slowly turned into curiosity and he crouched in the darkness, determined to solve the nocturnal mystery. It was not much of one. Soon he realised that the poor souls were scavenging for food, but mostly for rubbish of all sorts to repair and sell back to their neighbours beyond the sewer. While his boots soaked in the foul fluid, the padre watched the piratical crew walk back and forth, carrying split stovepipes, torn machinery belts, cooking pots and broken earthenware to the Quarter. At the same time their children would loiter about a group of soldiers, begging a coin or a cigarette politely but half-heartedly: they knew there was little chance they would receive it.

It could take one an eternity of punishment and one still might not admit to one's spiritual failings – but then it could all well happen in an instant: surrounded by the spectacle of destitution, Father

Simeon felt a transformation take place inside him.

'I thought this retreat was my Calvary,' he mumbled. 'But, in truth, it was meant to be my road to Damascus.'

It had taken him more than three years in Asia Minor for his nationalist and religious blindfold to fall off and for him to notice the poverty and despair of that other part of the populace – he would have been less surprised had he discovered a new continent. It was the fear and resentment that emanated from the backwaters of that asymmetric society that hovered over the acts of unspeakable cruelty perpetrated by the enemy, he understood. As if we had not committed our share of crimes, he also thought, recalling the massacre again with a chill. Indeed, he concluded, the enemy was, after all, as human – or as inhuman – as they themselves were.

'Not only the right one,' he said shaking his head, 'but both my eyes must have been made of glass not to see it.'

He watched the Muslim crowd go about its ghostly trade, and they reminded him of a note penned in the margin of a page with indelible ink: an undisciplined scribble next to the ceremonial line-up of typographic characters, sometimes useful but more often unwelcome, yet impossible to erase. He needed only another moment to convince himself entirely: *this* was his lost flock. He could, at last, become the missionary of the futile dream of his youth. He tried the words quietly: 'The Apostle of All Anatolians.' It sounded majestic. He made an effort to get out of the sewer but it was impossible to climb the soft sides with both the heavy knapsack and the burden of his years on his back.

'Help, friends!' he called. 'In the name of God.'

A group of men carrying an iron bedstead over their heads stopped and looked in his direction.

'Over here!' said the padre, waving his hand.

Only then did they notice the comical sight of the bearded man in the deep sewer, struggling to keep his backpack above the surface so that his liturgical para-phernalia would not suffer the desecration of shit, and they started laughing. Rather than being offended, Father Simeon laughed with them.

'You can either leave me in the depths of the pit until I grow wings, or you can give me a hand and save me and yourselves too.'

They did not quite understand what he meant in his clerical enunciation, but they did put down their pitiful booty and pull him out.

'Come with me,' he told them.

He set off in a hurry. They were so intrigued they followed him, but at some distance on account of the foul smell of his clothes. When they reached the church another obstacle awaited – Father Simeon laid a stubborn siege but it was impossible to force open its heavy doors. It was the Muslims who showed him how to get in, through a breach in its fortress walls behind dense ivy. The secret passage led him into the sanctuary.

'Back!' he ordered. 'This is the Holy of Holies and only a priest has the right to enter.'

They obeyed. Father Simeon asked for a lantern and when it arrived he explored the sanctuary alone and with humble veneration. It soon became clear to him that when the doors were locked and the windows boarded up so long ago, the church had been left to the mercy of scavengers – perhaps the same people who were with him now. 'Savages,' he muttered to himself. 'But I shall lead them to the light.' The altar table was still there, possibly because it was too heavy or too big to fit through the opening in the wall, but he could find nowhere either the tabernacle or the Gospel. He ran his hand along the dusty table top.

'The Lord does not live here any more,' he declared. 'We have to invite Him back.'

What the looters had left behind, time had treated with pagan contempt. The altarpiece must have been one of the first items to be dismantled and carried away, but the bishop's throne was still there, the torn strips of its velvet canopy dangling down like the branches of a clematis. Only a few broken pews had been left behind, a psalmist's lectern and the largest of the candelabra which now lay on the floor. While he surveyed the devastation of the nave Father Simeon maintained a calm silence, but the fists in his pockets were clenched in religious anger. When he approached the dark form that somehow had found its way to the narthex, he could suppress his horror no more: the brass baptismal font was brimming with rats. He began to cry.

Defeated by the enormity of the task ahead of him – namely the restoration of St Gregorius Theologus body and soul – the padre sat on the steps of the Royal Doors and contemplated the vast emptiness. A moment later he was tapped on the shoulder and handed an extraordinary item. His fingers recognised it before the light of the lantern confirmed its identity: heavy and immaculate, the Gospel lit up his face with the glow of its twenty-four-carat gilding. Praise be to the Lord! The scavengers had saved it from the rodents. He held the priceless gift close to his chest and his eyes watered again – he had at last arrived home. It was after a moment of respectful silence that his unwitting congregation enquired whether he would be interested in buying it.

CHAPTER 4

They had been tended with ample polish on each vamp as well as a globule of spit, before the camel-hair brush commenced its resolute attack. It withdrew only when the leather pair had regained the forgotten splendour of its youth and the shoes now deserved their place next to the rest of the uniform: the mended knee-socks with the green garters, the pair of ironed shorts, the starched khaki shirt with the badges and pins, the immaculate blue scarf, the broad-brimmed hat. The mayor inspected the items arranged on his desk one last time before undressing to his underwear; his civilian suit and shirt he placed with care on the hanger. He was trying to fit into the miniature shorts when the door opened behind him.

'If there is no age limitation to being a Boy Scout,' a voice said behind him, 'there ought at least to be a weight one.'

The mayor made a face but did not turn around – instead he breathed in and buttoned his flies as fast as he could. Saved from the lacerations of the Anatolian sun by the blinds and curtains of his bureaucratic career, his skin was soft, pale and covered with tufts of dense hair that spilled out of his string cotton vest. Having done up the buttons, he buckled on his belt and only then did he release his belly with an exhalation.

'Who let you in?' he asked with his back still to the arrival.

The schoolmaster closed the door and walked towards the Victrola.

'As a public servant, your door should be open to all the Sultan's humble subjects.'

'Haven't you heard? The empire is no more.'

'Even more so in a republic.'

The mayor kneaded his forehead and let out a deep sigh. A lifetime in the civil service had taught him how to steer the boat of his office clear of codes of practice. But the war had accelerated the collapse of the Ottoman Empire and brought about a political state of affairs whose novelty scared him: the damn Expeditionary Corps had pulled the carpet from under his feet. Oh, how he missed the Ottoman past.

'I want to know what genius first came up with the idea of elections,' he said.

Mr Othon lifted the cover of the Victrola and looked inside, arching his eyebrows.

'Our wise ancestors.'

The mayor continued to prepare. He picked up his scarf and folded it into a triangle. This he arranged over his shoulders so that one corner hung down from his nape, while the other two he tied in a neat knot over his chest. His dressing up with such seriousness and attention to detail indicated that this was more than a spare-time activity; it was an important voca-tion. He curled his lip.

'The ancients also believed that the sun was a man riding a golden chariot,' he said.

After a quick search through the stack of records

the schoolmaster placed one on the turntable.

'Your cheap Victrola is no match to my gramophone,' he said while turning the crank.

He contemplated the wobbling rotations of the bent record with his hands in his pockets.

'When I lent this Galli-Curci to you she was straight as a blade.'

Standing in front of the mirror, the mayor gave the mahogany cabinet an indifferent look.

'It must be the heat. You didn't say I had to keep her in the icebox.'

The other man made a fitting grimace.

'Are you still planning to run for office?' he asked.

'It's too early in the day to talk politics.'

At that moment Amelita Galli-Curci began to repeat a coloratura again and again. The schoolmaster had to give the tone arm a light push to deliver the great soprano from her torment.

'This record is scratched. I bet your cat slept in the Victrola again.'

The mayor checked himself in the mirror. He slanted his hat a tad to the side: perfect.

'Not her fault. Handling phonographic records is not an instinct nature has provided her with.'

'Oh yes,' said the schoolmaster. '*A Scout is a friend to animals*. I remember that being in the manual somewhere.'

The mayor nodded in confirmation.

'Scout law, clause six.'

Once he had finished dressing he searched for his Scoutmaster's cane. It was not in the drawers of his desk or in the filing cabinet – what had he done with it? Mr Othon watched him with spite.

'And remind me again where it says that a Scout can stab a man in the back?'

The last time he had the cane, the mayor remembered, was the previous week – he had used it to remove the cobwebs from the corners of the ceiling. Maybe he had put it with the feather duster by mistake?

'Imagine that once we were friends,' Mr Othon said with contempt.

It did indeed seem as if a geologic era had gone by. But in truth it was only a few weeks since the two men had turned from bosom friends into sworn enemies. Gone were the times when they would meet in the *lokanta* to recover from the vertigo of the afternoon slumber with the help of a cup of aromatic tea and the backgammon board. Or when they would make the long weekend journey to Smyrna to watch a play by a theatrical company from the motherland, and later frequent the finest establishments for gentlemen of their calibre.

Yes, they had been friends in those days but, at the same time, a fierce competition had always seethed under the surface. Once, when the mayor had shown up wearing new espadrilles, the schoolmaster had travelled overnight to the capital of the province and returned the following day with a fine pair of English leather riding boots; some days later, when the latter had bought a round of *raki* for everyone in the *lokanta* to celebrate the end of school term, the former had retaliated with exorbitant absinthe . . . They both agreed that the world existed so that one could catalogue its infinite constituents in order of size, merit or importance, and then proceed to acquire the best of everything for oneself. It had been a bloodless if not unamusing contest, until the day the French beauty was caught in its crossfire.

The mayor found the bucket with the cleaning materials; his cane was under the dustpan. He brushed it against his shorts and held it under his arm while bending down to adjust his garter. His inflexible spine reminded him of his age. He had joined the Scouts ten years earlier after receiving by mistake a pamphlet in the post addressed to a young namesake of his. The humanitarian ideals of the Movement had stirred the last dregs of integrity in the bottom of his unredeemable conscience and he had fallen head over heels for it. He had created a large troop from the boys in the town and organised vigorous outdoor activities. The schoolmaster had joined up briefly, too – calculating he would quickly overtake his friend in rank, no doubt, the mayor thought wryly – but the prospect of spending his Sundays in the company of the demons of his working week had soon become too heavy a cross to bear.

The mayor, on the other hand, revelled in it. Having read about the first jamboree in London, he had begun saving up in order to attend the next with some of the boys. (It was not his private luxuries he was economising on – he was setting aside funds from the municipal chest.) His recent engagement, however, had meant that he might have to postpone his Scouting pilgrimage: his fiancée wanted a child.

'Some friend,' said the schoolmaster.

Still kneeling, the mayor suddenly felt that the

heaviness of his belly threatened to topple him.

'I asked you to be my best man, didn't I?' he replied, steadying himself.

Mr Othon responded with a curse; it fell wide of the mark, only making his foe smirk with bravado.

'*A Scout smiles and whistles under all difficulties,*' the mayor said. 'Scout law, clause eight. It would do you good to rejoin the Movement, Othon.'

The schoolmaster clenched his teeth.

'You and that suffragist, that French —!'

The mayor pointed his cane at the door.

'Public hours are over. I have a serious matter to attend to.'

He left the room ahead of his erstwhile friend. In the square a contingent of Boy Scouts awaited him under the sun. Walking towards them, the mayor searched his pockets for his whistle. Battered by the winds, the tamarisks on either side of the street stood naked like skeletons; their flowers had been swept off the square and piled up against the walls, the thresholds and drains, rotting. A swarm of silent rooks had taken the place of the foliage. The mayor shuddered at the sensation of the changing season; he blew his whistle and the Scouts lined up, holding their staffs at their sides. When they were ready he gave the Scout salute, clasped his hands behind his back and commenced the inspection.

The boys' uniforms were starched, ironed and smelled of lavender. One boy carried a wooden snare drum the mayor had bought some time ago from the ringmaster of an Armenian circus. It had belonged to Hieronymus, their mercurial macaque, whom his trainer had apparently killed one day in a fit of anger after the monkey had bitten his hand. It was an uncomplicated but effective lie fabricated to cover up the truth, which had to do with the uncomfortable sin of sodomy. What the mayor did not know was that, having had enough of the human jungle, the macaque had one day made its daring escape from the affections of its keeper and had lived since in a nearby *madrasa*. The mayor wondered where the circus might be right now – he had not heard from the troupe for quite some time. He stopped in front of a boy whose shirt was missing a button.

'Take a stone out of one of its buttresses,' he said, 'and even the Great Wall of China would collapse.'

He tapped his cane against his palm while considering an appropriate punishment for the boy's untidiness.

'After the parade, tenderfoot, you will semaphore your patrol leader the complete first page of the *Anabasis*.'

He completed his review without further reprimand and returned to the middle of the line-up.

'Attention, Scouts!' he ordered. 'What is the Pledge?'

The boys chanted: 'On my honour I pledge that I will do my best to do my duty to God and the King, to help other people at all times and to obey the Scout Law.'

The mayor nodded with satisfaction.

'Who is the standard-bearer today?'

A Scout First Class came forward with a face savaged by acne. On his sleeves and pockets was sewn the evidence of a fanatical commitment to the Movement: the badges of ambulance man, pathfinder, rescuer, tracker, forester, weatherman and artist. The mayor observed the boy with pride; once again he tried to reconcile his embezzler's lack of morals with the ideals he tried to bestow upon these youths – once again he failed.

'The flag,' he said.

The boy took out a paper Greek flag he had sketched and coloured the previous night himself, and he attached it to his staff.

'Don't forget to burn that as soon as the soldiers go,' said the mayor. 'We are proud citizens of the Turkish Republic now.'

The boy nodded. His superior consulted his pocket watch: the brigadier was late. He bit his lip. The parade had been organised to honour that old mule and he . . . The distant noise of a ripped exhaust interrupted his malicious reflections. In a minute an officer in a threadbare uniform appeared, riding an old postman's motorcycle. He rode around the square until he spotted the line-up, whereupon he sped towards it. The mayor followed the progress of the backfiring motorcycle with a frown.

'I was expecting the brigadier,' he said as soon the motorcycle came up to him.

The officer on it killed the engine, dismounted and set the motorcycle on its stand. He saluted.

'He sends his apologies – I am his Chief of Staff. I will be honoured to attend the festivities on his behalf.'

To the mayor the news was a slap in the face. As the local representative of the Sultan he was unaccus-tomed to the insult of the cold shoulder – another shortcoming of democracy, he thought. His gloom about the change of season intensified.

'Democracy will never last,' he said. 'Who wants to

spend time stuffing paper into a ballot box when a bullet could achieve the same result?' He pushed back his hat and scratched his forehead. 'So be it,' he added and faced his troop of Scouts. 'Attention!' he called out. 'Dip the flag.'

The acned boy lowered the flag as a token of respect to military authority. Major Porfirio made an effort to salute gallantly the pitiable colours – fixed with drawing pins on the dented Scout's staff, creased and small, the watercolour flag seemed to mock him. The Scoutmaster called out another order.

'Scouts, face right!'

The boys carried out their drill in impeccable coordination. The noise of their feet against the gravel startled the rooks on the tamarisks and some flew off croaking towards the church. There was a bad winter ahead, the mayor thought before blowing his nickel-plated whistle.

'Ready to march!'

Another brief whistle and the young automata were set in motion to the accompanying sound of the monkey drum. Immediately they began to circle the square, it became evident that their daily drilling for more than a week had paid dividends: no one broke step or fell behind, despite the briskness of the march. Feeling proud, the mayor directed his guest to the shade of one of the trees.

'The aim of the Movement is to provide opportunities for developing those qualities of character which make one a good citizen,' he began. 'Honour, self-discipline, self-reliance, willingness and ability to serve one's community.'

Major Porfirio contemplated the marching children with sadness. Ahead went the desperate flag, followed closely by the drum and then the rest of the contingent. In their starched khaki uniforms and broad-brimmed hats they reminded him of the pawns on the medic's chessboard. He sensed he should say something in response to his host's grandiloquence.

'These are indeed the fundamental principles,' he attempted.

'It is what Plato has called an education in virtue from youth onwards,' the mayor continued. 'It makes a man want to be a perfect citizen, by teaching him how to rule correctly and how to obey.'

'Obey,' Major Porfirio echoed. 'That is important, naturally.'

'The methods of Scouting are based on the natural desires of youth. By giving them practical and attractive outlets, it turns them to socially valuable purposes. The young Scout is unaware of what lies behind his training – to him it's just a game played with his comrades.'

The boys completed another circle round the square while the drum shooed away the last of the rooks. The flight of the black birds strengthened the presentiment weighing on the mayor's shoulders all that morning, and he forgot his speech.

'Things used to run like clockwork before the war . . .' he said with a sigh.

Major Porfirio raised a pair of tired eyebrows in response to the mayor's lament. He, too, attempted to assess life before the Great War that had spawned the Anatolian campaign. How bad had it been? He was surprised to discover he could not say for certain: the shock of the defeat had lessened the misfortunes of the past. He observed his host with the mistrust of an amnesia sufferer told by a stranger they were related. Was the mayor a potential convert to the Socialist Cause? While trying to decide, the major grabbed the first banality he could lay his hands on.

'The wheels of history creak along.'

The mayor shrugged at the flavourless comment. He blew his whistle and the Scouts began to sing a triumphal anthem – but it was not as successful as their drills. The rehearsal the evening before under the guidance of the schoolmaster's baton had gone well, but the boys had clearly not practised their singing in concert with marching, as the mayor had specifically asked Mr Othon to do, and the Scouts started falling out of step. The mayor looked down, embarrassed by the spectacle and angry at his former friend.

'May the Devil sing at his funeral,' he murmured. 'This is a carnival parade.'

Next to him the major had not noticed, still considering the possibility of a new recruit; he decided to test the waters.

'Some say a national flag is a shroud with colours,' he remarked, seemingly in a casual way.

The ageing Scoutmaster gave him a protracted look. He could not care less what flag flew on the roof of the Town Hall as long as he occupied the office inside, but such a comment from an army officer was surprising. He thought no more of it; the deterioration of his parade was of greater concern at the moment.

'Yes, of course — the violence,' he said in a hurry. 'There was perhaps no reason for it.'

The fraud left the idealist standing under the tamarisk and rushed to assume the command of his troop. When he returned the Scouts had stopped singing and resumed their silent parade. Round the square they marched, and sweat started to soak their khaki shirts under the armpits, round the airtight collars, over the fronts with the badges of merit. The mayor nodded appreciatively until the foul smell of the sewer, blowing from the direction of the Muslim Quarter, cut short his joy.

'This would be a fine town,' he said, 'if only it were in Europe.'

Ever since Air Lieutenant Kimon had seen Major Porfirio set free the gelding, he had found himself in possession of a delicious yet burdensome secret. It was like an old treasure he had to safeguard until a trusty evaluator for it could be found. The crime itself had not been significant — at least not according to his civilian reason. But an officer prepared to risk his career for the sake of a mistreated horse without testicles must be possessed by an unpredictable humanity. What else was this secretive man capable of? The airman raised his eyes to the azure vastness of the evening sky and recalled the discussion that had taken place between him and the major that night in the camp some days earlier, which had lit the still burning fire of their mutual and deep antipathy. His thoughts of revenge slowly gave way to the boredom he always felt when his feet were in contact with the ground.

He looked at the dust, the stones, the gravel of the street almost with scorn – how he longed for his biplane now. Beyond the edge of the town a sand-storm hissed.

He examined his burns from the crash: they were healing, albeit slowly. The fire had licked his cheeks, the nape of his neck and hands, but had failed to over-rule the privilege of his beauty. A fly touched down on the crust of blood on his forehead but took off before his palm had the chance to crush it. Yes, it would be fun to see the major humiliated – the spec-tacle of such a proud man disciplined . . . Chuckling at the thought, Air Lieutenant Kimon continued his walk.

Presently he heard a coo: a cage hung from the eaves of the grocery; inside, four pigeons flopped about, stupefied by the heat. While he observed them with an empty mind, the airman felt the urge to urinate. Because of his condition, he had to find a quiet spot. He decided to cut across the municipal park. As soon as he entered the overgrown common, a secret orchestra of birds broke into song. He unbuckled his trousers behind a large palm and directed his stream on to the scales of its trunk. When he finished he threw stones at the high branching spikes until he had collected enough dates. He ate with relish, and only when he had finished did he notice that his actions had silenced the birds. The sweet fruit had made him thirsty and he went to look for water. He took a path shaded by cypresses, which became narrower and darker the further he went, until he came to an iron gate enfolded in overgrown ivy and surmounted by a cross spattered with bird droppings: it was the town cemetery. The gate creaked on its hinges, and he walked across a bed of dry poplar leaves that cracked under his boots like eggshells. Everything was covered with moss: the stone crosses, the urns, the praying angels, the roofs of the mausoleums. Something moved across the fallen leaves – a snake or a bird? His eyes caught sight of a slow army of snails and he followed them to a fountain filled with stagnant water. He skimmed the slime with the edge of his hand and, while he quenched his thirst, the songbirds resumed their song.

The great hero being taught a lesson. Air Lieutenant Kimon thought again about the major with an involuntary clenching of his perfect teeth. Why, he might even lose his place among the staff – now, that would be better than the time his squadron leader had landed in a bog and his triplane had flipped over. At the far end of the cemetery he saw the big house that was his ultimate destination. He entered via the back garden, making his way through the vines with the unripe grapes, the lemon trees, the sprigs of coriander. In the house itself the doors and windows were open, surrendering their curtains to the playfulness of the wind. On the veranda a terracotta pot lay in pieces and in the salon the airman discovered the culprit: a cat sitting in an armchair was clawing its precious upholstery. In the marble-tiled drawing room the aristocrat leaned over the grand piano and fingered the ivory keyboard. By the time he heard the steps behind him he had convinced himself to inform on the major.

A voice said, 'The only place one can listen to good music these days is in the brothel.'

Brigadier Nestor made the sign of secrecy with his forefinger, while grinning agreeably.

'Please don't tell the mayor you saw me. I am supposed to be busy reviewing the artillery.'

When the invitation to attend the Scouts' parade had arrived two days earlier, the brigadier had welcomed it with as much enthusiasm as an order to surrender. On reflection, he had decided to spend the morning draped in the red satin of Violetta's sheets. Air Lieutenant Kimon saluted him.

'At ease, lieutenant. As far as I know we are both charged the same. Therefore, you may treat me as equal while in the confines of this establishment.'

The airman remembered his own secret; this was his opportunity.

'My brigadier, I would like a word.'

His superior checked his watch.

'Not now, son. I have an even more important job than' – he winked – 'the review of the cannon. One should never let a wise sibyl[*] wait. Come and see me tomorrow.' And with that Brigadier Nestor bade his subordinate farewell.

Ever since his arrival in the town the brigadier had been hearing stories concerning the necromancer wife of the Armenian grocer. Apparently, the woman possessed such remarkable paranormal abilities that she was known across the Levant. Brigadier Nestor was told that disembodied voices would echo across the

---

[*]Any woman in Greek and Roman mythology possessing prophetic powers, supposed to be given her by the god Apollo. The sibyls lived in caves or near streams and prophesied in a frenzied trance.

room during her séances, various objects come afloat, musical instruments play spontaneously, carnations materialise from her mouth . . . The list of her achievements was impressive. As soon as he had heard about her the brigadier had begun to think of his late wife. Perhaps the distinguished seer could help him whisper her the last farewell.

The Armenian grocer had been waiting. Standing in the crotch of a forked cobbled street, his two-storey house was shaped like the prow of a battleship. A small balcony occupied by flowerpots jutted out from its narrow front, over a street lamp nailed into the wall. There were shuttered windows on both of the plastered side walls, but only one door which opened into the left prong of the street. When he saw the officer the grocer snuffed out his cigarette and put it in his pocket.

'You are very fortunate, my brigadier. Tonight is a new moon. Souls like darkness – the darker the better. Come inside.'

The night moved slowly down the cobbled street, inundating the whitewashed façades one after another. The Armenian moved aside. No sooner had Brigadier Nestor crossed the threshold than he had the sensation he had been transported to a mysterious world. His host picked up a heavy oil lamp and shone its conspiratorial illumination into the darkness.

'Follow me, friend,' he said. 'But watch your step. There are spirits around. They have refused to return to the underworld after one of the séances, and they can be mischievous. It is difficult to get rid of them.' He gave his customer a sidelong glance. 'Sometimes it feels as if my wife and I run a hotel for lost souls.' The creaking of a door emphasised his advice. Brigadier Nestor could not help but gulp. Leading the brigadier through the macabre steps of a choreography devised to exaggerate a customer's superstition, his host felt a professional satisfaction under his dispassionate countenance.

It was a large house, but after a few minutes there the brigadier wondered whether they were walking in circles. They went up and down staircases several times, along narrow corridors where an out-of-step echo gave the old officer the impression they were being followed, and through doors the Armenian would open with some key from the bunch on his belt and lock immediately behind them (so that the wandering souls would not contaminate the rest of the house, he explained). The cobwebs against the brigadier's forehead and the noxious smells persuaded him he was taking leave of the material world. Finally, they reached a door at the top of a spiral staircase.

'My general,' a voice said when the two men entered. 'Welcome. Leave your authority outside and come in.'

The brigadier removed his cap and coat and bowed with reverence. The medium's parlour was a circular room where dark drapery covered the wall from end to end, and the ceiling, too. The woman was sitting behind a small round table with a crystal ball on it.

'You may sit,' she ordered.

Having received the officer's cap and coat, the grocer showed him to a chair and retired. With a quick glance the seer could tell her customer's submission to super-stition was almost total; they could now begin.

'I hold no answers myself, general – I am merely a servant of the spirits. It is they who will give you the answers you require.'

The elaborate charade had affected the brigadier's reason but not his humour.

'But *you* will receive the fee.'

His host stared him out of his sacrilegious wit. It was time to demonstrate her metaphysical powers. Shrouded by her arcane dress, her feet pressed the pedals of her secret machine and the small table began its extraordinary levitation. The trick succeeded in silencing the brigadier. A moment later a whiff of perfume entered the parlour.

'State your name, spirit,' the necromancer requested.

No sooner had she said it than her countenance began to distort. When she spoke again her voice was huskier.

'*Conte Alessandro di Cagliostro.*'

One had to give her credit at least for being well read. She had chanced upon the infamous adventurer in a book she had borrowed from the municipal library. One of the countless charlatans for whom the Renaissance was to blame, the self-proclaimed count had excelled in anything from forgery to fortune telling. Posing as a physician, hypnotist or freemason he had travelled throughout Europe, peddling his elixirs of immortal youth. Eventually, he had been seized by the Inquisition and condemned to death as a heretic, but his sentence had been commuted to life imprisonment. Impressed by his résumé, the Armenian necromancer had installed him as her favourite conferee from the afterlife.

Brigadier Nestor was displeased to make his acquaintance.

'But I am here to communicate with my wife, madam. Not some lesser aristocrat.'

The count took issue.

'You command your troops well, general. Let us see whether you would be as competent with the legions of demons too.'

The brigadier shuddered.

'You seem to speak our language impeccably for a foreigner, count. Your syntax is impeccable and you appear to have no accent whatsoever.'

The spirit let that comment pass.

'I bring greetings from a person who keeps you in the safe of her heart,' it said through the medium.

Brigadier Nestor assumed a sombre mood.

'Tell her she's the love of my life, too. I cherished her and I always will.'

'Cherish,' the count said scornfully. *'You have committed adultery.'*

Brigadier Nestor shifted on his chair.

'It was a long time ago. Back then I was −'

'Repeatedly. All your long matrimonial life.'

The officer realised that it was impossible to outfox a nearly bicentenarian nobleman.

'Are you sure that this is Count Cagliostro, madam?' he asked the medium. 'My mother-in-law happens to be dead, too.'

The Armenian woman had no time for impertinence.

'Do not mock the proceedings, general. You may find that death rids one of one's humour.'

The senior officer complied. But since his meeting

with the journalist there had been something else he also meant to ask the spirits.

'Will I find fame, count?'

The medium's answer was as prompt as it was ambiguous.

'Your achievements will one day be known to the world, general.'

The prophecy brought the massacre to the brigadier's mind; that was one achievement he precisely did not want the world to know about. He was still contemplating the answer he had been given when the spirit spoke again.

'Beware, sir. Some vultures circle above your head. Others walk alongside you.'

The brigadier pleated his lips. The spirit was referring to the thief and the traitor in his army, no doubt.

'Who are they? Give me their names!'

By now he should have known that the Divine Cagliostro was not in the habit of offering straight answers.

'A plain tunic conceals the truth well. One with insignia does it better.'

Brigadier Nestor was losing his patience. Nevertheless, he attempted another crucial question.

'Will we ever see our homes again?'

The spirit of the Italian adventurer was about to oblige him again when gunshots were heard not very far away. The officer jumped out of his chair and drew his revolver.

'I have to leave, madam,' he said and checked his handgun: it was loaded. 'Something is happening. Where's my cap?'

'General!' the medium stopped him with her haunting voice. 'You cannot go yet – the spirit is becoming irritable!'

Another shiver went down Brigadier Nestor's spine.

'I apologise, but this is an emergency. My presence may be required.'

The situation called for a deadly weapon from the seer's armoury of tricks. She extended a finger. Behold – its tip began to emit a flickering light that appeared to come from underneath the skin. The brigadier froze; he stared at the inexplicable miracle with bulging eyes.

'What is it . . . that the count . . . wants, madam?' he asked, hypnotised.

There was a hint of derision in the necromancer's voice when she answered.

'For you to pay me first, sir.'

CHAPTER 5

The first incident had been an impulse caused by panic: he had run out of host for the Eucharist and the cook had refused to help him. Since the beginning of the retreat, food had been rationed and there were orders not to waste a single loaf of bread. But the cook was a big-hearted man and the two of them could come to an understanding, he had said. So, when one morning the brigadier was out on a scouting mission, the cook had sent him to steal the sugar. It had been easier than he had anticipated; the liturgical cross on his chest had proved to be the master key to every door. When next he ran out of consecrated wine it took him a mere few seconds to subdue his conscience, and he had raided the Chief of Staff's private stock. After that came the medic's expensive razor . . . He and that profiteer of a cook had become partners in crime.

The only time things had almost gone wrong was while he was searching for the brigadier's beloved cigars. A snake had somehow crept into the lorry and snapped its jaws an inch from his thieving hand. He had crushed it under his heel in a rage of religious proportions before leaving some time later with the precious loot under his tunic. He now took a moment to consider whether the evil serpent had perhaps had some sort of ominous significance – but he quickly dismissed such a pagan notion. He had absolved himself entirely of guilt by arguing that what he stole were luxury items one should do without in normal life, let alone in a dire situation like the present. Naturally, he would never do anything that would jeopardise the safety of the soldiers. His unorthodox practice was, in fact, only meant to secure their salvation – the spiritual one, that was, the one that mattered the most.

Father Simeon heaved a sigh and hugged himself; it was cold inside the church. He threw another piece of wood on the fire that burned in the middle of the empty nave. The flaking murals on the walls stared down at him with stern ascetic eyes. Sparks took flight from his rudimentary fire and burned out a few feet above the ground. Squatting on the cold floor of his new residence, the padre studied the booty of the night's operation – a pair of patent-leather riding boots with silver spurs, and a ceremonial sabre with a tasselled gold cord on its engraved scabbard – and could not suppress a sense of pride not dissimilar to that of a professional burglar. That morning the information had reached his ears that the brigadier would be devoting his evening to the unnameable wantonness of the villa on the edge of the market: it was the perfect opportunity. Ever since Father Simeon had touched the golden covers of the Gospel shown to him by the Muslims, an intoxicated reaction had taken place inside his brain that remained undiminished: the sacred book must be his. He had only to procure the necessary funds.

It had not been an easy undertaking. Brigadier Nestor had been fuming about the disappearance of his cigars and had set a series of cunning traps in order to catch the thief. Of the labyrinthine stratagems the padre had encountered in the Town Hall, the most impressive had been the invisible thread of silk stretched across the first-floor landing and tied to the big toe of the snoring guard. A close second had been the bucket of yellow paint balanced precariously on top of the door to the conference room. There were others too, but the padre had managed to evade every single one of them.

He thought that the boots and sword ought to be enough to buy him the ancient Gospel. Nevertheless, he prepared himself for some obstinate haggling in the Muslim Quarter the following morning. The fire in front of him was burning out and he had no more wood left. He wrapped himself in his greatcoat, leaned against one of the columns that supported the dome of the church and closed his eyes. Despite the cold he felt like a child going to bed on the night before Christmas.

The night of the new moon was supposed to act in his favour, but he could hardly see where he was going: the corporal felt his heart palpitate under his tunic like a trapped animal. He had been waiting so long for this moment, watching the waning moon with impatience every night; that evening it had at last disappeared. Apart from a patrol of sleepwalking soldiers there was going to be no one else around. The bugle had long since commanded the night's blackout; street lamps had been extinguished, curtains pulled across windows, and the town had sunk into a celestial darkness. The corporal had waited until the grandfather clock in the house where he was billeted had sounded the hour of midnight and then he set off. It was in moments like this he felt the cost of his communist beliefs: he would have found useful the illusory encouragement of a prayer. He went, nevertheless.

The absence of light meant he had escaped his shadow, but the sound of his boots followed him closely. The plaster walls echoed every step. He stopped and removed his boots, tied their laces together and hung them from his neck. He continued in his torn woolly socks, less comfortably but more quietly, pricking up his ears; the only sound other than his heartbeat was the night rustle of the tamarisks. He must be in the market, he guessed, feeling around with his foot. He had noticed the cobblestone pavement there before, but he did not know exactly where he was – it was impossible to read the signboards on the shops or the names on the street signs. His mind recalled the map that was in the back pocket of his trousers and which he could not read in that darkness. He concentrated: his quarters . . . the street that passed in front of the whorehouse . . . the park . . . The square should be round the next corner.

But it was not. He stood still to catch his breath. Though he had only been walking, he felt his chest swell as if he had been drilling for hours. He smelled the open sewer – was he headed for the Muslim Quarter? That was not on the painstaking route he had laid out for his escape. But it was too late to go back; the corporal pushed on reluctantly, as the brief calls of an owl added to the gasps of his agony. A moment later he admitted he was lost.

Apart from the map, he carried in his pockets like talismans the *billets-doux* from his secret love from Salonika. In his backpack, more pragmatically, were a few tins, a blanket, some bottles filled with water, a bayonet to defend himself and the Party's pamphlet explaining surplus value – his idea was that, if he were captured by the enemy, that last item could become his passport to freedom, something to help assure them that he had nothing against them: he was an internationalist and a proletarian. He stopped, put down his backpack and listened. He thought he had heard something. No; there was no one. He was preparing to start again when he saw it: a pair of yellow eyes, glowing in the dark like distant headlights, aiming at him. He stood as if mesmerised and for a while nothing happened. But the moment the corporal softly, stealthily attempted to walk away, the padre's dog began to bark at the top of its voice.

He ran. It was difficult with the weight on his back and the pair of boots dangling from his neck, but he managed several hundred yards before, inevitably, he had to abandon his pack. Suddenly his plan was not to reach the coast any more – he would be happy to make it to the hills. The urgency of the situation had robbed him of his reason. Without food, water or means to protect himself from the cold he could not survive on the Anatolian plain for long. But right now a short-sighted sense of survival made him all sort of promises. Where was he? He turned sharply round a corner and immediately stumbled on an obstacle that must have been a flowerpot from the way it sounded when it broke to pieces. Still after him, Caleb paused briefly; the noise had intrigued the animal. Was someone throwing stones at him? When he was positive no one was, Caleb continued his pursuit.

He was in high spirits. This was not what he had expected on such a cold night; as a matter of fact, there was very little to do in this town at any hour of the day. There was that infernal cat he had spotted wandering from the *hamam* to the Town Hall and back — but no sooner had he tried to chase her than the townspeople had started throwing stones at him and he had to retreat with his tail between his legs; what a dishonourable defeat. Never mind; tonight he had happened upon a most excellent form of entertainment. He hung out his tongue, gulped and began to bark with renewed ferocity.

Limping from the knock against the flowerpot, the corporal ran as if he were drunk. The blindfold of the moonless night forbade him any choice in his escape route. He ran until he reached an impasse whereupon he turned around and, feeling about, tried to discover another way. A moment later he splashed across a ditch. His nose told him it was the sewer: he was entering the Muslim Quarter. As a final act of despair he dropped his boots in the conduit before plunging into the sordid darkness.

All that while he swore at his bad luck — but not for an instant did he regret his decision to desert; in the storm of his panic the apparition of his female correspondent did not stop flashing in his eyes like lightning. True, he had never received a photograph from her despite his repeated entreaties, but he had fashioned her face from her handwriting as well as her turn of phrase. Specifically: long raven hair, possibly straight (his method was not exact science), almond-shaped eyes, strong long nose, stubborn lips . . . Admittedly, the object of his platonic affections resembled somewhat the artist's rendition of an Egyptian queen, a crumpled newspaper clipping he kept in his wallet, where one ought to carry the photograph of one's sweetheart.

What his pleading and curses had failed to achieve was suddenly accomplished by the sound of a distant whistle. The dog stopped, pricked up his ears and wagged his tail. Good, Caleb thought, more were joining in his nocturnal game.

The animal had alerted the patrol. He could hear them at this moment, still far away, rushing. He barked again to direct them towards himself. His voice was their lighthouse in the darkness and it was not long before their lanterns shone at the other end of the narrow alleyway.

'Halt!'

The corporal did the opposite. There were shots in the air and the guards scrambled to arrest him, shouting to each other over the walls to coordinate their hunt. But it was difficult, even with their lanterns and the help of the dog. The maze generated a tumult of deceptive echoes and shadows that not only led the soldiers astray, but also caused exchanges of friendly fire. Fortunately there were no casualties, but more time was lost this way, as lengthy quarrels broke out among the pursuers who had experienced the proximity of death. Those were opportunities the corporal exploited to his advantage, going deeper into the heart of the slum. By now his socks were torn and the soles of his feet should, in all likelihood, have been bleeding. But somehow he had managed to shake off the soldiers and the dog too. Had the smell of so many men perhaps tricked the mongrel's nose? In any case, the door to his hope had opened a crack. Concealed from the rest of the town by the adobe walls of the outer quarter, the houses in its heart were an assortment of nightmarish constructions comprised of wooden boards, sheets of tin and pieces of tarpaulin that were nailed, roped or stitched together to precarious effect. When the corporal stopped and spun round, looking for an exit, people began to emerge from the shacks holding candles and lamps, while more faces peered at him from windows without panes. The corporal felt like an explorer encountering an unknown tribe. And then something more extraordinary happened: a hand stretched out and offered him a lit lantern. He received the precious gift and was about to thank his saviour when the noise of the patrol restored his panic.

The pursuit resumed but now the corporal, too, had the benefit of light. With its help he emerged a few minutes later from the labyrinth. But a hissing bullet abridged his exhilaration. It bored through the flesh of his right arm and, coated with his blood, went on to smash his precious lamp to pieces. Against the dark sky the corporal saw the gigantic dome of St Gregorius Theologus. A flickering light – the embers of a fire? – was coming from its nave. The young man recalled the rumour that the padre had moved in there. 'I am saved,' he mumbled, panting.

★　　★　　★

243

It was a delicious dream, the kind he had not tasted for years. He was still in town but instead of his army uniform he wore his old cassock. Time had passed – he could not exactly tell how long – and there had been changes. There was no slum any more, but modest stone houses with pleasant gardens; the vainglorious *hamam* had been demolished, and a small park stood in its place; the brothel had been converted into a school where girls were taught home economics. Furthermore, the open sewer had been covered and the pestilential smell that once pickled the town was finally gone. It was all the result of Father Simeon's pastoral labour. The crowning glory of his remarkable achievement was to reveal itself promptly. Indeed: no sooner did he ring the cracked bells than from the Muslim Quarter a sea of pious converts flocked to the restored church.

There was also something strange about his dream. Wherever he went he carried on his shoulder a large ugly crow – the way Father Simeon understood it, it must have symbolised his unremitting guilt for not having achieved the clerical ambition of his youth of becoming a missionary. But he had redeemed himself at last and there was presently the proof in his dream: the crow opened its wings and flew off his shoulder. Father Simeon, Apostle of All Anatolians, contemplated it with tranquil eyes . . .

There was a knock on the door. The padre's ears barely registered the distant sound and he continued to dream. The crow flew above the dome of St Gregorius Theologus, letting out little shrieks. There was a second hammering on the door – but again Father Simeon

244

refused to abandon his precious dream. Where was he? Oh, yes; the crow of his guilt. There it was, flying away, soon to disappear for ever – what a splendid sight. But, unexpectedly, the bird turned round and came straight back, perching once again on the priest's hunched shoulder. Father Simeon began to weep.

'The massacre,' he sighed in his sleep. 'Will You ever forgive me, Lord?'

There was another knock on the door. This time the padre had fewer reasons not to wake up.

'Go away, demon!' he shouted in the direction of the door and pulled his coat over his head in one last attempt to resist the advance of consciousness. 'And tell your superior that *my* commanding officer is Our Lord Jesus Christ!'

But the thumping continued. Finally, the padre stood up and threw his greatcoat over his shoulders. He walked towards the narthex like a sleepwalker, removed the piece of wood that propped the door shut and opened it. He rubbed his eyes and squinted: on the steps of his church stood the corporal. Father Simeon thought he was still dreaming.

'If you are here for a confession, my son,' he yawned, 'say two "Our Fathers" before going to bed and one more first thing in the morning. Then come and see me.'

The corporal staggered back and forth on the church steps. He appeared not to have his boots on. The padre looked more carefully. Indeed: he was wearing only his socks and those were in tatters.

'Let me in, Father. No act of contrition will save me from this mess.'

Only then did the padre notice that the corporal was holding his arm: it seemed to be bleeding.

'You need medical assistance,' he said. 'I have nothing here.'

'Father, you have to hide me.'

'Cotton . . . dressings . . . carbolic . . .' mumbled the padre.

A whistle sounded somewhere in the dark and the corporal's head twisted round as if pulled by a spring. He listened: his pursuers were still in the alleyways of the Muslim Quarter.

'Please, Father.'

Father Simeon put his hands in his pockets. He was wide awake now. His instinct had always been to help the needy.

'But this could be serious. The medic has –'

The young soldier dismissed the padre's worries gallantly.

'Nothing to worry about. I get deeper cuts from shaving.'

He tried to wipe the sweat from his forehead with the hand that had been pressing his wound, but only managed to smear his brow with blood.

'Please, Father.'

Another of the padre's instincts was to comply with the law. There had been certain exceptions lately, of course – no need to go into that at the moment. But the present situation on the steps of the church concerned a true and unmitigated crime.

Father Simeon said timidly, 'I am the moral compass of . . . Any decision that . . .'

Then he remembered the items he had stolen from

the brigadier's quarters that were at that moment inside the church – what if the patrol were to conduct a search? The risk was too high.

'Impossible,' he mumbled. 'It would be a crime . . . And I an accessory.'

A cold wind blew past him and entered the church through the half-opened door. The fire on the tiles of the vast nave flickered. Tiny sparks shone in the corporal's desperate eyes. The padre looked down.

'There is nothing I can do for you, my son.'

There was shouting in the Muslim Quarter – probably an argument among the soldiers. Then a dog began to bark. That was Caleb, the padre thought fleetingly, before returning to his torment. Oh, cruel God, why are You testing Your humble servant? He, too, was sweating now.

'I advise you to give yourself up,' he said. 'Where would you go in your condition?'

The corporal gave his arm a glance, as if it were something he had picked up in the street. His sleeve was soaked in blood.

He said, 'I'm a deserter, Father.'

In the distance the argument ended and only the barking of the dog could be heard; it was coming closer.

'Even if I helped you . . . There is nothing but wilderness out there,' said the padre. 'It wouldn't be long before the jackals –'

'The jackals will be more generous than the firing squad.'

'I promise to speak to the brigadier. He is a very reasonable man. It is a miracle that the circumstances have not driven more men insane.'

The young man felt a numbness spread down his wounded arm. He was tired; all this was not meant to happen.

'I only wanted to go home, Father.'

The padre tried to smile, but the gravity of the unfolding tragedy was too great; he only managed a caricature of his intended expression.

'Home. Of course. You are young. Our country needs men like you. After the catastrophe of this war men like you −'

'I beg you, Father.'

A slight sense of impatience came over the cleric.

'Yes, yes. I will do everything in my power to help.'

Caleb appeared at the end of the street. He lifted his head like a pure-bred hound and sniffed the air: his master was over there. Father Simeon placed his hand on the young man's shoulder.

'The risk is great. My position . . . delicate.'

The dog came towards them. He had had an excellent play, and was grateful to the man for it. He came wagging his tail, tired but pleased. At both ends of the street lanterns swung in the dark.

'Mother,' the corporal started shaking. 'Oh, Mother.'

Father Simeon was quietly glad his own torment was coming to an end.

'Ask the Lord for forgiveness. Only He −'

The corporal rushed down the steps of the church in a last attempt to escape. But he was surrounded; driven into a corral of bayonets, he knelt down and remained silent. Someone had been carrying his discarded backpack; he emptied it in the middle of the street and searched through it. From the scant provisions he picked the communist pamphlet and put it in his pocket. Then he tied up the corporal, gave the padre a grateful salute and the soldiers took the deserter away.

Not far away Major Porfirio lay on his cot – the commotion had awakened him too. When he heard the patrol pass under his window, marching in silence, he immediately guessed what had happened. 'Fool,' he murmured. 'The end was so near . . . One way or another.' Then he blew out the lamp and went back to sleep.

A futile candle stuck in the neck of a bottle lit the interior of the shack, a wretched dwelling comprised of a single room without partitions. The floor was laid with dry clay. The furnishings, old and discarded objects repaired by an ingenious hand, gave the impression of sick animals that had crawled in there to die. In a corner was a large piece of earthenware filled with water: the sink. A string of onions hung from the rafters that supported the vulnerable roof. Across the room a mattress stuffed with dried husks was placed directly on the floor; a rough blanket hid the clandestine couple well, but offered little protection from the cold. Annina pulled the blanket over her neck.

'Tell me when it's time,' she said. 'I don't want Madame to wake up and find I'm missing.'

Yusuf tucked her up and ran a pair of fingers over the blanket across the woman's chest, playfully.

'Don't worry – the rats tell the time better than a Swiss clock. In the morning they always go back to the church.'

He was not joking. As soon as the sun hid behind

the hills the town surrendered to the anarchy of the rats. All night the shuffling of their feet, their squeaking and munching would be heard over the rooftops. But the first rays of light were enough to make them abandon their posts, take flight and hide in the Byzantine vaults of the church. Was it a bestial instinct brought into play by dawn? A divine intervention to render unto the people the town which was theirs? Or the fact that any rat found in the open in broad daylight would be crushed by a merciless spade?

The young maid attempted to stop the rattling of her teeth.

'I am a little cold tonight, my love.'

Yusuf sprang out of bed.

'No problem. I'll bring you the hot-water bottle.'

He found the spirit stove and boiled some water. Then he took the pot and disappeared into a dark corner of the shack where Annina heard him rearranging some of his rag-and-bone man's loot. When he returned he wore across his chest a vulcanised rubber inner tube.

'In a minute the bed will be as hot as Hell,' he promised.

Annina shivered at the blunt mention of the nether-world.

'Don't say that on a night like this, my love. It makes me scared.'

Yusuf arranged the inner tube under the covers before getting into bed again.

'Why? You'll go to Paradise – for sure. Hell is for the rich and the murderers.'

'I am thinking of that poor soldier.'

Yusuf agreed.

'Poor, yes. He may go to Paradise, or maybe Hell – God will decide.'

That night's incident had excited them both and they could not go back to sleep.

'It was so nice of you to give him the lamp.' In defiance of the cold the woman took her hand out of the covers and stroked her lover's face. 'My kind Yusuf,' she whispered.

The Arab kissed her fingers.

'But I have no light now,' he said modestly. 'And he's in prison.'

Annina nodded.

'He must be a very desperate man to attempt such a thing.'

'He's a fool. He stood no chance.'

'Only a man in love could be so desperate,' continued the Frenchwoman.

They were like two people looking at an embroidery but from opposite sides: she was impressed by the romanticism of the human impulse, but all *he* could see were loose threads and ugly knots.

'No chance,' said Yusuf. 'Wolves, brigands, no food. Impossible.'

'The call of love lured him like the Sirens,'[*] insisted Annina.

---

[*]Sea nymphs who had the bodies of birds and the heads of women. So sweet were their voices that the mariners who heard their song were lured into running their boats aground on the rocks. However, when Odysseus sailed near their island he managed to escape their trap by plugging his men's ears with wax and having himself bound to the mast of his ship.

The Arab was familiar with the ancient myth.

'Then he should have plugged his ears.'

'Oh, my cruel Yusuf. Love is a song coming from within.'

She did not have to tell him all that. His leonine roaring aside, the Arab served the demanding master that is love like a tractable slave. He had met Annina, the light of his eyes, at the end of a long and adventurous journey that in retrospect seemed to him like a pilgrimage of some exalted purpose. In truth he had left his home, a small village in the land of the Nubians not far from Aswan, in search of work. Annina knew the story; Yusuf was only ten when he had found his first job: carrying rubble at the site of the first Aswan dam. At twelve he was already working in a Pharaonic quarry, splitting granite from dawn until those hours of the evening when he could no longer see the luxurious steamboats on the distant river. He often talked to Annina about his home, with yearning and adulation in equal measure. 'The best place in the world,' he would say. 'The houses swim in the sacred Nile. One day I'll take you there.' If only he knew then what a hard pit his succulent words hid at their core. Less than forty years later, in the dusk of his life, construction of a bigger dam would start at Aswan, and an enormous artificial lake would ultimately inundate his beloved birthplace.

In any case, with his hammer and wedge the adolescent Yusuf had managed to carve himself a simple life. And he would still be living there now had he not been singled out by tuberculosis before his sixteenth birthday. The disease had mauled the defenceless boy without mercy. When it had gone away two years later he was left with a hunched back and contorted ribs, which compressed his lungs and made it difficult for him to breathe: Yusuf could work in the quarry no more. For a long time he wandered across the Levant, doing menial occupations: street sweeper, bootblack, tool sharpener. What fuelled his feet was not so much a desire to live in foreign lands as the unshakeable embarrassment caused by his deformity. After a few weeks in a place, when the people would start recognising him in the street, he would become convinced that their stare was directed towards the unbearable ballast he carried on his shoulders: they were all fascinated by his hump. Such was the frustration of his misconception that he had once walked into a butcher's and begged him with tears in his eyes to relieve him of his burden with the cleaver.

He had finally found refuge from the world in a remote *madrasa* where he was apprenticed to its nonagenarian gardener with a melancholy macaque, the only beings not to notice his crooked back. A secret never revealed to him was that his saintly patron was blind as a mole, while the reticent monkey had enough predicaments of its own. Under the old man's auspices Yusuf not only discovered his vocation in life, but also shed at last some of his bashfulness – enough at least to permit him frequent visits to the nearby town. It was in the Armenian grocer's that he had met the Annina of his dreams. He had been attracted by the magnet of her eyes and she, in turn, by the geography of his parched skin – perhaps it had also helped that at the time she had been reading her mistress's copy of *Notre Dame of Paris*, and had been moved by the character of the tortured hunchback Quasimodo.

Under the covers Yusuf searched with his freezing toes for the hot inner tube.

'Sea for fish, desert for camel, road for man,' he said. 'That soldier had to be patient.'

His lover snuggled up to him and kissed him on the shoulder.

'You have crossed deserts yourself, haven't you?'

The Arab smiled in the dark.

'But I'm a camel – can't you see the hump?'

The woman slapped him across the face tenderly.

'Your life reminds me of a book, my love.' She scratched her head. 'I think it was called *The Life and Adventures of Robinson . . . Croesus*.'

Yusuf raised his head.

'I know him – king, yes?'

'No. He was a sailor.'

The man shrugged his shoulders.

'Then I don't know him. The sea takes many men every day.'

'It is the true story of a brave man. I wish I could have met him – what stories he would have to tell.'

Jealousy gave the Arab a little pinch and he buried himself in the blanket.

'It's late. Now we sleep.'

He had already fallen asleep when a moment later Annina tapped him on the shoulder.

'I think we ought to pray for the poor soldier.'

Yusuf yawned and shook his head submissively.

'Very well. He needs many prayers. You pray to Jesus, I to Allah.'

And so they began to pray, quietly, each in their own tongue, until their exhaustion silenced them both and ordered them to sleep like a strict parent.

CHAPTER 6

The following morning the town awakened to the blasts of a torrential rainstorm. While the people slept, a westerly wind had begun to blow inland from the sea, foretelling the imminent meteorological violence. In a steady stream of salty air it brought to the town calcified seashells, withered sponges and dead starfish, an incessant aquatic hail that lasted until the sloped roofs began to resemble the burial grounds of the ocean floor. It was now time for the birds that spurned migration to get their annual come-uppance; the crows rushed to hide under the narrow eaves. Soon the rain started, building up strength fast, with an illogical spite. After the lashing of the autumnal winds, rain had arrived to give the hapless tamarisks their *coup de grâce*, stripping them of the remains of their foliage.

The town writhed under the weight of the water. Tiles slipped off roofs, drainpipes clogged, flower-beds were swallowed by the mud – but the worst was yet to come. As the sun shone above the hills – briefly: it disappeared behind the heavy clouds soon afterwards – the rain flooded the open sewer and turned the Muslim Quarter into a nauseating swamp. Its inhabitants fled their homes ahead of the tide of foul smells and pestilence, and found refuge on the higher ground of the town square where, barefoot and in their rags, they stood shivering, waiting for the storm to pass. From a window on the top floor of the Town Hall the medic watched the silent, ghostlike figures soak in the rain.

'By the end of the month,' he diagnosed, 'several will have died of pneumonia.'

He returned to his work. In the middle of the room the corporal sat on a chair with his hands tied behind his back, his feet hobbled with chains and his head bent forward, resting on his chest. He was alive – but fatigue and the failure of his midnight attempt had taken the shine from his eyes. A battered metal box with a faded red cross was on the table; the medic used a pair of scissors to cut his patient's sleeve above the chevrons. Blood and pus had coagulated on the surface of the skin, making the wound seem like a strange flower. Having cleaned the injury, the medic held the arm gently with one hand and studied the damage caused by the bullet with a magnifying glass.

'Entry point,' he said, as if dictating to an assistant taking notes. He looked on the other side. 'Penetrating. Some damage of the triceps.'

After a while he smiled with relief – it could have been worse. He searched through his medical box.

'They never had to do this to the Great Houdini,' he said. 'You're even less of an escape artist than a chess player, corporal. This will sting.'

He poured antiseptic over the wound and watched as the acid burned through the dead tissue with a hissing noise. The medieval pain brought the corporal back from his stupor.

'Medic,' he cried, clenching his teeth, 'you've never

257

forgiven me for the time I forced a draw on you.'

His opponent at chess poured more antiseptic over the wound, even though it was not necessary. Promptly, the corporal squeaked.

'It is a well-known fact that the English Opening is for cowards,' the medic said. 'Every other game ends in a draw.'

The vial of acid in the medic's hand persuaded the patient to stop reminding his curer of his only success. Outside, the rain thumped the window like an angry customer and water slowly crept in over the sill. A soldier with a small round head and the unconcerned expression of a ruminating animal sat on a stool by the door with his rifle propped against the wall. The medic looked at him: he had removed his boots and socks and was rubbing his toes.

'This man has to be taken to the infirmary,' the medic said.

'Out of the question.'

The medic looked into the guard's eyes: there was so little matter in them he thought he could see the bone behind. Compassion was not an innate human quality.

'At least untie his hands. He has to be operated on.'

The soldier again shook his head in refusal.

'The brigadier has given strict orders.'

'I cannot treat him like that. Unless you want him to die of gangrene.'

The ruminant shrugged its shoulders.

'As long as it happens on that chair. A soldier who abandons his post deserves whatever he gets.'

The rain subsided briefly and the wind took over.

Tiles slipped off the roof of the Town Hall and crashed to the courtyard where the marble bust stood.

'Medic,' the corporal said. 'Before the operation I want you to read me something. In my pocket.'

The medic searched his patient's tunic, but the love letters were nowhere to be found.

'All documents have been passed on to the brigadier,' the guard said. 'He is personally in charge of the investigation.'

The corporal let his head drop forward again.

'My love,' he sighed. 'I failed you.'

The medic patted him on the shoulder before soaking a pad of gauze in chloroform.

'If you did all that for the love of a woman I would do better to operate on your brain.'

The corporal did not laugh.

'You don't know what love is capable of, medic.'

'I know it won't deflect a bullet.'

The medic placed the pad with the anaesthetic over his patient's nose and mouth. A moment later the corporal was fast asleep with a curious smile on his face. The medic looked at his friend with pity and then his eyes rested on the gauze daubed with the generous dose of chloroform: it was enough to cause cardiac paralysis. A dark idea immediately took the doctor's soul unawares. The poor fool, he thought; I would perhaps do him a great service if I let him spin in that dream for ever . . .

It was only a momentary lapse but one of enormous significance to his conscience – the irreverence of his thought surprised him. But he recovered quickly, telling himself he had taken the Hippocratic oath and he had no intention of violating it. Without further existential musings, he removed the lid of the canister with the sterilised tools and went to work. It was a routine operation save for the awkward position of his restrained patient. At some point he had to squat and bend backwards in order to reach the inside of the arm where the exit hole of the bullet was located.

'I have operated under some highly adverse conditions in this war,' he said while inserting the scalpel, 'but I never expected to perform my duty like a car mechanic.'

Not far away, in the church, the padre was dressing. He had passed the night attempting to exorcise the demons of his decision to refuse the runaway shelter. He had failed. He was still shaken by the dramatic events. The wind broke against the walls of the church like waves upon a rock. Father Simeon tied the laces of his boots and began to wind his puttees around his legs, murmuring to himself.

'But he had committed a crime – according to army rules.'

He was not accustomed to questioning his faith. He thought that the Lord ought to know by then that every decision he made in his life was ultimately intended to confirm His glory – so why was He bent on driving him insane? Having finished with the puttees, the padre slung his braces over his shoulders. It had started to rain again.

'It wasn't myself I was thinking of last night,' he mumbled. 'No, Lord. It was *You*.'

The wind whistled through the broken stained-glass

windows. Father Simeon felt as if a breach had been made in the fortress of his virtue. He covered his ears with his hands.

'This wind . . . Almost stronger than the trumpets of Jericho.'

Somewhere in the dim corners of the church the dog was chasing rats, but they were too canny for him. The padre contemplated his companion. Caleb stuck his muzzle in a hole in the wall.

'Virtue,' said Father Simeon. 'What a rat. Try to catch it and it eludes you. Leave it alone and every night it comes round to chew your ears.'

He buttoned up his shirt. There was nowhere to hang his clothes, and his tunic, like the rest of his uniform, lay on the dirty floor. He picked it up and beat it with his hand; a cloud of dust enveloped him and he began to sneeze.

'My life I handed over to You,' he continued his bickering. 'Body and soul. See this glass eye? For Your glory, too.'

He was caught in the whirlpool of his argument and nothing seemed to pull him out. The weather inflated his malaise. The bulwark stones of St Gregorius Theologus repelled the attacks of the rain but a cold wind had found its way in through the broken windows. It vented its anger upon the religious debris scattered over the floor. The fire he had built in the nave had long since been extinguished and Father Simeon shivered. His thin tunic offered little protection.

'The temptations . . . Oh, so many. When one is surrounded by . . .'

Now he was opening the bottom drawers of his

frustration, taking out mothballed stories of his youth he had almost forgotten.

'*You* should understand, Lord. There is always a Mary Magdalene to anoint one's feet.'

Even at his age, and with his eye injury, the evidence was there to support his thesis. Not only had he been the spiritual leader of his village but also the most handsome among the male members of his parish. And his sermons had never failed to induce a tear or two among the pious women. There had been numerous occasions . . . He stopped and raised a finger.

'But *I* never succumbed, Lord,' he said proudly.

The ingeniousness of his faith was that it somehow led to happiness through the denial of pleasure – and, even, through the espousal of pain. Father Simeon recalled how as a young cleric he used to practise self-flagellation, a crude but efficient way to purge his mind of sin. That was a very long time ago, of course. Since then he had developed the mental ability to catch the Devil's spies before they could infiltrate his deepest thoughts.

'All I want is to spread Your word to these heathens. And I need the gospel Bible to do it.'

Caleb yelped and pulled his muzzle out of the rat hole in the wall. His bark travelled across the nave, entered the narthex and a moment later was heard coming from the opposite end of the church. Enticed by the echo, the dog abandoned his game and trotted towards the altar, wagging his tail, expecting to find one of his kind there.

'I need that book, and the church and the icons,' Father Simeon said stubbornly. 'And I need the wine for the communion, and the oil, and the candles, and . . .'

He raised his eye to the mural far above his head: the eternal dome sat on an array of windows whose circle of light, even on such an overcast morning, made the austere face of the Pantocrator seem poised in mid-air.

'For what is faith without the power and the glory?' the padre asked Him.

He must have received a satisfying answer because soon he began to feel that his guilt was abandoning him, the way it had happened after the earliest thefts. No sooner did he pick up his greatcoat from the floor than a rat ran out of its sleeve and disappeared behind a pillar. Father Simeon held his coat up to the light: there were large holes across the chest and along the hemline.

'Virtue is like a rat. Precisely.'

Before putting it on, he shook the heavy garment to ensure it contained no other intruders. Then he put on his kepi. The weather did not seem to be easing its anger. Father Simeon was glad − it meant there would be fewer soldiers in the streets. He hushed the dog with a single word, cupped his hand behind his ear and listened attentively. Satisfied there was no one else in the building, he knelt down and lifted one of the heavy mosaic tiles. In a secret hole in the floor, wrapped in a piece of tarpaulin, were Brigadier Nestor's ceremonial sword and his riding boots with the silver spurs. He could not resist untying the string and having a quick glance before leaving. The shine of the polished metal and the expensive leather lit up his tired face – the precious Gospel would soon be his, without a doubt.

'Do you know who Zephyrus was, orderly?'

The young man shrugged his shoulders – he had no idea. Brigadier Nestor made his disappointment known with a series of nods.

'A pity when one doesn't know one's history. But almost a crime to be ignorant of one's mythology.'

His orderly's face lit like a red light; he continued polishing his commanding officer's belt and holster with a hard brush.

'Because mythology is more than history, son. It's also science. Take for example the west wind blasting us all morning. Our ancestors would say that Zephyrus was responsible for it. The son of a Titan and the goddess of the dawn. Also, he was married to Iris, goddess of the rainbow.'

Brigadier Nestor looked out: more clouds were gathering above the defenceless town. He pursed his lips.

'His brothers were Boreas and Notus,' he resumed with less enthusiasm. 'The gods of the north and south winds respectively.'

The boy finished the polishing and next began cleaning his superior's revolver. He stuffed an oiled handkerchief into a cartridge chamber, pulled it out of the other end and did the same in the other holes of the rotating cylinder. The inside of the barrel he cleaned with a worn toothbrush. He was meticulous in his task, which in actual fact he performed once a week despite the pistol having being used only once during the ill-fated expedition.

A long time had gone by but the young orderly still remembered the incident in all its terrifying sounds and brutal imagery. Frightened by a snake, one of the mules of the baggage train had thrown itself into a ditch, snapping its leg. Brigadier Nestor's lorry happened to be passing by and the old man had witnessed the accident. He had given the boy his pistol and the order to take care of the matter. It might have been easier to ask him to cut off one of his own fingers. Such had been the orderly's reaction that his comrades had turned the situation into a joke and anthologised it since in the echoing gossip that went the rounds of the bored brigade perpetually, without ever losing its capacity to amuse. He had hesitated when he had placed the muzzle on the suffering animal's forehead, and he had cried when he had finally pulled the trigger. The wide idiot's eyes of the mule, its enormous teeth, the desperate braying: it had been a cold-blooded assassination, no matter what everyone said.

Pensively, the soldier tended his superior's kit, while the brigadier continued to pace the room, absorbed in his mythological meditations.

'. . . Zephyrus was also a courier of the gods. If our ancestors were here today they would reason that this wind out there now carries a divine message.'

A bolt of lightning struck the rod on the roof of the Town Hall, making the windows shake. The young orderly cowered instinctively. The electric discharge seemed to rip open the canopy of the desert sky and a biblical downpour was unleashed. Suddenly Brigadier Nestor felt tired.

'This meteorological message probably says the gods

are not happy with the situation,' he said, rubbing his chin.

His orderly had worked hard to transform the abandoned conference room into a comfortable residence. The dust sheets had been removed, and the furniture had been polished until the wax had restored its nineteenth-century glory. The floor had been mopped and waxed too, the nails that stood up from the boards had been hammered back in and carpets had been brought from other rooms to clothe the majestic immensity.

'And neither am *I* happy,' the brigadier added. His breathing was getting heavier. 'Any news?'

It was the seventh time he had asked since he had woken. The seventh reply he received was also negative: no, Major Porfirio, who had been put in charge of the search for his boots and sword, had not yet returned. Brigadier Nestor waited nervously. He was convinced that the deserter – although the man denied it – had stolen and sold them, probably in return for instructions as to how to make it across the hills. Water dripped from the ceiling into pots placed across the room. The latest stolen items had no practical value, but they had always been of great sentimental importance to the senior officer. He had been presented with them at his graduation from the Military Academy, he told his orderly again, one of the happiest days of his life.

'The year was 1881,' the brigadier said in a melancholy voice. 'I was twenty-one.'

Since he liked to imagine his illustrious career as an orchestral symphony, that would have been its overture. Likewise, the Anatolian retreat threatened to become its dishonourable finale — but maybe the unscrupulous journalist could help him write a last-minute heroic coda . . .

Anyway, at the graduation ceremony, he reminisced aloud in the presence of his orderly, he had shaken the hands of his tutors, saluted the generals attending, kissed the hem of the flag and delivered a valedictory speech of such patriotic fervour that it had roused his fellow graduates. Just one look at his graduation uniform had always been enough to remind him of that glorious afternoon. Suddenly Brigadier Nestor's eyes darkened and he interrupted his happy narrative.

'My hound ate the aigrette only a few months later,' he said.

It had been the first of a series of accidents that, little by little, had ruined his dashing outfit. Brigadier Nestor recounted the others for his orderly's benefit.

'One year I forgot to spread camphor in the wardrobe and the moths drilled into the tunic and trousers without mercy — in the autumn I gave them to our gardener to dress the scarecrow. And the last time I was home from Anatolia, my grandson thought the cap was a chamber pot.'

The young soldier finished his chores. Brigadier Nestor put on his belt, picked up his revolver and unexpectedly placed its muzzle to his temple; he could smell the lubricant.

'If I am not mistaken, the last time this pistol was used was to deliver a mule from its torment. Sometimes I feel it will be next used for a similar reason.'

He squeezed the trigger. The empty cylinder turned and the hammer hit with a dull sound.

'Maybe,' the old man said and searched for bullets.

By the time he placed the loaded pistol in its holster he had also charged his optimism a little. On the edge of the conference table lay the communist pamphlet found on the corporal; the brigadier riffled through it.

'So. If it weren't for Cerberus[*] that Bolshevik would have slipped away right under our noses.'

'Caleb, my brigadier.'

Brigadier Nestor nodded.

'That canine deserves a decoration for extreme vigilance.'

The rain continued but with less intensity. The brigadier walked up to the window and stood watching the rain with his hands clasped behind his back. Heavy clouds hovered over the tiled roofs, but beyond the limits of the town the sky had cleared and the sun was already drying the hills. Feeling as if his feet were made of stone, the old man collapsed in one of the leather armchairs.

'We've stayed here too long,' he said with a sigh. 'To avoid smelling your feet you must keep moving.'

In actual fact they had arrived in the town only a few days earlier. The lorry repairs were almost finished, the animals had rested, and enough provisions had been requisitioned to last the final march to the sea – the brigade was going to be on its way soon. The orderly left the room, only to return a minute later and inform his superior that the air lieutenant was there to see

---

[*]Cerberus was a dog with three heads and a dragon for a tail that guarded the entrance to the underworld.

him. Brigadier Nestor remembered the appointment with misery.

'Give me a moment.'

It was time for his dose. That morning, without even getting out of bed, he had reached for the old cigar box under his cot and filled the syringe. Over the past few days his chemical desire had increased steadily. It seemed as if a fire had broken out in his viscera that threatened to consume his heart unless he constantly flooded his veins with morphia. At present, the quantity he required to retain his sanity doubled every other day and the frequency of the administrations tripled. But even so, at night his mind would still travel back to the massacre – it seemed to come to him more vividly nowadays, the horror of his decision. In addition, his fascination with classical mythology had spawned a new and peculiar nightmare: every time he blew out the lamp Brigadier Nestor braced himself for the assault of the Furies. And sure enough, every night they would come. The three avenging deities would ascend from the underworld to pursue him without mercy, their wings flapping, the snakes in their hair writhing, their eyes dripping blood. All night they would torment him, lashing him with whips and burning him with torches.

By now he had given up sterilising the needle over the burner. Brigadier Nestor pulled it from his vein and sank in an armchair. He let the empty syringe slip out of his torpid hand and watched as it rolled away on the polished floor. Outside the rain still menaced the town. Under his skin the drug galloped. He recalled the séance he had attended the previous evening – what had the

Armenian seer said? *Some vultures circle above your head; others walk alongside you.*

'That Black Sea witch was right,' he muttered.

He remained in the armchair motionless and exhausted for what seemed like a great length of time. When he turned his eyes to the clock on the wall he discovered that only a few minutes had passed. He waited patiently while the drug inflated his mood even further; then he shouted in the direction of the door. Promptly the airman entered.

'Come, lieutenant. But I'm afraid I have very little time – an interrogation to take care of. I guess you've heard.'

The young officer saluted and removed his cap.

'The arrest, yes.'

Brigadier Nestor remained seated. He hit his fist on the arm of his chair with bravura.

'Indeed. Enough is enough. It was about time I cleaned my bed of ticks.'

'Your bed?'

'The brigade, son. Of criminal elements.'

The airman nodded.

'It's a happy coincidence. That's exactly the reason I have come to see you – the extermination of ticks.'

Thanks to the drug Brigadier Nestor was euphoric.

'The atheist Bolshevik attempting to hide in the church. How's that for an irony?'

Air Lieutenant Kimon was anxious now to share his knowledge.

'Divine justice, brigadier.'

'Because the padre is a buttress against corruption,' continued the senior officer. 'Sometimes, I admit, he gets on my nerves, but overall he is an indispensable part of this unit. Both he and the dog.'

'Caleb?'

'Cerberus,' the brigadier corrected him. 'He smelled the Bolshevik from a mile away. If the Tsar had a few like him he would still be lounging in Yalta. What was it that you wanted to see me about?'

The airman came closer; his excitement made him tremble a little.

'I may have a piece of information that could be of some relevance to the case.'

Brigadier Nestor raised his eyebrows and haltered his euphoria.

'Right. Enlighten me, lieutenant.'

At last the airman released the poison of his secret. When he had finished he felt a sense of relief. There was a jug of water on the vast conference table. After being granted permission, he filled a glass from it and gulped it down.

Brigadier Nestor's first reaction was not to believe him.

'Porfirio? An officer of his abilities? Impossible.'

'I saw him free the horse with my own eyes, brigadier. I have twenty-twenty vision – certified.'

'But you cannot be certain. The rainstorm, the night . . .'

The airman stood stiff as a statue; he was not trembling any more.

'It was him.'

While Brigadier Nestor twisted the tip of his moustache in silence, the morphia stirred the contents of his brain like a ladle. Suddenly another of the seer's warnings popped to the surface: *A plain tunic conceals the truth well; one with insignia does it better.* At once the brigadier felt as if he were sinking in quicksand, and his hands gripped the arms of the easy chair impulsively.

'*Et tu, Brute?*' he whispered. 'I must be senile not to have seen it.'

Indeed: the regular appearances of the inflammatory handbills, the absence of witnesses regarding the thefts. Being his Chief of Staff the major could easily have entered his lorry without suspicion. And the diversion he had created by claiming that his own wine and razor had been stolen, too – those internationalists were a shrewd bunch. Brigadier Nestor had solved the mystery that plagued his command. After such a long time – the handbill inquiry had been going on for almost three years – he would have expected to feel triumphant. Instead, his feelings were akin to those on the day of his daughter's wedding: a strange sense of loss. The major was a kind of son to him, the one his precious wife had failed to honour him with, he thought. And now . . . Could Porfirio be the leader of the Bolshevik conspiracy within the ranks? He called his orderly.

'Send the patrol to arrest Porfirio,' he ordered gloomily. 'And search his quarters inch by inch.'

The rain granted the town a short reprieve. The wind died away and the clouds anchored over the roofs of the town, laden and quiet, like a fleet of men-of-war with their gun ports open. Now was the time for the townspeople to run their errands. A human torrent clogged the muddy streets: men with skinned carcasses over their shoulders, sacks of potatoes or bundles of firewood; women holding live chickens tied by their feet; and among them a pair of newlyweds carrying an iron bedstead over their heads. The stench of the flooded sewer covered the smells of the market but no one seemed to notice. But the armistice of the weather did not last. Mr Othon was on his way to the *hamam* when the rain restarted with a thunderous broadside. The crowd immediately scattered. In the panic of the retreat, the schoolmaster found shelter under the awning of the grocery. Leaning on a broom, the Armenian watched the rain from the door of his shop.

'If this continues much longer only an ark will save us,' he said.

The schoolmaster wrung out his drenched hat.

'This is the worst autumn in living memory. And the storm isn't over yet – when I left home the barometer was still falling.'

The grocer crossed himself.

'Lord, help us. Maybe the Adventist was right, after all.'

He was referring to the American pastor who during the Great War had stayed briefly in town on his way to Mesopotamia. He was a young man of worldly elegance and so much wisdom for his age that one could be forgiven for mistaking it for arrogance. He had told the people that he was an amateur archaeologist who dreamed of discovering the Tower of Babel, but spent more time preaching the tenets of his denomination than planning his search. He believed in the Second Coming of the Lord Jesus Christ, which he insisted was imminent, and in the observance of Saturday as the Sabbath. When one evening the towns-people invited him to a dance he looked at them with a disapproving stare and said that that was an activity second in wickedness only to theatregoing. Another time he had explained to the schoolmaster how the human body was the temple of the Holy Ghost and therefore one should refrain from eating meat and smoking tobacco. The latter, whose idea of nirvana was a morning spent in the *hamam* followed by a full *narghile* and a large plate of *fricassée de poulet* from Violetta's hands, had not forgotten the man either.

'I still believe he was a spy for the Allied Powers,' he said.

He sat on the creaking bench outside the grocery and began to knead his crumpled white hat back into shape – it had been a birthday present from Violetta and it could not but recall her to him now. But his happy reminiscence was obscured by the shadow of a heavy cloud: he would never forgive the mayor.

'That Anatolian Beau Brummell! The hell with him.'

The rain streamed down the awning. The dirt street was a thick swamp where empty pallets and barrels floated, and the broken wheel of a cart. Further up on the opposite bank of the swamp someone was trying to find a crossing. The more he searched the more the rain kept coming down and the swamp turned into a faster torrent flowing towards the town square. Suddenly he plunged into the turbulent current, but what he believed to be a shoal was in fact a floating plank and he began to sink in the mud.

'Help!' he cried.

The grocer and the schoolmaster had been watching his frustrated attempts with bemusement.

'Fool,' Mr Othon said. 'He'll have the honour of being the first man to drown this year.'

The man struggled to stay on the surface of the violent torrent. He grabbed the floating plank that had lured him in, but had to let it go after a moment because it was leading him away.

'Help me, good Christians!' he cried again, choking.

'He is talking to you, grocer,' said the schoolmaster. 'I haven't said the Lord's Prayer in eleven years.'

The Armenian rushed to the steps of his shop and held out his broom. With a desperate effort, the drowning man managed to swim a few feet and reach the salvation of the broomstick. The grocer and the schoolmaster helped him out of the deadly mud and sat him on the veranda of the grocery. It was not until they wiped the mud off his face that they recognised him: it was the padre.

'Thank you, my brethren,' he said when he got his breath back. 'I've been making a habit lately of almost perishing in your waters.'

He was shivering. The Armenian brought the brandy bottle.

'Did you mistake this swamp for the Red Sea of Exodus, Father?'

Father Simeon drank the alcohol.

'God knows, my powers are nothing like Moses'.'

The red-striped canvas over their heads was filling with rain; the padre looked at it with mistrust.

'The weather is after me like a hound.'

The grocer pushed the awning with the broomstick

and it emptied on to the street. Then he returned inside the shop to inspect the leaks in the roof.

'One day man will be able to change the weather at will,' said the schoolmaster.

The padre had another sip of brandy.

'Impossible. The skies are the realm of the Lord.'

'There have already been experiments of limited success – dynamite attached to balloons detonated in the clouds to induce precipitation.'

Father Simeon gave him a sidelong glance.

'You sound like a heretic.'

'No; like a scientist.'

The padre puffed; science again. Even in that desolate place that God Himself threatened to abandon, science had crawled in. He wanted to leave the shelter but the torrent forbade him.

'You are not going to tell me that you believe the theories of that German too?' he asked.

Mr Othon moved a little on the bench to avoid a drip from the awning.

'I would, if I could understand them myself. Einstein is without a doubt the greatest scientist since Newton – perhaps even greater than him.'

The padre slammed his brandy glass on the floor.

'Newton was an enlightened Christian, not some mystical Semite!'

Mr Othon contemplated the wet bearded man sitting with him on the veranda with wonder. He could not help but feel he had come across a prehistoric fossil. A moment later a raft with armed soldiers passed in front of the grocery and interrupted his thoughts. Navigating with the help of a long pole, they approached the veranda and asked Father Simeon whether he had seen the major that day. The padre seized the opportunity to ask a favour. He had not met him, but would they take him back to the church? The patrol said they were on an important mission that could not wait but agreed to put him down on the first bit of dry land.

It took him a long time to reach home. By midday the whole town seemed to be sinking into the swamp that overflowed with litter, drowned animals and the excrement of the open sewer. When he finally climbed the steps of St Gregorius Theologus, Father Simeon was exhausted and wet to the bone. He let out a sigh of relief but it quickly proved a premature reaction. No sooner had he opened the heavy door than he was confronted with a repulsive spectacle: the rain had flooded the bowels of the church and the floor was carpeted with the corpses of thousands of rats. Quietly, the padre closed the door again and squeezed himself under the narrow eaves outside. Protected from the rain, he unbuttoned his tunic. The parcel was wrapped in several layers of tarpaulin, which he began to remove with trepidation. After a few wet sheets the rest were dry – thank God. Holding the precious medieval gospel close to his heart, he waited for the storm to pass – it should not be long: beyond the town the weather had already cleared and a faint rainbow was running across the sky.

CHAPTER 7

The creaking of the bed almost lulled her. From the direction of the garden came the chirping of birds bathing in the rainwater of the brimming cistern. As was her habit on such occasions she stirred her eyes lazily across the walls. But a strange thing happened today: the row of tall meridian windows seemed to shed new light on the room. She was surprised to discover from where she lay several details she had not hitherto noticed: secret chinks in the polished wooden floor, microscopic holes in the delicate web of the drapery, green rust on the brass hinges of the oak door. It was not until she raised her eyes to the high ceiling that her innocent curiosity turned into sadness: the slow crumbling of the stucco relief had also gone unnoticed for quite some time.

It was a work of baroque extravagance, one of the unexpected pleasures that had been installed in the house for the sole purpose of indulging the artistic whims of its occupants and guests. Others were the spiral staircase with the carved handrail, the magnificent marble floor of the downstairs salon and the modest fountain with urinating cherubs in the garden. She contemplated the ceiling. Under layers of thick cobweb emerged acanthus leaves, birds with broken beaks, headless gypsum snakes, monkeys whose tails had fallen off. She felt as if she were not in her bedroom but in a public space – a theatre perhaps or the waiting room of a railway station. Her sentiment was as new as it was unsettling . . . For the first time in her life Violetta questioned the purpose of her situation.

While she did, the bedstead continued to creak. It was made of galvanised steel tubes, primed and painted white, so that placed against the wall it seemed like a berthed dreadnought. The frame supported a red mattress whose springs also creaked to the rhythm; every time the heavy bedpost hit the wall it brought down more flakes of plaster. For a while Violetta listened to the noise and then spoke up.

'What a pity this house ended up a brothel. It is even grander than your old church.'

Panting and heaving, the mayor paused and wiped the sweat off his brow; he was wearing only his string vest and his socks. Somewhere under the rest of his clothes scattered over the floor was a copy of the Kama Sutra. When he found the heavy volume he studied a different illustration and tried again.

'Impossible,' he said after a while with exasperation. 'This is a great book, but it suffers from a bad translation.'

He remembered a contortionist he had watched once at the Armenian circus who could twist himself into extraordinary positions.

'It would be easier to tie myself up into the Gordian Knot.'*

---

*Gordius was a peasant who became king of Phrygia after an oracle had said to select as ruler the first person to drive into town in a

He had come across the rare manuscript in the municipal library during one of his periodic attempts to clean up the room. He had only had to leaf through it to discover that he had been leading a life of unbearable triteness. He had immediately signed the book out on permanent loan to himself and did not omit to bring it along every time he paid Violetta a visit. But his efforts to taste ecstasy had met with very limited success. Conceding defeat once again, he now lay next to his lover and let out a deep sigh. Violetta repeated her comment about the church.

'That place is a rat-hole,' the mayor replied wearily.

Soaked in the sweat of his earnest but futile efforts, his cotton vest stuck to his chest. Underneath, his lungs felt like a pair of deflated balloons and he started to take in deep breaths. In the garden, the birds chirped happily.

'How come I've never seen a rat in *your* house?' he asked between gulps.

'The cat,' answered Violetta absent-mindedly. 'Yusuf brings her over a couple of times a week for a small fee.'

The mayor hit his fist on the iron bedstead.

'Damn Turk. So that is what he does when he's supposed to be fumigating her ticks. If there was law in this town I would have him arrested for embezzlement.'

---

wagon. King Gordius dedicated his wagon to Zeus and placed it in the grove of the god's temple, tying the pole of the wagon to the yoke with a rope of bark. The knot was so complex that no one could undo it. According to legend, whoever succeeded in untying the knot would become the ruler of all Asia. Many tried but failed. When Alexander the Great also failed to untie it, he drew his sword and cut it through.

The woman rolled her head on her pillow and looked in the direction of the windows. The buoyancy of the breeze lifted the long drapes off the floor and caused their flaxen fishnet fabric to ripple. Violetta thought of the sea; she had not been to the coast for years. A competent swimmer, she used to spend summers on the Côte d'Azur when she lived in France, where she swam an entire nautical mile in the nude every morning before breakfast. From the hotel terrace she would later watch for hours the foam of the gentle undulations, the diving seagulls, the sailing boats travelling across the horizon.

'*Enfant,*' she recalled sentimentally, '*je croyais que leurs voiles étaient les ailes d'un ange en train de se baigner.*'

Next to her the mayor was still on the subject of the cat.

'Besides, that animal is for the rodent control of *municipal* buildings. Any private user should first lodge an application with the office of sanitation – and pay the appropriate fee. What did you say?'

Violetta's silk kimono was on its hanger next to the bed. Abandoning her reminiscence, she stretched her plump white arm to reach it, put it on and propped herself up on the pillows.

'The office of sanitation is the closet where you keep the mop and bucket,' she said, tying the ribbon of the oriental robe about her waist. '*N'est-ce pas?*'

The mayor offered a grunt in place of an articulate reply. Bathed in sweat as he was, the breeze made him shiver a little. But he knew his lover liked to keep the windows of her bedroom open and he did not complain. He began to finger the ribbon of her kimono.

'Have I told you the story of this garment?' he asked amorously.

In fact he had, countless times. The kimono was among the spoils of an infamous game of poker, which had begun on a pleasant evening years before in an exclusive Smyrna hotel, and had lasted twenty-one hours and seventeen minutes. The final round had turned into a bloody duel between the mayor and the captain of a merchant vessel that had just arrived from the Far East. The latter was a bearded giant with cardinal cheeks, a sexual passion for card games and more mettle than actual wealth. A cabin boy he had brought along to the game in order to mix him the sensual cocktails he had first tried in Shanghai and Macao had soon been ordered to carry over from the ship anything that could be bet on the fateful game. Soon a treasure was piled up both on the table and the floor around it, the likes of which one could only have seen in the hold of a Barbary corsair. Among other items were a bag of silver coins, a concertina with a smiling turbaned face painted on its folded bellows, a scrimshaw opium pipe, said kimono (an article of great associative value to the captain, because it used to belong to a geisha who had taught him the pleasures of poetry or the poetry of pleasure – the mayor could not remember which), two human heads bought from the aborigines on the island of Borneo and the ship's gyrocompass in its brass casing. That accurate instrument had been a most unwise stake, the mayor told Violetta. A week after the momentous game the vessel had hit shoals in the Red Sea and slowly sunk. All the crew had managed to abandon ship apart from the captain, who had gone down with it in the time-honoured manner, cursing geophysics until the last moment: he had never understood adequately how to correct the readings of his pocket compass for magnetic declination. The mayor had read all about the tragedy in the news, without being able to suppress his sense of guilt. Back in the game, when all this was still known only by the Fates, the last drops of the mariner's courage had finally been squeezed out of him when the mayor had laid on the green table the shares of the Co-operative Association. The captain had dropped out. A moment later his dismay had transformed into lunacy when the mayor had cruelly showed him his hand, a measly pair of deuces to the captain's mighty full house. The mayor had to hire three horse-drawn carts to carry his winnings back to the town, which he had then stored in the impregnable vaults of the Town Hall and gradually offloaded.

Violetta sighed; the retelling of the story bored her. Besides, there was something else on her mind.

'What will they do to that man?' she asked.

At first the mayor did not understand whom she was referring to.

'It's two men now – they arrested the major yesterday, too.' He ran his hand over his belly. 'I used to think of him as a nice fellow. But he turned out to be a communist conspirator.'

His pocket watch was on the commode next to the bed; he opened its gold cover and read the time.

'I have to leave. Nothing in this town moves without me pushing it.' Then he noted his lover's anxiety. 'Don't worry, my dear. The brigadier is a reasonable man.

Othon is harder on his students than the old man on his soldiers. They suffered enough, what with the retreat and the desert.'

He started to gather his clothes from the floor and put them on without brushing off the dust. He dressed with a child's gratifying abandon when he is beyond the reach of maternal strictures.

'Can one see them?' Violetta asked.

Her lover stopped whistling and frowned.

'I don't think they would have the time to receive visitors. They should be occupied with the interrogation.'

'Interrogation . . . Will they be treated violently?'

The mayor resumed whistling. Looking in the mirror of the dressing table, he tied the knot of his striped necktie.

'I have no doubt the brigadier will use his full powers of persuasion,' he said when he was done with the knot. He buttoned up his shirt and contemplated his reflection. 'I need a new collar.'

Violetta put her arm under her head.

'Send the shirt over. Annina will do it for you.'

The sun came out briefly and then disappeared again, leaving the memory of summer behind. The mayor sat on the edge of the bed to tie up his laces when the words prodded him over his back:

'Maybe I should take them some food.'

The mayor paused – he was confused.

'Who?'

'The prisoners.'

He went back to tying his laces.

'Oh, I am sure they're well looked after.'

Violetta said, 'Even the church rats eat better than those soldiers.'

The mayor curled his lip. He turned and touched that little bit of her shoulder that emerged from the covers before it vanished under her fierce scarlet hair. Her locks looked like a bush set on fire but her skin was cold. It was the contradictions of her body that captivated the mayor's senses. They had been together for some time now, but making love with her still made him feel like an explorer travelling through an uncharted territory.

'Listen, my dear. We are civilians. Even *I* have no authority over —'

A small songbird with brown wings and an ash-grey breast had arrived at one of the windows. Violetta put her finger to her lips and hushed her fiancé. He, in turn, gave the newcomer an indifferent look before hooking the chain of his watch on his waistcoat and putting on his hat. Having chirped a few notes the bird flew off the sill again.

'*Jolie*,' Violetta sighed. '*Que fais tu dans ce désert?*'

The mayor thought he understood.

'I love you too, very much. But I do have to go. Duty calls.'

He kissed her on the forehead. As soon as the door closed Violetta felt as if a large redundant piece of furniture had been taken out of her room — the truth was that she did not love him any more. Her thought returned to the two army men. The major she remembered well as her customer — a proud and courteous man, if somewhat detached, with a predilection for self-satisfaction she had often noted over the years in the priests among her clientele. Had he spent time at the seminary? she wondered. On the other hand, she was uncertain whether she had offered her services to the corporal. That meant nothing, of course; there had been so many soldiers . . . She would have felt a professional pride now if it were not for that sinister premonition of late.

'*La mort*,' she murmured, lying in the damp bed of her lucrative craft. '*Elle nous suit comme l'ombre de l'après-midi*.'

When the soldiers smashed the lock and stepped into the room they had the impression they were entering a monastic cell. The major's chosen quarters were an abandoned attic with a low ceiling and a sole circular window. He had arranged his cot so that the light of dawn would wake him as soon as the sun rose above the hills. For the rest of the day the room would slowly descend to an arctic dusk made all the obscurer by the sloped roof, and one could only navigate with the help of a bright lamp. They found neither the sword nor the pair of boots with the silver spurs, but they did notice a pair of loose floorboards, and when they lifted them they discovered the crate filled with books and the ancient mimeograph the Chief of Staff used to print the handbills. They had barely had time to congratulate themselves before the door opened and Major Porfirio walked in. Calmly, he raised his arms, and there was no sign of surprise in his eyes whatsoever.

In the Town Hall Brigadier Nestor awaited the return of the soldiers with a nervousness that had put him in a continuous orbit round the conference table. Several times he halted to check his watch, but such was his preoccupation that his eyes did not register the time. Nor could he abstain from the poison of the recent revelations, which he drank with abandon. For the corporal he cared not; a deserter was a coward whether the army was in retreat or not – it was discipline that had kept them alive so far. And let themselves not forget: they were not safe yet. The enemy could still be pursuing them. It was imperative then that he make an example of the corporal. Besides, thousands had died so far; one more . . . The floor creaked under his polished boots.

But his indifference and military reason seemed to run out when he considered his Chief of Staff's fate. He murmured, 'Damn you, Porfirio. The last thing I needed was another ghost hovering over my grave.' He coughed. 'But even if I have to have it, why does it have to be yours?' He began to feel nauseous and a moment later his left foot fell out of step with the right and he had to grab the table to steady himself. As he leaned over, his morning coffee poured out of his mouth and on to the polished surface. He looked at the vomit dispassionately and did not attempt to clean it up – he had come to terms with the consequences of his disease a long time ago. He pulled a chair closer and landed on it with a sigh; he had attempted to exorcise his morphia addiction several times since the beginning of the withdrawal but its arsenal of symptoms had defeated him. Diarrhoea, sleeplessness and fever had all been thrown upon him without mercy. And then the pain: his bones, his muscles, his abdomen . . . The medic had warned him that it would be difficult. It had proved, in fact, impossible. Bowing to his disease's wishes once again, he shouted through the closed door that he did not wish to be disturbed, and did the short walk to his trunk where the tools of his torment lay hidden.

Some time later he opened his eyes and looked out of the window: a group of soldiers was crossing the square in a brisk manner. Walking among them with his hands tied behind his back but his head held high was his Chief of Staff. Still delirious, Brigadier Nestor imagined that his heart was a pincushion where life had stuck countless needles; some were many years old, others more recent: the village massacre for example, or his wife's death and the collapse of the front. Now another was being pushed in, one that bore Porfirio's name. There was a knock on the door.

'I said, I don't want to be disturbed!'

His orderly informed him that the major had been arrested and that a variety of evidence had been seized. Brigadier Nestor asked him to bring it in. His orderly set the crate with the books and the mimeograph on the floor. Before leaving he noticed the vomit on the floor, but his superior's stare pushed him out of the door. A moment later there was another knock.

The old man puffed impatiently, 'What now?'

Instead of his orderly's voice he recognised that regional accent in the reply.

He groaned. 'Demon of my soul . . .'

After hiding the syringe he raised his voice and conceded.

'Come in, my friend.'

It was indeed the journalist. He entered, rubbing his hands with exhilaration.

'Dramatic developments, my brigadier. What more could we have asked for!'

His arrival was like the entry of a new character on stage, entrusted with moving the plot forward. But if this were acting he was an untalented artist, for his role exuded more vulgarity than pathos. Brigadier Nestor felt a sensation not dissimilar to an empty stomach. The tin cigar box with his hypodermic syringe and the morphia was on his lap; he squeezed it involuntarily.

But the war correspondent was not acting – he was genuinely happy about the arrests. He began to explain how the two conspirators would add the necessary vigour to the articles he was preparing for the press. His argument was without doubt intelligent and of great importance – the senior officer could tell that much. But Brigadier Nestor's heavy intoxication, as well as his paternal grief over his Chief of Staff's perfidy, were all his mind could accommodate at that moment. The journalist noticed the old man's indisposition.

'My brigadier? Are you well?'

Brigadier Nestor rubbed his eyes.

'It's nothing – only homesickness.'

'Then it should be cured soon. And your arrival in the capital will be nothing short of a Roman triumph.'

'A triumph?' The old man raised his eyebrows. 'But we have been defeated.'

Now the other man took a seat, as if the words he was about to say were too heavy to bear standing.

'The Nation mourns, of course . . . This campaign has indeed been a disaster.'

Suddenly he waved the thought aside with his hand and regained his earlier buoyancy.

'But that is for my colleagues on the political pages to discuss,' he said smiling. '*My* personal concern is the human factor.' He slammed his palm on the table. 'And *I* declare your adventure a triumph of the human spirit!'

The brigadier was both impressed by the abrupt shift in the other man's tone of voice and also a little frightened.

'It will be impossible to find much glory in our story – unless you are a writer of fiction.'

'Ah, modesty. It always hints at a great man.' The journalist took out a notebook and made a note. 'Have you realised the parallels between your journey and that of Xenophon's Ten Thousand?'

'The *Anabasis*? That was an extraordinary feat. We are not worthy of such a comparison.'

The journalist smiled again with infinite tolerance and returned his notebook to his pocket.

'Who really knows what happened back then? Given time and a good narrative people will believe you could circumnavigate the globe on the back of a dolphin.'

'Lack of evidence also helps,' the senior officer added.

His reason was coming back at last. The injection had given him some euphoria, but recently there had been a change – after such a long acquaintance with the drug, he could tell that the sense of tranquillity that followed every use like the rainbow after a shower evaporated ever sooner. As a matter of fact, today it had gone unnoticed. What underworld was he going to enter now? And if not the morphia, what would pull him out of it, even temporarily? The journalist took out his Kodak from the pocket of his jacket.

'This invention has put myths to rest,' he said. 'Its evidence is indisputable.'

Brigadier Nestor contemplated the camera with scorn.

'A fine piece of equipment. As useful to the journalist as to the pornographer.'

That infinitely kind smile again.

'Now now, my brigadier. Do not let your dejection blind your judgement. You still ought to be able to tell a friend from a foe.'

The brigadier did not fail to see the threat. But what could this minion threaten him with? He decided to ignore the comment.

'Myths are wild beasts,' Brigadier Nestor said. 'They normally live in an exotic wilderness, but we educated people only encounter them in the cage.'

He stood and balanced himself before walking to his cot. Under his pillow was his *Lexicon of Greek and Roman Myths*. He brought it back and placed it on the table. The war correspondent gave it an impatient look.

'My myths are kept under lock and key,' the brigadier said and tapped the cover. He raised his finger and aimed it at the journalist. 'But you, friend, want to let them loose.'

The journalist tried flattery.

'The story of this brigade will one day be taught in schools.'

Brigadier Nestor recalled his grandson. He wondered: will I ever see him again?

'There are enough lies in the curriculum already.'

It was time for the journalist to use his bloodiest weapon. He put down his camera on the conference table, took out his notebook again and turned its yellowed pages ostentatiously.

'In your case, my brigadier, truth would be an even fiercer beast than myth.'

His patience had been exhausted. After closing his notebook and placing it next to the camera, he began. He said he had already interviewed several soldiers for his articles and they had all extolled the brigadier's leadership. They believed they owed him their lives. They knew what fate many an army unit had met following the collapse of the front. Why, the journalist was of the opinion that their devotion was not dissimilar to that of the praetorians of ancient times. Brigadier Nestor listened to the praise with increasing suspicion. He possessed the elementary wisdom to know that it was being handed out too generously to be honest – and he was not mistaken.

'And many have told me,' the war correspondent said, 'that surrender is not an option.'

An arrow pierced the brigadier's chest.

'One can never trust the enemy to treat prisoners of war according to the international treaties,' he said nervously. 'Surrender is not a decision to be taken lightly.'

The journalist nodded.

'Especially those responsible for the massacre of civilians. One could understand the degree of anger, the desire for revenge . . .'

'I said nothing about any massacre,' the brigadier snapped, and reached for the notebook. 'It's enemy propaganda — whom did you talk to?'

But the war correspondent was faster. He hid the notebook in the inside pocket of his jacket.

'A journalist never reveals his sources, my brigadier. Basic rule of my profession.'

The brigadier lacked the strength to sneer at the lesson in ethics.

'That is sensitive military information,' he mumbled. 'It's not to be disclosed . . . It never happened.'

It was a vague defence. As during battle, he knew when he was beaten. Brigadier Nestor stood and paced around the room in silence.

'What will the punishment of the conspirators be?' asked the journalist.

The brigadier went to the crate. He picked up one of the major's books and turned to the contents page.

'Thirty-three lashes? One for every chapter of *Das Kapital*?'

Humour was not one of the journalist's strengths.

'Consider your reputation. They will have to be tried here and the sentence carried out.'

'That could wait until we returned home — a proper court-martial.'

'No. It is of paramount importance. Consider the discipline of the troops. What will happen if others decide to follow their example, or if they escape?'

The senior officer shrugged.

'Let them all go to Hell.'

'And we don't know how extensive the clandestine network is — what if their comrades attempt to free them?'

Brigadier Nestor collapsed in an armchair.

'It would jeopardise the rescue of the whole brigade,' continued the journalist. 'We cannot take any chances.'

Brigadier Nestor buried his head in his hands: the bombardment had begun to weaken his defences.

'What do you want from me?'

The war correspondent stood up and walked over to where the old man had been shipwrecked.

'Only to make you immortal, my brigadier.' He touched him on the shoulder. 'Besides, taking those men home would only prolong their torment. The court-martial will not be any more lenient.'

This was also true. But it subtracted nothing from the fact that the brigadier would be staining his hands with his favoured comrade's blood.

'A trait of human nature,' Brigadier Nestor said. 'What a criminal a man who has never pulled a trigger can be.' He rose to his feet. 'So be it. I will suffer Tantalus' punishment.'[*] He went to the anteroom and

---

[*]Tantalus was the king of Lydia and son of Zeus. When the gods once came to dine at his palace he decided to test their omniscience by killing his only son and serving him at the banquet. Realising the nature of the food, the gods restored his son to life and devised a terrible punishment for the king. He was hung for ever from a tree in the underworld and afflicted with tormenting thirst and hunger. Under him was a pool of water, but when he stooped to drink the pool would sink from sight. The tree above him was laden with fruit, but when he reached for it the wind blew the branches away.

told his orderly: 'Clean up my quarters and find me four officers for court-martial duty.'

The distant sound of the military drums on the evening the brigade had arrived in town had made Violetta's skin crawl. Only she and her maid knew the reason for her morbid sensation. It was a secret she had kept locked in her memory for many years, and one she had not even shared with her indefatigable confessor, the late priest of St Gregorius Theologus.

Paris had been the arena of her fame. How she arrived there and from where, even she had almost forgotten. Once she had been admitted into the Babylon of the *belle époque* with its overnight parties, its busy cafés, the proliferation of couture houses and variety shows, she set about excelling in every facet of society. She received more invitations to exclusive functions than the talented artists of the day contracted venereal diseases, and she attended them all – often two or three on the same evening, when her trim black landaulet (a present from an early admirer) could be seen rushing down the cobbled boulevards. It was not vanity that fuelled her glamorous style of life but common sense: in her profession one had to make a name for oneself, and fast.

It had worked because in addition to her enterprising brain she had a physique to match, and she quickly built a large enough fortune to emancipate herself from the prejudices of a patriarchal society. Alas, Paris had also turned out to be the scene of her downfall. It began when she violated the foremost principle of her occupation: she fell for one of her clients. It was inexcusable, even when taking into account the dashing appearance of the man in question: the silver moustache that joined the fertile sideburns, the dome of the well-fed belly, the manicured fingernails, the infinite wardrobe.

At any rate, it had been a phantasmagoria of an affair, when Chinese fireworks went off at any pretext (their first candlelit dinner, their first month together, his first gift of a diamond necklace), *bals masqués* for a thousand guests were organised at the drop of a hat, weekends spent in the country, artists commissioned to paint Violetta's portrait (she favoured one done by a Fauve, because it extolled her unabashed curves). But the fantasy ended when in a moment of weakness she had the imprudence to declare him the love of her life.

He exercised his acquired rights to abuse her with ardour. She could not even smile at anyone without receiving later at home as many slaps across the face as the number of smiles she had dispensed that day, while listening to her master's assorted fulminations. Violetta endured these and other more serious and humiliating punishments for a year. Then, on the evening of their first anniversary, sporting a black eye and a broken rib, she left the bedroom of her tormentor, went down to the reception, picked up the bronze bust of Voltaire, hero of the Enlightenment, from its gypsum pedestal and carried it back to her room, where she brought it down several times upon the head of the last man she would ever truly love.

One would think such a brute would hardly be missed. But Violetta knew he was going to be, because he happened to be a junior government minister. The following morning she announced the news to Annina.

'If I were honest with myself,' she had said without remorse, 'I would have cracked my own thick skull, and a long time ago. For falling in love.'

Neither of the women ever mentioned his name again. They buried him in the garden and the same evening they left Paris. Before the week was over they had sailed from Marseilles, on an odyssey that finally brought them to the small Anatolian town. There Violetta lived beyond the reach of the police but not of her nightmares. Many a night she would hear the beat of a phantasmal drum and then see at the far end of her room the shadow of the *guillotine*.

She had developed an extreme aversion to executions. She could not read about one in the news without her hand starting to shake and her throat becoming dry: the name on the page could well have been hers. Accordingly, when she heard of the arrest of the two soldiers, she vowed to help them in any way she could. It was perhaps a sense of unusual camaraderie that drove her, but definitely not atonement, for after all these years she still felt no remorse for her crime.

She knew that the padre of the brigade had taken up residence in the abandoned church. Given the mayor's refusal to help her, the army priest was her only other hope. Thus, she took the road to St Gregorius Theologus filled with suspense – it was not going to be an easy mission. She had prepared for it with the utmost care: a delicate lilac gown with a high neck and long pleated sleeves, plus a wide cummerbund and matching gloves, while she had managed to subdue her scandalous hair only by employing six combs and eleven pins. When she had finished she inspected herself in the dressing-table mirror. Deciding that her assumed modesty was so overdone that it could impede rather than assist her cause – padres, too, were men, after all – she applied a few subtle strokes of vermilion to her pneumatic lips. Now she was ready for battle.

Father Simeon was sitting on the floor, polishing his glass eye with a piece of cotton daubed with alcohol. As soon as their eyes met, the woman knew she had been right to anticipate a difficult negotiation.

'Mary Magdalene,' the padre greeted her coldly. 'Your visit is a desecration of this place. What do you want?'

Violetta felt exhausted by the merciless embrace of her corset. She had not worn it since that almost fatal evening at the Smyrna Theatre when she had recognised among the audience an old customer of hers from Paris. She had escaped the auditorium under the cover of the darkness of the first act and had never set foot in Smyrna again.

'You have to help me as regards a very important and just cause.'

Father Simeon blew the cotton lint off his glass eye and put it in as casually as buttoning up his shirt.

'And what mutual interest may a servant of the Lord have with a renowned harlot?'

'The salvation of two lives.'

The padre understood. He rose to his feet with an effort and rubbed his legs, which had gone numb from sitting cross-legged.

'Their lives are in God's hands.'

'Not quite. They are in the hands of the general.'

Father Simeon gave her a softer look.

'He wouldn't listen. Authority deafens officers more than cannon fire.'

Violetta came closer. The clicks of her heels echoed across the vast empty church.

'I implore you, Father.'

A shaft of light from the dome illuminated her like a spotlight on a stage. Father Simeon took a few steps back, as if retreating from a wild animal.

'Perhaps there is a way.'

He stroked his beard, looking down in order to avoid the blinding glow of her amazing dress, busying himself with the eternal patterns on the tiles. He knew what he had to do, but would he have done it if this woman had not come to see him? Maybe the Lord was giving him another chance, he decided. He moves in mysterious ways, indeed, the padre thought; sending a woman of loose morals . . .

Violetta interrupted his thoughts.

'I will come with you, Father.'

The padre shook his head.

'No – it would be better if I went alone.'

She bent down to kiss his hand but he withdrew it. What was actually modesty the Frenchwoman inter-preted as antipathy, but she received the insult with forbearance. She picked up the train of her lilac dress and started towards the door. Father Simeon's voice stopped her before she had reached the narthex.

'Wait. I haven't dictated my terms yet.'

Violetta turned and offered him a wide smile.

'*Mais bien sûr. J'aurais du le savoir*. After all, men are men.' She walked back. 'Agreed,' she said, without waiting to hear the demands.

It was Father Simeon's turn to smile condescendingly.

'I will help you only if you confess your sins and take Holy Communion.'

She agreed to his request with no more enthusiasm had he demanded, as she had expected, her professional services gratis. The padre led her to the steps of the altar where he instructed her to kneel down.

'I'm a Catholic,' she warned him. 'We do things differently.'

Father Simeon hushed her with his hand.

'At least you are not an idolater. Just repeat what I say.'

It was some time since he had instigated an auricular confession. They began by reciting the Lord's Prayer and then he asked her to recount her sins for him. She satisfied him with a small fraction of last year's harvest.

'Is there anything else?' asked Father Simeon.

'No, Father.'

The padre looked into her blue eyes. For an instant he thought he understood why so many men wasted their lives away committing carnal sin.

'Are you sure?'

'I am, Father.'

Father Simeon nodded with contentment. Next to him was his greatcoat. He unfolded it and picked up the heavy precious Gospel; he began to read.

'*Peace be unto you. As my Father hath sent me, even so*

send I you. Whose soever sins ye remit, they are remitted unto them. And whose soever sins ye retain, they are retained.' He motioned to her to stand. 'Now go. And I promise to do everything in my power to help those sinners.'

He was alone again. Now it was his turn to kneel before the Royal Doors to pray for the forgiveness of his own sins, and for help from Him in persuading the brigadier to show mercy.

CHAPTER 8

'Major?'

The only light was coming from the small window in the sloping roof — it was not enough to illuminate the whole room; the evening was approaching fast. Already the moon was up, resembling a shining sickle. It was a clear sky and the stars would soon be coming out too. Major Porfirio tried to open the window, but the damp winters had warped it and it would not swing wide. He blew the cigarette smoke through the crack; in the frosty night it almost turned into white crystals. Only a few days ago the brigade had been lost in the desert, tormented by thirst and sultriness; now the rains threatened to drown them and you could not sleep without your coat on. A few days earlier he was also a decorated hero and the revered leader of his men.

'Major?'

This will be a century of change, Major Porfirio thought, and his memory stopped randomly at some news items he had read some time ago in the papers: *Industrial Revolution set to reach farthest corners of Europe . . . Electrification of countryside imminent . . .* And had he not read somewhere that a regular airmail service had begun in America and some parts of Europe too? He shook his head in awe. A letter sent to, let us say, Moscow that would arrive within a week — why not even a couple of days? He had been told that the flight lasted about thirty hours, but that was only because the aeroplane flew during the day – what if it could fly at night too? He attempted the calculation in his mind but did not complete it: that aeroplane reminded him of the air lieutenant.

He was surprised he did not feel hatred towards him – in an unusual way he was, in fact, grateful. The aristocrat had shown the true colours of the ruling class, the major thought, and reconfirmed his faith in his political beliefs. But it will not be long now, he reassured himself – the start had been made in Russia. *A spectre is haunting Europe* . . . No sooner had he repeated the first words of the Manifesto than his face darkened despite the brilliant crescent of the moon that cast its light upon him through the window: he would not witness the fulfilment of that dream. Contemplating the infinity of death, Major Porfirio shuddered a little. For he did not believe, of course, in the immortality of the soul – but how many actually do, in front of the firing squad? he wondered wryly. Perhaps if he had had a spouse . . .

'Major?'

Had it been a mistake not to get emotionally involved with somebody? It was not a conscious decision, he did not think. He enjoyed the occasional company of women and – although neither at the frequency nor with the enthusiasm of some of his colleagues – the visit to the brothel too. On the other hand, he had never come across a female acquaintance who could comprehend his burning fascination for his profession. How lonely he would invariably feel after a while with any one of them. The Party had been the answer to his intellectual concerns, but his emotional needs had withered like unwatered flowers. Maybe if he had a child, death would not be so terrifying – a part of him to live on.

'Comrade Porfirio?'

The major thought he heard a distant voice; he turned around.

'You said something, corporal?'

In a corner of the room, beyond the reach of the moonlight, the corporal squatted with his back against the wall.

'Could you please move a little, major?'

The officer frowned.

'Move?'

'The light, major – you are blocking the light. I am trying to read.'

Major Porfirio moved aside. The shaft of moonlight stretched as far as the corner of the room, and the young soldier held up a bundle of handwritten pages.

'They are from her,' he said with pride.

Immediately, Major Porfirio recognised the letters of the commissar from Salonika that had seduced the young soldier into joining the Party. Lighting a cigarette, the major contemplated his subordinate.

'I wrote her a letter. The brigadier will see it gets delivered together with the prayer rug I picked up for her.'

The officer smoked in silence.

'He promised. In the letter I explain what has happened. Otherwise, if she doesn't hear from me, who knows what she might think.'

The moonlight fell over the pages, the gesticulating hands, the young desperate face. The dim blue glow made him seem already dead.

'Killed in battle would be the obvious thing, of course. But that's not how the mind works, is it, major? More likely to assume I forgot all about her. Or that there was someone else back home all along – a wife perhaps. It's only human to be suspicious, isn't it, comrade?'

His superior did not reply.

'She should not live her life in bitterness. I think that was more than a friendship, major.' He looked at the pages with love. 'Who would have thought two people could feel so close to one another only by correspondence?'

Major Porfirio finished his cigarette and dropped it to the floor. He looked at its glowing end for a while before pressing it with his boot. In the far corner of their prison the corporal still talked.

'In my letter I say I risked my life to be with her – because I could not wait. But I don't want her to think it was her fault in any way. That's how love is, I write. It follows its own reasoning.'

When the major lifted his boot there were only a few specks of burning dust that had refused to die.

'The brigadier says she can have my medal – it's something. I want her to be proud of me.'

He remembered that he and the major had talked about returning their decorations as a protest against the imperialist war and bit his lip.

After a moment he asked timidly, 'Comrade, do you mind if I don't –'

'Not at all, corporal.'

'Something to remember me by, you see.'

Major Porfirio lit another cigarette and took a long draw.

'What . . . was her name?'

'Coralia,' replied the corporal and his face beamed.

'Beautiful.'

'I think so too, my major.'

From the other side of the stuck window the moon shone brighter than ever; the stars too were out now. The major could not see the square, but it was quiet out there and he assumed a curfew had been imposed in advance of the early-morning execution. He looked at the floor: the embers of his last cigarette had finally died out.

As the rubber cuff began to inflate and press his naked arm, Brigadier Nestor closed his eyes and let out a sigh of impatience.

'Do we have to do this every time?'

The medic ignored him. He continued to squeeze the bulb until the cuff was fully inflated and then he let the air slowly escape. While listening to his stethoscope his eyes watched the graduated rod of mercury. A moment later he deflated the cuff and removed it from his patient's arm.

'Systolic one hundred and sixty, diastolic eighty-five,' he said. 'Hypertension.'

Brigadier Nestor rolled down his sleeve.

'I feel fine. Some diseases would never have existed if the medical profession had not been invented.'

The medic instructed him to open his mouth.

Knowing the procedure by now, the old officer exposed his tongue. The medic touched it with his finger and narrowed his eyes.

'The fact of the matter is that your arteries are pumped up like automobile tyres. It is yet another reaction to your' – he stopped in order to find the right word – '*medication*.'

He asked the brigadier to close his mouth and returned the sphygmomanometer to his battered metal case. Then he rummaged through its contents and held up a rubber tube.

'You should reduce your intake. Or else I shall have to push this down your oesophagus and cannulate your stomach.'

'In that case, you'd better enter through the opposite end and evacuate my bowels too. Sometimes I feel as if I were about to explode.'

'Constipation is another side effect of your addiction.'

This time he had chosen his words unwisely. Immediately, the old man's face deformed to an unpleasant expression.

'The only thing I'm addicted to,' he snapped, 'is the classics.'

The medic did not contradict him. He returned the cannula to his box and took out a large vial of morphia. Brigadier Nestor licked his lips in an almost involuntary reaction.

'You've been a first lieutenant for too long, medic. I am promoting you to captain. Tell the quartermaster to sew you new shoulder boards on.'

The medic washed his hands in ethanol and shook them dry.

'My career is the last thing you should worry about now, brigadier. Besides, I have no intention of staying in the ranks.'

Brigadier Nestor was privy to his subordinate's noble aspirations.

'Oh, yes. The founder of the Order of Discalced Physicians. Even more so. When you're dying of hunger, the war pension will be the blessing you'd never receive from God for your charity.'

The medic tried to smile.

'Your words amount to blasphemy – or, worse, misanthropy.'

Brigadier Nestor took the morphia bottle and unlocked his trunk. While he was hiding it under the clothes, the medic watched him. After a while he could hold back no longer.

'A summary court-martial is not perhaps the ideal way to administer justice.'

That morning, in a trial which had lasted less than three hours, a tribunal of officers presided over by the brigadier had found both of the accused guilty of high treason. It had taken the court another two minutes to sentence them to capital punishment.

Brigadier Nestor closed the lid of his trunk and locked it.

'That will be all,' he said and hung the keys from his neck.

The medic rapped on his metal case with his fingers.

'Hasn't the enemy killed enough of our men already, brigadier?' he asked. 'Do we have to add more casualties ourselves?'

The brigadier hid the string of keys under his tunic and buttoned it up.

'If you were not my personal physician I would have you arrested as an agitator.'

The young doctor let out a bitter chuckle.

'My job is to save lives. Of all sorts – heroes' lives and cowards'.' He began to raise his voice without realising it. 'And traitors', deserters', comrades' and foes'. Saints' lives and sinners' too.'

The brigadier looked at him with pursed lips, waiting for him to finish. Then he spoke up.

'As long as I'm the commanding officer of this unit, *I* will be making the decisions. Both the good and the bad ones.' Then he offered the medic the olive branch of a smile. 'Now, it is late. If I don't go to bed soon I'll end up in the infirmary. And neither of us wants me there.'

The young man saluted sternly and turned to leave.

'Doctor,' the old man called, 'let me have some cotton, please.'

The medic cut a piece and gave it him before leaving. The brigadier felt lonely. All that day he had been trying to justify his decision to himself – that it was according to the military code, was the best excuse he could think of. Every one of his wars had opened a hole in his heart, which he had tried to plug with his reason. But it had been impossible. Feeling the last drops of his compassion slowly drain away he gave up, sat on the edge of his cot and began to remove his boots. There was a knock on the door. Brigadier Nestor let out a sigh of weariness and gave permission to enter. It was the padre.

'What brings you here at this hour, Father?'

Father Simeon closed the door and approached the end of the long conference table. He nodded nervously.

'Yes, yes. At this . . . the eleventh hour, indeed.'

'Well?'

Father Simeon squeezed the edge of the table with both hands and took a deep breath.

'A confession, my brigadier.'

Brigadier Nestor raised his heavy eyebrows.

'A confession?' He misunderstood. 'Listen, Father. When all this is over I promise to sit down with you and try to remember every damn sin I ever committed.'

Father Simeon stopped him.

'No, no, my brigadier – I know where your sword and boots are. I am confident I can get them back. But you'll have to give me a little time.'

Brigadier Nestor put down his boot and raised his eyes. His long stare only increased the padre's nervousness.

'If you have any idea where the stolen goods lie hidden, you only have to tell me and I will see they are recovered. It is hardly your obligation.'

Father Simeon felt the sweat run down the palms of his hands.

'Oh, but it is, my brigadier. Because *I* placed them there.'

'What are you saying, Father?'

The padre bowed his head. There was a pool of sweat on the lacquered table top under his hands. The time had come.

'I am the thief. Those possessions of yours and the major's . . . I stole them all.'

He had said it. He took a few unsteady steps and collapsed on to a chair under the weight of his shame, his heart beating fast. He buried his head in his hands. I am not worthy of Your love, Lord, he thought – how could he not have seen earlier the error of his ways? No matter how charitable the purpose, the way he had gone about achieving it . . . Two men had to be sacrificed in order for him to comprehend. A sudden hearty laugh interrupted his thoughts of sincere remorse.

'Well done, Father. I admire your gesture. Very noble indeed – taking the blame.'

The padre raised his head.

'No, brigadier, it is nothing but the truth.'

The old officer continued to laugh. Father Simeon had no option but to invoke the name of his god.

'I swear in the name of my Lord Jesus Christ.'

Brigadier Nestor stopped laughing and looked him in the eye. A moment later his lips formed an ambiguous smile.

'Even if it were true, Father, it would make no difference now.'

'But why?'

'Because the men have been sentenced for high treason, not stealing.'

He bent down and pulled off the second boot, then threw it on the floor.

'Are you guilty of that too, Father?'

Father Simeon felt like a drowning man crying for help whom no one could hear. He started giving a long account of his loathsome actions since the beginning of the withdrawal. Not only was his narrative chronologically accurate – he remembered exactly the day and time of each unlawful entry – but also he could name every item in the brigadier's trunk he had come across during his searches for valuables: the black uniform for evening receptions, a bundle of letters and postcards held together by a rubber band, a big bottle of some sort of medication. Sitting on the edge of his cot, barefoot, Brigadier Nestor listened. The more he looked at the padre, the more he thought the poor man resembled a shipwreck on a distant beach. He was still not entirely convinced he was the perpetrator of the thefts, until Father Simeon mentioned the dead snake.

'It was a long snake with grey skin and a pattern of yellow diamonds,' he recalled.

'Well, Father! You too will burn in Hell like the rest of us.'

The padre blushed but did not stop. He wanted to explain his actions. He said he knew he was gambling with his soul but he did it for the glory of God. His erratic speech of apology continued for some time. He was honestly remorseful but, when asked by the brigadier, he refused to reveal the name of his collaborator, the cook.

'It's not important. It's not the timber's fault if a house catches fire.'

After his surprise had subsided, Brigadier Nestor began to see the sincerity of the cleric's despair. He wished he could pat him on the back, but the padre was standing too far away and the brigadier was too tired to stand up again. Instead, he shrugged his shoulders.

'You'll have to learn to live with your demons, Father. The way I have to.'

There was not enough strength in the aphorism to lift the padre's heart.

'You deny me my right to repent, brigadier. I regret what I have done – you have to believe me.'

Brigadier Nestor took off his braces and began to remove his breeches.

'But I do. And I pardon you.'

Father Simeon hit his fist on the table.

'No. I have to be punished!'

Brigadier Nestor stopped undressing and scratched his head.

'Oh, I see. Say one hundred "Our Fathers".'

'You don't understand, my brigadier. You will be doing me a favour if you arrest me.'

'Arrest you? For what? It is true that at the time the thefts took place I would have hanged you with pleasure. But now I have more serious business to attend to.'

The padre's protestations only annoyed him and he soon silenced him with his hand.

'A commanding officer should know where the limits of discipline lie. Do you have any idea what the arrest of the chaplain would do to the morale of the troops? A padre stealing?'

Father Simeon bowed his head. He had failed.

'I know my men are not the most religious bunch,' continued the brigadier. 'They are no Crusaders. But still, the collapse of the ultimate moral authority . . . No, it is out of the question, Father.'

'Perhaps if you spared the life of the corporal? He was only a pawn.'

313

Brigadier Nestor shook his head.

'Pawns too are to be taken in a game of chess.'

'By killing that corporal you condemn *me* to eternal Hell, my brigadier. If only I had helped him that night.'

'You did the right thing. But if you do not think so, your present regret is sincere – even I can see that. I am sure God will forgive you, Father.'

'Repentance is not as easy as one assumes.'

'I'm very tired,' the brigadier interrupted him. 'You will have to excuse me. Please go, Father. And find some other way to make amends.'

Once the door closed the brigadier stared at it and shook his head.

'With fools even greater than myself, we never really stood a chance.'

He threw his breeches on to a chair and fell back in bed. If there was one good soldier in that piratical crew, he thought, it was Porfirio. He folded his hands behind his head and for the first time ever he called his Chief of Staff by his first name.

'But we'll meet again, Leonida. I have the feeling you will be stoking my fire down in Hell.'

He had almost forgotten; he stood up again with effort, carefully blocked his ears with the cotton the medic had left him and shut the windows that faced the square. Satisfied there was no way he would hear the rifles at dawn, he lay at last in his cot and let out a deep, mournful sigh.

The medic hung his metal case on the hook behind the door. His white smock also hung from it, and he stood looking at it with a vacant gaze. It was torn under the arms and speckled with blood. The bell of his stetho-scope hung down from a hole in its pocket, like the head of a dead snake. On the inside of the smock, at chest height, something was written with a pen: he had copied the Hippocratic oath into all his work clothes. The more he stared at it, the more his smock turned into a map of his present disappointment.

His room was the old office of the local chief of the Ottoman gendarmerie; the rest of the station housed the brigade infirmary. It was a single-storey adobe building of whitewashed walls with a pitched tiled roof and a wooden sentry box out front. It had been abandoned soon after the Expeditionary Corps had landed on the Anatolian coast, when the gendarmes had fled to join the army of Turkish nation-alists that was already being assembled in the interior. On the wall behind the chief's desk where the portrait of the Sultan had once hung there remained only a rectangular stain: the mayor had taken the picture down and hid it in the storeroom of the Town Hall to await the outcome of the war. When the situation had seemed to turn in favour of the Expeditionary Corps, he had ordered a large portrait of the King of the Greeks in a gilded frame but it had not arrived. Since the collapse of the front he was glad it never had.

The medic turned away from the door and went across the room, trying to take his mind off the execu-tion. The mayor had told him everything about the last occupant of that office: the chief of the gendarmerie had been an amiable man who procured a great enjoyment from life. He had the suntanned face of a diligent farmer, which he held several minutes

315

every morning in front of the mirror while applying beeswax and combing the tips of his moustache and long eyebrows upwards. He had loved his occupation – but more with the random passion of a clandestine lover than the devotion of a good husband. Like the schoolmaster he, too, preferred to pass his day in the garden of the *hamam* sucking at the mouthpiece of his *narghile* rather than sit behind his small desk. The town put up with his ways because he was an ingenious investigator and a natural solver of riddles.

The medic sat behind the desk and rested his elbows on it; it wobbled. He picked one of his old medical journals from the neat pile on his desktop, tore off a yellowed page, folded it several times, then wedged it under the lame leg. He consummated his professional blasphemy by throwing the journal into the rubbish basket. A moment later the weight of his action hit him. His vocation seemed to have little purpose – for the first time since he had embraced medicine he was questioning his ability truly to better life. Many diseases had been conquered, of course. Without doubt life expectancy had been greatly extended since the beginnings of civilisation. But his science's success in prolonging life meant that a human being would now also have the opportunity to experience more misery. Better if one lived happily into one's early twenties than to have to suffer the suppurating wounds of a long life: war, famine, the death of one's children before oneself, the incapacity of old age. He thought of life as a clever torturer who is meticulous in keeping his victims alive for a long time. The medic rested his face in his palms that still smelled of ethanol. He used to believe it was enough to cure sickness to bring happiness. The light in the lamp on his desk flickered and he turned the knob to let out more wick. His thoughts went again back to the stranger who haunted his quarters, the chief of the Ottoman gendarmerie. Where was he now? he wondered. Dead, perhaps? According to the mayor's anecdotes he did not sound like a man suited to war – but who ever was?

He immediately received his answer: Major Porfirio, of course – and the brigadier. *They* saw no evil in causing human suffering. It seemed to them as natural and indomitable a process as the rain. He did not understand their ideological differences, nor did he care to find them out now. Instead, he simplified their clash in his mind by thinking of the two men as the opposite ends of the same magnet: neither one better than the other and for ever irreconcilable. He felt tired and began to undress without getting up from his chair. No noise was coming from the other rooms. There was silence outside too, until the boots of the patrol overseeing the curfew broke it briefly, walking down the road. At last the medic stood up to remove his breeches. Dressed only in his underwear, he carried the lamp, followed by a moth, to his cot. He had only just lain down when the nurse appeared at the door. The medic gave him a blank look.

'Are you asleep, doctor?'

'Come in, nurse,' the medic replied wearily.

In the near dark his assistant removed his apron and hung it on the peg behind the door. Feeling his way, he came and sat on a chair next to the window. The moonlight illuminated the side of his body the way a schoolteacher would use a globe to demonstrate how night follows day. The nurse took out a handkerchief from his pocket and wiped his forehead.

'Stifling,' he said and sighed.

The medic raised his head.

'What?'

'The night, doctor – humid.'

The torrential rain had passed, leaving behind large pools of slowly evaporating water. The town was enveloped in a thick warm mist and a boundless cloud of marauding mosquitoes. The smell of the open sewer was now worse than ever, but the troops had lived long enough there not to notice any more. The nurse craned his head and looked out the window at the moon.

'Those mosquitoes are the size of aeroplanes,' he said.

He was a man with the capacity to maintain a cheerful disposition even in the eye of the worst catastrophe. Whether it was absolute bravery or pure simple-mindedness the medic had not decided as yet. The nurse became serious.

'I'm worried they will spread malaria, doctor. There's no quinine left.'

'There is no need. They are not anopheles.'

The nurse shrugged his shoulders and rolled up his sleeve to scratch his forearm above his anchor tattoo. He began to hum. The medic covered his eyes with his arm and shifted in his cot.

'How are the patients?' the doctor asked.

His question let loose his subordinate's eagerness to talk. He began to unroll a long catalogue of medical information as precise and orderly as if it were not a labour of his mind but actually inscribed on paper – he had never learned to read or write but he was blessed with a librarian's memory. The medic listened silently, with his arm still over his face, until the nurse interrupted his recounting and suddenly changed the subject.

'That corporal did not like horses,' he said.

His superior did not react.

'They say he tried to run away because of a woman,' continued the nurse.

The medic lifted his arm from his face.

'He seemed like a decent enough fellow,' the nurse said and scratched his cheek. 'I'm sure the brigadier has considered all avenues before making his decision.'

The medic could not stop a snicker escaping his mouth.

'The brigadier is a –'

He wanted to say that the old man was an incurable opiate addict whose condition worsened by the day, but through the fog of his anger he saw the dire consequences of the truth if the rank and file found out. Under the circumstances the brigadier was not unlike an effigy whose supernatural authority had to be preserved if he were to sustain everyone's hope of salvation, the medic thought. Besides, the revelation would contravene the principle of medical confidentiality. The medic was pleased that his present disillusionment had not, after all, erased his professional ethos completely.

'Yes, all avenues. I suppose you are right.'

'We owe him our lives.'

'Our lives – indeed. What about the patient who had the trepanning?'

His assistant was disappointed: he would rather have discussed the arrests.

'This morning,' he replied, 'he was telling me how he had won a battle in Austria more than a hundred years ago. In a place called . . .'

He scratched his head but could not remember. The medic raised his head a little.

'Austerlitz?'

'Yes, doctor. How do you know?'

The medic let his head rest on the pillow again.

'Increasing paranoia. Delusions of grandeur. Prepare him for another operation tomorrow.'

Against the moonlit window the nurse's head nodded in acknowledgement of the instruction. He looked at the pools of water in the street: heaps of slowly drying mud rose above the surface like islands seen from afar. The spectacle reminded him inevitably of home.

'I hope I'll see it again.'

The medic turned his head in his direction.

'What was that?'

'My island, doctor. It's been over a year since my last leave.'

His superior sighed.

'Oh, it will still be there.'

The nurse always talked with nostalgia about the crumbling walls of the medieval fortress that still resisted the advances of the sea with the eternal strength of their masonry, about the heretic monastery in the mountains that stood even higher than the nests of the ernes on the cliffs, about the quiet fishing villages built of pebble and seashell along the jagged coast.

'There is a small hospital in the capital,' the nurse said. 'But not enough staff.'

The medic could not sleep.

'I see.'

'There's one doctor who suffers from lumbago and cannot operate any more, few nurses and an intern who never got his degree.'

'Is the doctor a specialist?'

His subordinate nodded.

'Veterinary medicine.'

After a moment's silence the nurse spoke up again.

'They can use all the help they can get.'

He explained how the mayor back home had used his influence to get him assigned to the Medical Corps.

'When I go back I will work in the hospital.'

It was very late. The nurse stopped talking and contemplated the moon with motionless eyes. Later, after he was gone, the medic covered himself with the blanket and slowly managed to sleep. He dreamed he was on an island of steep cliffs and secret coves, fishing boats lying on the beach like bathers, and he listened to the sound of the sea. Then he dreamed he was sitting barefoot at an iron coffee-shop table outside a medical office and stuffing his shoes with the sheets of an unread newspaper so that they would keep their shape.

PART 3

The Sea

CHAPTER I

In the afternoon a strong sun came out that baked the thick mud left behind the receding floodwaters. When the clay began to dry an extraordinary event took place: the earthen streets of the town, the yards, the common and the gardens all turned a radiant red. First to notice the fantastic transformation was Yusuf. The Arab was in the main square, sweeping with a broom the spot where the two soldiers had fallen, when the dust under his slippers had begun to change colour. He sincerely thought then that a sinister miracle was happening, namely that the blood of the executed was staining the town. He gripped the broomstick and palpitated with supernatural fear.

'*A'uwudhu billah iminash Shaitan ir rajeem,*'[*] he prayed.

He was not the only one to feel that a terrible evil was descending upon their small Anatolian town; soon others saw the change from their windows, and like sleepwalkers rose from the bed of their afternoon nap in their underwear, their gowns and nightcaps, wearing an expression of credulous amazement. They climbed down the stairs, opened their doors, came out into the street barefoot and dazed, and watched in silence as

---

[*]'I seek refuge in Allah from Satan the rejected.' (Arabic)

the bravest ones scratched the caked earth with their fingernails to convince themselves it was not an illusion of the sun: the mud indeed stained their hands.

'We're cursed,' the Arab said. 'The blood of the innocent is drowning the town.'

At that time the schoolmaster was in the grocery. The draught from the open door carried in the commotion and he put down the almost empty brandy bottle.

'Whom are they going to shoot now?' he sighed.

On the other side of the counter the grocer slept with folded arms and his head against the shelves; Mr Othon gave him a look and decided not to awaken him. It was only when he stood up that he admitted to himself he was drunk. That morning at the execution he had tried once again to speak to Violetta but his old flame had rebuffed him. He had found refuge in the grocery, where since midday his despair had demanded alcohol and the Armenian's hand had provided it. He staggered to the door of the shop. Outside, soldiers were joining the townspeople and the unrest of the crowd was increasing. The schoolmaster gave them a scornful, intoxicated look.

'I loved her,' he hiccuped. 'I admit it. Now, leave me alone.'

No one paid him any attention. The earth reflected the sunlight and the walls of the houses also turned red.

'This town is going to Hell,' Yusuf said. 'Allah isn't pleased.'

It was a terrifying sight that was made worse when the wind began to blow and a cloud of red hissing dust arose and attacked the people. Everyone rushed to find shelter – apart from the schoolmaster.

'She's the Devil,' he stammered from the veranda of the grocery. 'Never ever trust a woman, friends. Especially one from France.'

In his hand he held the brandy bottle; he took a swig at it. The wind blasted his face with dust but he did not seem to care. The red dust entered the shops and the houses through the open windows, the entrances and balcony doors, settling on the furniture and the carpets. At last the schoolmaster began to understand what was happening but still looked around him with serene curiosity. Behind him the grocer was running to the windows to shut them.

'This is not Hell,' Mr Othon mumbled. 'Not being loved, that's Hell, my fellow citizens!'

He took another swig at the bottle but it was empty. He threw it away with contempt and stepped forward, but where he thought the step was his foot found no support and, falling from the height of the veranda, he landed face down on the hard red mud.

From her bed Violetta listened to her maid's feet against the floorboards, dashing to defend the house from the attacks of the whirlwind, and turned her head towards the shut window. 'The ten plagues,' she murmured and, adjusting the cold compress on her forehead, she spent no more time thinking about the natural occurrence. Instead her mind returned again, the way it had constantly done since earlier that morning, to the execution.

The army priest had failed to save the two lives –

he had been her last hope. On her way back from the square the town had seemed to her smaller, as if the foundations of the houses had sunk several inches under the weight of the official crime. She had not expected the event to affect her to this extent; she wished now she had not witnessed it. She cupped her ears: the memory of the volley of rifles still sounded so real it could be a thunderclap of lightning striking the rod on the roof. And no matter how firmly she commanded her mind, she could not drive the images out of it – it was like trying to shoo a cloud of flies away from a stagnant pond. Somewhere in the house a heavy shutter banged against the window; the Frenchwoman heard her maid climb the stairs, enter the room and latch it.

But there was one idea that had been born before the shame of the trials and executions, in fact even before the arrival of the army in town, and at that moment it was fighting for Violetta's attention. Outside, the wind was loosening its grip. It soon left for the desert and a sparkling red dust began to fall quietly over the Anatolian town. Without putting aside her grief, Violetta considered her plan apprehensively. She need not have been afraid – it soon became clear to her that hers was one of those ideas that were more difficult to conceive than carry out. After an hour in deep thought her timidity of the previous weeks now seemed ridiculous. Having made up her mind, she reached for the silver bell on her night table. Annina answered her call in a state of uncontrollable panic.

'What a disaster, Madame! The curse of the dead is falling on our heads.'

Her mistress put the bell on the table with an affectionate smile.

'Calm down, my little one. That dust is a curse only to my coats. Have you closed the windows in the room with the wardrobe?'

Her maid assured her that she had taken care of it in ample time; her precious clothes were safe. Talking as if she were a general in charge of a citadel under siege, Annina said that she had also blocked the gap at the bottom of the exterior doors with wet towels and the chimney of the unused fireplace in the salon.

'But the rosebushes are at the mercy of the dust, Madame.'

Her mistress nodded.

'I always thought that garden was too beautiful for such a forsaken place.'

The red dust continued to fall outside, settling on the roofs, the trees, the sidewalks. Looking out, Violetta began to understand how such a spectacle could be mortifying to the ingenuous. After her secret departure from France, she and Annina had sailed to the port of Naples where they had disembarked and waited for another ship to continue their passage – a practice they would repeat several times, in order for any police that might have pursued them to lose their tracks. During Annina's prolonged stay in bed, to recover from a tenacious seasickness, her mistress had taken an excursion through the Campanian countryside with some ephemeral lover whose name or face she could not recall any more. But she did still remember their visit to ancient Pompeii, the silent walls and collapsed colonnades of temples and theatres, the baths, shops and houses but, above all, the remains of hundreds of victims scattered among the ruins, remarkably preserved by the rain of ash and cinder that accompanied the eruption: men, women and children, aristocrats, freemen and slaves, gladiators in chains, animals. An ordinary town like this, she thought. The re-enactment of the disaster in her imagination made her flesh crawl. She turned to Annina who was still standing at the door.

'Start packing, *jolie*. It is time we left this hole.'

Annina did not understand. Did Madame mean they were moving away from the town altogether? She opened her mouth to ask why but her mistress stopped her.

'But first go and tell the mayor I want to see him.'

The gravity of her manner warned her maid not to ask any questions. The girl withdrew, closing the door of the lavish *boudoir* softly behind her. Violetta got out of bed and put on her robe. In one of her monumental closets she found an empty box and then set about carrying out her decision. First, she picked up her rare kimono, folded it with affection and placed it in the bottom of the box, with a feeling similar to lowering the body of a loved one into its coffin. Once the start had been made the rest of the items did not cause her such a sentimental reaction. In the back of her wardrobe she found the fur coat made from eleven foxes and the wide hat with the bunch of pearls arranged like grapes. The embroidered umbrella with the silver handle was hanging from the rail. She emptied her jewel box on her bed and found the golden garter with the amethysts.

The box was almost filled when her maid informed

her that the mayor had arrived. Violetta instructed her to show him into the drawing room and to let him know she would be seeing him shortly. As soon as the mayor saw his lover he knew something was wrong: she was neither dressed nor made up. He wedged himself into a narrow armchair and wiped his face with his handkerchief.

'Terrible, terrible,' he gasped. 'That dust. Infernal! But can you believe that some simpletons are talking of abandoning the town?'

Violetta tied the belt of her robe.

'The execution shocked them,' she said.

The mayor returned his handkerchief in his breast pocket.

'Of course. A regrettable event. I am sorry my people had to witness it. All these years I tried to keep the war away from them. And I succeeded until last week.' He shrugged. 'In any case, my love, those two were enemies of the State.'

Violetta contemplated her lover with a hint of contempt, and reassured herself she had made the right decision.

'Enemies of the State. Of course.'

The mayor felt her bitterness.

'The army is leaving and things can now go back to normal. The war is over.'

The Frenchwoman contemplated the dust falling outside her window.

'*Plus ça change, plus c'est la même chose,*' she reflected.

The mayor was exasperated.

'In the name of mercy, woman. Start speaking the language of your future husband.' He stood up and paced round the room. 'You've lived in this place long enough to have learned it.'

He orbited around his fiancée like a planet, casting his shadow over her robe: he wondered what had happened to the kimono he had given her.

'The only words my clients wished to hear,' she said, 'were exclamations of appreciation at their manhood.'

The mayor curled his lip.

'Othon was right. You *are* a suffragist.'

She removed her ring and threw it in with his other gifts. Only then did the mayor notice the box at the woman's feet.

'I believe all these belong to you,' she said. 'You should send your men for the bathtub. It is too heavy for me and Annina to carry downstairs.'

The mayor frowned.

'The bathtub? But . . . what about us?'

Ever since the beginning of their affair he had tried several times to teach himself his lover's language but his impatience and laxity had caused him to fail. That afternoon, for the first time ever, he had no trouble understanding her words perfectly when she spoke up again:

'*Notre histoire est finie.*'

Air Lieutenant Kimon made his way through the crowd and fled from the square with his hand over his mouth. As soon as he turned the corner he vomited against the wall. While leaning over he heard the pistol deliver the *coups de grâce*. He could not then prevent a second discharge of brown matter from his stomach splashing over his boots.

He had helped to send the major to his death. His intent had only been to humiliate him a little. How could he have known he was a conspirator? Him, a fervent militarist. He had found him excessively self-important and self-righteous, that was all. Now that he knew, it was easy to attribute the seriousness of his manner to the man's ideological vigour. Air Lieutenant Kimon spat out the last of the bitter contents of his mouth. He did not think a man deserved to die because of his beliefs – no matter how naive they were. Because he thought them more as naive than dangerous. Indeed, the word Bolshevik did not stir fear in him the way it did in other people. He was confident enough to believe that it would be easier to unmake the pyramids of Egypt than reform the ranks of society – and he was rich enough to afford a first-class ticket out of the country if it ever came to that. Of course, there had been the recent situation in Russia, but that would surely not last.

No; the Chief of Staff's convictions did not bother him. It was authority he simply had a grudge against. He had meant to embarrass the man – the way the practical jokes he had played at the Flight Academy had mocked his instructors. Air Lieutenant Kimon thought of those days of innocent fun with longing: less than three years had passed, but the happy memories felt as old as his days at primary school. He wiped his mouth with the back of his hand. How sorry he was . . . An insolent voice interrupted his grief.

'A historic occasion. One feels humbled to have witnessed it!'

The airman turned round: it was the war correspondent.

'What?'

'The last dead of the war.' The journalist raised his
hands in the air. 'God willing, of course.'

His camera hung from a strap round his neck like
a powerful amulet. He noticed that the airman was
looking at it.

'It's all captured here – for future generations.'

Air Lieutenant Kimon removed his cap and passed
his hand through his hair. He was struggling to keep
more bile from his stomach from rising to his mouth.

'Perhaps future generations would rather forget this
disaster.'

The journalist cast his eye over the airman's boots
which were covered with vomit.

'I don't agree, lieutenant. Historians, students, the
descendants of those heroes . . . They will all need to
understand what happened.'

'And you will endeavour to explain.'

The journalist confirmed his destiny with a nod.

'Both the glory and the suffering.'

For a while neither man spoke. But the journalist
could not hold back his excitement for long.

'Conspiracy, a desperate act of love, an elusive and
unpatriotic thief, a great leader. It'll be the best story
written about this unfortunate war!'

Air Lieutenant Kimon put his cap back on.

'The story of two men shot.'

'Yes, what a culmination – as in a Greek tragedy.'

In the town square the crowd had begun to disperse
in silence. Air Lieutenant Kimon contemplated the

naked tamarisks, the wall of sandbags against which the two men had stood, the firing party now slinking away.

'There was little glory back there earlier on . . . I hope you took enough photographs.'

The correspondent shrugged.

'Bad things happen whether one is there to photograph them or not.'

The airman remembered the dispatches he had read without much thought throughout the war: the elegant descriptions of battle, the sobriety of the text, the explicitness of the photographic plates.

The journalist said: 'It was a practice of barbaric nations to execute the bearers of displeasing news.'

The mayor wandered down the streets without direction, lost in the sadness of his thoughts. He felt humiliated and terrified. His rejection by his fiancée had caught him unawares; he still could not understand why it had happened. Yes, he knew his asthmatic performance in bed would never win him laurels, but she had repeatedly assured him that coitus had long ceased to be a source of satisfaction to her. He looked at the box he carried in his arms. What about his gifts? They were the finest clothes and jewellery he could afford – or, rather, the best the town budget could buy. Despite her returning them he still thought of his lover as most ungrateful. With his hand he felt the expensive fabrics and lifted one or two, half expecting to find his heart underneath. How could she do this to him?

The red dust fell over him and settled on the items in the box: the diamond tiaras, the velvet slippers, the

Compagnie des Indes porcelain figurines – there was a thick layer of dust over them when the mayor came out of his stupor and looked round. If this was his town he could not recognise it. The once whitewashed walls, the swept pavements, the trees and lovingly tended gardens had all turned red. The mayor shuddered. A few people stood under the eaves of the shops and watched the event in a daze, their initial panic having turned to surrender. The mayor looked at them the way he would observe a multitude of ghosts. He hitched up the box with the extravagant gifts and took the road to the Town Hall. Not long after he saw a man lying in the middle of the road and, despite the coat of dust, he recognised him.

'Othon?'

When he received no reply he put the box down and knelt beside his old friend. Holding his breath he placed his palm on the schoolmaster's back. He was relieved to discover he was alive.

'Can you hear me, friend?'

But neither the schoolmaster's lips nor his body made the slightest move. The mayor felt a vague sense of guilt sneak inside him. He turned his former friend gently over and cleaned the dust from his face with his fingers. The infernal dust still fell inexorably. Behind it the afternoon sun baked the earth like a kiln. Some time later the schoolmaster opened an eye a little, then shut it again.

'Take your dirty hands off me, traitor.'

The mayor wiped the sweat off his own forehead; his hand left a red mark on his furrowed skin. He felt an immense sense of relief.

'Thank God. I thought —'

He held the schoolmaster's head in his arms: it felt as heavy and lifeless as a slaughtered animal's. The schoolmaster was unshaven, his hair was dirty and his breathing seemed to be coming from very far away.

'Go away,' Mr Othon said. 'Leave me alone.'

'What happened?' Then the mayor smelled the alcohol. He shook his head. 'If this is over Madame Violetta, I can tell you —'

The schoolmaster's lips were distorted in a mocking smile.

'No. I'm only trying to pickle my liver.'

He shook off the other man's hands, rested on his elbows with much effort and squinted round him with disapproval. The doors and shutters were shut and there were people standing under the verandas. They paid no attention to him; they were watching the dust come down in silence.

'I hope I live long enough to watch her go to Hell,' he said. 'And you, holding her hand all the way.' He scratched the ground with his nails and scooped up a handful of red dust. He studied it closely, nodding. 'After that I could die in peace.'

He threw away the dust and wiped his hand on his trousers — he was recovering his senses quickly. The bottle he had been drinking from lay beyond his reach.

'Pass me that bottle,' he ordered.

When the mayor gave it to him the schoolmaster grimaced: it was empty.

'That figures. He stole my woman, he steals my brandy too.'

The rain of dust was petering out. The air began

to clear but remained hot: it blew from the desert. The mayor sat carefully on the ground and broke the news of his rejection to his friend. His account was quiet and melancholy, but what eased his pain a little was him knowing the story would have a healing influence on his friend. He was correct. The schoolmaster's spirits seemed to rise so much that at some point the mayor would not have been surprised if his old rival had suddenly risen into the air and started floating several inches above ground.

'You were always a fool for love, mayor,' Mr Othon said. 'Take my word for it: she's not worth it.'

The mayor gave him an injured look.

'Perhaps she was too good for this place. An angel who crashed on Earth.'

It was the other man's turn to tend to his friend's injuries. He said that the mayor's statement was extreme hyperbole. The woman was, after all, a prostitute. Yes, he had loved her once too, but what could you expect from a bachelor condemned to abstinence? Her bed was the garden of earthly delights – that much was true. But marriage? His friend had been lucky to get out in time – could he imagine the ridicule that would follow him, a state official, everywhere in Anatolia?

'Things are changing, Othon,' the mayor said. 'I have the feeling I won't be an official for long. When the dust of this war settles there will be elections. A man of Christian descent will never be allowed to retain his post.'

Mr Othon grinned.

'The unsoundness of your fiscal decisions over the

years might also have something to do with it.'

The mayor gave the box with Violetta's gifts a long sorrowful look.

'I regret nothing. All I will ever have to remind me of her will be a box of clothes and a bathtub.'

A morbid sensation cast its shadow over him, fleetingly, like a cloud passing overhead. He brushed off the dust on his jacket with his fingers. The dust storm had stopped and the townspeople were emerging from their shelter.

'I tried not to take sides in this war – for our town to be neutral. And, in fact, everything was fine until those devils came marching in.'

He raised his head and turned it left and right. All he saw was a panorama of misfortune: the cracked clay earth, the shop fronts buried in dust, the square where the executions had taken place.

'Armageddon . . . Many are preparing to go. The arrests sowed the fear of death – this morning's executions made it grow. And then came all this dust.'

The schoolmaster threw away the empty brandy bottle.

'I'm not staying here much longer either.'

'You are leaving too?'

The schoolmaster nodded and removed his shoe; he turned it upside down and emptied the dust.

'I've decided to follow the army back to the motherland.'

'The motherland? But you were born here.'

'You wouldn't know it unless I'd told you. Nothing left for me here to call it home.'

The mayor bit his moustache; the news increased

his gloom. He slowly became aware of muffled talk around them and pricked up his ears: it was the townspeople, animatedly discussing their plans for departure. The schoolmaster continued.

'Besides, I don't think it's safe to stay. There have been executions and evictions elsewhere already. Our number could come up soon.' He raised his hands. 'It's understandable – the principle of revenge.'

'We harmed nobody.'

Mr Othon shrugged.

'We harboured the retreating invaders.'

At that moment the smell of the open sewer blew in their direction and opened a hole that finally sank the mayor's hopes.

'This place is truly cursed,' he said, turning his head to gaze at his once delightful kingdom. 'Maybe Hell *has* come to the surface, after all.'

Once they had interpreted the dust storm as a supernatural sign, the townspeople began to discover mystical meaning in all the events that had taken place in their peaceful town recently: the arrival of the brigade, the rising of sewage in the open conduit, the autumnal flood, the executions. It was obvious: they were clear warnings they had to leave before worse could happen. The schoolmaster did not try to dissuade them – he was leaving himself too. But he did attempt to persuade them that there was no supernatural pattern about the random phenomena. In vain. He turned to the mayor.

'Don't tell me you believe that nonsense, too?'

He was not prepared for the mayor's reaction. While Mr Othon had been giving his lecture a sudden realisation had overtaken the civil servant. The mayor's shame for the embezzlement of the town funds, his sadness for the loss of his love, his fear of punishment by his new superiors, had given way to a heroic determination. The mayor brushed his trousers and buttoned up his jacket – the confusion of his life had put itself instantly in order; the compass of his life had come at last to rest. He straightened his tie and folded his lapels neatly.

'My fellow citizens,' he said, raising his voice. 'I am here to help you.'

They all listened in silence: he was their leader: he had met his destiny.

He had given his speech and received many warm handshakes when he called to mind the schoolmaster's question.

'It doesn't matter what *I* believe, Othon. It's the democratic view of the majority. Therefore it becomes my obligation to lead these people to safety. Damn it, am I not the head of this municipality?'

'And those poor souls are so terrified they will follow you like Moses,' the schoolmaster said.

The mayor smiled.

'They'd better; I know the safest route to the coast.'

He was not boasting. Once, in the early days of their courtship, he and Violetta had set off on a romantic Sunday excursion. On the hills outside town they had lost their way and instead of the road they had led their cart down a deep and narrow valley that no one in all likelihood had ever set foot in. Then they had travelled across a dried-up salt lake and along a wide precipice from where they had all of a sudden caught sight of the sea. The mayor interrupted his narrative; that old adventure reminded him of his ex-fiancée. He turned and kicked the box at his feet with contempt; it went rolling across the street, scattering on the red dust sparkling ornaments, expensive fabrics, high-heeled leather pumps. He resumed: yes, he could guide his people, and the army too, safely through that secret path to the sea – he would only need a little help from his trusty Scouts. Having said this the mayor sanctioned at last the evacuation of the town.

CHAPTER 2

It was a heavy bicycle with a frame of tubular steel and large galvanised wheels with rubber pneumatic tyres now long deflated. Its seat was made of hard leather with a pair of springs underneath that aimed to deliver the rider from some of the cruel punishment of the bumpy Anatolian roads – but that bicycle had not travelled over dust or pothole for some time now. When the gearbox with the crank that drove the magneto of the radio-telegraph had been crushed (by a piece of the roof of the headquarters during the enemy bombardment on the first day of the counter-attack), the situation had demanded extreme and urgent innovation: communications with the defending battalions along the front had to be restored at any cost. The orderly had found the bicycle placed against the wall outside the farmhouse where the brigade command had been established and with little skill and more patience he had adapted it so that it turned the magneto. He checked the time, sat on the worn seat and slowly began to pedal.

From the door to the conference room came the sound of deep snoring: the brigadier was still asleep. The rear wheel of the bicycle gathered speed and a belt made of leather braces hissed and set the clanking armature of the magneto in motion. The orderly looked outside the window of the Town Hall: in the square the Arab was sweeping the dust where the two conspirators had fallen earlier that morning with a broom. The orderly felt his flesh crawl. His sleeves were rolled back, exposing a skin that was burned by the sun and covered with crusts of blood from the trivial injuries he had suffered over the last months. It was nothing compared to what one could witness in the infirmary. He contemplated how fortunate he had been to be assigned to attend the Chief of Staff and the brigadier. He did not have to remind himself he owed it to the major; a weighty feeling of shame pressed his heart and he averted his gaze from the macabre spectacle. But would not everyone choose a duty as far away from the front as possible, given the opportunity? While he considered his response, he carried on pedalling.

The sun came out and from his seat on the bicycle the orderly witnessed the terrifying spectacle of the town turning red – it haunted him no less than it did the townspeople: he, too, came from a small place where the laws of physics were subordinate to those of superstition. All he could do was cross himself. The magneto was working fast now and he jumped off the bicycle. Rubbing his buttocks he sat at the radio-telegraph and put on the headphones. He keyed a brief message, then held his breath and listened, turning the dial a little from time to time, while the magneto slowed down. They were not far from the coast, he thought. Perhaps . . . When the magneto stopped, he removed the headphones with an expression of disappointment but without surprise.

In the square, civilians and soldiers came out of

houses and shops and inspected the red earth. From this distance the orderly could not hear what they were telling each other. He sat on the bicycle and started to pedal again. While the heavy machine gathered speed, a violent windstorm broke out and the crowd outside scattered. The young man contemplated the autumnal fury of nature with timid eyes: the wind was shrouding everything in red dust. The pedals turned under his boots and the rusty chain rotated the rear wheel noisily. He felt he was carrying out a ritual that had as little purpose and meaning as the daily raising of the flag. He stopped to shut the window and then started to pedal again, feeling the sweat on his back and under his arms. From behind the door the sound of snoring ceased. The orderly sat at the radio-telegraph again.

He was about to give up when he thought he heard something through the interference. He turned the dial carefully with a trembling hand as if he were trying to pick herbs in a patch of nettles. It was not until the wind outside had dropped that he was able to hear it clearly. On a piece of paper he jotted down a series of dots and dashes. Following a few brief exchanges he threw away the headphones and burst into the conference room without knocking. The brigadier was on his cot. Holding up the piece of paper with the deciphered Morse broadcast, the orderly shouted: 'Our brothers . . . Out there . . . At last . . . We're saved!'

Under the blanket Brigadier Nestor did not stir. As was his habit, over his nightshirt he wore his greatcoat with the collar up to protect his ears from the cold, and on his head the woollen nightcap his wife had knitted with the blue glass charms to exorcise his nightmares. Having stopped snoring some time ago he lay as comfortably and quietly as a deeply buried fossil. His orderly shivered.

'My brigadier?'

But, again, his commanding officer gave no indication of hearing. The young soldier had convinced himself of the worst before he even stretched out his arm and touched him. When the officer shook the hand off with a jerk of his shoulder, the orderly jumped back. Brigadier Nestor sat up and removed the cotton he had plugged his ears with before going to bed.

'What is the meaning of this, orderly? Did I tell you to wake me up?

The soldier still shook from his fright.

'My brigadier, thank God. I thought you were –'

'Dead?'

The old man at once turned to the window: it was over. The view of the empty square filled him with remorse.

'I'm afraid not. Even though it appears to be easier to die in this hell than have an hour's sleep in peace.'

The orderly had undergone such an alarm that he had almost forgotten the reason for his intrusion. When he did remember, his excitement returned. The brigadier strove to understand the boy's incoherent account. As soon as he learned that contact had been made with the remnants of the expeditionary force that had fled to the islands, he started laughing – but not because he was happy.

'The gods play with me like Idomeneus,[*] he said bitterly.

The young soldier stopped talking and watched him in puzzlement. But he did not have the opportunity to find out what his superior was referring to because the latter jumped out of bed with a nimbleness he had not demonstrated for a long time and issued his order: they were leaving the town.

The preparations went on through the night, and at dawn the brigade was ready to march. The dromedaries were arranged in a long train and the reins of each animal were tied to the tail of the one before. The mules were fed and watered, the tanks of the lorries were filled and the stretchers with the wounded were loaded on to them. Very little equipment was to be carried on that final stretch of the journey; most of it was left behind, including the artillery guns that had made it across the desert. Their breechblocks were removed and their carriages were broken to pieces, while the last unfired shells were pushed off the edge of a deep ravine at the outskirts of the town. When the brigadier came out of the Town Hall that morning the town resembled an endless scrapyard. In addition to the field guns, scattered everywhere were spare

---

[*]Idomeneus, king of Crete, was one of the bravest Greeks in the Trojan War. On his way back from the war he encountered a violent storm and promised the sea god Poseidon that if he arrived home safely he would sacrifice the first living thing he met. Although the first to meet him when he landed was his own son, Idomeneus still carried out his vow.

engine parts, wooden cartwheels, empty petrol cans, tents and camp beds. For a moment Brigadier Nestor surveyed the landscape of defeat: on the roof of the Town Hall the flag of the brigade flapped like the wings of a vulture. Despite his previous night's sound sleep, a heavy sense of exhaustion sat on the brigadier's shoulders. It remained there until the sound of an approaching engine scared it off: his lorry with his orderly behind the wheel came towards the gate of the Town Hall.

The troops were lining up in the square, in a bustle that bore no resemblance to the previous day's events. The wall of sandbags against which the two conspirators had stood had been unmade overnight, and the bloodied dust had been cleaned. In the courtyard of the Town Hall, in the small garden where the marble bust was, were two wooden and unmarked crosses over a patch of recently churned earth. Brigadier Nestor observed his army with feverish eyes – that morning he had taken the largest dose of morphia ever, but it had yet to take effect.

The soldiers had found their companies and the horsemen had taken their positions, when the crowd of civilians entered the square led by the troop of Boy Scouts. Despite being informed of the townspeople's decision to follow the brigade – for which he had given his consent – the brigadier was still taken by surprise. Every man, woman and child seemed to carry as much weight as their donkeys, while their oxcarts were so heavily laden with the rest of their belongings that their wheels turned furrows in the street like ploughs. There were tables and chairs, wall clocks and framed portraits, sleepy canaries in cages, cooking pans, filled wardrobes, bedsteads. Lost in the human herd were also bleating sheep, cackling chickens and cows that mooed. Brigadier Nestor knitted his brows; the spectacle would be as comical as a carnival parade had it not been a desperate exodus. Dressed in his Scoutmaster's uniform, the mayor signalled to the crowd to halt and came forward. On his shoulder he carried the turntable of his Victrola he had removed from the mahogany cabinet which was itself loaded on to one of the donkeys. He saluted cheerfully.

'At your command, my brigadier.'

The old officer clasped his hands behind his back. From the steps of the Town Hall he gave the crowd a scornful look and tapped his foot on the marble.

'We are not going to the bazaar, mayor.'

The mayor turned and looked at his fellow citizens with surprise. Seeing nothing strange he shrugged his shoulders.

'How else would we pay for food and lodging where we're going, my commander?'

Contemplating the crowd and the Scoutmaster, Brigadier Nestor remembered the Byzantine monarch who would blind ninety-nine of every hundred prisoners and leave the one to guide the others home.

'Don't worry,' he said. 'The motherland shall provide for you all.'

There was nothing the mayor could do. Quietly he placed the delicate mechanism of his beloved Victrola on the steps of the Town Hall and gave it a fond farewell look. The brigadier gave orders to slaughter all the animals and instructed his men to place the townspeople in the middle of the column, so that they were protected in case of enemy attack. But the mayor and his Scouts joined the vanguard, because they would be leading everyone to the sea.

Brigadier Nestor had climbed into his lorry when Father Simeon asked to see him.

The brigadier had forgotten about him. He had not seen the padre since the night before the executions when he had come to beg clemency for the two men. That night, in fact, Father Simeon had visited the condemned men's cell to pray with them and offer them the sacrament. The major had declined, but the corporal had partaken of communion with great humility. It was some sort of consolation to the padre's soul, tortured by remorse for that night at the door of St Gregorius Theologus when he had refused him admission. But his relief had been temporary; the following dawn, as he administered the last rites over the bodies of the two soldiers, his depression had returned and it was crueller than before.

'My brigadier,' he said from outside the lorry. 'A word, if you please?'

Brigadier Nestor looked at his watch.

'Please make it brief.'

Father Simeon climbed on to the back of the lorry. It was a while since he had been in the brigadier's mobile quarters, yet everything seemed to occupy the same place: the heavy trunk, the stove, the table laid with maps, the leather holster hanging from the crossbar of the tarpaulin. Brigadier Nestor sat on the edge of his cot. There was still a thick layer of dust on those items that had not been carried to the Town Hall when the brigadier had taken up his residence. It prompted the padre to recall their desperate journey through the desert almost with fondness. That was the time when the enemy was the Devil, when evil was what they escaped from and good was where they were headed. The padre longed for the simplicity their lives had attained during their brief desert adventure. The suffering, the shortage of food, the desolation: it all truly purified the soul, as any hermit would know. Why did it matter whether the troops came to his pitiful tent of a church or not? Gradually, unbeknown to themselves, each man was turning into a little saint. If only they had never come across the town but had gone wandering through the desert for ever . . . Because the death of the flesh was so trivial compared to the exaltation of the soul, Father Simeon thought. When he spoke up his voice trembled a little.

'My brigadier, I ask permission to stay behind.'

The officer inflated his chest and sighed. Then he removed his cap and scratched the crown of his head.

'What is the problem this time, Father?'

The padre looked around him for somewhere to sit but the back of the lorry was so cluttered up with the brigadier's personal effects that he could not do so without somehow trespassing upon the officer's privacy. Standing, he felt like an accused man in the dock pleading his case. But as soon as he opened his mouth the words came as easily as the air he breathed. He talked about his lifelong dream of becoming a missionary, his loss of courage to fulfil his ambition as a young priest and the subsequent doldrums of his insignificant parish. His life had been like that of a horse yoked to a water pump, he said, made to circle the well all day long. There had to be more a cleric could do – did not the brigadier think so? The officer contemplated the standing man in silence. Yes, the padre answered himself, there had to be. He had volunteered for the campaign three years ago, having had no idea what he was looking for, but he had found it at last: his vocation was to stay in that town that had no priest and be the shepherd of its people. As soon as he heard this the brigadier raised his brows.

'Haven't you noticed the crowd outside, Father? In a moment there will be not a single Christian left here.'

'The Muslims, my brigadier – *they* are my flock. I intend to establish a holy mission and convert those lost souls to the true faith.'

Brigadier Nestor twisted the tip of his moustache. It was a ridiculous proposition: no sooner would the enemy arrive in town than the padre would be dangling from a rope – but at the same time he saw what a torment the cleric was in and he pitied him for being alive. He licked his dry lips.

'Don't worry about the locals, Father. They don't know it yet, but they are the victors in this war.'

'But they worship a lie, brigadier. What about their souls?'

Brigadier Nestor searched for his cigars. It was a while before he remembered that the padre had, of course, stolen them some time ago.

'It is often healthier for the soul to believe a lie than to search for the truth.'

'You talk like a casuist.'

'No – like a patriot. Or else we'll all start running in circles like the cat chasing its tail.'

They would never agree on that; Brigadier Nestor let it pass.

'Are you quite sure of your decision, Father?'

The padre nodded.

'I believe it is my destiny, my duty and my penance.'

'Your spiritual guidance will be missed.'

Father Simeon smiled bitterly.

'I wish that were true. My sermons sent more soldiers to sleep than the bugle sounding lights out.'

The brigadier looked the cleric in the eye and for an instant thought he detected the beginnings of insanity. He knew that expression: he had seen it many times before in the mirror, while in the height of his morphia stupor.

'Very well. You may stay. The army is grateful for your services.'

He stood up and lifted the lid of his trunk. From the tunic of his folded parade uniform he unpinned a medal and held it out to the padre.

'I cannot remember what this was for, but it couldn't have been for anything braver than your decision, Father.'

Father Simeon raised his hands in refusal.

'No, no, my brigadier, I cannot accept it. If there is any reward to be had I shall receive it from other quarters.'

The old officer shrugged and threw the medal back in the trunk. When he offered his hand the padre shook it warmly. The moment the priest jumped off the lorry the dog came up to him, wagging its tail. Father Simeon smiled and patted it on the head.

'Of course you can stay too, Caleb. And as soon as

you learn how to light candles I promise to ordain you as my deacon.'

Padre and dog watched the lowering of the flag from the roof of the Town Hall and then the bugle sounded the order to march. Like the heavy carriages of a train pulling out of a station, one after another the files of troops and civilians slowly began to leave the square.

Yusuf walked behind the dromedaries, carrying a large suitcase in either hand; he was sweating but still whistling. The pack animals travelled quietly, leaving behind a continuous trail of dung. Occasionally, Yusuf moved aside to avoid one of their noisome deposits and then he rejoined the path of the long narrow column.

'Just as I thought,' he said. 'The smell of the town is coming along, too.'

Beside him Annina walked with the mayor's cat in her arms. She too was panting. She wore a long skirt of black brocade that was as effective as a slave's fetters: it trailed behind her, grazing the dirt and stones of the path and was often caught in the briers. The next time Annina stopped to free her dress from a buckthorn, Yusuf puffed with impatience.

'That dress is too long. One ought to wear trousers in the mountain.'

His lover lifted the hemline of her heavy skirt and stepped over the briers.

'I am fine. The day women start wearing trousers they will also start to fight in your wars.'

There was little talk among the others. The noise was mostly from the lorry engines up ahead, from the creaking of the leather saddles, the clanking of sabres, rifles and water bottles and, of course, the treading of feet and the snorting of the horses. As the thousand runaways crossed a shallow ravine where a cool stream of rainwater flowed into a sharp cleft in the rocks, a cloud crossed the sky and masked the sun for a short but welcoming instant. The vultures had long noticed the winding human line that made its way across the hills like an enormous snake, and followed it quietly from high above. Some time later a whistle was heard and the muleteers halted their animals. Yusuf put down the suitcases and sat on them. Annina joined him and he began to stroke the cat in her lap.

'We're going to the sea, cat – more fish there than even you could eat.'

The cat closed her eyes and purred, digging her claws in the thick brocade. Suddenly the birds flew off the trees and scattered in the sky. A moment later the great vultures arrived, sat on the branches and folded their wings: standing still they resembled the heraldic emblems of ancient kingdoms. Annina pulled a silken handkerchief from her cuff and wiped the sweat off her lover's brow.

'*Mon petit* Yusuf. You are the bravest man I've ever known.'

The Arab inflated his chest and grinned with mock pride.

'The bravest gardener in Anatolia,' he said.

They held hands over the sleeping cat. Not far away Violetta, dressed in a chiffon jacket and holding her organdie parasol, stood on the crest of the hill and contemplated the horizon. The coast was still out of sight; there were only hills as far as she could see. Covered with dried hay and speckled with trees and dark shrubs, the landscape was like an endless leopard skin. The Frenchwoman suddenly remembered an excursion she had taken with the mayor before the war. Could it be they had come this way that day? She recalled a view as majestic as this and the same sense of tranquillity that she was experiencing now. Perhaps, she thought.

She had not forgotten the executions but felt a superstitious relief that she had left the site of that hideous crime. But the town had until now been an excellent hideout. Where should she go next? She had to plan her journey ahead. Indeed, she had already begun to draw lines in the map of her mind when her maid interrupted her.

'Madame? We have something to tell you.'

Violetta turned round. She only had to glance at the couple holding hands to guess their decision, but she let them speak just the same. The young pair announced to her the plan they had come up with after many nights of deliberation in Yusuf's shed: they were going to go to Egypt. They had thought everything over even before the decision was taken to evacuate the town: Annina had her savings and Yusuf knew a relative who could help him find a job. They would follow the army to Athens and sail out from Piraeus.

'We are going to get married and live in Alexandria,' Yusuf said.

'I'm so happy for you, children,' Violetta said. 'Cupid's arrows don't have to feel to everyone like the martyrdom of St Sebastian.'

She wished them luck with all the sincerity of her heart, but that did not stop a stealthy loneliness from creeping under her jacket. She turned towards the glorious view of the hills to avoid betraying the feeling, but it kept pressing her chest like a tight brassiere. Annina noticed the shadow of melancholy under the delicate parasol.

'But, Madame, why don't you come with us?'

Her mistress pleated her lips and raised her eyebrows – she was genuinely surprised.

'*Moi?* Alexandria?'

'There're many rich there,' Yusuf said. 'Merchants. Captains. Lots of money.' He lowered his voice. 'And they all need a woman, Madame.'

'Yusuf says it's such a cosmopolitan city,' Annina added. 'You won't feel out of place.'

Violetta pinched her chin. It was less a gesture of contemplation than a valiant attempt to stop her tears – her maid's dedication was so moving.

'And where there is lots of money there is a shortage of love,' she said. '*N'est-ce pas?*'

She was referring to the chances of her, too, finding true love in the famous Egyptian city. But her young maid thought she was hinting at her business prospects, and nodded with heartfelt animation.

'And I could still go on working for you, Madame.'

Violetta let the misunderstanding pass. She admired and felt responsible for the young couple who had worked for her so diligently.

'No, *jolie*. A married woman has no place in my parlour. Besides, as time goes by I wither while you blossom. What would my clients think when they make the comparison?'

'True,' Yusuf said. 'She'd be bad for business.'

Annina elbowed him in the ribs.

'*Oh, Madame. Tu es la plus belle femme du Levant.*'

Her mistress frowned comically.

'*Et pourquoi pas de toute la Méditerranée?*' she asked.

She was still considering her maid's offer when the whistle sounded and they had to rejoin the caravan. Soon the column was moving again. After the ups and downs of the earlier stretch, the trail now ascended towards the crest of a hill that dominated the landscape like an impenetrable fortress. It was a narrow trail, and several times the mules, stupefied by their burdens and the afternoon sun, tottered and came close to the edge before the drivers brought them to their senses. Stones rolled down the steep verge and clouds of dust rose from the wheels of the lorries struggling ahead. One of the rev-ups awakened Brigadier Nestor from his tormented sleep. He sat up in his cot dazed, rubbing his eyes with his fists. With disappointment he realised that the lorry was moving: they had not yet arrived. He moved aside a flap of the torn canvas and looked out. Leading the column was the troop of Boy Scouts.

'And in the end,' he said, 'a bunch of boys and a grown man in shorts save the day.'

He shut the flap and turned to look at the dim interior of his lorry. Everything was there: his trunk, the stove, his table with the maps, his holster hanging from the roof. For a moment he treated himself to the idea that he had never ordered a massacre, that the brigade had not marched into the town, that his Chief of Staff was still alive – perhaps it all had been a dream. But no sooner did he make his wish than he answered it himself with a cruel, uncontrollable snicker of self-ridicule. He was almost behaving like a child, he thought, who when faced with danger covers his eyes in order to make the evil go away. Presently, the driver's hatch opened and his orderly looked in, puzzled.

'My brigadier?'

His superior checked his laughter and gestured for the young soldier to carry on driving.

'Watch where you're going. I don't want my bones buried in this Field of Blood.'

The hatch closed and the back of the lorry was dark once again. The coffee smoked in the pot and Brigadier Nestor filled his cup. But he could not drink it without remembering the major, the cups they had had together, their discussions, his paternal advice to him, the cigars they had smoked. The old officer sighed as if he were carrying a heavy burden up that steep slope himself.

'A disaster,' he muttered. 'What a disaster.'

Had he really had that shot of morphia earlier that morning in the Town Hall? He could hardly believe that he had: he felt so tired . . . Breathing heavily, he decided to have another. The syringe was in its usual place but he could not find the rubber band anywhere. He removed his belt instead to tie round his arm – but first he had to boil the syringe. The stove was cooling down; he had to build the fire up. He took the scoop and dug it in the bucket but came up with more ash than coal.

'Orderly!'

The hatch opened.

'I need coal for the stove.'

'I'm afraid there isn't any, my brigadier.'

Brigadier Nestor narrowed his eyes.

'Don't tell me it was stolen, too?'

359

The lorry slowed down.

'No, my brigadier. We ran out.'

Brigadier Nestor raised his hands more out of resignation than annoyance. But even that simple gesture was difficult to execute: his arms felt heavy and he so powerless . . . A voice inside him told him to hold on; it would not be long now, the coast was near. He had saved his men. He thought of the padre and his decision to stay behind – how he, too, wished he had gone insane! Perhaps the next shot of morphia would be the one to tip the scale of his reason once and for all – Brigadier Nestor's idea of insanity was of a happy oblivion. He was prepared to use the syringe without boiling it when he noticed the box in the corner: it contained Major Porfirio's clandestine books. He called to his orderly.

'What is this doing here?'

'The evidence from the court-martial, my brigadier. I thought you wished to keep it.'

Brigadier Nestor lifted the hot plate with the pair of tongs and dropped one of the books into the embers of the stove. While he waited for it to catch fire he picked up a few other volumes and turned the pages absent-mindedly. He threw another book in the fire before returning the rest to the box.

'But who would want to live in a world run by philosophers?' he wondered.

His orderly turned round.

'Maybe I could ask the cook, my brigadier – there's coal in the field kitchen. If we stop for a moment.'

'No – no more stops until we reach the coast.'

Brigadier Nestor shut the hatch and placed the syringe in the pot. Waiting for the water to boil, he rolled up his sleeve and tied his belt above his elbow. He injected the morphia and threw the syringe on his cot beside him. 'A disaster,' he stuttered. His eyelids flapped a few times and then shut. 'What a dis . . .' At that moment he thought he heard noise outside and half opened his eyes. He could see nothing. He stretched out his hand, feeling along the tarpaulin for the flap. As soon as he moved the cover aside the sunlight burned his eyes: the lorry had reached the top of the hill and there ahead of them was the sea. Brigadier Nestor squinted at the sun. Through the curtain of his addiction, he saw on the shore the standing doorposts of ancient mausoleums amid pieces of fallen columns, several private temples slipping slowly into the sea, and a few sarcophagi ravaged by the centuries, half sunk in the sand and inundated by the oscillating waves. In the gulf beyond the coastal necropolis he made out a small fleet comprised of a dreadnought and a few destroyers. And far beyond them he thought he saw the faint shapes of distant islands: it was the motherland! But his elation lasted for only a moment; soon he began to suspect that the ruins, the sea, the ships and the islands, too, were all an unkind deception of the morphia. He let the flap drop and in the absolute darkness of the lorry he felt desperately under the covers not for the vial with the drug or his precious letters from home, but for his *Lexicon of Greek and Roman Myths*. When he found it he embraced it, and embracing it he fell back on his cot and closed his eyes.

EPILOGUE

It was several hours after the departure of the long column of soldiers and civilians, a long time since the dust raised by feet, hooves and wheels had settled and the neighing of the pack animals had faded, and much longer after the smell of exhausts had cleared and the stench of the open sewer had returned, that the forgotten inhabitants of the Quarter finally mustered the courage to emerge from their slum. They crossed the pestilent moat around their neighbourhood, tiptoed towards the silent market and pressed their faces on the glass to see inside the shut windows, while the bravest chanced as far as the square where they were confronted by an awesome sight: scattered across the open space were the carcasses of slaughtered animals, many pieces of expensive furniture and count-less bundles of clothes and dusty rags. For a while they dared not touch them in case someone would accuse them of stealing, until they realised there was not a living soul around. In the courtyard of the Town Hall they came across two Christian crosses over a patch of turned earth and puzzled over them for a while, trying to understand why these dead had not been buried in the cemetery behind the municipal park where everyone else used to end in the past. Only when they noticed that there was no flag on the mast

362

of the Town Hall did they convince themselves that they were truly alone in the town, and so climbed the marble steps that led to the heavy double doors of the bygone authority. They felt the chill of the official tiles on the bare soles of their feet, heard the echo of their whispers with suspicion, and then they began to search the rooms for valuables. There was a lot – but little that they could carry: neither the mahogany floors nor the cast-iron railings of the gallery would have been easy to pull out, and they would have had to break the marble conference table into several pieces to get it out the door. In the library they threw to the floor the rare manuscripts and Phrygian papyri and climbed on them to search behind the cobwebs of the shelves for secret compartments, but there were not any. They were pulling apart an invaluable Gutenberg Bible in case it hid a key to a medieval trapdoor somewhere in the municipal building, a book that centuries earlier a monk had saved from the library of the patriarchate during the sacking of Constantinople, when the unexpected tolling of bells sent a chill down their spines.

They followed the sound to the Christian church whereupon they gaped up at the belfry where the enormous bells swayed, and for a moment were convinced they were witnessing the machination of the ghost of some Christian saint, until the tolling stopped and the door of the church opened and they recognised the priest. He walked out with his arms spread wide and a demoniacal smile on his face, followed by the dog. No matter how he tempted them with salvation, begged them with tears in his eyes, or threatened them with eternal hellfire while calling himself the Apostle of All Anatolians, he only managed to frighten the children with his proclamations. They decided that the poor man had lost his reason for good and that there was nothing they could do for him, and the crowd resumed its search with increased ardour. By the time they reached the Frenchwoman's house they had worked themselves into a frenzy. The greedier burst into the bedrooms and attacked the armoured safes with their crowbars; the more contemptuous came up with the most profane acts they could think of to honour the corrupt regime of the mayor that had sentenced them to eternal poverty and sickness; the angrier began to burn, tear or break anything they could salvage from the hands of the looters; while the sensible headed for the kitchen, the pantry and the cellar searching for food. It was midnight when they had finished. They lay under the stars and put the children to sleep with sweet myths, like the one about the glorious warrior whom a king had imprisoned, and how the latter's daughter, having fallen in love with the hero at first sight, saved him by adding opium to the wine she gave the guards to drink, before cutting her blonde hair to add to the rope he used to escape. At dawn the poor villagers found the few buffalo that had survived the bayonets of the soldiers, yoked them to their ancient carts which they had loaded with the abandoned treasures collected the previous day and, seeing that the tracks of the army led west to the coast, they themselves left the town for ever in the opposite direction, where a fine October sun rose slowly above the Anatolian hills.